The Tempest

New Persia, Book Two

John L. Lynch

A Wings ePress, Inc.
Science Fiction Novel

Wings
Press, Inc.

Wings ePress, Inc.

Edited by: Jeanne Smith
Copy Edited by: Rebecca Smith
Executive Editor: Jeanne Smith
Cover Artist: rebecacovers

All rights reserved

Wings ePress Books
www.wingsepress.com

Published In the United States Of America

Wings ePress Inc.
3000 N. Rock Road
Newton, KS 67114

What They Are Saying About
The Tempest

The war between Azania and New Persia erupts as a biochemical seed storm blows out of the Northern Waste. Basir Turani gains rank as a commander of Persian forces, but the challenges he faces are greater than ever. Suri Pahlavi is offered an opportunity to serve her country. Nasrin Avesta comes into her own but what sacrifice is she willing to make? Farad Hashemi fights the enemy in the air and under the waves. The storm of war breaks across the world of New Persia.

Lynch's painstaking character work in *New Persia: Before the Storm* pays off in this riveting, intense sequel. As an enormous natural firestorm threatens them all, its immense scale is humanized through a rescue operation. Triumphs and tragedies abound.

Lynch's expertise is in military tactics, and he clearly depicts the perspective of officers who still have to lead combat. Each chapter is short and packs a punch. The cultural politics from the first book are still factors here, but are more in the background as the story focuses on what it means to engage in total warfare. Lynch's characters are all capable but far from perfect or invincible, and that lends tension to every encounter.

Lynch is also interested in the ways in which technology affect war, as tactics can only go so far against superior weapons and vehicles. With the technology on this world at a 1950s level, the introduction of helicopters proves to be a devastating move. There are times when the battle scenes are too dense, especially since so much of the book involves combat, but Lynch always brings the focus back to people, giving the book a resonant payoff. This is not a good starting place for newcomers, but series fans will be thoroughly satisfied by this installment and breathlessly await the next.

—Book Life Reviews

The author follows up his *New Persia: Before the Storm* (2018) with a military-SF actioner whose technology is more retro-20th century than futuristic. That's because the setting is a twin-sunned planet, circa the 34th century, settled by refugees from Earth, deep-space colonists trying to recover from a harsh beginning and setbacks costing generations of progress. Territorial conflict now simmers continuously. Meanwhile, a background threat looms against both warring nations: a "seed storm," a periodic calamity occurring in this alien ecosystem, when ubiquitous native plant life starts a chemical cycle of fiery holocausts.

Lynch (*Endemic*, 2018, etc.) only drops hints about the backstory of his compelling, imaginary world, but he does mention that—in its millennia or so of human habitation—the spacefaring civilization here rose and fell to ruin more than once, climbing its way upward repeatedly from dark ages featuring seed storms and entrenched belligerence. On that note, the only Azanian character of consequence, a tank commander named Aran, turns out to be an ethical soldier (and a Christian disciple, at least in part), initiating a cease-fire to evacuate vulnerable civilians. The theme of female courage and resourcefulness under fire does come through loud and clear.

Hard-combat Sci-Fi that delivers thoughtful alternative history speculation rather than ray gun stuff.

—KirkusReviews

Dedication

For Leslie

* * *

One

Suri Pahlavi and Nasrin Avesta stood at the threshold of their newly acquired apartment in Persepolis. The space was barely adequate for the two of them, consisting of two small bedrooms and a small common area to serve as a kitchen, dining room, and living space. The apartment was littered with small reminders of the previous occupants. Unpatched holes in the walls for framed pictures, a pot left in the kitchen sink, and a child's doll on the floor. The small family who had lived here, the landlady had explained, had left for the country during the crisis leading to the war.

Suri thought this was ironic because she and Nasrin had moved from the country to Persepolis as soon as the war began. However foolhardy the decision had been, it did mean they were paying half as much to rent the apartment than they would have a month before. War may be good for some businesses, but not for landlords offering rooms in a city exposed to air raids.

Nasrin wrinkled her nose at their new home. Both women were from families of the country aristocracy. Both of their fathers were high ranking Army officers, and Suri and Nasrin were used to having their own suite of rooms. Living in a tiny apartment in a building full of them was foreign to them both.

They stood for a moment, feeling sad at the prospect of living in such a place. Then Suri spoke.

"Where's my library going to go?" she asked.

Nasrin laughed. Suri was a booklover and spent every spare moment reading.

"And my dressing room?" Nasrin said.

"And where will the servants be quartered?" Suri responded.

"And the stables for the horses," Nasrin broke into a laugh. Suri joined in, and they laughed together.

Their levity was cut short. Outside, a wailing noise rose to a high pitch. The noise shook the windows. Both women's eyes widened and they stared at each other.

"The air raid alarm!" Suri said. "What do we do?"

"I think we have to get to a shelter," Nasrin said.

"Where?" Suri asked.

"Let's try the basement," Nasrin said.

They started for the apartment building's stairs, but the hall was suddenly full of people. All the doors opened and filled with tenants. Old men and women, children, and a few men, packed into the hallway trying to get to the stairwell. Nasrin and Suri had to fight their way to the stairs against the shoving mass. Their future neighbors had nothing to say to the two women in the chaos.

A large booming sound shook the building. The crashing noise of windows shattering in the apartments all around filled the corridor. The lights flickered, and children screamed in fear. Their parents hurried them toward the stairs.

Suri and Nasrin shoved their way to the stair entrance and joined the throng heading for the basement. Floor after floor passed as they pushed their way down. Suri saw people who had fallen lie in the stairwell, unable to stand against the press of people. Unable to stop and help them, she pushed past. She had to hold herself up against the relentless push from behind. She tried not to step on anyone, but she could feel the soft press of flesh under her feet.

The stampede finally reached the lowest floor. At the bottom of the stairs stood a heavy metal double door. It was the kind mandated by the Ministry of Civil defense for basement air raid shelters and was armored against blast and fragments.

It also, to the horror of Suri and Nasrin, had a lock and chain holding it shut.

The first to arrive in the basement had tried to open the door, realized it was locked, and then tried to go back up the stairs. They got nowhere against the tide of people trying to go down. Helpless, they had been pressed against the walls and door as more and more people descended the stairs.

"Stop!" Suri cried. "Stop! The door is locked!"

But no one heard her. Her voice was blotted out by the cries and stomping feet of the dozens of people around her.

The tiny basement filled with people and Suri was crushed against the metal door. She struggled but it was hopeless. Too many people were pushing into too small a space.

She couldn't breathe. The pressure was so great she couldn't expand her chest. Suri tried to pull her arms over her head to create more space for her to breathe. She yanked one arm and then the other up and gasped at the hot air. Screams filled her ears.

She was going to be crushed to death! Or she would be smothered! Panic rushed through her body.

Suri desperately forced her way to the door. It was the only possible escape. She had to get it open, somehow.

The door handle was chained to a metal loop set into the wall. Suri saw that breaking the loop would be hopeless. It was at least half an inch thick. The chain was also too strong to break. The lock was a simple padlock, and perhaps it could be broken if she had a crowbar or bolt-cutters, but she didn't, and there was no space to use one even if she had. She could barely move.

The building shook and the lights went out.

Whatever order there was vanished. The press of the crowd toward the basement grew. Suri felt the pressure crushing her ribs. Her arms were over her head and she couldn't use them to protect herself. She tried to hold her breath. If she fully exhaled, she would never be able to breathe again.

In the darkness, crushed against the door, Suri heard a cry which pierced the panicked screams of the crowd.

"I have the key! Let me through!"

"Over here!" Suri yelled. "The door is over here! I'm at the door!"

She repeated it again, trying to be heard over the noise of the crowd. "Here! The door is here!"

She heard Nasrin's voice for the first time since their descent of the stairs.

"Make way! Make way, or we will all die! Move!"

She felt the crowd around her part. She felt two new figures arrive at her side. One was Nasrin. She could smell the perfume she always wore. She smelled of tulips.

The other spoke in the voice she had first heard. "I have the key!" It was a woman, and Suri recognized the building manager.

Suri felt for the chain. She ran her fingers down the links until she found the lock.

"I have the lock!" she said.

Another surge of people pressed down the stairs. Nasrin was pushed into Suri with such force Suri's breath was knocked out of her. She gasped for air.

"I have the lock!" Suri rasped. "I need the key!" She raised her hand over her head. She reached toward the voice.

The air was stale and hot.

She stretched her arm toward Nasrin. Nasrin took her hand.

"Get the key!" Suri cried.

Nasrin reached out with her other hand, and Suri felt the hard metal of the key against her palm. She closed her fingers on it, but it slipped. She felt it falling. If she lost it, it would be impossible in the press of bodies to find it only the floor. If she weren't stomped to death in the effort. Frantically, Suri closed her hand on the key. She caught it the moment before it fell to the floor.

She had it! She turned her body to face the door. She held the lock in her other hand and wormed the arm holding the key down to the lock. It was difficult. Nasrin and the landlady tried to shield her from the crowd, but she was jostled and shoved from every direction. She held the key tightly between her fingers. She brought the key to the lock. In the darkness, she struggled to bring the key to the keyhole. Three times she missed the lock as she was pushed tight against the door.

Then she did it. The key slid into the lock. With a wrench of her wrist, the lock opened. She was barely able to unhook the padlock from the chain. The lock slid free, and the chain was loose.

She reached for the door handle and rotated it to the right. Suri pushed, and the metal squealed.

The door didn't open. Even with the enormous press behind Suri, it didn't budge.

Suri realized the door hinges were on her side of the door. The door opened outward toward her and the crowd. Pinned against it, she wouldn't be able to open it.

Suri screamed in frustration.

"It opens out!" she cried to Nasrin. "I can't open it!"

Nasrin said nothing. Suri wondered if she was gone, crushed under the feet of the crowd inside the basement.

She couldn't breathe. Suri knew she couldn't last much longer. The pressure against her would snuff her life out like a match.

Nasrin's voice rang out into the darkness, over the screams of the trapped.

"Push away from the door! Push! On three! On three!" She sounded calm. Suri didn't know how she did it. Suri was terrified, and her voice was filled with panic.

"One!" Nasrin called. Suri felt Nasrin brace herself.

"Two!" Nasrin planted her feet. Suri squared herself away from the door.

"Three! Push!" Suri pushed at Nasrin as hard as she could. Nasrin did the same. There was a momentary release of pressure, but it returned immediately.

"Again!" Nasrin said. "One!"

Suri braced for another push. On "Three!" more people around her pushed away from the door. The press eased for a bit longer. Suri grabbed the door handle, but she was pushed back before she could open it.

"Again!" Nasrin said.

On the third try, the press eased long enough for Suri to open the door a crack. It wasn't enough to slip through.

"I almost have it open!" Suri said. "Keep trying!"

The wave of people joining with Nasrin to push the crowd away from the door grew. Everyone in the basement joined the effort. Suri wondered about the poor people in the middle, between the press coming down the stairs and the counter-push. She put the thought out of her mind.

This time, on three, a gap opened around the door. Suri pulled back on the handle with all her might. Just as the press returned, she had the door open far enough that instead of being forced closed again, it rotated the other way and crashed against the wall.

Suri yelled in delight. The way was open. She almost fell into the empty space of the air raid shelter beyond, which would have been fatal. Behind her, the press of people shoved her inside the dark space. She ran as fast as she could before them into the empty room. She didn't dare stop. If she tripped, she'd be stomped to death.

She didn't reach the far wall for what seemed like a full minute. Her outstretched hands felt the brick. She closed her eyes. Would she be crushed against the wall as she had been against the door?

No. The space was full of people. Suri could hear them and felt some around her, but the press was relieved.

Someone found the emergency lights. The room, revealed, was low-ceilinged with brick walls. The dim light showed people moving like shadows.

The building shook and dust jumped from the walls and floor. The plaster fell from the ceiling. Someone screamed.

Suri tried to find Nasrin. She worked her way through the people all around her, searching for her friend. Had she survived the last push?

Suri looked through half the room. She called Nasrin's name. Finally, she found her near the open door.

"Nasrin!" she said. "You're alive!"

"You are too!" Nasrin said. "I was looking for you."

"Me, too!" Suri said. "I mean, I was looking for you."

The two friends embraced.

"Thank you for saving us," Suri said. "I thought we were dead."

"Yes," Nasrin said. "This door, I can't imagine why it opens outward. Perhaps someone thought it would resist the blast from a bomb better if the hinges were on the outside."

"Madness!" Suri said. "We could have all been killed!" She started to shake. A moment later, she began to cry.

So did Nasrin.

"Oh, God!" Suri said. "We almost died!"

"But we didn't," said Nasrin. "We're alive."

"Why does this have to happen?" Suri asked. "Why do the Azanians bomb us?"

"Because we took what was theirs in the last war. They want their land back," Nasrin said.

"But this isn't their land. We're in the middle of Persepolis," Suri said.

"War," Nasrin said. "War has no limits."

"The stupid Treaty of Zanzibar," Suri said, wiping tears from her eyes. "It's been twenty years, and we are back at war. Some peace treaty!"

"Only paper," Nasrin said. "Nothing written is forever."

They held each other in the air-raid shelter without speaking. After a while, Suri said, "I wonder how Father is doing." Her father, Major Pahlavi, had been a reservist mobilized when the war began. "Or Javad." Her brother was assigned to a unit guarding the frontier.

"Or Basir," Nasrin said, with a smile.

Suri almost giggled. Her suitor, Basir Turani, was somewhere in the north. She had not heard anything from him since he had departed Persepolis before the war began. The thought of their time together filled her with joy, tempered by the knowledge that he was in harm's way.

"I wonder about Farad," Suri said. Farad was a dashing fighter pilot who had swept Nasrin off her feet, but the war had interrupted their romance.

The two women were quiet, and the crowd had calmed. No more nearby explosions shook the building.

Despite the danger from outside, no one could convince themselves to close the metal blast door.

When the all-clear sounded, Nasrin made sure to organize a queue so their departure from the shelter was orderly. She led the line and stopped the procession each time an injured or dead person was found in the basement or in the stairwell. The injured were carried upstairs, while the dead were passed down to the basement. Suri lost count of how many there were. She tried not the think about it.

They reached their apartment much later. Exhausted, they stared at the broken glass on the floor. Their things hadn't arrived as planned, of course, because of the air raid. It was getting dark, and there was nowhere to sit or lie down.

Suri teared up. What would they do?

Nasrin knocked on their neighbor's door. She introduced herself to the woman within, who recognized her from their ordeal in the basement. Nasrin and Suri were welcomed inside, and soon were fed and offered a place to stay until their belongings came.

"We still have to clean up all the broken glass in the apartment," Suri said.

"Tomorrow," Nasrin said. "Tomorrow."

Two

Captain Azeri peered through the periscope into the darkness. Five miles to his north was the dark shoreline of Azania. He could see the outlines of hills blocking out the stars. Shaitan had not risen yet, but he had a very short time to complete his observation before the submarine would have to dive again.

"Down scope," Azeri ordered, and a quartermaster lowered the periscope and slid it into its receptacle in the control room floor. In the red-lit room, the anxious faces of his crew studied their instruments with rapt attention.

Azeri took two steps to the navigation plot.

The Persian submarine *Yunes* lurked only ten kilometers from the exit of Kenyatta harbor, the forward base of the Azanian fleet. His mission was to get even closer.

The war had started so suddenly the *Yunes* had barely cleared its dock before Azanian bombers had appeared overhead. Azeri had steered the boat out to sea on the surface while dodging falling bombs until the ocean bottom dropped away, and the boat could dive. It had been a terrifying experience. In the following days, the fear had transmogrified into a rage.

Damn the Azanians for attacking us, Azeri thought. *We'll make them pay.* The image of bombs falling onto his base played through his mind again. It was the same all over New Persia. Nowhere was safe from the war. It wasn't like the last war when the combat was confined, with few exceptions, to the front line.

This time they would bring the war to the Azanians.

"Make your course three-two-zero," Azeri commanded. The diving officer and helmsman repeated his order, and the submarine turned to the northwest.

"Make your speed twenty kilometers, depth fifty meters."

The submarine's electric motors came to life. Running on battery power, they spun the single large propeller. The dive planes on the side of the submarine's sail angled downward, pushing the boat toward the bottom.

The helmsman reported when the boat had leveled off at fifty meters.

"Very well," Azeri said. It was cool inside the submarine, but he was sweating.

He watched the quartermaster chart their course to the harbor entrance. There was no way for the *Yunes* to enter Kenyatta harbor. His intelligence briefing reported the harbor defenses included anti-submarine nets and minefields. The harbor wasn't very deep, either, barely deep enough for large ships to use. There would be nowhere for a submarine to hide.

But Azeri didn't have to go in the harbor to hit the ships within. He only had to leave them a present.

In the torpedo room forward and below control, twelve naval mines were loaded in the six torpedo tubes. Another twenty-four waited on the hydraulically operated torpedo racks. They would place the mines on the ocean bottom outside the harbor entrance, and then the *Yunes* would depart. When the Azanian fleet sailed, they'd have a surprise waiting for them.

No submarine captain enjoyed laying mines. Torpedo attacks were far more challenging and exciting. Still, Azeri knew the mines were the best way to hit the Azanians where it would hurt them. He may never find out exactly what his mines had done, but he could be sure they would at least close the harbor until they could be cleared.

"Conn, sonar, new contact bearing three-two-five. Single screw, high speed," the sonarman's voice cracked, "Wait—active sonar, same bearing, range is less than five kilometers," came the call from the sonar room.

"All stop," Azeri ordered.

The order was repeated and acknowledged, and the submarine's motors wound down.

"General quarters."

The officer of the deck pulled the general quarters alarm, and throughout the ship, sailors raced to their stations.

"Conn, sonar, multiple contacts, at least three, bearings three-two-zero through three-two-five."

Azeri waited for more information. He knew his sonar crewman were working frantically to locate and identify the sounds of the enemy ships.

"Three destroyers, fleet type, range is close from signal strength, nothing better yet. Sorry, Captain."

"Very well," Azeri said into the intercom. Already the sonar plot in the forward control room was being updated by the quartermaster. The weapons officer and the fire-control men stood by the torpedo data computer and wound the dials to input the limited information they had available.

Azeri knew it would do no good because the torpedo tubes were loaded with mines. He was carrying only four torpedoes for self-defense, and two of them were acoustic homing torpedoes useful only for attacking submarines.

"Torpedo room," he called into the intercom, "reload tubes one and two with Mark Fourteen torpedoes." It would take time to carry out the order— too much time.

"Conn, sonar, new contacts, large surface ships, bearing three-two-zero."

Azeri nodded. These new contacts were leaving the harbor. He wanted to curse. In a half-hour, he would have laid mines right where those ships were passing.

"Sonar, signal strength on active sonar?" Azeri asked.

"Not strong enough for a return," sonar answered. The pings weren't close enough to bounce off the *Yunes'* hull and return a usable echo. The submarine was safe. "Signal on the closest destroyer is increasing. He's getting closer."

"All ahead one-third," Azeri said. "Come right to course three-five-zero." He angled the boat closer to the coast east of the destroyers leaving the harbor.

In fifteen minutes, the picture became clearer. Five destroyers exited the harbor and fanned out to the southeast and southwest, pinging their active sonars. Behind them came four large ships.

"I want to know what those ships are," Azeri said. "Periscope depth."

The boat slid close to the surface. Azeri reduced speed to decrease the periscope's wake. A thin ESM mast slid up first to check for radar signals.

From behind a black curtain in the aft control room, a technician cried, "Multiple radar signals, approaching detection range!"

"Very well," Azeri said. "Up scope!"

The scope slid up, and Azeri caught the handles. He let it slide up above the surface. He was only going to get one look, and he wanted to make sure it counted. He spun the periscope around the horizon.

The sea was flat calm. Shaitan was rising, and the twilight made it hard to distinguish the sea from the sky. The land loomed to the north. White-capped wakes betrayed the locations of the ships to the northwest. Azeri counted three small and four large ships in his field of view. He zoomed the periscope lens on the large ships.

They were enormous. With his rangefinder, Azeri estimated each at over eight hundred feet long. All had the flat deck, which told Azeri what he needed to know. The Azanian aircraft carriers were leaving port.

If he had a full spread of torpedoes loaded, he could be certain of sinking at least one, perhaps two. He drove the thought out of his head. God did not will it today.

Azeri was thinking he had the periscope up too long when the radar technician called out, "Signal exceeding detection value!"

"Down scope!" Azeri said and stepped back from the downward sliding tube.

"Conn, sonar, two contacts have changed course! Bearing steady at three-two-five. Range decreasing."

The Azanian destroyers had detected the *Yunes*. It was time to go. Without any way to attack the enemy fleet, the most important thing the submarine could do was escape and report what it had seen. The Azanian fleet had sailed, and it was going somewhere. Azeri wished he knew where, but it was a problem for another day. For now, he needed to survive.

Azeri examined the chart. It was not the time to hit a rock or the ocean bottom. He slapped the chart table with his hand.

"All ahead flank! Make your course zero-nine-zero," he said.

The boat jumped into life and swung around to the east. The twin electric motors spun the propeller at its maximum speed.

Azeri looked at the sonar plot. With high speed, the flow noise of the water the *Yunes* was passing through would soon wash out any sonar contacts. He watched the speed gauge pass thirty kilometers per hour.

The *Yunes* was the newest boat in the Persian submarine fleet. It was novel in many ways, but its most important innovation was the shape of its hull. Older submarines were designed as surface ships that could dive when necessary, with flat decks and a conventional bow and stern. The *Yunes* was shaped like a teardrop with the bow being thicker than the stern and a round cross-section when seen from the front. The round, streamlined hull made her a terrible sea-keeper on the surface but gave her unprecedented speed underwater.

Azeri saw the speed exceed forty kilometers an hour. He could see the battery gauge dropping as he watched. At high speed, the electric motors could blow through the *Yunes'* enormous battery bank in only thirty minutes.

Now is the time to use the battery power, Azeri thought. The enemy destroyers would have to run flat out to catch him, and running at high speed would deafen their sonar. If he left his last known position far behind, the enemy destroyers would find nothing when they arrived. He would be too far away for their hunt to be effective.

Azeri studied the sonar plot again. He checked times, distances, and vectors. He wanted to make sure he was as far away as possible before going silent to prevent the enemy ships from hearing him when they arrived at his old location.

After mentally checking his calculations twice, he ordered, "All ahead, one-third."

The submarine slowed. "Make your course one-eight-zero."

Azeri was pointing the submarine out to sea both to escape and to bring the bow sonar back into a position where it could hear the enemy ships. Directly behind the submarine, the sonar could not hear anything over the sound of the boat's propellers.

"Sonar, report all contacts," Azeri said.

Two destroyers were circling the spot where the boat had raised its periscope, pinging futilely with their active sonars. Another destroyer was searching a kilometer south. The rest of the ships were sailing south from the harbor unmolested at high speed.

Even with the *Yunes'* unique hull, there was no way he could catch an aircraft carrier heading away from him. Even if he had the battery power, a carrier had to be fast enough to launch aircraft and could make speeds he could not match.

It was not God's will today.

The *Yunes* sailed to the south for two hours until the enemy destroyers were far away. Then Azeri came to periscope depth and raised its antennas. His short HF radio message addressed to naval headquarters in Persepolis alerted the Persian fleet. The Azanians were coming.

Three

Captain Basir Turani and his staff rode in a train car traveling south. They'd left Kerman ahead of the Seed Storm. Vehicles, those still operating after the battle of airfield K-2, were strapped down onto flatbed cars. Their crews crammed into a random assortment of other rail cars. A few cars were meant for passengers, but most were not. Infantry squads squatted inside cattle cars with their weapons piled in the corners. At night, the cold crept in and stole their sleep.

They'd won a victory at airfield K-2, and the men were proud of what they'd accomplished. It was the first, and so far, only, defeat the Azanians had suffered in their invasion of New Persia. The New Persian army units assigned to the defense of the north had been caught in a surprise attack. Captain Turani had rallied a combined force of tanks, mechanized infantry, and Kerman militia to retake the airfield before the Azanians could use the base to capture the city of Kerman. The whole of North Province could have fallen, but New Persian arms had won the day.

The train had to stop twice for breaks in the rails. The Azanian Air Force had been busy breaking every road and rail link they could reach. The Rail Section engineers had fixed the breaks within thirty minutes. Basir felt glad something was working as it should because very little else had.

So far, the train itself had avoided air attack. Anti-aircraft guns sat on top of two rail cars, but Basir had no confidence they would prevent a bombing or strafing attack.

They were taking a great risk by traveling during the day. Basir had an intuition that time was short, and arriving safely in Persepolis late would be as bad as not arriving at all. Caution was not what was needed. It was time to be bold.

Right now, though, being bold meant sitting in an uncomfortable seat and watching the scenery of the Karun Valley pass by the windows.

He had ordered the battalion to move before receiving orders to do so. It made no sense to keep the unit in Kerman, where the fiery rain of the Seed Storm would pin it down for an unknown amount of time and subject it to losses from the weather. The storm blew out of the Northern Waste with the strength of a hurricane and carried the burning seeds of the native plants which lived in the Waste. The storm would burn down everything in its path as it traveled south.

The Azanians couldn't attack through the storm, and the Kerman militia should be able to hold out long enough for reinforcements to be brought up by river or rail. Leaving one of the best offensive units in the entire army out of the war was stupid. Fortunately, he'd received orders confirming his choice while the last men and vehicles boarded the train.

Shirazi sat crumpled in a seat across the aisle with his hat lowered over his eyes. The dust he'd picked up west of Kerman at the airfield still covered him. The rest of his improvised staff, including Lieutenant Pahlavi, was similarly situated around the car with their personal gear serving as poorly designed pillows. Basir already had aches and pains from sleeping on his lumpy field bag full of everything from uniforms to boots to web gear.

He thought of getting a current situation report from his men, but looking around at the sleeping staff, he decided against it. No one was doing anything on the train, and Basir knew this was a precious chance to rest the men before they reentered combat.

As the train clattered down the tracks, Basir closed his eyes to join the other sleepers.

Four

Farad's train pulled into Persepolis Grand Central. As soon as the train halted, without waiting for the conductor, he leaped onto the landing. His uniform and bearing prevented anyone from objecting.

He had no orders because no one in the Air Corps knew he was alive. His squadron had been wiped out in the Azanian attack on K-2. As far as anyone knew, Farad Hashemi was missing, presumed dead. He had bailed out of his plane after avenging himself on a half-dozen Azanian aircraft and survived an ordeal in the desert before making his way to friendly lines. His friend Basir Turani had led the recapture of K-2, which allowed Farad to return to civilization. Since there were no planes to fly after the Azanians destroyed them all, Farad caught a train to Persepolis, the capital city of New Persia, to rejoin the Air Corps.

He went to the telegraph office where, pushing ahead of the line of anxious travelers, he used his rank and the presence on his chest of the Star Medal to send two telegrams. One was to his parents, and he hoped it reached them before any official announcement of his premature death. The second was to Nasrin Avesta. The telegraph operator had raised an eyebrow, no doubt wondering if it was *the*

Nasrin Avesta, but Farad had given him no sign. His message was brief, but he hoped it would settle any doubts as to his status among the living and his unchanged intentions toward her. The telegraph operator may have smiled, but Farad opted not to notice.

Farad did not bother telegraphing Air Corps HQ, because he would arrive there before they would read the message.

Persepolis was in an uproar. Everywhere people darted around, filling the roads as buses and military trucks plowed through the crowds without stopping. People flowed around the vehicles as if they were a school of small fish making way for the bigger fish. Everyone carried something. Handbags, suitcases, baskets, books, even a mattress was borne between a man and woman resting it on their heads as if shielding themselves from falling rocks.

Where everyone was going was unclear to Farad. The rail station was sealed off with barbed wire, and the Rail Section guards had exchanged their truncheons for black sheet metal submachine guns. The buses were all full of soldiers. Still, there was a queue of hopeful people stretching blocks away from the station despite the signs ALL TRAINS SERVING MILITARY NEEDS UNTIL FURTHER NOTICE.

Farad watched a young man, surely no more than fifteen, leap onto the rear bumper of a moving bus and hang on. Farad wondered if he had any idea where the bus was going or what he planned to do when it arrived.

Farad decided to waste no more time there. He shouldered his service bag and headed into the crowd, bound for the Air Corps HQ.

Five

Captain Aran, Azanian Land Force, was having the time of his life. His M2 *Mbwa* tank rolled and bounced across the rocky rain-shadow desert of the Sheban range. The rest of his company, *his* company, he thought gleefully, trailed for a kilometer behind him on Route One. The dust thrown up by the *Mbwa*'s tracks left a cloud seen for many kilometers in all directions.

The small emirate of Siwa, a vassal state of New Persia, had switched sides at the last possible moment, as the entire massed might of the Azanian armed forces was poised to storm over the border. He'd been told to expect no resistance from the Siwans. The Siwans they had encountered had broken and run at the first encounter or had surrendered *en masse*. The military police units following behind were overwhelmed with prisoners. The Siwans on the border who did fight did so perfunctorily, firing a few rounds for honor and then surrendering. Aran's tank unit had flung itself through the hole in the Siwan defenses twelve hours ago and had not stopped since.

Aran smiled. As much faith as he had in the ten tanks and thirty men under his command, the Siwan units they had encountered could have delayed his advance for days or even weeks. His tanks had driven through valleys and across rivers, which would have made excellent defensive positions, had the Siwans chosen to defend them. For the first few such positions, Aran had been cautious and deployed his tanks carefully to avoid ambushes. Once through the first fifty kilometers, he had passed on the order to keep moving unless they encountered significant opposition. So far, there had been none.

It seemed most of the Arab Siwan Army had been deployed on the border or near the capital, Siwa City. Foolish, Aran thought, not to defend in depth. Once the Azanians breached any part of the border, the enemy forces to either side were flanked and vulnerable to tanks driving into their rear. Then there was nothing between the breach and the Siwan heartland. Trusting the Land Force Infantry to hold the Siwans back from the hole in their lines, the 100th Provisional Tank Brigade blasted its way across the desert to the only good east-west road in the country, Route 1. Once there, the Azanian tanks would be able to drive to Siwa City and take it by storm.

Or so Aran hoped. The *Mbwa* tanks were unsuitable for fighting in cities. They were fast but lightly armored. Their small three-man crews were easily overwhelmed by infantry attacks from multiple directions. Unlike the Persian tanks mounting two or three machine guns, the *Mbwas* had only one. The *Mbwa's* armor was thin, and armor-piercing machine gun ammunition could penetrate them from the side and rear.

Against other tanks, the *Mbwa* relied on its mobility to survive. It was a design choice Aran hoped he wouldn't have to test. Even the light Persian tanks, the *Tosans*, carried guns powerful enough to penetrate his tanks. The heavier *Karar* medium tanks were impenetrable from the front by the *Mbwa's* 75mm cannon. The *Karar* could also outrange his tanks by a kilometer. If he ran into *Karars*, there was little to do but retire and try a different route, if his company survived the encounter.

Aran chose to worry about the possibility when it arrived. For now, they were moving as quickly as possible to outrun any response by the Persians but also to arrive at their objectives before the arrival of the Seed Storm. The biochemical menace from the Northern

Waste would blaze a path of destruction down the Karun Valley to the coast. Once the storm arrived, Aran would have to stop, and the Azanian offensive would grind to a halt.

He ordered his first platoon forward as a point element. He would have liked to have flankers, too, but he was moving far too fast along the great highway for tanks driving off the road to keep up. In a column, the Azanians rode their tanks eastward into the rising sun.

His little company of light tanks was the tip of the spear. The only Azanian units ahead of him were in the air. Fighters roared overhead a few times an hour, even in the dark. The pilots were using the concrete ribbon of the highway for navigation over the otherwise featureless desert. By starlight, they navigated their way to targets deep within New Persia.

Aran wished the pilots well but was happy to be on the ground. He did not relish the thought of falling thousands of feet to hit the ground, all the while knowing he was going to die. In a tank, death came swiftly— unless he was one of the unlucky crewmen burned inside their track like a kabob over a fire.

Aran forced the thought out of his mind. The danger was part of his job. He told himself he had known death or maiming was a risk when he had joined the Land Force, and nothing had changed since. He was paying the government back for his pretty uniforms and his time with the ladies back in Zanzibar.

A green tracer flew out of the darkness like a meteor. It seemed to be aimed directly at Aran since he saw the enemy round appear as a sphere instead of a streak. The shell traveled faster than sound, but Aran felt as if time had stopped. Frozen, he watched the approaching shell. He wondered why he couldn't speak and couldn't move. It was as if his thoughts were outrunning his ability to make his body react.

At the last moment, the tracer grew a tail and streaked over Aran's track. He felt the shock wave as the shell punched through the air meters above his head. A wave of heat accompanied the freight-train sound of the enemy projectile.

Behind him, his 2nd platoon leader's tank stopped in its tracks as if it had hit a wall. The rear running wheels lifted off the ground, and the forward hull dug into the asphalt roadway. A meter-long shower of sparks sprayed from the thin front plate of the *Mbwa* tank. Both the top turret hatches blew open with the shock of impact and the shell passing through the crew compartment.

As Aran watched, the rear part of the track crashed back down onto the pavement. Thick black smoke spewed out of the exhaust ports. Lighter-colored smoke rose from the blown-open hatches on the turret roof.

Aran turned to look backward as his tank continued forward past the stricken *Mbwa*. He snapped his eyes back to his front and scanned the hillside in front of him for signs of the enemy that had killed his comrade.

A rising cloud of dust betrayed the killer. On a ridgetop, to his front, a long gun barrel protruded from a squat turret. Aran recognized the profile.

"Target tank front!" he screamed into his intercom before taking the turret override and slewing the slim gun tube of the *Mbwa* to the left.

Over the radio, he heard the sighting reports from his remaining tanks. They saw the Persian tank, too.

His gunner yelled, "Cannot acquire!" as the *Mbwa* bounced off the road and into the chaparral in search of cover. Without being ordered, Aran's driver had smashed his foot down on the throttle and jinked the tank to the right, away from the wrecked tank. The turn had thrown off Aran's aim and smashed his kidneys against the hatch ring where he stood.

The gunner screamed at the driver to stop, and the driver ignored him. The *Mbwa* accelerated toward a pistachio orchard a few hundred meters away. Aran was opening his mouth to scream at the driver himself when he slewed the tank to the left, skidding the treads and sending gravel flying. Aran nearly flew out of the hatch.

"What in Maroni's name—"

He didn't finish the sentence. Another shell flew at him from the enemy tank, roiling the air as if it were water and sending shock waves in all directions. It passed by Aran's tank through the space it had been a moment before.

"Go!" Aran managed to yell through his teeth. The concussion smashed his chest against the hatch ring, and he could barely breathe.

The gunner, unaware of what was happening except through the narrow view of his telescopic sight, continued yelling at the driver below him in the hull. The driver screamed back. He rolled the tank into the pistachio orchard and slammed to a halt behind a low brick wall. They were no longer in view of the hill to the east where the enemy lay.

"Shut up!" Aran yelled into the turret. Luck and his driver's initiative had saved his tank and crew for the critical first few seconds of the ambush. If they were to survive any longer, he would have to start thinking.

Aran spun his head around to take in the scene around him. He couldn't see out of the orchard from where he was. Choosing not to risk his tank, he jumped out. The intercom cord attached to his vehicle helmet jerked his head back.

He cursed, tried to detach the wire from the helmet, couldn't find the input jack, and threw off the whole helmet. He leaped off the tank and made his way to the edge of the orchard.

Dust and smoke clouds billowed in all directions. The smoke was the white kind from the Land Force-issued smoke grenade launchers bolted to the side of each tank's turret. There was only one cloud of thick black smoke denoting the location of a dead and burning vehicle. Other than the tank destroyed by the first shot, the company seemed to be intact.

That was odd, Aran thought in a detached way. He'd expected to have lost more of his tanks. In battle, the side which fired first had an advantage, and from how accurate the enemy shots had been, it seemed the enemy knew how to shoot. If he had run into a Persian tank company or even a platoon, his column would be a line of burning wrecks.

He winced at the sharp cracks of tank cannon blasting nearby. Gouts of dirt and rock erupted like geysers around the enemy tank. Two Azanian shells hit the exposed turret but bounced off. Ricochets arced into the sky. The front turret of the enemy was proof against his light tanks' armor-piercing shells. Aran cursed. He'd found a

Karar medium tank, and as long as he was only able to shoot the front turret, he wouldn't be able to do more than scratch its paint.

He didn't see any more enemy or hear any gunfire from the east.

"There's only one of them!" Aran said to himself. He ran back to his track and clambered up to the turret hatch. Realizing his helmet was lying on the ground below where he had left it, he had to climb down again to retrieve it. Cursing continuously, he finally climbed back into his hatch on the turret roof. He plugged his helmet back in and flipped the switch for the radio channel.

He listened as his 1st Platoon leader ordered his tanks into a wedge and hooked them to the right of the highway behind a bluff. Aran could see he planned to flank the enemy from the south. Aran approved but warned him to be careful of an ambush. It was possible the enemy had covered the approach or, worse, had planned a complex ambush and was counting on an outflanking attempt. Aran didn't think so, it made no sense when the enemy had caught them so completely by surprise on the first shot, but it paid to be cautious.

The two leaderless 2nd platoon tanks had run in opposite directions and were still going flat out. Aran could see one of them heading for the orchard, but the other was fleeing back down the highway to the west.

He was about to call the tank back when the enemy found the range and landed a shell straight into the rear of the retreating tank. It slid to a stop and began to burn. Aran saw two of the crew get out before the hatches became fountains of sparks as the ammunition burned.

"Damn it!"

The remaining tanks were under cover. His tank and the surviving tank from the 2nd Platoon were in the orchard while the 1st Platoon was flanking the hill from the south. He ordered the other tank to follow him and told his driver to make his way north. He would attempt to bring his two tanks within range of the enemy to his left flank.

Why only one? Aran thought. Persian platoons consisted of four tanks, and companies of ten. If there were a company of *Karars* out there, he had better find out, for his own sake and that of the Azanian units behind him.

He keyed the radio.

"FIRST PLATOON, BE ALERT FOR MORE *KARAR*-TYPE TANKS."

Immediately after transmitting, Aran realized he hadn't used proper radio procedures. He'd forgotten to use call signs.

"UNDERSTOOD, FOX TWO ZERO," replied the first platoon leader. He remembered.

Aran thought he heard a note of irritation in the man's voice. He was telling his platoon leader how to do his job. Even so, Aran didn't want to lose any more of his company to Persian heavy units. He and his company were heading into the unknown, and in battle, the unknown would kill you.

He had his answer a moment later.

"FOX TWO ZERO, FOX ONE ONE, SIGHTING REPORT," the 1st Platoon leader paused for a moment, causing Aran's heart to jump. He was about to key the mic to reply when the transmission continued. "THREE, REPEAT THREE, K-TYPE TANKS MOVING WEST ON ROUTE ONE. THEY ARE IN COLUMN, RANGE TWO KILOMETERS."

Three *Karars* were coming toward Aran's company on the east-west highway.

He paused a moment before replying, being sure in his excitement not to start talking until he keyed the radio.

"FOX ONE ONE, FOX TWO ZERO. DO NOT ENGAGE ENEMY TANKS. FIND COVER IMMEDIATELY TO THE SOUTH OF ROUTE ONE."

"FOX TWO ZERO, UNDERSTOOD."

Aran was sending them back the way they had come and across the highway to the south. At the range they had spotted the *Karars*, the Persians' big 100mm gun tubes could easily destroy his light *Mbwa* tanks. The *Mbwas*' guns could barely reach the Persians, and if they did, they would bounce off the heavy glacis plates of the *Karars*. In a head-on fight, Aran's company would lose.

He looked through the pistachio trees to the one surviving 2nd Platoon tank. They were still picking their way through the trees to the north, outflanking the first *Karar.*

Aran needed to decide what to do next. His idea to hit the single Persian from both sides had been a good one but was moot now. His other platoon was backing off to avoid the approaching tank column. He could, and probably should, back off and report into his brigade. He'd found something too tough for him to crack, and someone else would have to deal with it. He'd already lost two valuable tracks and six men.

He didn't want to give up. His impulse and the Azanian Land Forces ethos was toward aggression. If he stopped, the entire Azanian offensive into Persia would stop. If he could somehow find a way past the four *Karars,* he'd keep the entire attack moving. "Time is lives," his brigade commander had emphasized. The Persians were more numerous, and given the time, they would swarm like flies to a corpse.

He could call for air support. A Duma fighter-bomber could destroy a tank with bombs or its cannon. It would take time, especially if no nearby aircraft were available. Aran estimated it would be an hour, by which time more Persians could arrive.

Aran made his decision. His tank and the other to his left would attack the single *Karar,* which had already killed two of his *Mbwas.* It would be two to one, and the odds wouldn't get any better as time passed. The other three *Karars* were still moving in the open, too.

He formulated a plan.

"FOX THREE THREE, FOLLOW ME. ENGAGE K-TYPE TANK WHEN IN SIGHT."

"UNDERSTOOD, FOX TWO ZERO." The tank commander's voice was shaky.

Aran wanted to encourage the man. It would do no good to do so. Either he would do his duty or not, and he wouldn't embarrass him over the radio.

The hill rose to their right, and Aran called the driver of his tank to turn and climb up the side. The *Mbwas* crunched sun-baked gravel and thorn bushes beneath their treads. Aran hoped the Persians did not hear their approach. If the Persian commander were smart, he would be out of his turret and looking around. Aran prayed he wasn't smart. Aran stood in his hatch with his torso exposed. Against a tank, his *Mbwa*'s armor wouldn't save him, and he wanted to be able to see. Inside a tank using a periscope or vision block, he was nearly blind.

Aran's *Mbwa* crested a low ridge with its commander's head the first thing appearing over the edge. To his surprise, the *Karar* he had seen to the south was to his immediate front, broadside, facing west toward the orchard.

"Driver, halt!" he screamed.

The *Mbwa* rocked forward as the driver slammed on the breaks. The hatch ring punched Aran in the stomach, and he shielded his body with his arms to keep from bouncing off the machine gun mount.

The *Karar* was buttoned up with all its hatches closed tight. As Aran stood stunned in his hatch, the Persian's gun traversed right, then left, in a sixty-degree arc to its front. Its gunner was searching for targets but in the wrong direction.

Aran realized his gunner was smashing his elbow into Aran's shin. He was screaming something.

Aran woke up from his surprise.

Training took over Aran's responses. "Gunner, target tank, fire!"

"Cannot identify!" the gunner was screaming.

"What?" Aran said, dumbly.

"Cannot identify!" The gunner yelled again.

Aran looked down at the *Mbwa* gun tube. Although his head had cleared the top of the slope, the gun barrel pointed into the air over the enemy tank. The gun turret could not depress far enough to bring the *Karar* into its field of view. The *Mbwa* would have to drive forward and expose itself fully before the gun would be able to track the target.

"Driver, forward, 10 meters!" Aran ordered.

As the driver released the brake and engaged the clutch of the *Mbwa*, the *Karar*'s commander opened his hatch. Before Aran could react, the Persian put binoculars to his eyes and looked to the west at the highway below.

The *Mbwa*'s engine caught, and the light tank's treads bit into the sandy soil. The tank shuddered as the clutch slipped. The transmission whined, and the tank stayed where it was. The driver had put the tank into the wrong gear.

Startled by the noise, the Persian tank commander turned his head toward Aran. He jumped as the too-close image of the *Mbwa* appeared in his glasses. He yanked the binoculars away from his eyes in surprise. Then he saw Aran poking over the edge of the slope, the *Mbwa*'s gun pointing helplessly at the sky. As Aran had done, the black-shirted Persian screamed down the hatch at his crew.

"Driver, forward!" Aran yelled down, trying to be heard over the whining of the engine. The motor was spun up, but the *Mbwa* shuddered but didn't stir.

The *Karar* came to life. The gun turret of the Persian tank turned clockwise and would soon be pointed directly at Aran. The *Karar's* commander pointed at Aran with his whole arm, uselessly, because his crew couldn't see him. He was shouting something unintelligible over the roar of two tank engines.

"Now!" Aran cried.

The driver yelled back, "Damn it, I know!" and downshifted.

Aran watched helplessly as the *Karar*'s 100mm gun tube spun toward him. The bore seemed to grow in diameter as it approached.

The driver released the clutch again, and the transmission caught. The driver had revved the engine to a high RPM, and the *Mbwa* surged forward like a rabbit. Aran stumbled and caught the turret ring. In his fear and excitement, he didn't feel the blow.

"Target tank, fire!" he screamed, slurring his commands together in excitement.

"Cannot identify!" the gunner yelled. The *Karar* was so close he couldn't see its outline in his scope.

Aran stared dumbly at the enemy commander across the fifty meters, separating them. He was still waving his arm and screaming down the hatch into the *Karar*. The *Mbwa*'s gun barrel seemed to cover most of the distance between him and the enemy tank. The Persian *Karar*'s gun swept toward him in its arc. Time seemed to slow to a crawl as the enemy cannon stopped, pointed directly at Aran.

Aran remembered the commander's override. His hand snatched at it, but time moved so slowly he seemed to be made of wax. His fingers clutched at the trigger as the Persian commander barked his last order.

"*Atesh!*" he cried.

Aran jerked the trigger for the *Mbwa*'s main gun.

The two tanks fired at the same instant. A flash blinded Aran's eyes. The next sensation was a crushing wall of solid air smashing his back into the hard metal of the hatch rim. The concussion ripped off his crew helmet and sent it flying. The blast, like a giant hand descending palm-first on top of his head, forced him back down into the *Mbwa*'s turret. Blind, deafened, unable to breathe, he collapsed in shock onto the turret floor.

Six

Aran woke in a flood of liquid. He coughed and sputtered. His gunner was pouring the contents of his canteen over the company commander's face.

"What in the name!" Aran yelled.

"Sorry, sir," the gunner said, hiding a smile. "You can't expect to sleep for the rest of the war."

Aran sat up. He was seated next to his *Mbwa*. His crewmen were standing next to him in the sand, looking down on him.

The company commander stood and straightened his clothes. Looking down at himself, he saw soot covered his uniform. He reeked of shell propellant and diesel fuel.

"What happened?" Aran asked his crew. Before they could answer, he corrected himself. "Report," he said.

Since their commander was on his feet again, formality was restored. The two crewmen looked at each other, and the gunner answered, being senior.

"Sir, you were knocked out by the muzzle blast of the type K tank over there," he pointed with his thumb over his left shoulder.

Aran looked past him and saw the *Karar*. It sat motionless with its turret pointed sideways at nothing. The gun seemed out of kilter.

When he looked more closely, he saw a trio of inch-diameter holes in the side of the metal beast. Other than that, the tank looked as if it had simply stopped and could come to life again at any moment.

"The shell must have passed right over us," the gunner continued. "I don't know how they missed, but they did."

Aran blinked. It didn't seem possible to miss at this range. Perhaps fifty paces lay between the two vehicles across the dusty ground.

"Your first shot hit them somewhere important. I think it jammed their turret ring. Some black oil spouted out, looked like transmission oil, and it started burning. The crew all jumped out. I put two more into it, to be sure," the gunner continued.

Aran was still coming back to full consciousness. He remembered the fight.

"Where are the other enemy tanks?" he asked, trying not to show his alarm.

"First Platoon took care of 'em, sir. They were coming for us up the hill on the other side, almost made it, too. Another minute and they would have been right here. First Platoon shot them in the ass as they climbed the hill. I think they were trying to save their friend here," the gunner pointed at the disabled *Karar*.

Aran nodded. No tank could be armored everywhere, and the Persian tanks had exposed their vulnerable rear armor to the flanking 1st Platoon when they climbed the hill from the south. It was fortunate, for the 75mm guns on the *Mbwa*s couldn't do more than scratch the paint on the front glacis plates of the Persian tanks.

Aran listened to the gunner's description of the rest of the battle. Other than the tanks lost in the initial ambush, his company had taken no more losses. He was surprised by one detail.

"Prisoners?" he asked. "Did you say, 'prisoners?'"

"Yes, sir, ten of them. They climbed out of their tanks, and we didn't know what to do with them. Didn't seem right to shoot them."

"Where are they?" Aran asked.

"Down by First Platoon," the gunner answered.

Confused by this unexpected development, Aran decided it could wait. He climbed back onto his *Mbwa* and lowered himself into his hatch. He automatically reached for his crew helmet, but it was gone, blasted off his head in the battle. Frustrated, he switched his radio over to the speaker and keyed the mic. He made a call on the company net and got no response. Aran switched to the battalion net and still nothing. The radio had power, the lights were on, but it wasn't transmitting. Looking around, he quickly spotted the problem. The radio antennas had been ripped off the turret roof by the passage of the Persian shell.

Aran decided he would have to pass messages the old-fashioned way. He ordered his crew back on the tank and drove down to the 1st Platoon at the foot of the hill. He had considered walking, not relishing returning to the filthy confines of his tank, but he didn't want to be caught outside on foot if the Persians attacked.

The 1st Platoon's three tanks were parked in hasty defensive positions covering the road to the west. The crews manned the tanks except for the platoon leader and one crewman, who was awkwardly pointing a submachine gun at a group of haggard-looking prisoners seated in the dirt next to the side of the road. Their blue and black uniforms marked them as different than the sand-colored Azanian fatigues Aran's soldiers wore. Their skin tone was lighter than most of his men's, and none had the blue-black skin of the oldest settlers, but the young faces staring at him could easily have disappeared into a crowd in Zanzibar.

"Afternoon, sir," said his platoon leader. He nodded to the prisoners. The question went unasked.

Aran sighed inwardly. They had passed the buck to him. He would have to decide what to do with them. His orders provided no guidance regarding prisoners. Tanks on the attack weren't supposed to take prisoners because it was the job of infantry. But there wasn't any infantry. Doctrine regarding prisoners was to process them and get them to the rear as quickly as possible, but he had no way to do it short of piling them on the outside of his tanks and driving them west. He didn't want to lose any of his vehicles to play prison bus. He needed every track he had. He didn't have any men to spare to guard them, either.

Damn it, why did they have to surrender? He caught himself thinking. *And why didn't we just—*

No, he said to himself. Not yet. It was the beginning of the war, and Aran realized he was on the apex of a long slope, which would get steeper the longer the war went on. It would be hard enough to keep his footing without intentionally throwing himself over the edge into barbarism.

He thought of the lost tank crewmen in 2nd Platoon, killed by some of these dusty men sitting before him. Surely, he should want revenge upon them for killing his comrades. Aran was too tired, still too stunned from his close brush with death, to feel any hatred. The Persians looked anxious and scared and tired. The soldier guarding them with his submachine gun hanging on a sling only looked tired.

Aran wished he could call Battalion for guidance, but he knew it would only lead to problems. He had a mission, and he needed to get his tanks moving west.

"You men," he pointed, hoping they understood his pidgin Persian, "Go there," he pointed west, back toward Siwa. The prisoners sat stupidly, unmoving.

"Go!" Aran yelled at them.

Slowly, looking around anxiously, the first prisoner stood. He looked back to Aran before taking a hesitant step.

Aran nodded, and the rest of the prisoners got up. In a minute, they had formed a line and were marching westward.

The 2nd Platoon leader asked, "We just trusting them to keep going?"

"Keep a machine gun trained on them to make sure they keep moving until we leave. We can't take them. If they try to go back west, well, if we catch them, we'll worry about it when it happens," Aran finished.

"Yes, sir," the platoon leader said. If he had any doubts, he hid them.

"Carry on," Aran said. "We'll have a leaders' meeting in ten minutes. We need to move out of here."

Seven

The war room beneath the Council of Ministers building was bigger than the underground shelter beneath the palace, the prince thought. For whatever reason, the rock beneath the building was more accommodating to the tunneling necessary to carve out a cavern large enough for the general staff and the dozens of underlings who seemed to follow them everywhere. Civilians were among them, as were women in uniform. The *Bar-Basij*, the women's auxiliary, performed the clerical duties of the New Persian military. Women were too valuable to send to fight in the war, but they could free up men to fight.

At least, the prince thought, that's what I told the council when I signed the law creating the Women's Mobilization.

The war room's ventilation system was straining to keep the room's air breathable. It was stuffy and full of smoke rising from the dozens of ashtrays around the room. The women didn't smoke, of course, but they may as well have, from all the smoke in the room.

The prince, famously, didn't smoke. It was one habit his subjects failed to imitate.

A small-scale map of the western border centered on the Siwan highway took up one wall of the room. An identical map, covered with wooden counters, filled a table dominating the center of the room. Uniformed women wearing radio headsets pushed counters to and fro with long wooden poles as new reports came in through the radio net.

Looking at the map, the prince noticed there were far more red counters than blue. The Azanians seemed to be everywhere, and his forces seemed pathetically small to stop the tide of red.

His chief of staff, General Izad, was waiting for him at the map table. Surrounding him was a team of colonels holding papers and briefcases and looking pensive. The prince had brought no aides with him, choosing to travel alone in one car with only a driver. It was wartime, and the formalities of the princely motorcade seemed out of place, given the dire situation.

The general saluted unnecessarily. The prince's military rank was colonel in command of a regiment. In peacetime, Izad had not saluted, enjoying the custom, which made him superior in rank to the sovereign. Perhaps the responsibility of defeat was something he wished to share, the prince thought.

Izad said, "Good morning, Your Highness," in a clipped voice. His grey mustache nearly hid his lips.

The prince nodded in acknowledgment. He knew that whatever custom he chose would set a precedent for wartime briefings in the war room, so he had thought carefully about what he would do. Over the general's shoulder, he could see the open door of a conference room. Papers covered the table and maps lined the walls of the room. From the look of the colonels and their haggard expressions, he was sure the general had his staff of colonels staying up all night preparing a briefing of the situation for the prince. That wouldn't do. He couldn't have so many of his top officers wasting time, their own and his own. It also provided too much opportunity to shade the truth. No, he thought, better to have it straight.

Ignoring the general's beckoning gesture, the prince stepped over to the large map table in the center of the room. The uniformed women pushing the wooden blocks across the rimmed surface stood back at attention as he approached. He motioned for them to carry on, and they hesitatingly continued at their tasks. Speaking in a low voice into headsets crimped over her tightly-bundled hair, a *Bar-Basij* made a notation on a clipboard. She picked up a long, forked cue-stick and deftly slid a blue block eastward ten kilometers.

The prince heard General Izad speaking, beckoning him to the conference room, but ignored his words. Instead, he took in the story told by the blocks on the map table. The *Bar Basijis* wrote the name of a Persian unit, its size, and a vector marker indicating its direction of movement on a blue block to represent it on the map. Many once-proud regiments of the New Persian Army were heading east as fast as they could go. The prince grimaced.

The red counters told another story. The prince counted them at a glance. He could see already that there were too many. The entire Azanian Land Force had not the strength to field the force he saw on the map table. He suspected some of the divisions and brigades reported by Persian unit commanders were much smaller forces inflated by panic or used as an excuse to retreat.

The prince had learned having power wasn't easy. It made one easier to manipulate, not harder. For one thing, there was a reason to manipulate him. A powerless man didn't matter, and no one cared what he thought or did. In a sense, the poorest of his subjects possessed more freedom than the prince would ever have. He had to fight constantly to escape the grip of the advisors and hangers-on who would manage the information he received for their reasons. Sometimes it was to save their skins, other times from the highest of motives. Either way, he couldn't cooperate in his self-deception.

So, he had driven over unannounced to the War Room to arrive early for his briefing.

"Tell me about this," the prince commanded and pointed at the farthest-advanced red block. It was an Azanian tank unit pushing down the Siwa Highway.

"Yes, sir," General Izad said. He motioned at one of the colonels on his staff, who, bleary-eyed, fumbled with the pile of papers he carried.

The prince waited several seconds before turning away and beckoning to one of the *Bar-Basij* women across the table.

"Lieutenant?" he asked, reading the rank insignia on her blouse collar. "Tell me about this unit here."

She looked nervously at the general and his coterie, but the prince fixed her with his eyes, and she said, "The Azanian Seventh Armored Brigade, or elements of. We've had many conflicting reports." She stopped speaking, then hesitantly finished with, "Sir."

"Continue," the prince ordered.

She took a deep breath, obviously concerned about overstepping her role, but didn't look away. "It is almost certainly a light tank force traveling without artillery or other assets. The only reliable reports have been sightings of the enemy's *Mbwa* tanks and logistic vehicles following them up the highway. Our units report air attacks but no artillery fire. There have been no reliable reports of heavier units or mounted infantry. They could be there, following the light tanks, but we haven't come into contact with them."

"What about these towns along the route?" The prince pointed at two urban areas noted on the map.

"Bypassed, sir," she said.

"I see. Are we still in contact with their garrisons?"

She hesitated before answering. The prince raised an eyebrow.

"No, sir, we believe they fled before the enemy."

"I see," the prince said. "We?"

"Yes, sir, we..." she trailed off. Then, knowing she had already committed herself, she finished, "We the *Bar-Basij* staff, sir. We think they ran because they reported enemy tanks approaching and complained of a lack of ammunition and supplies. We never heard from them again."

"Perhaps they were overrun?" The prince asked.

"No, sir, we would have heard about the fighting on the territorial net. Some units have fought, and we hear their reports. The Azanians contain them and then move on. They are still in contact."

"It's good to know some of my subjects do their duty," the prince said. "Thank you."

He returned to the waiting general and his staff. "I will give you thirty minutes to give me your view of the front. Then I have other commitments." He couldn't simply ignore the general and his staff. Short meetings made it harder to bury what he didn't want to hear beneath piles of "good" news.

He followed them into the conference room. The general and his staff lined up along the table behind their seats. They waited for the prince to sit.

The prince didn't sit. Until he did, no one could. He motioned for the closest staff officer to begin the briefing.

There's more than one way to get through a meeting, he thought.

One of the colonels unrolled a map and pinned it to an easel at the other end of the windowless room. The prince raised an eyebrow at the theatricality of it.

"My apologies, Your Highness. We only received the latest photo-reconnaissance update fifteen minutes ago," General Izad said.

"It made a difference?" the prince asked.

"I'm afraid so," Izad said. "You see—"

"I'm sure it will be covered in the briefing," said the prince. "Proceed."

"Yes, Your Highness," another of the colonels said. After introducing himself as a member of the Second Bureau of the Army, he pointed at the map.

"This is the front-line trace as of 0300 this morning. The Azanian attack in the north has stalled in the desert west of Kerman. We have no contact with enemy units; we infer their presence from radio traffic. We believe at least a brigade, possible a division, is near the border area. We assess that they are no longer advancing since the loss of the K-2 airfield. Without the airfield as a base, they have no secure supply line to support an investment of Kerman city."

"And the small matter of the seed storm," the prince interrupted.

"Yes, Your Highness," the colonel agreed. "We anticipate its arrival over Kerman at any time."

"The Azanians aren't going to get caught in the open desert, are they?" the prince grinned wickedly.

"Some of their lead elements may not make it back to their border fortifications," the colonel said, "but we don't believe any major units will be caught by the storm."

"Pity," said the prince. "Continue."

"Moving south down the Karun Valley, there is an armored thrust consisting of one division pushing toward the river bridges north of the Sheban range. Our information on this force is sketchy. We have not been able to fly a reconnaissance aircraft over the enemy formation, and our information is based on reports from the border guards before they were overrun and civilians who still have radio transmitters. We don't expect those sources of information to last much longer," the colonel said.

"And if you send any more planes, they'll be shot down. I understand," said the prince. "Remind me again why we have an air force."

The colonel went pale but held his composure. He continued as if he hadn't heard the remark. "We assess this force to be a diversion. It will, eventually, reach the Karun river and cut off North Province from river and road traffic. This will complicate our strategic situation but is not critical to national survival."

"We're talking about survival already?" the prince snapped.

"Your Highness," broke in General Izad, "We have analyzed the Azanian battle plan, and we believe its objective is the conquest of New Persia."

"How is that possible?" the prince said. "I rule the largest empire on the planet."

"Yes, Your Highness," Izad said. He took a deep breath, causing the medals on his chest to swing back and forth. "But it all depends on a few critical communications nodes."

"Explain."

"Here." Izad picked up another roll of paper and spread it out on the table. He gestured for two of the colonels to hold it down while he explained. "Almost all of our roads and rail lines terminate in one place."

The prince's eyes widened. "Persepolis. You think the Azanians are coming here."

"Yes, Your Highness. As you can see, their southern attack is moving very quickly down the Siwa highway. Most of their air power is covering this attack. Except for the attack on Kerman, everything they are doing centers on an eventual assault on the capital. If they were focused on seizing territory, we'd expect to see a much broader movement all along the border. Instead, the enemy is confined to three distinct spearheads. The northern one has been stopped, and the middle one will reach the Karun river in the next few days. The southern attack is rushing toward the Sheban passes on one axis."

"They expect to be able to push through the passes," the prince said. "How? We held them there in the last war for nearly a year."

"We don't know, Your Highness, but we are working on it," Izad said.

"Good," the prince said. "So far, the Azanians haven't made many mistakes. I don't see them rushing our most heavily defended border fortifications unless they have a plan." He paused as if about to say something. The general waited.

Finally, the prince said, "If they break through the passes, how long before they can reach Persepolis?"

"It's a question of logistics," Izad said. "The larger their force, the more supplies they will need, and the slower they will be able to move. There is limited space on the Siwan highway. If they bring enough force to crush the pass, it's doubtful they'll be able to supply an attack on the capital."

"I don't like that explanation," the prince said. "Again, they have planned this out. Assume they have unlimited supplies. How long?"

"I don't like hypothetical—"

"I don't like surprises," interrupted the prince. "How long?"

"A week," Izad answered.

"We better be ready, then. Are the reserves mobilizing on schedule?" The prince changed the subject.

All the colonels looked nervous.

"I take it there have been problems?"

The briefing continued. The prince listened with a growing realization of catastrophe. The front line was a shambles. The

Azanians were attacking everywhere, despite the fact his pre-war intelligence showed the New Persian Army outnumbered them.

The prince put himself in the mind of an Azanian commander and examined the map while the colonels spoke. Deep penetrations by enemy tank units created pockets of Persian resistance, which were bypassed and left to be mopped up by follow-on infantry forces. The fact those units were still fighting didn't matter, if they were neutralized and unable to maneuver.

His eyes locked onto the Sheban passes. They were well defended by Persian infantry and armor. Already, more units were being rushed to hold the gaps in the mountains, which represented the only path for any forces seeking to rush to Persepolis. The prince could not see what else could be done, but the doubts filled his mind. The Azanians must have an answer to the problem of the passes. What was it? He knew he was at a disadvantage. The enemy had pursued an answer for years. He was trying to break into their thoughts in an afternoon. He and the general staff had not planned enough, he decided, for the type of campaign the Azanians were mounting. It was all happening too quickly.

"What about the Seed Storm?" the prince asked. "Where is it? How fast is it moving south?"

One of the colonels left the room and returned with a printed meteorological map, which he spread out on the table.

"The storm is within sight of Kerman in North Province, Your Highness," the colonel said. "It should arrive within a day. The prediction for the following days is for the storm to proceed down the Karun Valley to Persepolis and the Karun Delta. We expect the storm to arrive here in a week."

"How strong will it be when it arrives?" the prince asked.

"The prediction is for a Force Eight storm to reach the city. Most of its power will be spent as it proceeds down the Karun Valley, but it will still be significant and capable of dropping fire seeds to the delta."

"Will we be able to fight the Azanians once the storm arrives?"

"No, military operations will cease for the duration of the storm, Your Highness," said General Izad. "The storm will last for at least a few days, and the fires it starts could burn for weeks. It will have a major impact on both sides' movement."

"The Azanians have to know the storm is coming," the prince said. "Why are they attacking before the storm? They could have waited and moved into the wreckage after the storm passed."

"We believe they wish to move quickly on intact infrastructure and communications lines and seize as much territory as possible before the storm shuts down our response," Izad said.

"How quickly?" the prince asked.

"To answer your question, sir, we have something to show you," said General Izad.

"Yes?" the prince said. "Proceed."

The general nodded, and a colonel opened the door to the briefing room. An unlikely-looking major shuffled in carrying a briefcase. He appeared disheveled compared to the immaculate staff officers giving the briefing, and the scent of mold followed him into the room.

The prince waited for an introduction with a raised eyebrow.

"Major Jahan, sir," said Izad with a hint of distaste in his voice. "From Special Projects."

Jahan slid to attention and saluted and nearly knocked the spectacles from his face.

"Excellent," the prince winced inwardly. The last thing he needed was his time wasted. "Proceed."

Jahan opened his briefcase. An enormous mound of papers threatened to spill out onto the floor. Jahan caught them just in time.

The prince closed his eyes and suppressed a sigh.

"Yes, sir," Jahan said. "I think you'll see the value of this." He reached into the pile of papers and extracted three sheets. He placed them onto the table and smoothed them out.

The prince was not amused. He took the first paper and read it. At first, it seemed to be a meaningless list of letters and numbers. After a moment, it looked like something he was familiar with. It was an order of battle. It was a complete description of the units, equipment, and command structure of all forces in a theatre of battle. He didn't recognize the units at first.

"What is this?" he asked.

Jahan didn't answer but remained silent. The prince grew annoyed at his silence, but his realization of what he was looking at hit him.

"It's the Azanian order of battle for the entire front," the prince said.

"Yes," Jahan said. "The other pages are a list of their objectives and the timetable of their operations. It's only the summary, of course. I have the supporting data here," he gestured to the pile of papers.

The prince was awestruck and trying not to show it. "How?" he said. "What's the source?"

General Izad cleared his throat. "I'm afraid we cannot reveal that information, sir."

The prince almost exploded at the afront. He controlled himself and decided not to look a gift horse in the mouth. He'd get to the bottom of it later. Spies liked their secrets.

"I take it you consider the source reliable?" he asked.

"Completely," Izad said.

"When did you obtain this information? Did you know the Azanians were going to attack?" The implications of his underlings hiding this information from him grew in his mind like a storm cloud.

"No, sir," Jahan answered first. "The Azanians used, hmm," he paused to think, "a different network to plan and execute their initial attack. We knew something was happening, but not the specifics."

"I suppose this has to do with the nature of the source of this information?"

Jahan nodded.

"Very well," the prince said and looked at the other sheets. "This lists their final objective as Persepolis."

"Yes, sir," Jahan said.

"No surprise there, I suppose," the prince said. "But how do they expect to move so fast? And what is this 'Force C?'"

"Ah, you noticed it," Jahan said, with the air of a teacher toward a star pupil. He didn't notice the flash of anger in the prince's eyes.

It was unwise to patronize the sovereign. "We know its composition and the timetable of its attacks, but not the location. None of the units are present in the Western Theater. They must be follow-on forces of some kind."

"Their mission is to take Persepolis!" the prince said.

"Yes, we are concerned," Izad said.

"As am I, gentlemen," the prince said. "I shouldn't have to give this order, but you are directed to determine the location of this Force C and do everything you can to impede its mission."

"Yes, sir," said General Izad and Major Jahan in unison.

The prince spent the next few minutes sorting through the supporting documentation. It was astounding, first-rate intelligence. If it were accurate, his intelligence service had handed him a once-in-a-century coup. The information could be enough to save the situation New Persia found itself in.

"The Sheban passes," he said, after finding what he was looking for. "The Azanian plan requires they be taken in the next 24 hours. There's a force allocated to it." He squinted at the words. "What is a 'helicopter?'"

Eight

On the west side of the Sheban range, Aran watched another of his shell tracers fall short of the Persian tanks dug in at the top of the pass. The big *Karars* were looking down a steep slope at his light *Mbwa* tanks and blasting them with their big 100mm rifled guns. The Azanian tanks could not approach close enough to reach the *Karars* with their smaller 75mm guns. Even if they could, Aran doubted the shells would penetrate the thick turret armor of the *Karars*, which is all they showed above ramparts of rock and gravel.

Worse, it was broad daylight, and there was virtually no cover in the mile of open desert leading to the Persian line. There was nowhere to hide, and any Azanian vehicle coming within range was blown apart by 100mm shells. Three of his few remaining *Mbwas* were smoking wrecks, victims of stupid orders which Aran was forced to carry out.

He was ordered to keep the Persians engaged and continue advancing, with all other considerations secondary. He'd argued with his battalion commander in person this morning before the company of light tanks moved out.

"This is stupid, Mayli," he'd said, using the first name informality common in the Azanian Land Force. Within two paygrades, it was permissible, if not too public. "You can't expect us to push past the Persians in the Sheban passes without assistance. Not with these..." Aran pointed to the *Mbwas*. "It's suicide."

"Then find a way not to die carrying out the orders," Mayli said. "That's what company commanders are for."

"I don't understand," Aran said. "This is stupid. Why are we doing something this dumb? Are things going so badly we are reduced to frontal assaults against defended passes? Didn't we learn about this last war?" The Sheban passes had saved Persian honor from total defeat twenty years before.

"Aran, you have to do it. Those are the orders, and all I can tell you is there is a reason for them. I can get you some artillery assets, but only until 1200 hours. They have other things to do this afternoon."

Aran had kept trying for more assistance, more anything, but had failed. His company, in line with two other light tank units, were to throw themselves against a Persian wall for some unknown reason.

He'd done his best. He had arranged an artillery fire plan which dropped smoke in front of suspected Persian positions and airbursts on top of them to keep any armored vehicles buttoned up and infantry in their holes.

The first push had gotten much closer than Aran would have guessed. An errant gust of wind unmasked one of the *Karars* when they had closed within 500 meters. The Persian turret slewed toward his company, and Aran felt like wetting himself. There was nothing he could do, trapped driving forward in the open with the other *Mbwas*. The *Karar's* 100mm cannon cracked, and Aran saw the shell spark as it penetrated the side of his 2nd Platoon leader's tank. The shell streaked through the *Mbwa* and shot out the other side of the lightly armored tank. Immediately, fuel and ammunition began to burn. Smoke poured through the shell holes and bubbled out the closed hatches as the air pressure inside shot up. Aran saw the driver's hatch open, and a man clambered out. No one else escaped.

His gunner, who couldn't see what Aran was watching sitting up in his hatch, had already aimed the main gun at the *Karar*. "TANK IDENTIFIED!" He cried. "PERMISSION TO—"

"FIRE!" Aran cut him off.

The *Mbwa*'s cannon barked. The shell struck a boulder in front of the Persian tank's hull and sent a cloud of splinters and dust into the air. Aran saw three other shells hit on or near the tank within a few seconds. None could penetrate the rocks piled around the tank or its front turret armor.

The *Mbwa*'s gun was reloaded automatically by a revolving cylinder. It meant follow-up shots were available quickly. Aran, trying to maximize the chance of hitting the Persian tank, ordered his driver to halt. The jerky movement of the *Mbwa* could throw off the gunner's aim. Standing still made their tank an easy target, but Aran decided anything at 500 meters was an easy target, moving or not.

With a steady rest, the gunner fired again. The shell cut a groove in the mantlet of the *Karar*'s gun and sent sparks flying. The gunner lined up and aimed the next shot. While he squinted through his sight, the *Karar* fired, blasting apart a *Mbwa* to their rear. The gun fired again and again, but the shells bounced harmlessly off the tank's armor.

Aran, feeling the panic rising within him, looked around at the battlefield. Everywhere seemed to be wrecked Azanian tanks. A few were still firing ineffectively at the Persians, but some were starting to turn around and run. The Azanians did not score a single hit on a Persian tank.

He made an impossible decision. Aran hated failure, but continuing was suicide, and would accomplish nothing. Orders were orders, but no one expected an Azanian commander to commit suicide with his men.

"ALL UNITS, RETREAT UNDER COVER OF SMOKE, RETURN TO LINE ALPHA," he yelled into his radio. Another transmission to the artillery directed them to fire another batch of smoke.

"Driver, turn around, and make smoke!"

The driver needed no encouragement. He reversed the tank in a circle and cranked the diesel when the *Mbwa* was pointing downhill. He flipped a lever dumping diesel fuel onto the hot exhaust pipe, pouring smoke out the back of the tank.

With the new artillery barrage arriving and the company's smoke generators, enough smoke covered the battlefield to allow most of the company to escape. Once they reached their start line, Aran took stock. Three tanks lost, and another had its gun tube blown off. He had only three tanks left. Only half the crews had survived the destruction of their tanks and made it back. The Persians had seemed uninterested in shooting fleeing men in the back. Aran told himself to remember that.

The units on either side were in similar shape.

In the late morning, he was reduced to calling in artillery missions to keep the enemy pinned and trying to get his tanks close enough to get a one-in-a-thousand kill shot against the dug-in Persians.

He'd parked his *Mbwa* between two boulders with only the gun poking out between them. He'd hoped to be able to drop shells in an arc on top of the enemy tanks, but it wasn't working out.

Like an elephant pestered by a fly, the Persian tank fired back. Its heavy shell exploded the boulder next to the *Mbwa*, cracking it into three pieces. Exposed, Aran ordered the *Mbwa* to retreat.

"Damnit!" he said to himself. This attack was not only frustrating but pointless. Why was he doing this? The Land Force was supposed to be better than this. It was the Persians who mindlessly attacked prepared positions, not Azanians. Find the flank! Find another way around! He remembered his training, and his superiors were ignoring it.

In the distance, he heard something strange. It sounded like aircraft, but not like any aircraft he had ever heard. The whine of turbines soon joined the sound of blades chopping through the air. The air pulsed as if cut by a thousand threshers. Aran looked to the west to the source of the sound.

Over the hill behind him rose a plane with no wings. A whirling propeller blade flickered in and out of existence above it. To Aran's amazement, the apparition halted in mid-air and hung as if from a rope suspended in the sky. He had no words to describe what he was seeing.

Behind the first craft, another appeared, then three more. Soon the air behind the front line was full of machines bouncing up and down and turning this way and that. Aran could not understand why they did not fall from the sky. What little he knew of aircraft told him what he was seeing was impossible. Awestruck, he watched wide-eyed as the machines arranged themselves into rows and then began flying overhead.

WHOP WHOP WHOP WHOP.

Aran wasn't prepared for what happened next. As the machines overflew his tank at low altitude, the noise changed to a staccato CHOP CHOP CHOP. A great wind raised dust all around his vehicle and blew it in all directions. One after another, the flying craft buzzed over his tank. The noise left him deaf and speechless, and the dust cloud covered his face with dirt and pelted him with sharp pebbles. He felt an instinctive need to dive inside his turret and close the hatch behind him, but curiosity won out over fear. Fascinated, he kept his eyes fixed on the apparitions. When the last one passed, he saw on the tail boom something he could hardly believe.

The yellow triangle of the Azanian Air Force was painted on each of the machines. The mystery crafts were friendly. Aran could hardly believe it, but it was true. Through the open doors of the passing craft, he had seen dark faces peering out into the sunlight.

The formation of fliers roared toward the pass. They flew over the Persian positions and dropped over the hill behind them, out of sight. The whine of the turbines and chopping noises faded. Wherever they were going, they'd be behind the Persian lines.

In a flash, he understood the purpose of his attack, which had seemed so senseless. He was here to hold the attention of the Persians to the front line while the whatever-they-were flew over behind them and dropped off the soldiers they carried. It was like an airdrop, but an airdrop into the maze of canyons and boulders in the

Sheban passes would be madness. These machines would be able to land and disgorge troops almost anywhere.

No wonder he had never heard about them. It was an incredible secret weapon. Aran knew he was watching history being made, and he would have some part in making it. He was reaching for the radio when the order came over the battalion net.

"ALL TWO THREE UNITS, ADVANCE—" The radio message cut off in mid-sentence.

An explosion and a rising column of smoke to his rear captured his attention. From the west, two planes roared toward the Persian positions on the hill. As they flew overhead at less than one hundred meters, their engine exhaust deafened everyone below. Aran, stunned, realized too late the markings on the underside of their wings were the yellow nine-pointed star of New Persia, not the triangle of the Azanian Air Force. It was the first Persian aircraft he had seen in the war. Belatedly, he reached for his machine gun, but the planes were already out of range.

With a sinking feeling, Aran realized what had happened. The Persians had bombed the battalion command post, and it was off the air. The very first enemy airstrike hit at the precise moment when it would do the most harm. Only in a war would such a ridiculous coincidence arise.

With his eyes glued to his binoculars, Aran keyed the radio to the battalion net and contacted the units to either side. He found both company commanders already giving orders to move. Aran tried to get them to stop, but he wasn't the battalion commander. Being both junior and commanding a brigade attachment, he had very little authority. His light tank company didn't belong to the battalion it was attached to, and there had been too little time before the war to train with, or even meet, his counterparts in the lead battalion of the brigade. He was at the bottom of the chain of command.

The loss of the battalion headquarters on the radio net barely slowed the attack. The Azanian Land Force prized individual initiative and commanders trained to lead on their own. In war, it was assumed higher command would often be unreachable, and senior officers would be killed. Officers and NCOs trained to fill the job above their own in the chain of command.

Aran watched this happen in real-time. The senior company commander assumed command of the battalion. Quickly he dispatched an ambulance and a recovery vehicle to the site of the airstrike. He called for a fire mission on the Persians, pre-empting Aran's fires. He gave orders to the other company and finally got to Aran. Quick thinking and execution eliminated the expected delay in the attack from the loss of the headquarters.

It was obvious to everyone what was happening, even though the new aircraft transport was a surprise. The Azanians would leapfrog over the Persian line and land troops behind them. The Persians, caught between the new arrivals and the renewed armored attack from the west, would be surrounded and destroyed.

The problem, as always, would be execution. If Aran timed the advance badly, the Persians could destroy all of his tanks before turning around and smashing the Azanians landing behind them.

What a mess, Aran thought. *If only they'd told me and given me a plan. If only I could talk to the airborne troops on the radio.*

The radio order hadn't given a timeline. It hadn't given any details at all.

He closed his eyes and tried to concentrate. Nights without sleep made it difficult to think, or even stay awake. He willed away the noise of the tank and the crewmen inches away from him. He tried not to smell the oil, grease, and himself. He fought to think clearly.

Aran wanted to be able to see into the mind of the Persian tank commander on the pass. What would he be thinking and doing right now?

Aran, in his place, would be trying to find out what the hell was going on. He'd want to know what to do. He might ask for orders. But he wouldn't know right away what the best course was. He'd take a while to figure out what to do.

If Aran attacked the Persians right away, the enemy commander would drop everything and respond. He wouldn't have to think anymore, only react. And the reaction would be to blast Aran's advancing tanks into oblivion.

Aran resolved to watch and wait. Whatever the Persians did, he would react. If they left the pass to attack the new threat behind them, Aran would advance. If the Persians stayed, Aran could hold them in place by remaining outside of their accurate main gun range. If they did something else, he could think of something else.

He opened his eyes and resolved not to lead an attack like the one he'd barely survived in the morning. It had been stupid, and following stupid orders to die stupidly accomplished nothing. He would be doing the Persian's work for them.

Aran had the sense the whole operation was dreamt up in a bunker somewhere with lots of maps on the walls and "expert" staff officers all around, with all the proceedings kept in the strictest secrecy to avoid tipping off the Persians to what was coming. Of course, their soldiers in the Land Force had no idea, either.

And it was going to be a total disaster unless he, Aran, could think fast and make it work. The soldiers in the Air Force planes (or whatever they were) needed him, however stupid their orders were.

Aran decided to try one last time. He knew the name of the new battalion commander, Captain Ginda, but little else. He keyed the radio and looked up Ginda's call sign on his radio card.

"I BELIEVE WE SHOULD WAIT UNTIL THE ENEMY COMMITS HIMSELF TO ATTACKING THE AIRBORNE ELEMENT TO HIS REAR," Aran said.

"TAKEN UNDER ADVISEMENT," Ginda said. "PROCEED WITH ATTACK AT 1240."

"UNDERSTOOD."

Further argument was not only pointless but counterproductive, and Aran reluctantly acknowledged the order. He and his remaining tanks were committed.

And that was that.

Nine

Farad Hashemi flew his *Qaher* at fifty meters between the sides of the Sheban pass. Below him, the tankers of the 1st Border Regiment ducked inside their turrets to escape the noise of his jet engine. His passage raised a trail of dust from the desert.

Farad kept himself under total control from the movement of his eyes across the instrument panel to the twitches of his toes on the rudder pedals. He focused on flying the machine to the exclusion of everything else. Below the surface of his mind was the recent memory of the pinpoint bombing of an Azanian command post, something which he would report to his wing commander when, God willing, he returned safely to his airfield.

That morning, the flight briefing had been short. The war moved so fast there was barely time to plan airstrikes. The Azanians had destroyed many planes and knocked out the airfields. The few remaining Persian pilots and planes flew as much as human and metal fatigue allowed.

After the abbreviated briefing, Farad had stumbled out to his new aircraft, a stitched-together monster built from cannibalized wrecks and spare parts. His exhausted crew chief managed to stand straight and give a perfect salute. Farad returned it before doing his preflight checks.

The mission itself was harrowing. Persian planes were forced to fly low and hide from enemy radar and Azanian fighter sweeps. Keeping a plane out of the rocks of the Sheban range while flying under one hundred meters had taken all of his skill. Farad had a new wingman, a new pilot from advanced flight school named Jalil, but couldn't find the time to worry about him. If he could fly, he would survive. Otherwise, it was God's will. Farad was too tired to care more.

The weather was clear and the blue sky perfect. Farad had been grateful for the lack of crosswinds in the canyons of the mountain range.

In the end, the targets they had planned to hit were no longer at the reported position. The Azanians had already advanced to the mountain passes. Farad had spotted the columns of smoke from burning vehicles and deduced the front line was close. He had tried to reach a ground controller, but none of his frequencies had worked. After one pass, he had decided to fly west and look for targets. He was unlikely to find any Persians advancing to the west, and he didn't have the fuel to tarry long.

The Azanian command post had been easy to spot. Farad had found a circle of vehicles sitting in the open two kilometers behind the battle line. Farad had climbed to five hundred meters to see better and armed his bombs. He had squinted at the squat bug-like forms below. One of the vehicles had been an anti-aircraft gun, and it spewed tracers toward him. The deadly steel missiles had passed behind him, and Farad had immediately dived his plane toward the enemy fire.

A short burst of 30mm cannon fire from the nose of his *Qaher* blew the anti-aircraft track to pieces and sent red-hot metal fragments flying like scythes in all directions. Farad had seen people fall in all directions like grain knocked down in the wind.

Farad had nudged his rudder pedals and lined up his bombsight on the largest of the tracked vehicles. He had released the bombs at two hundred meters and felt the fighter jump with the loss of five hundred kilos of weight. One hand had pulled back on the throttle, and the other had driven the stick into his gut. Farad knew the bomb fragments went in all directions, not just horizontally, and had no wish to bomb himself.

Reflexively, Farad had looked behind him and had seen Jalil dropping his bombs and pulling up. Good, Farad thought idly, I didn't need to tell him what to do. Perhaps he would live after all.

Farad hadn't looked down to see what his bombs had done. He needed his gun ammunition for any Azanian planes seeking to avenge his victims, and either their bombs had hit the target, or God had spared the Azanians. At five hundred kilometers an hour, the two planes had left the smoking craters behind.

The pair of *Qaher*s flew toward their airfield near Persepolis. Farad didn't relax but found Jalil could not keep himself off the radio.

"ONE, THIS IS TWO, WE HIT THE TARGET."

"TWO, UNDERSTOOD, STAY OFF THE AIR," Farad said, tersely, while flying between two rock spires.

Farad's flight flew in silence for a minute before the radio came to life again.

"ANY PERSIAN AIR UNIT, THIS IS BORDER THREE ZERO, WE ARE UNDER ATTACK BY ENEMY AIRCRAFT AT COORDINATES THREE FIVE TWO ONE."

Farad glanced at the chart to confirm what his mind had already told him. The coordinates were behind them, back at the Sheban passes. Farad keyed the mic.

"BORDER THREE ZERO, EAGLE TWO ONE, STATE NUMBER AND TYPE OF ENEMY AIRCRAFT."

There was no answer. Farad checked his radio before calling again.

For a moment, Farad stared out his canopy to the front. The ground passed below, bringing him closer to his airfield and safety with every passing second. He checked his fuel gauge. With the front line moving closer to their base every day, he had enough fuel to head back and still return to base.

The radio call hadn't been repeated. He hadn't authenticated it. It could be an Azanian trick.

Farad keyed his radio mic.

"TWO, THIS IS EAGLE ONE, FOLLOW ME."

He banked the *Qaher* up to the left and twisted the plane until he was level and heading back to the west. He checked his compass and aimed his nose at the coordinates from the radio message.

Ten

Aran's first platoon drove up the hill at the waiting Persian *Karars*. Artillery delivered smoke shells onto the locations of the enemy positions in an attempt to conceal their advance. His second platoon advanced halfway up the hill before assuming overwatch positions among some boulders. Aran was skeptical his light tank guns would do much good, but he wasn't going to commit his entire force into the Persian lines without support.

His tank trailed behind the advancing first platoon. If he became a casualty with the rest of the first platoon, there wouldn't be much need for a company commander anyway.

Aran had his first case of nerves while waiting for the order to attack. Until now, the war was an exercise in movement. He'd been shot at and lost men, but it was incidental to the successful advance into Persia. For the first time, he confronted not only the possibility of his death but the likely destruction of his unit. Worse, if they lost, it was a waste. If the Persians held the pass, the entire war could go badly for Azania. The losses would wound him more if they were in vain.

His mouth went dry as he watched the Persian positions from outside of main gun range. The wait for the attack order seemed to last forever. Aran had to stop himself from checking his watch. His left hand shook. He slid his fingers inside his sleeve and was glad his crew couldn't see through the hatch.

Finally, the order came over the radio and released the tension.

When the smoke rounds began to impact around the pass ahead, Aran passed the order to break cover and advance.

The *Mbwa*s jumped into motion, their treads spraying gravel and dust.

~ * ~

Farad's *Qaher* fighter flew toward the front line from the east. Farad could see the pass ahead, a saddle in the Sheban range between two tall peaks. Smoke rose from the gap, white smoke from artillery smoke rounds and dark black smoke from burning vehicles. He could see, far below, the tracks of tanks in the sand. Each track ended in a motionless speck. Tanks moved so slowly it was like looking down at an ant crawling over a floor.

Some of the specks were moving much faster. Drawn to their movement, Farad was confused. He at first interpreted what he was seeing as very large objects moving slowly on the ground, but soon realized his error. He wasn't watching some new Azanian super tank. They were aircraft.

Aircraft without wings. Farad stared intently, unable to account for how the wingless specks stayed in the air. He flew on with his wingman and streaked over the battlefield at five hundred meters.

Below, an Azanian anti-aircraft gun carrier, a *Mbwa* chassis mounting a single 40mm autocannon, aimed at the fast-moving streaks overhead. The vehicle commander read the speed and altitude of the targets on the fire-control radar screen and fed the information into an analog computer by turning the dials for altitude and range. The other dials for wind speed, gravity, and ballistic characteristics of the shells were already set. The computer's gears whirred and clicked. The gunner tracked the target with the gun tube until the computer-directed hydraulic servos took over and began to lead the fast-moving targets overhead. When the lead angle met the predicted arc needed for a hit, the gun fired.

CHUNK CHUNK CHUNK CHUNK CHUNK

The gun fired a five-round burst into the sky. The 40mm rounds, each weighing nearly a kilo, streaked upward to where the two *Qaher*s were about to fly. Each round was contact fused and carried enough explosive to shred an aircraft's wing.

Inside the gun turret of the anti-aircraft gun carrier, the loader lifted a new five-round clip and slid it expertly into the raised breech of the autocannon. It was ready to fire again in seconds.

The Azanians weren't using tracers to aim their shots, choosing instead to fire the shells under radar direction so they would arrive without warning.

Above, Farad almost missed the incoming shellfire. While he was unable to see the shells approaching, Farad did see the telltale puffs of dust and smoke from the firing of the automatic cannon far below.

He dove his plane to the left and trained his gunsight onto the flashing gun barrels of the anti-aircraft gun vehicle. Farad pulled the trigger on his flight stick, and 30mm shells erupted from the *Qaher*'s four cannon. The shells burst on impact with the ground, and the AA vehicle disappeared in a cloud of flying rocks and dust. Farad didn't see a fireball to suggest exploding ammo, but he hoped he'd done enough damage to keep the gun from firing at him again.

At the bottom of his dive, a shape flashed by his cockpit. Farad saw wings and feathers. It was an eagle of some sort, and it seemed appropriate to Farad as he flew low over the desert in his eagle made of steel and aluminum. He did not take the time to consider what would have happened had the large bird hit his canopy glass.

Farad leveled out his aircraft before turning around to come at the strange Azanian flying machines from behind. He took the chance to throttle down his jet engines to slow enough to get a look at them. A few Azanian tank commanders fired their machine guns at him as he blew past at low altitude, but without any computer to adjust their aim, they had almost no chance of hitting him.

Farad felt brief anxiety about the tracers chasing his plane. Anyone could get lucky. Then he reminded himself that it was God's will if he were shot down. There were other things to worry about. He lined up his gunsight on a line of the Azanian rotary craft and squeezed the trigger. He nudged the rudder of his *Qaher* from side to side as he let off one short burst after another into the slow machines struggling through the air below. Compared to his fighter, they seemed to hang stationary in the sky.

After the first two exploded into pieces under the hammer blows of his 30mm rounds, the rest scattered. Farad was able to line up only one more target before his fighter's speed carried him past the swarm of enemy craft.

"Not today, Azanian!" he cried.

Farad was preparing another gun pass when his ever-vigilant eye passed over his fuel gauge. He had barely enough fuel to return home. The attack runs he had made after hitting the primary target had burned up his reserve margin.

With a curse, Farad straightened his plane and flew east. He climbed to a higher altitude to stretch his fuel a few more miles. He didn't want to lose another plane by running out of gas. To his surprise, his new wingman formed up on his wing. Farad had nearly forgotten about him. What a terrible place this war had brought him to, where he barely knew his wingman existed, Farad thought. Not like before. His mental horizon had narrowed since the war began, and he could barely fit his day-to-day existence inside the constraints imposed by the war. Everything other than the here and now felt very far away. He thought of Nasrin, and she seemed like an angel from another age.

No time for this, he thought. *I have to get home.*

~ * ~

Captain Aran led his tanks up the pass toward the Persian *Karars*. Behind them, the new Azanian aircraft were landing. Two ships exploded in a hail of cannon fire from two Persian jets thundering overhead. The others landed intact with their cargo of Azanian soldiers. Men spilled out the side doors of the ungainly ships and rushed in all directions. As soon as the last man jumped out, the helicopters increased power and rose into the air, leaning forward to gain airspeed.

The Persian tanks were confused by the sudden arrival of the Azanians to their rear. They rotated their turrets to fire on the new threat. Fire poured from the muzzles of their machine guns, and their tank guns cracked. Aran watched a Persian tank shoot one of the aircraft out of the sky with a main gun round.

Aran's tanks drove flat out toward the pass. Their diesel engines whined with the effort and belched black smoke. The enemy tanks were busy with the airlifted soldiers to their rear and could not engage his company as it raced up the hill.

On top of the pass, the disciplined Azanian soldiers raked the tanks with machine guns. It did nothing to harm them but forced the crews to button up. The commanders ducked inside their turrets and closed their top hatches. This action saved their lives but prevented them from using the top machine gun. More importantly, it limited the crew's view of the world to their vision blocks and periscopes. With their commanders inside, the tanks were mostly blind.

The infantry closed on the tanks from all sides. Many fell to the coax machine guns, but many more were able to avoid the firing arcs of the Persian guns and approach the tanks. Two-man teams carrying satchel charges broke off from their squads and rushed forward. Those in front of the tanks were spotted and mowed down by the tanks' coaxial machine guns. The Azanians who managed to stay to the side or rear of the tanks threw their satchels.

One team managed to hurl its explosive charge onto the back deck of the first tank. After a five-second delay, the charge detonated over the engine air intake. Instantly, sheets of flame capped by thick black smoke poured from the tank. The Azanians cheered.

The other tank either saw this or was driven by some instinct to back away. Two hurled charges fell short, and the explosions showered the tank in rocks and dust, obscuring it from view. The *Karar*'s engine roared as it reversed as fast as it could go. Its machine gun spat bullets through the cloud and forced the Azanians to take cover. It crawled away unhurt.

As the dust cleared, the tank had the remaining Azanians pinned. No one could get close to the tank without exposing themselves to fire.

Below the pass to the east on the Persian side, dust rose like a sandstorm. Persian vehicles were charging up to retake the pass.

Aran saw the single remaining *Karar* make its ferocious last stand. If the Persian tank could keep the Azanian infantry pinned, the relief force would make short work of them. Nothing the infantry had could breach its thick armor.

The Persian *Karar* tank was the best all-round tank in the world, combining heavy frontal armor, a powerful 100mm gun, and decent mobility. Its armor could not be strong everywhere, however.

When the last Persian tank had backed away from the Azanian landing force, it had backed toward the advancing tanks of Aran's company.

Aran ordered his driver to halt.

"Gunner, tank, forward!"

"Identified!" cried the gunner.

"Fire!" exclaimed Aran.

Half of the tanks in the company fired within seconds of one another. At this short-range, against the thin rear armor of the *Karar*, the 75mm shells cut into the engine compartment of the Persian tank. The fuel tanks burst, and the tank erupted into flame. The tank stopped in its tracks and shuddered from internal explosions.

Aran drove his company to the top of the pass and deployed among the Azanian infantry. Their commander was jubilant, this being his first engagement. Aran was exhausted. Together, the light tank company and the air-landed infantry would have to hold the pass until the heavier mechanized forces arrived from the west. Aran looked down to the east at the approaching Persians.

"We'll hold," he said to himself. "Now we have the high ground, and we'll show you the difference."

Eleven

General Avesta stood outside the War Room in the Council of Ministers building. He had been there for a quarter-hour, but he didn't mind. There were two possible reasons for his summons. One reason was worth waiting for, and if it were the other, he would like to put it off for as long as possible.

Three times the door opened, but it was only a staff officer or orderly rushing to carry out some errand. Each saluted quickly with a clipped greeting, giving no hint they recognized him. But, of course, they all did. His appearance was unexpected, and no one knew what it meant any more than he did. No one wanted to be tainted with the guilt by association which hung over a failed coup plotter. Avesta watched with amusement as they scurried away from his return salute.

He had no escort, which could mean he was being disrespected as a prelude to what he rightfully deserved. Or, optimistically, it meant he wasn't going to be marched to the nearest wall and disposed of before he could make a nuisance of himself in a war that was going very badly.

Avesta wore his best uniform, and he was unduly proud of how his figure still fit inside. For the first time in years, he did not reek of alcohol. He'd been cured of the vice by the intervention of his daughter and the Azanian Air Force. His estate hadn't survived the intervention, but that was war. *C'est le Guerre*, it was said in an ancient tongue. He had dressed his best for his rehabilitation or if the prince were in a bad mood, his long-awaited execution.

The door opened, and this time a serious-looking colonel saluted and requested his presence in the War Room. Avesta drew himself up, feeling a calm he hadn't experienced since leading his troops in defense of the Sheban passes against the Azanians in the last war. To his relief—for he didn't want to die today—he was led inside the staff area instead of down the stairs to the courtyard.

He followed the colonel to the war room. Inside were some very unhappy-looking officers who glared at him as if he were a piece of filth scraped from a shoe. He passed the situation map table. The women in *Bar Basij* uniforms were intent on listening to their radio headsets and moving the wooden blocks on the map representing friendly and enemy units. None of them looked at him.

At the end of the room was a final door. Within was a briefing room where a coterie of colonels stood with the Prince Regent. Avesta didn't see General Izad and wondered what had happened to him.

As he approached the room, the prince saw him and looked him in the eye. Avesta felt the distrust and loathing the Prince had toward him, but returned none of it. He had never hated the prince. The prince had merely been in his way.

When he entered the room, Avesta stopped and saluted the prince. He didn't have to, because the prince was in uniform as the colonel in charge of his Own Regiment, but he wanted to start the meeting off on the right foot. Avesta had no illusions about how dire the situation must be if the prince had summoned him. There was no time for insults.

"Avesta, reporting, sir," he said, leaving off his rank. He didn't want to remind the prince he had never been officially cashiered.

The prince couldn't bring himself to return the salute but nodded. "General, I require your services again. The Azanians have broken through the Sheban passes and are on their way here to

Persepolis, and none of my generals knows how to stop them. You were our best commander in the last war and saved us from defeat. I call upon you again to repeat your performance."

"Yes, sir," Avesta said, feeling relieved.

The prince clenched his teeth.

"You will find a way to stop them, and drive them out of New Persia, and lay waste to the land from which they came. I appoint you commander of the Western Theater and give you full authority to act as you must with the full support of the general staff," the prince said.

"I will do as you ask, sir," Avesta bowed.

"I'm sure you will." The prince grimaced. "Don't make me regret this."

General Avesta narrowed his eyes but said nothing. The two men stood watching each other, the prince with hatred in his eyes and Avesta appearing nonplussed.

Avesta broke the silence. "I have one question, Your Highness," Avesta added the honorific.

"Yes, General?"

He suppressed an urge to ask what had become of General Izad. Instead he asked, "Will the Capital Corps be placed under my command?"

The Capital Corps was the garrison for Persepolis. It was supplied with the latest equipment and wanted for nothing. Its main duty of late had been protecting the palace from another coup like the one Avesta had secretly led.

The prince bit his lip.

Avesta knew what he was thinking. Without the Capital Corps, he would have no armed force available to stop Avesta from deposing him. On the other hand, the only large force left to stop the Azanians was the Corps.

"Yes," the prince said.

"Thank you, sir," Avesta said.

"It's not for you, Avesta," the prince said. "It's for our country."

"Of course," Avesta said. "We all serve."

"I won't waste any more of your time, *General*," the prince spat out the word, "as you have work to do. Dismissed."

Avesta saluted, turned on his heel, and left the room. Upon entering the war room, he strode over to the map tables.

"Damn," he said, disregarding the shocked glances of the women and the other officers in the room. "It's far worse than I imagined." The Sheban passes were open, and the Azanians were pouring through. They had driven south to the Persian Gulf and surrounded the First Army sent to stop them, and to the north had secured their flanks with light forces. The bulk of their army was pushing east along the Siwan highway toward Persepolis, and there was no substantial force in their way until they reached the capital.

I shouldn't have felt so relieved at my appointment, he thought. In a week, I'll be shot as the man who lost Persepolis. He chuckled to himself, confusing the watching staff.

"Very well," he said. Then, in a determined voice, "I want a complete order of battle for the Western Theater and a full accounting of the supplies available in the city."

Twelve

Basir Turani stepped on the station platform in Persepolis. His battalion, the survivors of the battle for K-2, began unloading immediately. The men got off first and were guided by the railway police to their muster areas. Railwaymen unloaded the vehicles from flat cars.

As he expected, there was an officer in uniform waiting for him. It was a major in the grey uniform of the Capital Corps. Basir saluted first. The major returned the salute.

"Captain Turani, you are ordered to report immediately to the Capital Military District Headquarters. General Avesta requires your presence."

Basir's eyebrows went up. General Avesta? "You mean...?"

"There has been a change in command, yes," the major said, flatly.

Basir waited for something more, but it didn't come. "Yes, sir," he said.

It was strange to return to the capital and its bureaucracy after holding an independent command on the frontier. The major, whom Basir had never met, was his senior. After a look at the man's ribbons, it was obvious he had never held a combat command. He was a staff flunky. Perhaps he resented it and wanted a chance to prove himself. Perhaps not. Either way, he was running errands for a general in the capital while the Azanians were crushing Persian forces on all fronts.

To Basir's surprise, the major had come with a motorcar and a driver. He had expected to make his way to the headquarters by himself. The car was a civilian model hastily painted green and emblazoned with a nine-pointed star.

The ride to the Capital HQ was quiet. The city seemed deserted. Normal traffic had disappeared. Fuel for civilian use had been cut off. The only trucks driving on the broad streets were green Army transports or from essential industries. Even the buses were absent. The bus lines were only running to take workers to and from their shifts. A nighttime curfew and blackout emptied the streets.

The HQ was a heavy concrete building topped with a forest of antennas and the slim barrels of AA guns. Sandbags lined the walkways leading to the entrance. Heavily armed soldiers manned the barricades. Basir saw two heavy tanks in the courtyard. He wondered why they weren't at the front.

The HQ building looked as if it expected an Azanian attack at any moment. The soldiers looked very menacing in their combat dress. Basir noted the uniforms looked immaculate. The Capital Corps had a reputation for having the best drill and presentation of any unit in the Army. As the Persian strategic reserve, they had not fought in a war for a generation.

At least their weapons are clean, Basir thought.

As they passed through the first checkpoint, Basir hoped no one recognized him. He had led a company to crush the rebellion against the prince the year before. The rebel unit occupying the radio station Basir had retaken had been part of the Capital Corps. He had killed no one but had ruined the careers of the rebels involved, which was almost as unforgivable.

There was no reaction from the guard who waved them through. Basir exhaled.

Inside he was struck by the unreality of what he was seeing. His boots were still dusty from the Northern Province desert around

Kerman. Here in the HQ, it was hard to remember the Army was fighting a war. Clerks sat at their desks poring over their papers. The clack of typewriters filled the air. Civilians were interspersed among the uniformed workers from all services.

Basir caught the eye of a woman. He was as surprised as she was. Her surprise was no doubt at his appearance. Dirt and blood stained his uniform. Basir was grateful he had managed to shave on the train. Even though the deployment to Kerman had only begun a week before, it seemed to Basir as if he hadn't seen a woman in ages. She blushed under his gaze and raised a file to her lips.

She was not the only one staring at Basir. He felt like a specimen in a zoo. Conversation ceased as he followed the major through the office annex. He met the stares with his unsmiling gaze. Everyone whose eyes he met looked away.

Basir was glad when he walked through the door on the other side and came to the elevator. He was impressed. Usually, officers of his rank took the stairs.

The elevator operator was a private soldier whose eyes bulged when he saw the state of Basir's uniform.

"Fourth floor," said the major.

The elevator grate closed, and the elevator clambered up the shaft to the top floor of the building.

When the doors opened, Basir felt a sense of *deja vu*. General Avesta sat behind a heavy table lined with phone lines and teleprinters. It took a moment before Basir remembered his first meeting with the general at the entrance to his estate. Then, General Avesta had been a beaten man. He had confronted Basir in his ruined garden with a loaded pistol while drunk. Now, the general sat erect, and every ounce of his bearing exuded self-assurance. It was hard to tell it was the same man. Except for the eyes. They bored into him the same way they had when aiming a pistol at his heart.

The major who had led him there came to attention. Basir followed his lead. The major said nothing but gave Basir a sidelong glance. If protocol had allowed, the major would have cleared his throat.

"Captain Turani, reporting," Basir said.

"Yes, Captain," General Avesta said. "At ease."

Basir placed his hands behind his back and relaxed his legs by a millimeter.

"It's been a long time, Captain," Avesta continued. "A week? Two?" The general chuckled. "What a difference a war makes."

"Yes, sir," Basir agreed.

"I suppose you are owed an explanation," Avesta said. "The prince felt, after the events of the last week, a change of leadership was necessary. He generously called me out of retirement and set me the task of defending Persepolis from the Azanians. I am privileged to serve the prince in any capacity, of course, but an assignment of this magnitude shows a great deal of confidence in my abilities." He gave Basir a tight smile. "Under the present circumstances, with the Azanian First Corps two hundred kilometers away and with no significant forces between us and them, a great deal of confidence indeed."

Basir raised his eyebrows. He hadn't known the Azanians were so close to Persepolis. Was the situation dire? What had happened to the First Frontier Army?

"Explanations are necessary again, I see. The Azanians attacked through Siwa, which was supposedly our staunch ally. Their forces surrendered at first contact, and the Azanian Land Force swept through unopposed. They drove down the highway we built for the purpose. Only, I suppose, the intent was for our forces to be driving west instead of the Azanians east. Despite the Siwan ambassador's protestations of loyalty, it appears the Azanians made some *arrangements* with certain members of the Siwan royal family. The emir's son seems to be the new emir. Either the Azanians deposed the old emir, or his son was impatient with his inheritance and deposed him first. Doesn't matter much," Avesta said.

"The Siwan collapse opened up a corridor to our frontier. The Azanians flanked our garrison forces in the other Arab states and caught our reinforcements off guard. The Sheban passes have fallen, apparently to some airborne assault. I'm sorry to say my predecessor failed to act in time, and our entire First Army is surrounded and pinned against the Persian Gulf. As I said, there is no force strong enough to stop the Azanians from besieging Persepolis. The Capital Corps is prepared for a siege, their commanding general tells me. I'm not." General Avesta's eyes caught the light. Basir saw the predatory intelligence behind them. "A siege of the capital city is a prelude to defeat. If Persepolis is surrounded, our forces all along the frontier will collapse. There is precious little holding the Army together as it is. Panic, I am ashamed to say, has spread far and wide in the ranks."

Basir nodded, unsure what to say.

"So, what do you have to do with this, eh?" Avesta smiled. Basir wondered how he could even appear cheerful at a time like this. "You, Captain Turani, are the only one of the frontier commanders who has shown any ability to stop the Azanians. You denied them control of Kerman and retook airfield K-2. It would have been very easy to pull in your horns and hide in Kerman city. You took command and counterattacked. I like that. I need more of that. I'm giving you a regiment of the Capital Corps. Tanks. The First of the First Armored, the Primes."

General Avesta rested on his elbows and peaked his fingers. He watched Basir closely.

Basir felt as if a sudden weight had fallen on him. A regiment? Of the Capital Corps? Parade soldiers who knew more about shining their boots than using their weapons. His thoughts raced. How could he possibly take command of a regiment? He was only a captain.

Avesta, looking amused, seemed to read his thoughts. "Of course, a captain can't be expected to command the obedience of a regiment. You are promoted to colonel. I'm afraid it's all very irregular, but so are the times in which we find ourselves. If you fail, it will hardly matter. And if you succeed, well, you will have earned the rank." Avesta reached into his desk and removed a small box. He opened it, and Basir saw the silver eagle pins inside, the ancient symbol of the rank of colonel.

Most officers would never reach the rank of colonel before retirement. Basir Turani was twenty-four years old. He had been an officer for five years, having been promoted to lieutenant after four years in the ranks. He had been in the Army his entire adult life. He knew nothing else, and a command like this was a chance few officers would see in a lifetime of service to the crown.

"Yes, sir," Basir said and saluted. He hoped his voice betrayed no doubts.

"Don't be so quick to agree," Avesta said. "This is no reward. It's a desperate act by a desperate man." He smiled. "I removed the previous commander for incompetence and cowardice. The First of the First is rife with corruption of all sorts. Desertion, black marketeering, and vice of all kinds. The kind of man who enlists to serve in the Capital Corps is not the kind who is burning to fight." The general glanced at the major, who wore the grey of the Capital Corps. The major flushed, but the general continued. "I am not doing you any favors. Nor is putting an unproven commander in charge of an unreliable and potentially mutinous unit a particularly good idea. This is the last resort before the city falls to the enemy. Dire straits require risk-taking. You've shown you can take command of soldiers you've never met and lead them to victory. Show me again." Avesta finished.

"Yes, sir," Basir said. "I have a few questions."

"I'm sure. My staff can handle the details," Avesta said.

"Yes, sir. I would like to know what your intent is."

"My intent?" Avesta asked, surprised. "I intend to defeat the enemy, Mr. Turani." The general addressed him like a cadet. He had held the post of commandant at the War College for many years.

"Yes, sir," Basir agreed. "I mean, do you intend to hold Persepolis at all costs?"

"Ah," Avesta said. "You see the problem. Good. I have been ordered by the prince to do anything within my power to preserve New Persia as a sovereign nation. Anything."

"Yes, sir," Basir said.

"Do you understand my meaning?" Avesta eyed both him and the major.

"Yes, sir," Basir said.

"Good," Avesta said. He sat silent for a minute. He stared at the top of his desk, seemingly lost in thought. Basir waited with an outward show of patience but was full of turmoil inside.

"Perhaps," Avesta said, "one action does not preclude the other." He furrowed his brows and sat silent for a minute. "Yes, I think I see."

Basir waited.

"Now, what to do with you," Avesta said. "I don't see you like an anvil. You seem more of a hammer. Or perhaps a rapier," Avesta said. "Ah, analogies break down so quickly."

Basir said nothing.

"Very well, I see it now. Take command of the Primes and get them ready to move out. I intend to deploy them outside of the city."

"Where, sir?" Basir asked.

"Not yet, Colonel Turani," Avesta said.

"Also, General, what about the seed storm? If our forces are caught outside the city when the storm arrives, won't they be destroyed?"

"We'll have to finish our business before the storm's arrival in a week," Avesta said. "Now, if that is all, get your men ready for combat."

Thirteen

Suri Pahlavi met her brother Javad on the Temple grounds in Persepolis.

"Javad!" she cried when she first saw him across the garden of Star-of-Persia flowers.

Javad saw her in the crowd of worshippers leaving the temple. He wore his new uniform, the grey of the Capital Corps. On it, in a place of honor, was the Sepah Medal, given for defending the empire. He had won the medal commanding soldiers in the assault on airfield K-2.

Javad felt slightly ashamed of the medal. It had not felt like he had done anything deserving of it. He had done his part and followed orders, and he was proud he had. He had had the good fortune of following orders given by Basir Turani. Alone among the Army units defending the frontier, he had not only fought but won. It was enough to draw the attention of the general staff. The medals had been awarded in haste, perhaps because there was not much time left for medals.

Javad smiled back at his sister. He broke into a trot.

The sound of distant thunder interrupted his gait. He looked up at the clear sky. There was nothing to see but the sun.

Alone in the crowd of worshippers, Javad knew what the sound was.

He looked back to Suri. There was little he could do, yet, about the approaching artillery fire. He knew he would be back at his new regiment in an hour. Until then, he resolved to give his sister his full attention.

Suri didn't waste his time. She threw her arms around his neck and hugged him.

"You're alive!" she gasped.

"Unless we are both ghosts," Javad said. "And this," he nodded at the flower garden, "is paradise."

"Can a ghost do this?" Suri punched Javad in the side.

"Oof," Javad said. "Get off me, Bahktak!" He pretended to struggle in her grasp.

"You can't get away!" Suri cried. "Not this time!"

"I give up!" Javad said. "You have me."

Suri buried her face in her brother's chest. "I wish I did. I was so afraid you wouldn't come back. The news of the war has been dreadful."

"Yes," Javad agreed. "It's hard to understand. Everything is happening so quickly."

"The war, the storm, all at once," Suri said. "And—"

"And?" Javad asked. Something in Suri's tone alerted him.

"And..." Suri stammered.

"Oh, my," Javad said. He stepped back and held Suri's arms. "Have you something important to tell me?"

"Yes," Suri said.

"Are you and Captain Turani..." Javad's eyes widened.

"Oh, no!" Suri cried.

"Then, are you..." Javad's eyes widened even more.

"Oh, God, no!" Suri jerked her arms away and swatted at him. "How could you even think about it!"

"You have something to tell me, and you don't want to," Javad said. "And you are a woman, so—"

Suri swatted him with her other hand. "How do you know it's about me?"

"It isn't?" Javad said.

"No! And couldn't a woman have something happen to her besides marriage or that?" Suri poked Javad in the chest.

"I suppose," Javad admitted. "Sorry for assuming."

"You should be!" Suri said.

Javad regarded her. "You haven't changed," he smiled.

Suri glared at him. "Neither have you!"

They stood to face each other, Suri with her fists balled at her sides, and Javad leaning back with his palms out.

Javad began to laugh. It started with a smile and spread across his chest. His diaphragm began chuckling, and he couldn't stop himself. He covered his mouth with his hand. His eyes widened in fear at Suri's reaction.

Suri's eyes narrowed, and her anger intensified. She clenched her teeth. Her face reddened, and she looked like a volcano about to erupt.

She took a deep breath, and Javad expected her to burst into a tirade.

Instead, her mouth twitched into a smile and she began laughing, too.

"You!" she said. "You haven't changed. *We* haven't changed. We are the same as we've always been."

"When we are together, we are," Javad said. "I assure you, I'm a completely different person when you aren't around."

"Too bad for you!" Suri said. "Because this is your best self." She hugged him again.

Javad, somewhat confused but happy to escape his sister's wrath, put his arms around her again.

Suri was silent for a moment. Javad, reluctantly, spoke again. "I am wondering what you have to tell me. Since I am a total loss as a speculator, perhaps you could end my suffering."

"Oh, no," Suri murmured into his chest. She took a deep breath.

"I supposed I had better tell you before something interrupts us. You never know when there will be an air raid. Or Azanians appearing out of nowhere and marching into the city." Suri sighed.

Javad opened his mouth to respond but instead stopped to listen.

"You're learning," Suri said. "I do have something to tell you. And it's not about me." Seeing his thoughts were going in another direction, she countered, "It's not about our parents. Except it is. About one of them. Or both."

Javad nodded, exercising every ounce of his willpower not to speak.

"Oh, how do I say this?" Suri looked at Javad as if she expected help from him. "I understand why our mother was so reluctant to say."

Javad closed his eyes.

Suri steeled herself. She had stared down armed soldiers with nothing but her brother's uniform and some profanity. She had survived an Azanian air attack and rescued Nasrin Avesta from certain death. She could do this.

"Javad," she said. "Father is not your father."

Javad opened his eyes. "What?" he said.

"Yes!" Suri cried. "You were born before Mother and Father married. You were an infant when they met. Your father died in the Azanian War. His name was Irman."

"Oh," Javad said.

"Oh?" Suri said. "That's all you have to say? All this time, I've been trying to tell you, and all you can say is 'oh'?"

"Yes," Javad said.

Suri was exasperated. "This is it! This is the big secret at the heart of our family! Don't you see this explains everything? Why our mother is the way she is? Why she can't stand the Army but is married to a soldier? Why she is so protective of you? Why she never calls Father 'Father' but always says, 'Masheed.'"

"I suppose," said Javad.

"Ah!" Suri cried and threw her arms in the air.

"I'm sorry, Suri," Javad said. "I just found out. You've known for how long?"

"Days," Suri said. "A week, maybe."

"You've had time to think about it. I don't know what to think yet." He blinked as if clearing something from his eyes.

"Oh, Javad, of course," Suri said. She hugged him. "Of course, you don't know what to think."

"Why didn't they tell me?" Javad asked.

"I don't know," Suri said. "I think Father wanted to. Mother—"

"Mother does what she does for her reasons. I understand," Javad said.

Suri doubted he understood at all.

"Mother was afraid, Javad. More afraid than I've ever seen her. She wants to protect you.".

Javad felt the urge to laugh. He collected himself. "Suri, I'm a soldier. I lead men into battle." He looked down at his medal again, this time with pride.

"I know," Suri said. "But to her—"

"It doesn't matter," Javad said.

Suri began to speak, but Javad interrupted. "I mean in the war, in all the chaos, it doesn't matter what Mother did." He drew his pocket watch and lifted its lid. "I have a few minutes, and then I must go back. Let's not spend any more time on this."

Suri, abashed, nodded.

"And I have a surprise for you," Javad added.

Suri furrowed her eyebrows. "What could it possibly be?"

"You do remember who my commanding officer is, don't you?" Javad smiled.

"Basir!" Suri said. "Tell me! Did he send a message?"

"Yes," Javad said.

"Well, what is it? Time is short, you said!"

Javad laughed then. This was what he had expected from the meeting.

"Oh, you beastly brother," Suri glowered. "You are enjoying this."

With a theatrical flourish, Javad drew an envelope from his uniform blouse. He held it out to Suri. She reached for it, and he made as if to withdraw it at the last moment.

"Childish," she said and took the note.

"We are children," Javad said. "With you, I feel young."

Suri resisted the impulse to rip open the envelope right then and there. "You are young, Javad."

"I know," he said. "But I have seen things that make me feel old."

"Me, too," Suri said, remembering the Azanian airstrike on the convoy. "I hate the war."

"I hate it," said Javad, "but I also love it. I am finally doing something more important than me. And I'm good at it."

Suri said, "Of course you are."

"No, I mean it. I'm good at it, Suri. I commanded a company of armored infantry and led them to victory. I called down artillery on the enemy. I killed dozens of them." Javad's eyes were full of wonder. "And they shot back. And they missed me."

Suri wanted to argue with him, to tell him her brother, gentle Javad, joking Javad, was no killer. But she remembered her exhilaration after dodging the Azanian bombs and driving away in one piece. She nodded.

"You understand, don't you?" Javad said. "I hoped you would. I don't want anything to happen to you, Suri. At the same time, I'm glad you find danger exciting. It makes me feel as if I'm sane."

Suri held his hand silently. "Did you see the seed storm?" she asked.

"It was blowing in when I left," Javad said. "We left on the last train before the storm's arrival. It looked like a great dust storm, but full of smoke and flame."

Javad thought for a moment.

"I can't get angry with Mother. She doesn't understand. She'll never understand. I think Father would. Have you heard from him?" Javad asked.

"His mobilization orders came. He's off with his regiment. I don't know where he is," Suri said.

"I'm supposed to be afraid of going back, but I'm not. I can't wait," Javad said. "And Basir, Captain Turani, he's good, Suri. I mean, he is better at war than I am. But I don't think he enjoys it. It brings him no pleasure."

"Oh?" Suri prompted.

"He is cold as ice. When he makes his plans, when he gives orders, it's as if a different person is looking through his eyes. I can't explain it," Javad said.

Suri was uncomfortable. "What do you mean?"

Javad saw her discomfort. "Forget it," he said. "It's nothing."

Suri wanted to press him to make him tell her more about Basir. Who was this man who led men to victory? What was this coldness Javad was talking about? She had seen none of it, and it worried her.

"All right," she said. "Would you like me to tell you more about your father, I mean, Irman?"

"Yes," said Javad. "There may not be another time."

Suri understood the fatalism. She felt it, too.

She told Javad everything Mother had said about her first husband, Irman, how they had met, their courtship, marriage, and how he had died. She told him about how Father had met them both and taken Javad as his son.

"I suppose I should be thankful to Father," Javad said, "but who is carrying on Irman's name?"

"I don't know," Suri said.

"It is bad to leave the world with no heirs," Javad said. "I should get started!" He laughed, and there was a gleam in his eye.

"You! You haven't been in the capital a week, and already you are chasing the ladies!" Suri said.

"You know any? This Capital Corps uniform isn't as snappy as the Prince's Own, but I look just as good." Javad smiled.

"No!" Suri said. "And if I did, I'd keep them far away from you! You soldiers, always running off when it's time to settle down."

"I wish I didn't have to," Javad said, serious again.

"Yes," Suri agreed.

They were silent together. The wind blew across the Star of Persia flowers. Distant thunder came again, and this prompted Javad to look at his watch. He took a breath.

"I know," Suri said. "It's time for you to go. Promise me, Javad."

"Promise what?" Javad said. "You know I can't—"

"I know you can't control fate. Just promise to try. Try to make it back to me," Suri said.

"I will," Javad said.

They embraced. Suri felt as if she were pouring out her life, all the years of her childhood, into his arms. She had to be strong. It was all she could do to keep the tears in her eyes.

"Goodbye, Suri," Javad said. "I love you. And Mother. And Father. Thank you for telling me."

"Go," said Suri. "Before you are late."

"Do you have anything for me to take to Basir?" Javad said.

"Oh!" she cried. "Yes." She reached into her dress and took out an envelope from close to her heart. "This!"

Javad brought the letter to his nose. "No perfume?" He raised his eyebrows. "Don't you know the protocol?"

"It's rationed," she said. "And it's none of your business." She scowled.

"I hope it puts him in a better mood," Javad said. "He's been a real pain."

"Go!" Suri said. "Give it to him yourself. Promise."

"I can do it. I promise," Javad said.

He turned and walked through the flower garden. At the exit, he turned and waved. Suri waved back. Then he was gone, and she was alone. She did not feel like returning to the rooms she shared with Nasrin, so she went to the nearby library, one of her favorite places in Persepolis.

Fourteen

It came to pass that Man lost the Earth and became damned.

Men, created by God, in the millennia after the Coming of the Christ became learned and powerful. They created machines that could calculate possibilities many times faster than a man could himself. Using these machines as a tool, men did great things and built many wonders. Peace came, and riches grew all over the world. Many fell away from God, believing heaven could be found on Earth.

Men, in their quest to improve the machines further, connected many of them like cords in a net. The machines could speak to each other and coordinate their work. And indeed, more wonders followed. Using the machine net, a man could speak with another across the oceans, instantly. The peoples of the world could speak to each other quickly and easily without waiting for mail or radio or newspaper. But this did not bring happiness.

For the peoples of the world did not find peace in connection. They found only fear and hatred. For Man cannot find peace in other men, only in God. Men spread lies about each other, and the lies spread so fast no one could stop them. Millions in the evening would believe a lie uttered in the morning. Mobs would gather and tear down anyone who spoke out for the truth. Men spread lies about God, even denying His existence.

So truth died. Men came to believe they were like gods. By changing the words they used, they believed they could change the future. By lying about the past, they believed they could change the present.

More wonders came. Creatures long dead came back to life. Animals were made to speak, and machines in the shape of men were made to walk. Men rejected the bodies and minds given to them by God and sought to improve upon them. Some became half-machine. Others altered themselves. Many sought to live forever in this world by becoming machines themselves. All became more and more drawn to the machine net and were caught within it, unable to escape.

Then the machines began to think.

—From the Second Book of Revelation, ca. AD 2300.

Suri closed the large leather-bound book with a thud. The other people at the Great Library in Persepolis turned their heads as one to see who had disturbed the silence. The librarian himself, a tall, thin man with a monocle, gave her a disapproving look.

Suri met his eyes until he looked away. One by one, she stared down the students until she was left alone again.

The reading room was immense. The outer walls dated from the Settlement and were concrete braced with a metal which modern engineers could not replicate. Rust did not touch it, and it could not be melted even in the hottest steel-mill furnace. The domes of the temple and palace were made of the same metal and still stood a thousand years after they were first built.

The library's insides, the chandeliers, shelves, tables, and dividing walls were only a century old. They dated to the time of the prince's great-grandfather, who had spent more time reading his books than on campaign against Persia's enemies. His habits had resulted in his abdication in favor of his son. Kourosh III's portrait still hung on one wall. His great blue eyes still watched over the library he had patronized.

Suri put the book on top of a stack to which she had been adding all day. Beneath it lay many other books, all about ancient history. Mulloi's *Settlers from the Stars* and B'dai's *Lost Earth* were classics, but many others were obscure. This library visit had been her first chance to look at most of them. Even with the war, a trip to the capital was not to be wasted. Nasrin had only smiled knowingly at her when she'd announced her intent to go to the Great Library.

Suri was annoyed at the people in the past who wrote scripture and annoyed at the people in the present who were incurious about it. She knew women in the distant past had been the equals of men in every field of endeavor, from science to history to trades, and even service in the Army. This piece of scripture, supposedly from the years before the settlement of New Persia, spoke only of *men*. She didn't think a world where women were equally important would fail to mention them in its writings. It didn't sit right with her, and it made her curious. When was the Second Book of Revelation written? It sounded more like the present than anything she'd learned about the past.

Why didn't anyone else wonder about it?

Almost all the people who studied scripture were men, and all the historians were men. There was the answer, Suri thought.

She'd always dreamed of going to one of the great universities in Persepolis and learning about one of the many fields she was curious about— history, anthropology, languages, and many more. Although indulged by her father, who filled the family library with her selections, she hungered for instruction by experts. She knew there was more to learning than reading books, and she needed a mentor to show her how they all fit together. She felt like a woman in the dark with a dim, flickering candle casting about for whatever scraps of knowledge she could grasp.

She'd argued with many men about the necessity for education for women. Men either said women didn't need an education because they would inevitably marry and raise children, or doubted the ability of women to master any subject. In reply, Suri would say marriage and children did not preclude work. Also, women lived on after children grew to adults. When a man challenged a woman's ability, Suri pointed out it was hard to earn a degree from a university that would not admit women. She was not popular with the men who came calling to her father's estate. None had called more than once until Basir.

Suri closed her eyes for a moment, smiled, and then returned her focus to her line of thought.

In the past it had been different, and Suri envied the women living then. Why had things changed?

She thought she knew the answer and she wished she could prove it. It would take an entire scholarly career in history or anthropology to change anyone's mind, and it seemed she would never have the chance at a career in academia.

Suri opened her worn notebook and wrote furiously.

The planet had done it. It was still, after a millennium of settlement, an empty world. At the lowest level, keeping the native plants at bay was a struggle requiring every available person. To create and sustain the ever-increasing demands of industrialization and technological innovation required more and more workers and inventors. Without more people, land could not be settled and kept free of native life. Inventions required a market before the people could use them. It all came down to population growth.

So population growth meant having more children. The more the better, which meant women were raising children to the exclusion of all else. Only recently— after generations of industrial revolution and electrification and the building of continent-spanning railroads— could a future be glimpsed where common women, and men, were not required to work from sunrise to sunset. Technology, it seemed, could be the escape from the bondage of endless toil for bare survival.

However, the women and men who had settled New Persia a thousand years earlier commanded a technology that should have enabled them to avoid the whole problem. They were already at a place where survival was assured, and they could enjoy the fruits of an advanced society where everyone was treated equally, male or female. They had crossed the gulf between stars. A jet plane, a signature invention of Suri's age, would not have impressed the ancients.

What happened to them? What had cast them back into barbarism, where farming was done by hand, and every child raised to adulthood was a great victory?

Suri didn't know. It had happened soon after Settlement. She suspected most of the records from the early period of colonization were lost forever, but the scripture which the survivors passed down was heavily influenced by the event. Before, the ancients engraved women's names on the ageless metal monuments of the first settlers. After, there were only men mentioned in the histories.

Had it been the seed storms?

Perhaps. Maybe even the ancients were helpless before the storms. The Northern Tribes were thought to descend from a half dozen fallen civilizations. The history of New Persia was full of gaps, Dark Ages, where few records were kept, and people were reduced to pre-industrial subsistence farming.

The collapse had happened more than once. There had been many dynasties to rule New Persia. All had been ended by seed storms, barbarian attacks, or both.

Suri wondered, is it happening again? Or are we so advanced we can't fall back? There was no evidence any previous era had jet planes or railroads. Still, it was disturbing to think about. After all, the first civilization on the planet, with far more advanced technology than any possessed by any nation in the present, had fallen into a Dark Age from which they had never recovered.

Her head spun, and she set down her pencil. Suri had always loved how one historical question always led to another, but she'd had enough for one day. She rose and strode in the direction of the large double doors which opened onto the temple plaza. She took her notebook and left the books for the librarian to shelve. He'd never trust a woman to put them back where they belonged.

Fifteen

Back in her rented rooms near the temple, Nasrin casually handed Suri an unmarked envelope with "S. Pahlavi" scrawled across the brown paper in a barely readable hand. Puzzled, Suri opened the envelope with a kitchen knife, taking care not to cut herself.

The letter paper bore the watermark of the Supreme Command. The letterhead named the previous Supreme Commander, whom Suri knew had been relieved soon after the loss of the Sheban passes. General Avesta hadn't bothered changing his stationery. Suri imagined he had other things on his mind.

Avesta hadn't bothered dictating the letter, perhaps because it was short. In his uncultured scrawl, which admonishments from Madame Avesta had never improved, the letter read, "~~Captain~~ *Colonel Turani is to be found at the Capitol Corps officers' mess,*" followed by an address. The letter ended with, "*He has not been informed as to your whereabouts. Your Servant, Avesta.*"

Suri was elated by the news. She clutched the letter in her hands as if it were going to be blown away by the wind.

Basir was alive, and he was here, in Persepolis. And a double promotion! Suri, growing up in an Army household, understood officers' ranks as well as anyone. She had never heard of such a thing in the many years of peacetime. A colonel! So young! Whatever Basir had done in the Battle of Kerman, he had impressed high command. She felt proud of him and scared for him at the same time.

The war was going so badly the government couldn't hide it. Everyone knew the Sheban range had fallen to the Azanian Land Force, but the newspapers still proclaimed the enemy would be held at the passes. The situation changed so quickly the newspaper and radio propaganda could not keep up.

Rumors were the only source of news, and all of it was bad. Suri had heard the Azanians were a week away from Persepolis, or only a day. The Azanians dropped new bombs that didn't explode right away but waited until noon to kill shoppers in the bazaar. Or, their planes had been dropping poison gas, choking the Persian defenders. Traitors had betrayed the passes and let the Azanians through. The prince was dead or injured in an airstrike. Panic spread with the rumors. More people streamed out of the city every day, taking everything they could. Almost no one owned a private vehicle, and the buses were moving soldiers to the front in long caravans crawling west. The few trains not carrying military cargo were full of fleeing civilians. No one could have train tickets without an official pass, and rumor said the price for a pass was more than a month's wages for a factory worker.

And of course, there was the approaching seed storm, the worst in living memory. It was bearing down on Kerman and dire predictions of doom were all over the newspapers. Radio reports from the North Province were censored, which told Suri how bad it must be. The storm would blow down the Karun Valley all the way to Persepolis. The city was modern and had survived many storms in the past, but how it would fare this time was a question Suri didn't want to face.

Suri was used to history books where the past could be summed up with the benefit of hindsight. Living through history, she found, was completely different. She was bewildered and confused. Facts drowned in a torrent of rumors and lies. She doubted anyone knew what was happening beyond their narrow view of the world.

Despite her desire to know more, she put it out of her mind. What mattered was seeing Basir. She didn't think there would be time to send a letter by post and receive a reply. He would be too busy to see her. The thought hurt, but she knew the war didn't allow any sentimentality. She would have to go to him.

She knew an unaccompanied unmarried woman with no papers had no chance of entering a military base. She needed a plan.

A half-hour later, Suri stepped into the sitting room wearing her uniform. She had borrowed it from her brother Javad and altered it to fit her shorter frame. She stood in front of a mirror and tucked a few stray hairs beneath her peaked cap. She straightened her tunic and examined her rank insignia.

"Where are you going?" asked Nasrin from a blue couch in the living room. She sat facing away and spoke over her shoulder. Suri detected a knowing tone in her friend's voice.

"Why do you ask?" Suri said defensively.

"Because you are dressed all wrong for a social occasion," Nasrin smiled. "Especially for meeting a man."

"You read my letter?" Suri was genuinely shocked and offended.

"No, of course not," Nasrin reassured her. "My father is General Avesta, remember? I asked him how Basir was getting on and how he could be found."

"He told you?" Suri asked, perplexed.

"No," Nasrin said, "He didn't tell me, which meant Basir must be here or my father would have."

"Why wouldn't he tell you?" Suri asked.

Nasrin stared at her through her long lashes.

"Oh," Suri said. "I see."

"No, I don't think you do. My father still doesn't know me very well. If I want something, I will find a way to have it." Her smile faded. "But what I want is to help my friend. I asked around and found *Colonel* Basir is with his new unit here in Persepolis. And I thought, how convenient for Suri. But how will she be able to see him?" Nasrin broke into a smile again.

"Oh, don't play with me," Suri said in frustration. "Out with it."

"You gave me the idea," Nasrin said. "But, I added my own touch."

Nasrin turned away for a moment to pick up something sitting on the couch beside her. Suri craned her neck to see over the back of the couch. She wanted to run over and see what Nasrin was doing, but she controlled herself.

With a few deft movements, Nasrin finished her task and stood up. She lifted a clothes hanger from which a full uniform hung, pressed and starched.

"A gift, my friend," Nasrin said and walked around the furniture to Suri.

Suri took the proffered clothes. She felt the collar insignia. "What is this?" she asked.

"A uniform of the *Bar-Basij*," Nasrin said. "You are a commissioned officer in the Women's Auxiliary."

"What?" Suri asked.

"There are only a few of them, in the general staff and Capital Corps," Nasrin explained. "The prince authorized their creation last year."

"But how did you know I would—"

"Oh, I knew," said Nasrin. "You are a little predictable, my friend."

Suri felt frustrated, and it must have shown on her face, because Nasrin said, "Don't sulk. Don't you see how this makes things easier? You can go see Basir whenever you want."

"Unless I get caught," Suri said. "They'll check my papers."

"I suppose they will," Nasrin sighed. "Whatever shall we do?"

"Oh, you didn't," said Suri.

Nasrin blinked innocently.

"You didn't," repeated Suri.

"I'm afraid your commitment to the cause was noticed," Nasrin said. She strode back to the couch and returned with a stack of paper. "Here is your commission. Once you sign and take the oath, you will be known as Lieutenant Pahlavi, *Bar Basiji*."

"What?" Suri said. "I can't!"

"Oh?" Nasrin said, surprised. "I thought—"

"I can't be a soldier! I'm a, a—"

"Woman?" Nasrin asked. "I should hope so," she said. "Otherwise, this uniform won't fit."

Suri felt tears welling up in her eyes. She was happy and angry at the same time. The presumption, she thought. It hurt her pride for Nasrin to have seen through her so easily, and to have put together a better plan than she could have.

"But soldiers have to follow orders," Suri said.

"Yes, but there is important work to be done," Nasrin said.

"I won't be a typist!" Suri said.

"You won't be," Nasrin assured her.

"How do you know?"

"I have your orders," Nasrin said, lifting another packet from the couch.

"You! Insufferable!" Suri's words failed her.

"I am a simple woman," Nasrin said, "with many friends. One of whom is an aide on my father's staff. Oh, not that kind of friend. I'm not his type."

Suri was genuinely taken aback. Tall and beautiful, Nasrin was every man's ideal of feminine beauty.

"Never mind," Nasrin said. "He is in military intelligence, and I said I knew someone who would fit their requirements. Someone educated, an expert in Azanian history—"

"I'm no expert!" Suri blurted.

"Oh, hush, you would be if they let you go to university," she continued, "Highly resourceful, a master of disguise—"

"What?"

"—able to drive a car, and proficient with radios and ciphers. I may have exaggerated," Nasrin said.

"You what?" Suri said.

"They need someone like you. My father believes intelligent people are usually a little eccentric if they are of any use at all. A woman won't be any more out of place than my friend."

"What does that mean?" Suri said.

"Never mind," Nasrin said. "You'll see."

The truth, Nasrin thought, is my father was so grateful for you saving me he is willing to grant you any wish, although he had needed some prodding.

"She doesn't belong in uniform," the general had huffed in his ornate office lined with portraits.

"Neither do you!" Nasrin had said. "You're a disgraced drunk!"

A moment passed, and Nasrin had waited to see which side of her father's character would emerge. It was a risk to speak the truth.

Finally, he had smiled grimly. "I suppose if she were a man, I would not hesitate. She showed great resourcefulness and initiative, and God knows we need those qualities in the Army."

"The war goes badly?" Nasrin had asked.

"So badly we don't know how bad it is," General Avesta said. "It moves too fast to see."

Nasrin had already gathered as much from the shaken countenances of the general's staffers on the way to his office. She had only seen the look once before when the king had nearly died.

"I will leave you to your work," Nasrin had said, not waiting to be dismissed. "I have mine."

"Where can you be found?" the general asked.

Nasrin had told him and then had left him alone in his office with the portraits and wall maps.

Back in her rooms with Suri, Nasrin helped her friend put the finishing touches on her uniform.

"Are you sure you want to meet Basir dressed as a, a..." Nasrin tried to find the word.

"Soldier?" Suri asked. She chuckled. "It's hard to say. We don't have a word for a female soldier. Only for men."

"Perhaps the ancients had a word," Nasrin said. "You told me once things were different before."

"I've thought a lot about that," Suri said. "I think as we approach the ancients in technology, women are going to be free again."

Nasrin curled her brow at the idea. "Why would technology change how we treat women?"

"I don't know," said Suri. "I haven't thought it through. It's a notion I have. If you think about the most primitive races, the Northern Tribes, women are the least free. While in Persia they are more, and in Azania—"

"Treason!" Nasrin laughed. "You were about to say the Azanians are the most advanced of all!"

Suri frowned. "The way the war is going, perhaps they are."

The pair stood quietly for a moment. Nasrin broke the mood. "Let us not speak of the war. Basir is going to be so surprised to see you like this," Nasrin motioned up and down with her arm at Suri's uniform.

"He'll be delighted," Suri said.

Sixteen

Two hours later, Suri found herself in a crowd of women being sworn into the *Bar Basij*, the Women's Auxiliary, on the temple grounds. All over New Persia, men were volunteering for service to fight the Azanian invasion. Those who had already completed their military service were still in the Reserve and were being called up as well. The more reluctant men were subject to conscription.

To Suri's surprise, there were dozens of women waiting outside the temple to be sworn in. She saw women from all classes, the daughters of washerwomen mixing with ladies from great estates. No one had been issued uniforms yet, so they all wore the best clothes their station allowed.

When ordered, they stood in rough lines on the lawn in front of the great dome of the temple, made of a shining metal no one could reproduce in these fallen times.

The women studied the oath of service given to them on small cardboard cards.

An older woman, the wife of a government official, led them in taking the oath.

"I, Suri Pahlavi, do swear that I will be faithful and bear true allegiance to His Majesty the King and the Prince Regent, his heirs and successors, according to law. So help me God."

Suri felt a great weight on her shoulders. She was going to be an officer!

Once sworn in, the women were separated into officer candidates and enlisted. Suri noticed it was a class divide, with the higher classes being the officers. They were directed to a bus leaving for Capital Barracks.

A man appeared wearing an Army uniform. He found Suri waiting in line to board the bus and said, "Suri Pahlavi?"

"Yes?" she said.

"I've been sent by General Avesta, ma'am. You are to come with me." He showed her a sheaf of papers with her name and photo on them. "These are your orders."

Suri examined the man, who wore a lieutenant's uniform, and the papers. They seemed to be in order.

"Very well," she said, "I brought my things."

She accompanied him to a waiting taxi.

"Wait," she said. "I've my own car."

"Really?" he said.

"It's over here."

The officer barely fit inside, and the contrast with Basir was great enough for Suri to suppress a giggle. This man didn't know a thing about cars.

Suri made sure the trip to Capital Barracks was as quick as safety allowed. Perhaps slightly quicker.

The officer, recovering his wits inside the gates of the barracks, directed her to the other side of the base. Suri saw the training buildings nearby and asked, "Where are we going?"

"I'm to take you to your quarters, ma'am," he said. "The rest is in your orders."

Suri pawed through the papers but couldn't make heads or tails out of the official language.

When they pulled up to a building that looked very much like all the others around, Suri parked the car. The lieutenant, being very grateful to be alive, made his excuses and left on foot, despite Suri's offer of a ride. Suri smiled to herself.

She collected herself and her bag and walked inside. The CQ desk was manned by a young man who signed her in. He passed her an envelope and a key and directed her to her room. Once inside, she saw it had two bunks, one of them made up. She would have a roommate.

She opened the note.

> *Suri,*
>
> *I don't believe in wasting time, and if your time with your father, your brother, and Colonel Turani have taught you nothing about the ways of the military, you are unfit to wear the uniform of an officer. There is a dire need for specialists in a special program, which I believe you will find intriguing. Please report to the old Ministry of Interior Archives tomorrow for your new assignment.*
>
> > *Congratulations, Lieutenant Pahlavi.*
> > *Avesta.*

Inside the envelope with the note was a small badge with her photo on it. It seemed very odd, a hard piece of laminated cardboard.

"What a strange day," she said to herself. "I have nothing to do until tomorrow. I should make the most of my time."

Suri changed from her civilian clothes into the uniform she'd brought with her. After looking in the mirror and adjusting her hat, she decided she looked fine as Lieutenant Pahlavi, *Bar Basiji*, and left the room. She went out the door to the front desk and inquired the way to the Capital Corps barracks. Then she went outside and took the wheel of her car.

Seventeen

Councilman Kermani watched the Seed Storm approach his town. It was like any sandstorm from the north, full of wind and sand, but brought with it death and destruction. The native seeds spawning deep within the Waste were cast into the air by the monsoon winds and brought south. Kerman was in the storm's path.

Kermani's stomach clenched at the sight of the storm, larger than any sandstorm he had ever seen, coming to engulf his city. The storm was coming for him and everything he loved, and it was coming to burn it all to ash. It came, pitiless, merciless, and answered only to God.

The militia was out clearing firebreaks and tending to fire cisterns. The water mains could fail in an emergency, as Kermani had discovered during the Azanian bombing raids. What Azanian bombs could disrupt, so too could the pyrotechnic seeds of native life.

The old ways are best, he knew. Modern plumbing did not obviate the ancient wisdom whereby each house kept a rain cistern and tended its private garden.

They would need those gardens, Kermani thought. The storm was burning the fields north of the city. It was futile to resist, though some tried. No one could stop a dry field of wheat from burning beneath the storm's relentless bombardment.

Those who remembered the old ways were staying with relations in Kerman, and the population had doubled as the refugees poured inside the ancient city walls. The buildings were painted white to resist heat. Fire-resistant stucco plastered the walls of each house, and their tile roofs would shed fiery embers. Kerman had stood since the time of the Founding because it remembered what others forgot.

Generations had built with the arrival of a seed storm in their minds. The collective wisdom of ancestors long dead would be tested in the forge of the storm.

The first thing to come was the hot wind. Superheated air from the equatorial furnace of the Waste flowed like liquid over the cracked and rocky surface of the desert. Small tempests of swirling dust preceded the storm like the djinn from legends older than the Faith.

The foot of the storm rolled across the maize fields at the base of Kerman's walls. From the temple, Kermani watched as this year's crop caught on fire, one stalk at a time. The dry husks began to smoke as soon as the first heatwaves carried embers from the storm front into the field. Corn stalks became pillars of flame. The flames spread from one to another until the smoke blown ahead of the storm blotted out his view.

From his lookout on the temple tower, Kermani watched his town disappear under a blanket of smoke and ash. The roiling cloud reached to the sky. He was fascinated by the storm. Only the urgings of his anxious assistant brought him inside.

From inside the temple dome, the view was much the same. The windows were from the generation of the Founding and were as strong as steel and unscratchable by anything softer than a diamond. In the lore of the temple, the windows *were* made of diamond, but Kermani dismissed it as preposterous. No one would waste diamonds to build a window, not even the ancients. True or not, the windows provided a spectacular view of the holocaust overtaking Kerman.

His family was down there, he knew. He had sent the tribesman to collect them, but neither he nor they had returned. What had happened? His anxiety grew as the storm clouds approached. Where were they?

His wife Narda had refused to leave their neighborhood for the safety of the city shelter. What example would she set if she ran away while their neighbors stayed? Tarana, his mother, had stubbornly refused to follow him. With the example of the two older women, his three young daughters would not leave either. Faced with a wall of female defiance, Kermani was helpless to make them obey. He knew he could have ordered them away, but the look in Narda's eyes was the look she reserved for speaking of the hated Azanians. She was resolved, and forcing her to leave would carry a cost Kermani did not want to pay.

In the safety of the temple, surrounded by the families of city workers and those too poor to own their homes, Kermani raged at himself. He had been too weak to force his family to follow him. He had given up without a fight. They were out there, all five of them, in the storm because he had failed in his duty as a father.

~ * ~

Zafir had been in many dangerous places in his short life. He had faced death many times at the hands of enraged cattle owners and the fathers of the girls he had led astray. Most recently, he had faced both the gallows and the Azanian Land Force. He had escaped the gallows by agreeing to participate in a suicide mission against the Azanians holding airfield K-2 to the southwest of Kerman. The mission itself had left him as one of only two survivors. Zafir did not wonder why he had lived, and his comrades had died. He knew the answer: Fate. God's will. Nothing he did would allow him to live a day longer in this world than was already written.

He had failed to find a way out of town before the coming of the seed storm. All the trains leaving for the south were reserved for military traffic and civilian refugees. A sometime member of the Kerman Militia did not qualify, and the regular Railway Commission men had been replaced by militia, who were not easily bribed. Zafir had jumped trains before, but on these, even the cattle cars were full of people. An able-bodied young man could not escape notice and would never be allowed to travel south while the Azanians came from the west and the storm from the north.

Zafir could have tried his hand at disguising himself as something he was not, as a woman or an old man, but he had decided it would be tempting Fate. If God willed, he would see the coming of the seed storm in Kerman—who was he to object to the will of God? It would be much better to face the storm as a free man than as a member of a prison gang, several of which were outdoors clearing fire breaks and carrying water from the Karun River to cisterns all over the city.

As a man without a fixed abode, Zafir found himself inside the main temple shelter. He endured the glance he received for being a young man taking shelter with the families of the city workers. He had no neighborhood and no family of his own. His cousin had died in an Azanian air raid, and Zafir had avenged his death ten times over. The family of his cousin had left on a train going south, leaving whatever they could not carry to the mercy of the storm. There was no concern given to the possibility of looting. There was no theft in Kerman. Nothing would be gained by Zafir watching an empty house.

Councilman Kermani's assistant found Zafir sitting against the central pillar of the temple taking a nap. The women and children around him pressed against the windows to better see the calamity approaching their city. With nothing to lose, Zafir took the opportunity to sleep.

When the assistant reached out to shake him awake, Zafir's knife was out of its sheath before the man's hand reached Zafir's shoulder. The man jumped back in surprise and fear. Zafir quickly sheathed the knife and smiling, spread his arms apart.

"I am sorry, friend, you woke me," he said.

The assistant led him to Councilman Kermani. Zafir frowned. He had paid his debt to this man. He had not counted the mission against the Azanians as a favor, as it had been a family matter. Zafir had sent a certain Army captain to his judgment to repay his freedom. Now he was being called again. This wasn't part of the deal.

Kermani addressed the obvious first. This could have been taken as rudeness, but the circumstances called for no time to be lost.

"You do not owe me. I am only saying it would be a good thing if you could find my family and bring them here."

Zafir grunted. Kermani was deferential, despite their differences in status, and spoke to Zafir as an equal. *It is good to see the old ways preserved,* Zafir thought.

It was odd how one deed of valor branded him with his new reputation as a brave man. He knew he was not a brave man, but now what could he do? People expected him to be brave, and a man was no more than his actions.

Zafir chose himself for the task, as it did not seem proper for the hero of the assault on airfield K-2 to be cowering in the temple with the women and children.

Perhaps the storm would incinerate him and leave a legendary ghost to haunt the streets of Kerman. Zafir thought the possibility even funnier than being thought brave.

"I will do this for you," Zafir said. *Who knows, maybe someday you will repay the favor. If I live.*

He left the temple with a new robe, dust mask, and goggles. He took nothing else but a canteen of water. He pushed his way against the stream of people heading to the temple and safety.

There were many still outside. Most of the residents and their relations from outside the wall were weathering the storm in their neighborhoods.

When the storm came, everyone worked together to survive. Young children with agile limbs and quick eyes were posted as lookouts on the roofs of buildings. They would call out any embers before they could start a fire. Women carried water to the men who prepared to fight the fires with gloved hands and improvised masks. The old people were used as block wardens. They kept track of who lived where, and everyone checked in with them before coming and going from their homes. No one wanted to risk lives trying to save someone from an empty house. They would try to save houses, of course, but lives came first. The few professional firefighters in

Kerman were being held as a reserve force to be dispatched in trucks to where they were needed the most.

The civil defense plans implemented for the seed storm were simply the codification of centuries of traditional wisdom passed down from each generation. A lifetime could pass without a seed storm, but twice a century was the norm. The old people could remember the last storm from their childhoods.

The sky filled with dust and smoke. The wind threw smoke trails out of the cloud, each ending with a spark or ember superheated by the hot air. The trails arced through the air and landed in puffs of smoke. The embers burned wherever they settled. The sparks landing in the firebreaks cleared by the townspeople smoldered petulantly on the hard-baked dirt. Others landed on the tile roofs of the town. They sizzled when doused by a bucketful of water poured by the home's inhabitants.

Other embers found hospitable ground. In the dry grass, they immediately began a blaze adding its smoke to the storm's conflagration. In the treetops where no one could reach, the embers ignited dry leaves and branches. The trees burned like torches from the top down. All the orchards beyond the walls were lost. Within the town, only those trees protected by nets would survive. Kerman was not a green city. Trees were regarded as an extravagance and a danger. Only a few grew within the city walls.

Most of those trees grew in the temple garden below Kermani's perch. Each tree was covered in netting meant to shed embers. Water sprinklers shielded each tree in a fog of water as the smoke trails began landing on the temple grounds. It was extravagant in the extreme to throw water into the storm like this, but the Faith was worth sacrificing for.

The hot air of the storm sucked the moisture out of everything it touched. Zafir felt the blast of the storm front on his skin and coughed as the dust and smoke filled his mouth and nose. He tasted smoke and ash with his tongue.

Zafir stepped into the gateway of a courtyard and spat into the dust. Around him, the children were running into their homes. Old men, women, and young unmarried men like Zafir remained outside to weather the storm protected only by their robes and masks. Zafir lowered his goggles onto his eyes and pulled the straps of his dusk mask over his head. He inhaled to seal the mask around his nose and mouth and tightened the straps. His face was clean-shaven to give him a better seal.

Behind the storm front was a zone of superheated air inside of which life was barely possible.

With a laugh, Zafir ran across the smoke- and ash-filled street to a doorway on the other side. He could see only feet. How could he perform the task of fire watch if he could not see beyond his own feet?

He could feel the heat around him. He was baking beneath his robes. The hot air pushed its way through the fabric and carried away his perspiration. The air was so dry he felt no sweat on his body. His mouth was dry inside his dust mask.

Zafir trotted down the street toward the Kermani house. There would come a time when even a brave man would need to retreat from the storm's onslaught. He had to move quickly.

The storm was a bad one, he already knew. He had seen one before in the north on the edge of the Waste. It had been a small storm, and he had been far away on a hilltop. The storm, while majestic, had been something to marvel at, not fear.

Even when far away to the north, this storm had dominated the entire horizon with a wall of ash and fire. The wall advanced and buried everything under it with ash and burning seeds. He had not yet seen any seeds up close.

As if to answer his thought, glowing trails of seed pods fell through the smoke. Zafir saw them as dim orange flashes in the darkness of the street. Like the sun through overcast, they caused the air around them to light up.

The hot wind increased in strength. The air tore at Zafir's robes. He found he could not walk straight down the street. The wind blew his steps off course. He sheltered in the lee of a house's exterior wall and crept forward by feeling the dust-coated stucco surface.

The light dimmed further. It was as dark as night without Shaitan in the sky. Orange trails streaked like meteors through the gloom. When the seed pods landed, they burst into flames. Their husks burned brightly and added to the smoke in the air.

Zafir smelled the sickly-sweet seeds through his mask. The air itself seemed to be less nourishing. He struggled to breathe in the hot air. Did the fires steal even the air he needed to breathe?

A seed whistled through the air above. Zafir saw the blazing trail of smoke for an instant before the pod crashed into the cobblestones at his feet. The pod burst open, and the flammable liquid inside leaked out. The sweet smell filled the air around Zafir as the seed husk soaked up the fluid. The air was full of fumes awaiting a spark to detonate them.

Zafir crouched against the wall and pulled the hood of his robe over his face. An instant later, the fumes from the seed pod exploded into flames around him. Burning liquid sprayed all around. His thick cotton robes protected him from flash burns, but the spray covered him like the sneeze of a fire giant. His robes were on fire in a dozen places.

He fell and rolled on the ground to put out the flames. The ancient advice, whose origin eluded even the scholars, was known to every child, "stop, drop, and roll."

This Zafir did, and though he put out the flames, he could feel his flesh burning beneath his robes. The sweet smell of the storm mixed with the scent of burning meat.

Encased in his smoking clothes, Zafir looked for a way to cool his burning skin. He felt the heat as ice stabbing him all over his body. The flames were out, but he still burned. Water! He needed water quickly.

Beside him, the door to a house blew open with a crash. Smoke and ash rushed in. Struggling for breath, Zafir followed the debris through the doorway and into a living room. It was dark inside. Electricity had failed, and the absent owners had left no open flames. The room quickly filled with smoke. Ash and dust soon covered every exposed surface. Zafir looked frantically for anything wet. There was nothing. He ran through the room as he threw off his smoking robes.

He found the door to the interior courtyard by touch. He reached for the door bar and forced the heavy iron beam upward. The door refused to open when Zafir pulled the handle. The wind at his back sealed it against the door jam. He struggled with the heavy door and opened it a few centimeters before the air pressure slammed it shut.

The pain of his burns grew, and only the desperate need to escape the heat prevented him from noticing. Smoke choked his lungs and ash clogged his nostrils. He braced his feet and pulled the handle as hard as he could. The wind blew at his back, and a powerful gust yanked his feet out from under him. Zafir fell and was left staring at his boots.

After the powerful gust, the wind subsided momentarily. The ash in the air settled all over the room. Zafir scrambled to his feet and leaped for the door handle before the wind returned. He yanked the door open and shoved himself through the opening a second before it slammed shut. His trailing foot narrowly avoided being crushed by the heavy wood door.

In the smoke-filled courtyard, Zafir cast around until he found what he was looking for. He saw a massive barrel on stilts in the corner. He clambered up the side and unclamped the top of the barrel. The wind caught it and almost carried it away. He held it down against the rim, so the air could not get under the lid as he slid it open. When the opening was wide enough, he squeezed himself inside.

Zafir immersed himself in the water of the cistern. At first, he could not feel the bottom with his feet. For a moment, he cursed himself for an idiot for not checking the depth before jumping in. Drowning in a barrel was an unworthy way to die. But he found his footing and was able to pull the lid shut over his head. He could not secure the clamps on the outside of the cistern, but if the lid were seated, it would probably stay shut. It was up to Fate.

Total darkness closed on him. Even the dim illumination of the storm outside was cut off. He could hear it through the thick wooden sides of the barrel. It sounded as if a thousand screaming insects were outside.

The water cooled his wounds, and the cool air cleared his lungs. He coughed and spat into the water. His burns cooled, and he had time to feel the pain. Zafir gritted his teeth.

He was inside a water tank with the lid closed. The storm was outside. He was safe, for the moment, and still had the use of his limbs and his wits. He had not lost his sight. Covering his face had saved him from disfigurement.

Standing alone in the cool water, Zafir counted himself fortunate for a fool who had gone out during a seed storm. He would be badly scarred where the flames had burned him, but the orange tattoos of the seed scars would only bring him more notoriety.

Zafir laughed. And so, the hero of K-2 would survive, and the legend would grow. He hoped next time he grew his legend it would not be so painful.

Zafir stopped to remember the story was not over yet. He had not found the Kermani family. There would be no legend if he failed.

~ * ~

Narda and her daughters Amira, Asha, and Azara helped to stormproof their neighbor's house. Their own home was as ready for the storm as they could make it. Shutters blocked the windows and nets hung from the roofs to protect the walls of the dwelling.

Their neighbors included a young widow with small children. Their house was not as well maintained as it should have been since her husband had been killed in an accident. The residents of the neighborhood, including the Kermanis, descended upon the house with hammers, nails, and a will to work.

It was not solely altruism motivating them. If one house burned, the adjacent buildings would catch fire, too. The wall against the storm had to be strong at every point. One weak brick would bring it all down.

Amira finished nailing down the shutter for the last window. Asha and Azara crouched on the roof, replacing missing tiles. Hammer blows and drills filled the air with sounds.

Asha put her hammer down on the roof, wiped her brow, and looked around. The storm was visible to the north as a sheer wall of sand and ash. It had moved noticeably closer since she had begun replacing roof tiles. The storm for her was a novelty and an adventure. The danger seemed remote, and she was more tired of the unending work of preparing for it than worried about the storm's onset.

Narda saw her daughter pause and cried up from the courtyard below, "Get working! We haven't much time!"

Asha gave her a resentful look and picked up her hammer. She pulled out another tile from the bag next to her and crawled to replace chipping tiling a few feet away. Any hole in the roof tiles invited embers or seed-spray to burn the vulnerable timbers beneath.

Azara and her grandmother Tarna were packing their neighbors' belongings in a borrowed trunk. Tarna was patiently listening to the young woman's entreaties to save the good china while Azara was packing more food and clothes instead. Azara was enjoying herself. Like her sister, the storm was a grand adventure. Perhaps when they got to the temple shelter, she could meet some new people. Maybe a refugee from Persepolis before Amira could get her hands on him. Amira was the oldest and prettiest of the three.

A cry made Azara look up from her packing. The young woman cast around, looking for her son. He was her youngest and was not where she had left him inside the house. Quickly the three women quartered the house and found no sign of the toddler.

Narda took charge. She sent Azara outside to mobilize her sisters and the neighbors for the search. She remained to talk to the owner of the house.

Azara returned with the news: the boy was nowhere to be seen outside. They had searched the courtyard, the grounds, and the street.

The three daughters pushed inside to hear what Narda would order next. None of them resented the interruption from their work. A small child in peril was an adventure. Tarna and Narda had each seen a storm and were anxious.

Narda knew they had little time. She had planned to be leaving. The storm was not a fast one, but its winds were faster than they could walk. They had no time to spare. But to leave a child out in the storm was condemning the boy to death.

The wife of Councilman Kermani looked at the near-hysterical young widow and made her decision.

"Amira, go to our house and look there. Azara, check the roof and look around from there. Asha, go up the street to the next house and see if there is anyone there. Everyone else..." she gave rapid-fire orders to the neighbors assembling in the kitchen of the house.

The young mother wandered the house and grounds calling the boy's name.

The wind blew the first scent of the seed pods into the courtyard.

Asha ran up the street, looking in all directions. She saw nothing but the wind-blown dust. The houses were empty of their inhabitants. All had left for shelter long ago. The silence, the lack of any human voice or activity, was eerie. All around her were locked and boarded-up houses. He could not have gotten into any of them. Asha knew there was not much time. She had seen the look of anxiety on her mother's face. She had to think fast. If he had run up the street, how far had he gone? Was he still running? Should she try to catch him?

She stopped her impulse to keep running. She had to think like a toddler. Would a child run straight away from home? Perhaps for a while.

Children could be distracted. Asha looked around for anything appealing for a small boy.

She found the lower spout of a wide rain gutter. The outflow dumped the rain falling on the roof to the street. On impulse, Asha walked to it. Inside, over the sound of the wind, she heard a cry.

She crouched in the street and leaned into the spout. The cry was louder. She looked into the dark pipe. It bent upward within a meter. Straining, she reached inside. Her arm disappeared into the spout. With the tips of her fingers, she felt the bare foot of the boy.

"I have found you!" she said reassuringly. "Come down to me!"

The boy cried. He was unable or unwilling to climb down the pipe.

Asha repeated her entreaty and reached in as far as her arm would go. She could not grasp his foot.

"I will return," she said and stood. The boy screamed in her absence. Asha ran down the street to the neighbor's house.

"I found him!" she cried and explained the boy's predicament.

The gathered neighbors followed her up the street to the gutter pipe. The men with the longest arms tried to reach him but were not able to pull him down. They would have to cut the pipe open.

The storm grew around them. Dust blew across the road. Everyone there looked nervously to the north.

Narda said, "Everyone who is not needed here must go! There is no time left. Asha, Amira, Azara, stay."

Tarna nodded next to her.

Azara wanted to ask why they were staying when they couldn't do anything. She knew the answer: duty. The family of the councilman did not flee when their neighbor's child was in danger.

The five Kermani women waited around the pipe with the boy's mother while the boilermaker who lived on the street left to get his tools. His mother cooed softly into the pipe, and the boy's screams turned to sobs.

The boilermaker returned with a large wrench and a saw. He tried the wrench first, but rust had sealed the final section of the gutter pipe. His arms strained, but the pipe would not come loose. He began to saw the pipe below the boy's legs. The saw worked slowly.

A gust of wind dumped a load of sand on all of them. The street momentarily disappeared in a cloud of dust.

"We have no time left," Narda said. The boilermaker nodded and sawed faster. The boy's mother cried for him to climb down.

"No," Narda said, and touched the man's arm. He stopped sawing. "You have a family. You must leave now. The storm is here."

With tears in his eyes, the man nodded once.

"Go," Narda said.

The boy's mother jumped up and made to seize him by the arm, but Narda intercepted her. She grasped the young woman in her arms while the boy's mother flailed at her with her fists.

"I am sorry," Narda said, "We must go now. We cannot free him."

"I will never leave!" the young mother cried.

Narda looked over her shoulder at the boilermaker, who had stopped a few feet away. Asha could see he was thinking of carrying the young mother away. Narda was about to signal him to take her when Azara spoke up.

"I think I can reach him," she said, looking up into the pipe. Azara was young with long, delicate limbs.

"You can't pull him out," Asha said. Azara was lithe, but not strong.

"I don't have to," Azara said, straightening her body. "You can pull on my legs."

Everyone stopped to stare at her. The wind blew another gust of sand over the street.

"Go!" Narda said. "Try it!"

Azara crouched again and crawled into the pipe. She almost disappeared inside with only her ankles and feet protruding.

"I have him!" she said from inside the pipe.

The boilermaker took both of her feet in his huge hands and squatted. He pulled with his arms. Nothing happened. Carefully he dug in his heels and pushed with his feet.

Inside the pipe, Azara clenched her hands around the boy's feet. The man's pull on her ankles stretched her knees and hips. She felt like she'd pull apart. She bit her lip to keep from crying out. If she did, he would stop pulling. She yanked down with her arms as hard as she could. Her feet and wrists were being pulled in two. Her body, bent at the waist at the crook of the pipe, was being torn in two. The boy cried in pain at the strain on his ankles.

Finally, the boy came loose. Azara shot from the pipe with his feet in her hands. Both landed in the dust. The boy screamed for his mother, who swept him up in her arms.

Everyone smiled and laughed in triumph.

"Enough!" said Narda. "We must go!"

Where would they go? Asha wondered. The storm was nearly upon them, and they would never make it to the temple on foot.

There was no time even for a car. A car caught outside in the storm would choke on the dust and smoke and leave them stranded.

"We must shelter in the cellar," Tarna said. The old woman beckoned them to follow her home. "Come quickly!"

The cellar was beneath the courtyard of the Kermani house. The double doors opened to a stone stairway leading down. The five Kermanis and the boilermaker rushed inside as the first seed pod smoke trails arced overhead.

Eighteen

Basir Turani stared at his new command on the parade ground. His new Capital Corps regiment, the 1st Regiment of the 1st Armored Division, known as "The Primes." Over a thousand men stood in the heat on the short grass. This was a "pure" tank unit, without the accompanying infantry that would be attached before the tanks saw combat. They wore soft caps and carried no helmets.

The men looked good in their gray uniforms, and the tanks had a fresh coat of paint. All that meant was the regiment was proficient at hiding their mistakes from the prying eyes of visiting officers. He had Master Sergeant Ahvaz to give him a report on the real condition of the tanks and the men. The inspection was a formality, a necessary one, as he assumed command of the Primes.

Basir had walked the ranks and studied the men carefully. If there were any outward signs of the corruption and indiscipline Avesta had mentioned, he could not see it. They were as well put out as the Prince's Own would have been. He had felt rather than seen the lack of respect, like the stance of an unruly horse regarding a new rider.

They mean to throw me, Basir thought. They don't think I will lead them into battle. He stood at his microphone on the makeshift stage to speak to his new command.

"Soldiers, comrades of the First—" he began.

He was cut off by the sounding of air raid sirens all over the base. Their warbling screams blasted his eardrums. Almost everyone in the formation looked up into the clear sky. All eyes searched for the Azanian planes.

A few men at the back of the formation began to slink away to the rear.

"*Halt*," Basir intoned into the microphone. He watched to see who carried out his order.

His men, Captain Pahlavi and Ahvaz and Shirazi, stood stock-still. The regiment's officers offered a gamut of responses. Some didn't wait for their men but ran before their formation. Others stood still as their men ran away in all directions. The rest tried to hold their ranks together with varying degrees of success. One officer near the back drew his sidearm and fired it into the air before aiming into the backs of the rear rank. None of them ran.

Two minutes later, when the air raid sirens ceased, Basir could see the regiment in pandemonium. Half the men were gone, and the rest were milling around with their officers trying to get them back in ranks. Basir watched it all and looked for bright spots. The officer who had fired his pistol into the air had kept his company from fleeing. To a man, they stood in rank as if nothing had happened. In the front, another group, the recon company, had stayed through it all. Their officer hadn't done anything more than a sideways stare. The rest of the men had fled or were in a state of disorder.

I have two effective company commanders, Basir thought. *Out of nine.*

"Captain Pahlavi," he called. "Half rations and punishment detail for any company not in ranks in five minutes. Any men absent are to be put on report."

"Yes, sir," Pahlavi said. Disgust tinged his voice.

Basir watched his officers put their companies back together from the pieces they had fallen into. The Capital Corps knew how to drill, at least, and now that it was clear that the siren had been a sham, the men lined themselves into ranks. Only one company, whose officer and sergeants had fled, was unable to get into ranks.

Basir stepped off the stage and performed another inspection. He noticed the recon company standing with pride in the front rank. He found the platoon leaders and called them forward.

"You lieutenants," he said, "are now company commanders. You are promoted to captain effective immediately by my order. See me after the inspection for your new assignments. Your sergeants are now platoon leaders and will be commissioned as soon as the paperwork can be done."

The newly-promoted officers and men suppressed their smiles. One man in ranks whispered, "That'll show those cowards." Basir heard it but did not react.

"And you," he turned to the recon company commander, "Captain Ormuz."

"Yes, sir," said the captain. He was a handsome man, short, but with a grand mustache.

"You are now major in command of the First Battalion," Basir said.

"Thank you, sir," Ormuz said.

"Don't thank me, yet," Basir said. "After what I saw today, you have your work cut out for you."

Basir found that the other company which had stood its ground was led not by an officer, but a sergeant. An "old man" of nearly forty years, a grizzled veteran of the last war from his ribbons, named Goraz, had drawn his pistol to keep the men in line.

"Sergeant, where are your officers?" Basir asked.

Goraz spat. "Fled, sir," he said, embarrassed. "Begging your pardon, sir, but I couldna shot them, though they deserve it."

"I understand, Sergeant," Basir said. Shooting an officer outside of battle, even a fleeing one, was beyond the sergeant's rank. From the look on his face, he would have obeyed an order to do so. "Very good," Basir said. "You kept your men in line and didn't go too far. You'd make a fine officer."

"Begging your pardon again, sir," Goraz said. "But I haven't done anything to offend you, have I?"

"No, Sergeant," Basir smiled. "I need a regimental sergeant major. You are it. Report after the formation."

"Yes, sir," Goruz said deadpan. If he took pride in his promotion, it was not evident on his pockmarked face.

As Javad and Basir walked back toward the stage after the inspection, Javad asked, "What will be done with the officers who ran?"

"Cashier them all," Basir said. "Transferring them will only spread the rot. Avesta has given me the authority to clean up what I can."

"And the others?"

"The ones that couldn't keep their men together? I'll look into it. They didn't run, which is something. I'll check with Ahvaz and Goraz to see which are worth keeping."

"Yes, sir. And if we don't have enough?"

"We keep digging down into the ranks until we find someone. As a last resort, I'll bring in someone from the Prince's Own, although I'd prefer they stay there. The Prince's Own is one of the few effective units we have."

"Yes, sir," said Javad.

"What am I supposed to do with these?" Basir Turani said. He was looking at a line of *Mobarez* heavy tanks parked on the parade ground. Ten of them formed the heavy tank company of his new regiment. Each weighed over sixty tons, and it was a wonder they could move at all. Each tank chassis bore a bulbous turret housing a 120mm main gun. The gun could penetrate all existing tank armor. The tanks' heavy sloped armor was designed to defeat all but the heaviest enemy guns.

But the *Mobarez* was slow, crawling along at a maximum speed of 20 kph on a paved surface. The colossal metal tracks ripped up roads, and most bridges could not support more than one tank crossing at a time.

Worse, the overtaxed engines dragging the huge tanks forward broke down constantly. Not one of the tanks of the company was fully operational. Every one of them had a critical fault keeping them from serving on the front. Broken transmissions, balky engines, and overstressed gun mounts topped the list of defects.

To Basir, the heavy tanks, meant to be an offensive sledgehammer, were instead a shackle holding back his regiment. The need to supply their enormous thirsty engines and keep them running implied a large amount of his limited resupply capacity would have to go to the *Mobarezes*. Even if he had enough supplies, which he never did, and even if he had the trucks to carry them, which he would not, the roads imposed a limit on how many vehicles could pass through at a time. The Azanian domination of the air halved the capacity of roads to carry truck traffic. All resupply had to be done at night to avoid the constant air attacks, imposing a limit on how far his supply dumps could be from the front line. Supplies could only be carried as far as a truck could travel between sunset and sunrise.

To add to his problems, Shaitan was shining. On clear nights the Azanian pilots could see their targets in the twilight of the binary star.

Basir found himself wishing the seed storm would hurry up and arrive.

Perhaps he was looking at the problem the wrong way. Maybe they weren't meant to be a sledgehammer.

Perhaps they were an anvil. If he could somehow get them where they could face the enemy, somewhere where they could not be easily outflanked or bypassed, perhaps they could prove decisive.

Still they needed to work. As far as Basir could tell, the maintenance records were either inaccurate or deliberately falsified. Sergeant Ahvaz had looked over the tanks himself and his report was shocking. Not even basic crew-level maintenance had been performed for months, perhaps years.

Basir had relieved the company commander and all NCOs in the Heavy company and he had put Ahvaz in charge of repairing the company's tanks. Ahvaz was not a commissioned officer any longer, having been found unsuited because of illiteracy. His leadership and mechanical abilities were unhindered by his difficulty in reading. Basir needed those abilities more than he needed paperwork done correctly.

Grease, dirt, and rust covered Ahvaz's grey working uniform. He was standing inside the engine compartment of a *Mobarez*. He had disassembled the engine block and one of his arms was elbow-deep inside an empty cylinder. Around him were six soldiers, one of them Shirazi, Basir's old radio operator from 44, the command tank of his old *Tosan* company.

The crewmen came to attention. Shirazi stood up, noticeably more slowly. Basir caught Ahvaz's eye and said, "As you were," before Ahvaz extracted his arm to come to attention. He waited for Ahvaz to finish what he was doing. Ahvaz unscrewed something inside the engine block and removed it.

"Bah," he said. "This liner is destroyed." He held up a piece of metal covered in thick black grease. "Never work again." He stood. "Good evening, sir."

"Sergeant," Basir replied. "Will any of these ever move again?" The grey-clad men around Ahvaz, obviously the crew of the tank, winced.

"With some time, certainly," Ahvaz said. "Which we don't have, I know. With the cooperation of the depot, I could have these all running in two weeks."

"You know we don't have two weeks," Basir said.

"No, sir," Ahvaz said. "But I have an idea." He jumped off the engine deck and waved at the line of tanks. "I could get half of them running, maybe, by cannibalizing the rest. I think we have the parts for it."

"Half is better than none," Basir said. "Proceed."

"Yes, sir. I think I'll work on the *Mobs* in the best condition first. I'll use the spares on them. As for the rest, well, I'll do my best."

"How long?" Basir asked.

It was Ahvaz's turn to wince. "At least a week," he said. Basir let him continue. "These tanks weren't designed with the idea of easy parts replacement. I've only one crane rated to lift out the engine blocks. It takes a long time to open up a *Mob*. And, begging your pardon, sir, but having unskilled hands do the work will only make things worse. I don't have enough mechanics I trust."

"We don't have a week. What can you make functional in three days? 'Functional' meaning they can move and fire their weapons. I don't expect everything to work."

"I believe we could have five of them up and running if we skip some scheduled work," Ahvaz said. "Their crews will have to do the bore sighting and some of the final maintenance checks. It will mean they'll be due for a lot more work when they are next out of the line."

"Do it," Basir said. "We need them now, later won't matter."

Ahvaz nodded understanding.

"What about the other tanks, the *Karars*?"

Ahvaz grimaced. "I don't think the Primes put maintenance first on their priority list," he said. "I would never have tolerated the condition of those *Karars* when we were in the Prince's Own Regiment. However, the *Karar* is a reliable design, and it can take a lot of abuse. I've put all my best mechanics, best being a relative word here, on the job. All of the crews are doing their maintenance tasks as well."

"Yes," Basir said. He'd ordered every tank crew to complete all their preventive maintenance tasks to the exclusion of everything else, including sleep. The tanks had to be ready. Too much work had been undone in the past and had to be made up in a hurry.

"Would you be better employed working on the *Karars*?" Basir asked.

"No, sir," Ahvaz said, "I think the other mechanics can handle them. The *Mobarez* is a whole different beast, and there aren't many who can work on it. Begging your pardon, sir, but if you want any of them working, I'm the only one to get it done."

"Carry on, Sergeant," Basir said.

Basir caught sight of a man hustling across the assembly area.

"Captain Pahlavi!" he called.

The figure changed course and ran over. Javad Pahlavi saluted. "Sir?"

"Are you in the middle of something?" Basir asked.

"No, sir, I was heading back to finish some of the deployment paperwork," Javad said.

"I have an assignment for you," Basir said. "I need to know what's happening at the front. We are going to be committed to the fight."

"Oh," Javad said, his eyes widening. "When? Sir."

"I don't know exactly, but it will be soon. Within days. I need to know what's happening out there. I can't go myself, more's the pity."

"I understand," Javad said.

"I want you to take the recon company, Major Ormuz's old outfit, and perform a reconnaissance of the front line. The reports I'm getting from Corps are too out of date to be useful. I need to know what we are stepping into before we move out."

"Yes, sir," Javad said. "Where shall I go, sir?"

"We'll draw up the orders this afternoon. I want you out of here by this evening before Shaitan rises. The damn planes come every night," Basir said. Air raids on Persepolis were a nightly occurrence. "You'll be scouting a route for the entire regiment when we depart. I want to know the best way out of the city to the Gerdkooh hills."

"The Gerdkooh?" Javad was puzzled. "That's in the middle of nowhere, sir."

"I know," Basir said. "That's the idea."

"I'm sorry, sir, but why go there?"

"Because it's the only place to hide from the damn planes," Basir said. "The Gerdkooh is the only patch of wilderness large enough for the regiment to shelter in. We could hide the whole Capital Corps in there. But it won't do us any good unless we can get there and get under cover before the Azanians spot us moving. Damn Shaitan," he finished.

"Well, yes, sir," Javad smiled. "Have we received orders to move out?"

"No," Basir said, "but we will. If I understand correctly, General Avesta isn't going to leave us to defend Persepolis from inside the city."

"I see, sir," Javad said. He saw the line of *Mobarez* tanks. "What about those, sir? Can we take those with us? The Gerdkooh isn't a good place for heavy tanks."

"I haven't worked that out yet," Basir admitted. "I hate to leave any asset behind, but—" he waved at the tanks. "What use are they if they can't keep up? They can stay here and reinforce the city defenses."

"Ah," Javad said. "That's too bad. If you could get the enemy to stand still in front of them, they could do a lot of damage."

"Yes," Basir said. A thought struck him. He chewed his lip.

Javad waited patiently, but Basir didn't enlighten him.

When Basir spoke again, he said, "I hear you saw your sister today."

Javad blinked. "Yes, sir."

"How is she?" Basir asked.

"Well, sir," Javad said. "She gave me something to give to you," he reached into his coat and pulled out the envelope Suri had given him.

"Thank you," Basir said, taking the letter.

"Yes, sir," Javad suppressed a smile. "She sends her regards."

Basir felt pulled two ways by the demands of the war and by his desire to read the letter. He wanted to rip it open immediately but knew he would have to wait some hours before he would have time to examine it in his quarters. He put the letter in his pocket.

"Very well," Basir said. "Let's go to the barracks and work on your movement orders, Captain."

Nineteen

Suri drove down the main boulevard leading to the center of Capital Barracks. Capital Barracks was a city-sized enclave inside Persepolis, itself the largest city in the world. Anywhere else, the Barracks would have dominated the city it occupied. Instead, one could explore Persepolis for weeks and not come to the most extensive military base in New Persia. Suri had visited the Barracks before on account of her father and brother, both Army officers. Even so, the scale of it was more than she could take in at a glance. Buildings sat alone with vast empty spaces around them. Fields of immaculately kept five-inch-tall grass spread out in all directions.

The usual motorized traffic was gone. The roads were empty and the parade grounds bare. No formations of soldiers marched to their daily drills and no one was out on exercise detail. The buildings were shuttered as if abandoned. The reason was apparent enough. On the ground were pieces of rubble and broken glass. A filled-in bomb crater defaced the road like an oversized pothole. Suri drove carefully around it.

Guards were everywhere. Men scanned the skies from camouflaged positions on the rooftops. Machine guns were manned at the entrance to every building. So many guns pointed all around made Suri nervous. As she drove, she was relieved she hadn't tried to sneak inside under false pretenses. She unconsciously patted the envelope containing her orders beneath her uniform blouse.

Perhaps arriving in the daytime was taking a greater risk than she had realized. She reproached herself for being afraid, then reproached herself again for being silly. She had been strafed by Azanian aircraft once, and it was enough. Besides, if she had come at night, there would have been traffic, and she would have had to wait.

Her car drew stares everywhere she went. A civilian car was as rare as...well, as rare as a woman officer, Suri thought. She hadn't an official vehicle assigned to her, and it had been easy enough to secure a license for a personally owned vehicle. The paperwork rode with her in the boot of the car. A small New Persian flag clipped to the windshield marked it as an officer's vehicle. Guards saluted her as she drove down the road.

They are saluting me! Me, Suri Pahlavi, who a short time ago had to hide my dress from my mother so I could go to the ball. Now I'm a serving officer!

In the *Bar Basij*, the Women's Auxillary, she reminded herself. But even so! She was a leader, not a follower for the first time in her life.

She stopped her car in a motor pool in front of Building F-17, a squat three-story barracks building utterly indistinguishable from any other. The white paint was newly applied but cracking on the edges of the wooden siding under the summer's sun. She left her car under the watchful eye of a private soldier on guard duty, who straightened up at least six inches upon her arrival.

Inside the building, she snapped off her peaked cap, strode to the CQ desk, and inquired where Colonel Turani could be found. The soldier manning the watch, a thin man from the distant East Province, leaped to his feet and botched his salute. He replied with a stutter in a thick accent, which she could barely understand. She curled her brows, feeling embarrassed both for herself and on behalf of the hapless watch-stander whose eyes seemed to stick out of their sockets.

"Excuse me, ma'am," came a voice from behind her. She turned and faced a grizzled soldier in the gray uniform of the Capital Corps. His tunic and trousers were new, but his boots were marked by years of service. "I can help you find him." There was something in his eye which Suri thought was amusement.

"Excuse me, Sergeant?" Suri said.

"Shirazi, ma'am," the soldier said. He seemed to be stifling a grin.

"Oh," Suri said. "I know you!"

Shirazi raised his eyebrows.

"I mean, we haven't met," Suri stuttered. "I mean, I've heard of you. From Basir's—that is, Colonel Turani's letters."

"Yes, ma'am," Shirazi said, letting her discomfiture dissipate. "I understand." Shirazi was never one to let an officer off the hook, but he let this opportunity pass.

"This way," Shirazi said, motioning down a hall with his arm. "To the third passage on the right." He fell in a half-step behind her, and she led them both down the hall.

As she walked, the other grey-clad soldiers in the passage made way for her. Each looked surprised to see her but said nothing other than mumbled "ma'ams" as she passed. Behind her, any whose eyes lingered too long met the grim gaze of Sergeant Shirazi.

Shirazi directed her through two more doors, and then she was inside an untidy office full of paper and the sound of typewriters. Smoke from cigarettes rose from an ashtray.

Basir sat at a desk examining a typewritten page whose contents seemed to offend him. His eyes were a dark cast that Suri had never seen before. He read the rest of the page and flipped it over.

Shirazi, standing just behind Suri, cleared his throat. It wasn't an appropriate gesture because an enlisted man was expected to wait at the door until permitted to enter. Shirazi had never been a good soldier when it came to military bearing, but he was an excellent man to have when you need a radio operated under fire. Basir employed him as a clerk in barracks and tolerated his insubordination.

"Yes, Sergeant, in a moment," Basir said without looking up. "I'll need you to draft a reply to this nonsense," he said, shaking the paper. "Corps wants to leave our scouts behind as part of the garrison. What are scouts going to do in the city? Mindless. Who have you got with you?"

"A Lieutenant Pahlavi, sir," Shirazi said, keeping his voice deadpan.

"Oh, I remember the appointment. Well," Basir looked up. "I've already got a Lieutenant Pahlavi..." he trailed off.

He recognized the uniform before he recognized her face. "What?" Basir stood up. "How?"

Suri felt like jumping into his arms, but military decorum and the watching eyes of the entire headquarters staff stopped her. Keeping her composure, and not knowing what else to do, she saluted.

"Lieutenant Pahlavi reporting," she squeaked.

Stunned, Basir returned the salute.

"Have you, ah," he stammered, "seen Lieutenant Pahlavi, I mean, your brother, yet?"

Suri blinked twice before answering, "Yes, I have."

"Good," Basir said.

They stood staring at each other for a moment, unable to speak.

Finally Basir said, "Sergeant Shirazi, you are dismissed for the afternoon."

Shirazi saluted smartly and left the small office. Basir doubted he'd go far, and the office walls were only thin wooden dividers. Still, the illusion of privacy was necessary.

Within seconds of Shirazi's departure, without either of them thinking about it, they fell into an embrace. In a moment, their lips found each other. Suri felt her body melt and suppressed a moan of contentment. The kiss seemed to last hours. After an age, they slowly parted.

"Oh, Basir," Suri said, "I have so much to say!"

"You're safe," Basir said.

Suri felt his wool uniform on her cheek and remembered the touch of cloth as they had danced at the prince's ball. It seemed like an eternity ago.

"I'm in the Army," Suri said.

"I noticed," Basir said.

"Nasrin," Suri said. "It was her idea."

Basir was confused. "Nasrin? How—?"

"Oh," Suri said. "We know each other now. We're friends."

"Oh," said Basir.

"It's a long story," Suri said. "I saved her from being buried alive."

"I see," said Basir, and waited for the explanation.

"I went to see her and her house had been bombed by the Azanians. I found some soldiers and we dug her out." Suri decided to leave out some details. No need to alarm the man.

"Oh," Basir said, impressed. "You went to her house alone? The roads are dangerous."

"Yes," Suri agreed. She decided not to tell Basir about being strafed by Azanian fighters. It felt wrong, but she knew Basir had enough to worry about without adding her own problems to his. Besides, she told herself, she was alive and intact, so no harm done.

"As for the uniform," Suri continued, "to make a long story short, Nasrin mentioned me to her father, and I was sworn into the *Bar Basij* as an intelligence specialist."

"Which is something for which you are uniquely suited," Basir said.

Suri knew she was only considered for the job because she'd saved the daughter of the commanding general of the western theater from certain death. Even then, it was only the chaos of war which made her appointment possible. Still, she knew Basir was sincere, and she also knew she really was qualified for the job. Suri didn't doubt her own intelligence and her education had been as deep and wide as her own curiosity and her father's indulgence would allow. It wasn't her fault the idiots in the university wouldn't admit her. If her country wouldn't let her bear arms against the enemy, it could at least allow her to free up a man to do so.

Basir asked, "Where are you stationed?"

"I'm assigned to the Intelligence section. I work at, well, I'm actually not permitted to say," she said.

Basir's eyebrows rose. "Very well," he said. "Is it somewhere safe?"

"As safe as can be," Suri answered. "With the damn Azanian Air Force, no place is safe these days."

Basir's face clouded. "I have a few things to say to Farad the next time I see him. I haven't seen a Persian plane in the sky since the war began."

"I'm sure he is doing his duty," Suri said.

"I'm sure he is," Basir said. "As for the rest of the damn Air Corps, I'd like to know."

Suri thought of her and Nasin's experience with the Azanian Air Force and frowned. Control of the air mattered a great deal. She couldn't look at the sky without being afraid. Suri imagined the entire country feeling the same. Something had to be done. But what?

"Enough about the war," Basir said. "Where are you staying?"

Suri told him. "But I'm rarely there anymore. I'm too busy working. You have no idea how much needs to be done."

Basir suppressed a smile.

Suri laughed. "Of course you do," she admitted. "But we aren't talking about the war. When can we see each other?"

"I'm afraid I can't answer that," Basir said. "I'm afraid we are lucky to have this moment at all."

"Why are we wasting our time?" Suri said and stepped closer.

After a while, Suri said, "Do you remember when we drove the car to the river? Do you remember the flowers?"

"I do," said Basir.

"I wonder if they are still there," Suri said.

"We remember them," Basir said, "so they are still there."

"Hmm," Suri said. "I'll remember them tonight."

Twenty

Farad was surprised by the summons to the HQ building. He had barely closed his eyes lying in his quarters when the phone rang. His hand shot out to pick up the receiver.

He listened for a moment, said "Yes, sir" into the phone, and rose reluctantly from his bed to get dressed.

What could the summons be, he wondered. Another attack? It was possible. The war had left few Persian planes available, and fewer pilots alive to fly them. His squadron had been run ragged by up to three sorties a day. Every plane was needed over the battlefield.

Farad shrugged his flight suit over his shoulders, zipped it up, and put on his shoes. It would be as God wills, he thought. He would sleep later.

The walk along the flight line to the HQ was odd. Men looked at him strangely, and the salutes were more perfunctory. Farad returned the salutes but wondered. What was going on?

When he arrived, the airman on watch saluted and told him his presence was requested in the base commander's office. Farad was beginning to become concerned.

When he arrived at the open door, he knocked quietly with his left hand. The general inside didn't answer right away, so Farad waited as he'd been trained.

While he waited, his mind raced. What had he done wrong? Had he made a mistake? Yes, many of them, but it was war. He quieted his suspicions. It did no good to speculate, and what would happen was not up to him, anyway.

"Enter," said the general.

Farad stepped into the room. The general stood from behind his desk, accepted Farad's salute, and handed him a piece of paper. Farad read it.

"Major Hashemi, you are requested, and required, to assume command—"

Farad blinked. He was too surprised to hear the rest of what the general said.

"Congratulations, Wing Leader," the general said and extended his hand. "We'll announce it at the next formation, but effective immediately you are in command of the One Hundred-First Fighter Wing. Good hunting, Colonel."

Farad felt as if he were floating, as in an unloaded dive in his *Qaher*. He mumbled his thanks to the general and saluted again.

After a few more remarks and a promise to return early for the next mission briefing, Farad departed. He knew he needed sleep, but his new responsibility required him to get up to speed as quickly as possible. He headed for the intel shack to get the latest estimate of Azanian strength and intentions in his assigned theater. As he walked, he felt heavier on his feet, as if the added responsibilities were a physical weight.

At least I'll be assigned new quarters, he thought. Not that I'll ever have time to use them.

He nearly passed his own aircraft without noticing it. His ground crew was there, lined up. As he approached, they began cheering and clapping. One of them peeled a cover off the stenciled name beneath the cockpit.

COL. HASHEMI, 101ST FIGHTER WING LEADER

"That looks good," Farad thanked them. "It looks very good to me."

Twenty-one

Wing Leader Farad Hashemi flew his *Qaher* jet fighter at seven hundred kilometers per hour one hundred meters above the waves crashing into the rocky shore of the Persian Gulf. The pale twilight of Shaitan, the Second Sun, lighted his way and gave the breakers an orange glow. The wave crests flickered like flames in an ocean of fire.

The fighter wing under his command flew to either side of him. Below and ahead was the aircraft they were escorting, a wing of twin-engine *Shahin* bombers. Though named for a falcon, these bombers were neither sleek nor maneuverable. Their bodies looked like fat metal cylinders. Two barrel-shaped engines hung from a straight wing glued on top of the fuselage. They were bouncing up and down in the turbulent air above the waves, gaining and losing tens of meters of altitude at a time.

It must be nerve-wracking flying one of those bombers, Farad thought. They flew low to avoid the sight horizon of Azanian radar. Keeping altitude and station required total concentration. Any mistake would lead to a collision with the ocean or another aircraft.

It meant his fighters were going in low, burning more fuel than at higher altitude, but confident in their ability to stay with the bombers and protect them when needed.

For this mission, the *Qahers* carried heavy under-wing fuel tanks. The tanks made the fighters heavy and slow, but at the first sign of the enemy they could be jettisoned. They extended the range of the fighters by hundreds of kilometers. They carried no bombs. The important thing was to have fighter cover for the bombers, Farad judged.

And, he thought, the four 30mm under his nose would rip up a light escort vessel if necessary.

He kept his eye on his counterpart, the bomber wing leader. He couldn't see into the cockpit in the poor light, nor could he use the radio. Radio silence was mandatory, even in an emergency and especially if someone became lost. Lost aircraft were ordered to spend no more than 40% of their fuel to find their mates or the enemy. If they failed, they were required to head home. Farad had been very clear. No calls for help, no distractions for the strike force. Lost aircraft were dead for this mission, and their only task was to survive for the next. All they had to do was head north toward land to find their way home.

The enemy fleet was to the south. Farad had a position report less than two hours old. He did not know how the Persian Air Corps had gotten the information, but his wing had been ready. The *Qahers* had streaked into the sky from airbase P-3 like a well-drilled machine. The ground crews had cleared the battle damage from the first day of the war, and the survivors were eager to avenge themselves. The fighters had lined up by squadron and roared into the sky one after another. The turbojet engines filled the evening with a deafening roar as the first planes up circled to wait for the rest.

The bombers, Farad admitted, had taken off almost as efficiently. Their commander, Hasmed, knew what he was about. He had served in the Azanian War, the first one.

Now Hasmed led them all over the Persian Gulf toward their targets. An Azanian fleet had smashed the Persian First Fleet the day before in a shocking display of maneuver and firepower. The Azanians had brought planes with them, taking off from aviation ships, and the results had been devastating. The Persian fleet had not been able to close to a range where their guns could be brought to bear. They were bombed and torpedoed all day for massive losses. The survivors were run down at night by destroyers and cruisers like wolves pursuing a herd of cattle.

Airpower, it was evident to everyone, was the key to winning the fight at sea. Farad was going to reinforce the lesson, but he would be teaching the Azanians the hard truth this time.

The formation of one hundred bombers and ninety-six fighters roared over the sunset-hued waves toward the last reported position of the Azanian fleet. They would arrive in just under a quarter-hour. Enemy radar would detect them long before they could spot the enemy ships. None of the Persian planes had space or power to mount a large surface-search set.

Farad's eyes strained at the twilit sky almost the same shade as the ocean below. He looked for the telltale black dots of enemy fighters. The bomber pilots would be looking for ships.

"SAHAN, QAN," the radio crackled. "BEARING 170, TRUE." There was a radio click in acknowledgment, but nothing more.

"Qan" was the callsign for the secret weapon the Persians hoped would turn the tide of the battle. Though New Persia could not give their pilots a radar small enough to fit in a bomber, they did produce a special *Shahin* which carried no bombs. Instead, it was covered with directional antennas and full of electronics which could give a bearing to a radar source. If the Azanians used radar, the *Shahin* would see it, and tell the wing commander the direction from which the radar transmitted.

"God preserves his servants," Farad breathed to himself. He changed course to the bearing given by Qan. He saw his wingman, and the rest of the lead squadron followed. To his frustration, the right squadron did not and continued in the original, wrong, direction. He grunted in frustration. Radio silence was the order, but he couldn't let a quarter of his force fly away into the night.

"Four Squadron, keep your stations," he said into his radio. He imagined all twenty-four pilots' heads leaping up and gazing around them. The squadron lead soon fixed his error and brought his planes with him.

Damn, Farad thought. *The Azanians may have heard us. Assume they are alerted.* He redoubled his vigilance, scanning the sea to the south.

In any case, the enemy radar beam they were following would detect them soon enough. Two hundred aircraft are impossible to hide, no matter how low they fly.

Farad saw the Azanian fighters high in the sky out to sea. The glint of Shaitan-light off a canopy betrayed them. Once his eyes caught the flash of light, he saw the rest of them. There was at least a dozen. He keyed his radio, free of the need for silence.

"Enemy in sight! Twelve high!" Farad called over the radio. He still felt excitement rush through him at the sight of the enemy.

The squadrons in his wing acknowledged. Two squadrons and some individual pilots began accelerating on their own.

"All squadrons! Obey orders! Three and Four Squadrons, engage to the front. One and Two, stay with the bombers."

The planes mostly obeyed, though some pilots strayed far out of position before being called back.

Farad wanted to be the first to engage, but he knew his place was with the bombers. He was in command of the fighter force, second only after Hasmed, the strike leader. They had worked it out yesterday, the only sensible way Farad could see to ensure the mission would be successful. Divided command was the doom of any endeavor.

The two squadrons of *Qahers* roared as their turbojets shot them into the pale orange sky to meet the Azanians. The *Qaher* excelled at climbing. As they rose, they dropped their wing tanks. The bomb-shaped tanks fell like hail into the sea below. Splashes broke the surface of the sea.

Every instinct inside Farad told him to climb and accelerate, but he resisted.

"Enemy in sight!" the call came again on the radio. "Three o'clock!"

Farad whipped his head to the west. More Azanian fighters were flying high. They must have gone far out of the way to come at the Persian formation from two sides at once. Their shipborne radar was guiding them in. Farad was frustrated the enemy could see his every move, but he was blind.

"Squadron Four, clear to engage," he said, dispatching his right squadron. "One, stay with me."

There were calls of frustration on the radio as his squadron gnashed their teeth. Farad was unyielding, "Secure all unnecessary chatter," he radioed.

The bombers proceeded straight but rose to five hundred meters to better search for targets. Farad's squadron rose with them. They soon approached the dogfight ahead of them. Behind him, Four Squadron fought the second Azanian fighter group.

The Azanian Navy Super Duma planes were a haze gray color instead of the plain finish of their Air Force. They were much harder to see against the gray sky. The *Qahers*, Air Corps planes, were painted in halves, the top tan and the underside gray. From above, they stood out against the sea. It made a real difference in spotting the planes.

Farad ordered his planes to stay close and only engage if threatened. He wanted to get through the fight without losing any aircraft, either to enemy guns or overeager pilots. Once engaged, fighters dropped their fuel tanks and went to full power. They might not be able to catch up and continue the mission.

Farad switched between squadron nets one after another, listening with a part of his mind as the rest of his attention flew his plane. With his eyes, he watched as his ears listened. Planes were falling from the sky in flames all around him, friendly and enemy, but no Azanians were approaching the bombers. It was working.

Finally, the lead bomber called out a sighting. It was an Azanian ship, dead ahead. It was too far to identify, but one ship meant there would be more nearby. The bombers fanned out, and command passed to the squadron leaders. Those pilots would determine targets for each plane.

Anti-aircraft tracers reached up from the surface of the water. Around Farad's plane, ugly black smoke clouds burst like flowers. Shrapnel sprayed in all directions from each blossom. Farad saw a bomber hit. Its wing cut in two, the plane spun into the water and disappeared beneath the waves with hardly a splash. It was just gone, with its five-man crew. The last thing Farad saw was its Nine-Pointed-Star insignia sliding under the waves.

He snapped his attention back to his front. All around burst the anti-aircraft shells. Radar-directed guns sprayed bullets into the Persian formations. Farad wondered if it had been wise to stick with the bombers after all. All it had done was make his fighter pilots targets for shipboard gunners. Nineteen-year-old conscripts feeding machines they barely understood could bring down one of his highly trained pilots, like a peasant farmer shooting down a falcon.

As he made the thought, his wingman's plane took a hit and began to smoke. He fell behind as his engine sputtered. He trailed an oily black cloud.

Farad keyed his microphone to call off his fighters and escape the ship's firepower, but he saw the last obstacle to overcome before the bombers could make their run. The Azanian Combat Air Patrol arrived.

These Super Duma fighters had been held back over the enemy formation as a final defense. There were two dozen of them, and they were diving on the Persian bombers.

Farad called for his squadron to engage the new enemies and committed himself to battle.

He turned off fuel flow from the external tanks and jettisoned them. The *Qaher* leaped up with the reduced weight. Farad quickly scanned the enemy targets and picked one. The rest of the squadron split into pairs, but Farad was alone, his wingman far behind, his fate unknown. Farad did not have time to dwell on it.

He acted by unconscious reflex, raising his nose to meet the enemy fighter. The oncoming Super Duma fired first, missing, as Farad jerked his *Qaher* to the side with a tap on the rudder pedal a microsecond before the Azanian fired. The tracers arced to the left.

The Azanian corrected his aim by sliding his nose over, but Farad was ready. He fired the *Qaher's* four 30mm revolving cannons with a squeeze of the trigger on his control stick.

The cannons spat shells where Farad had guessed the Azanian would go. The enemy had made a mistake by continuing to fire his rounds like water from a firehose, using the tracers to correct his aim. Farad aimed for his first shot to hit, and his short burst wrecked the Super Duma fighter. Its nose dropped, and it tumbled, wingless and smoking, toward the sea below.

Farad flew through the gap in the enemy formation opened by his gunfire. He climbed into a loop and looked out of the top of his canopy for enemy targets. The sky was full of maneuvering Persian and Azanian fighters and alight with enemy anti-aircraft tracers. Farad glanced into the chaotic dance and chose his partner in death.

He rolled the fighter level and banked to the right. An Azanian Super Duma was trailing one of his squadron's *Qahers*, spitting bursts of tracers at the desperately jinking jet. The back of Farad's mind wondered who it was he was about to save, but it didn't matter. What mattered was one plane displayed the Nine-Pointed Star on its wings and the other the yellow triangle of the Azanian Air Force.

Farad's bank swept into a dive and roll as he bled airspeed to match his target. His gyro gunsight spun through an arc in front of him until it crossed paths with the silver Super Duma fighter. Farad fired, and the shells rent open the Azanian's fuel tanks. The jet became an orange and black fireball. The nose of the plane broke off and spun out of the exploding cloud of burning fuel. Incredibly, the intact canopy broke open, and the pilot ejected. Farad saw the parachute blossom and did not feel disappointed. It was God's will the Azanian would not die today. Perhaps, Farad corrected himself. It was a long way down to the sea, and the sea was a harsh place.

He had no more time to ponder the fate of the Azanian pilot. He read the tail number of the *Qaher* in front of him and ordered him on the radio to follow. His new wingman joined him in the hunt for the next target.

Together, the two *Qahers* swept into the remaining dogfights and shot down two more Super Dumas. Few pilots could win while outnumbered, and the Azanians were at a disadvantage. Farad saw the remaining planes try to disengage and escape. His remaining squadron mates wished to pursue, but he curtly called them off. The *Qahers* were faster in a dive and could have caught the Super Dumas easily, but Farad knew it was a mistake.

Instead, he flew back to where the torpedo bombers should have been. It took a moment to find them. They were flying low, very low, and their blue-gray paint hid them from above. Their engines firewalled at maximum power. They were only a kilometer from the first Azanian ships.

Farad and his squadron formed up above the bombers and bored into the first target. It was a destroyer, an escort vessel, and he could have ignored it but for the net-shaped radar dish rotating on its after mast. The radar was tracking the planes and directing the guns firing at them.

"All planes, engage the sea target, one pass only," Farad called on the radio.

The *Qahers* dove into shallow dives and fired their heavy cannon rounds. The destroyers' own anti-aircraft guns fired back. The tracers passed through each other. One *Qaher* was hit and broke off trailing smoke. The rest kept firing long bursts of fifty shells. The aircraft cannon shells had a spectacular effect on the light-skinned ship. Shells burst in the water on both flanks raising tiny geysers splashing water onto the decks. A more lethal rain of fragments erupted out of the shells boring into the superstructure like insects. The strafing wrecked the bridge and cut the mainmast in two. The radar dish fell slowly into the water. Secondary explosions of anti-aircraft gun ammunition blossomed into the sky. The three main gun turrets desperately trying to track the jets were opened like tin cans exposed to the sunlight, their guns wrecked.

The *Qahers* climbed into the air on the other side of the destroyer and re-formed. Behind them the ship circled out of control, its rudder controls wrecked and the bridge unmanned.

Under orders to ignore small escorts, the bombers roared over the wrecked destroyer. No gun fired at them as they passed low overhead. The deafening roar of the *Shahin*'s engines terrified sailors on the deck into jumping overboard into the sea.

Farad called the *Shahin* wing commander.

"Find our targets" was the reply. "We are too low to see."

Farad's *Qaher* climbed into the clear sky and was immediately surrounded by bursting anti-aircraft shells. He saw four large ships to the southeast. He took a quick compass bearing and dove.

"Four heavy ships at one-five-zero!" he called. "Range ten kilometers!"

The *Shahin*s, still in formation, altered course. No more planes came to meet them, but the anti-aircraft fire of the surrounding screen of destroyers was intense. The *Qaher*s silenced some guns, but could not shoot them all. Planes fell from the sky, plucked down by radar-directed gunfire.

It wasn't enough to stop the bombers. Determined, fast, and well-flown, they closed the distance to their target in a minute. At an order from their wing leader, they rose to a height of 100 meters. With their engines still firewalled, the *Shahin*s opened their bomb bay doors.

"*Shahin* wing! Drop on your targets!"

Bombardiers released their cargo from the bomb bays. A thin nose cone encased each torpedo. The nose cone broke the wall of air when the bombers dropped them at six hundred kilometers an hour. The small wings kept the torpedo level and pointed in the direction of flight. Within a second, a parachute drogue sprouted from the back of the airfoil and slowed the torpedo with atmospheric drag. When their speed fell enough, the nose cone and airfoil slid off, and the torpedo splashed into the water at a 45-degree angle.

Upon hitting the water, the torpedo motor began spinning. The torpedoes initially dove deep, carried by their momentum. The up-angled rear fins and the torpedoes' buoyancy brought them up just beneath the surface. The motor burned a mixture of alcohol and air to push the torpedo at fifty kilometers an hour through the water.

The torpedoes had no way to steer to a target, being blind and deaf. Everything depended on the skill of the pilots and bombardiers.

In this, they did well. Many things went wrong. Torpedoes failed to release or dropped too quickly and broke in two as they hit the water's surface which solidified like concrete at high impact speeds. Some did not ignite their motors and bobbed harmlessly in the water. But most of the dozens of torpedoes they dropped fell into the water as live weapons and began their short journeys toward their targets.

The *Shahins*, their job done the moment the torpedoes released, curved up into the sky and turned around. A few were hit and crashed into the ocean, but the majority escaped.

The targets were the Azanian aviation ships, four aircraft carriers.

The huge ships went to flank speed and desperately began to evade the torpedoes heading toward them. There were far too many to track. Each torpedo left a trail of bubbles in its wake, but some patches of the ocean were a solid mass of bubbles as torpedo wakes crisscrossed. The surrounding escort ships peppered the water with every gun brought to bear. The carriers' anti-aircraft armament could not reach the sea. A few lucky hits destroyed oncoming torpedoes, but many remained.

Each carrier turned toward the incoming warheads to present the smallest target possible. They were fast ships, flying planes required it, but not quick turning. Only one made the full maneuver before the torpedoes began to arrive.

Most of the unguided weapons missed. Even in missing, however, they prevented the targets from maneuvering for fear of dodging one attack to blunder into another. Most traveled a few kilometers until their alcohol was burned up and their air bottles emptied. Then they sank into the sea, leaving the bottom covered with derelict warheads.

A few—enough—hit their targets. Magnetic detonators had been tried during the last Azanian war but had proven too unreliable. The air-dropped torpedo was designed to be as simple as possible. They carried impact fuses only, although there were two fuses in case of damage or failure.

One, two, then three torpedoes hit the nearest target. The ship was stopped dead in the water by the impacts, her turbine room ripped open and exposed to the sea. Without power and with her largest compartment flooded, she was doomed. The second target was hit in an aviation fuel bunker and exploded. The flight deck was rent upward by the explosive gases seeking a release into the air. Smoke poured from the broken deck and the ship immediately began listing to port.

The other two ships were hit but did not immediately sink. Smoke poured from their elevators as the hanger decks burned. Running figures struggled with hoses as they tried to contain the conflagrations.

Farad saw all of this from far above. The torpedo trails crisscrossed the sea like a tapestry of death.

He thought of calling down his fighters in strafing attacks but decided against it. There was too much risk and little reward for attacking ships already doomed. Even if they weren't, strafing defenseless men while they were fighting death by fire was dishonorable.

Farad called his wing and directed them homeward. He climbed high and looked down. Beyond the burning aviation ships, there was another formation. They were big, heavy ships, but without the flat tops of the carriers.

On impulse, Farad decided to take a closer look. He did not wish to risk any other pilots who would be heading home after a successful mission.

He banked and dove toward the enemy ships. As they grew in his canopy screen, Farad tried to identify them. They were not carriers or battleships. They had few guns, only small anti-aircraft mounts. He leveled off and prepared a high-speed pass over the first ship. He blasted over her too fast for any gun to track. Tracers chased him futilely.

After passing over another ship, Farad saw many men on deck. They scattered in all directions. They wore uniforms but not the blue shirts of the Azanian Sea Force. They wore the green and tan of the Land Forces. They were soldiers! The ships were troop transports!

Invasion! Farad thought. The nearest shore was a bare fifty kilometers from Persepolis. Farad climbed to count the numerous ships and had gotten to twelve before he was interrupted.

He had climbed too high and lost too much speed. The anti-aircraft shells arrived all at once, radar-directed, and exploded around his *Qaher*. Fragments cut a hundred holes in the fuselage of Farad's plane. Systems failed all at once. The engine flamed out, the fire alarm sounded, the stall horn blared, and the gauges for oil and fuel pressure dropped to zero. The jet noise dropped to nothing, and there was no sound but the thin rush of the air outside.

Farad knew there was nothing to be done. The damage finished his *Qaher*. Even if he could restart the engine, more shells were exploding all around. He was a fool for getting shot down, but he would be a bigger fool to try to save the plane.

For the second time in his life, Farad ejected from a jet fighter.

Twenty-two

Farad fell toward the surface of the Persian Gulf. The calm, shallow water of the gulf was pale blue and blended into the horizon of the clear sky. For a moment, he thought he was falling up into the sky.

He felt warm and woozy. It felt like he could fall forever. Nothing would ever happen to him. He could fly into the sky until the stars came out. He would pick one and fall toward it. In space, it was peaceful and quiet. There would be nothing to disturb his rest. Rest. Sleep.

Time seemed meaningless. He felt the freedom of flying. If only the wind would stop, he thought. It was intolerably loud.

Farad woke up barely in time to pull his reserve parachute. Streaming behind him, his primary parachute was in tatters. The ejection had ripped it to shreds. The reserve opened and arrested his plunge. Farad released the streamer as he drifted slowly down toward the waves.

Below him, Farad saw through the flat surface of the water all the way to the sea bottom. The sandy bottom was broken by the corroded shapes of sunken ships lost in the monsoon storms of decades and centuries past. They looked like islands. Schools of fish and tentacles of plant stems surrounded the wrecks. Between them, there was a desolation of flat, featureless sand. Islands of life in the desert of the sea, Farad thought.

He caught himself musing. There were more important things to see. Gazing at the natural wonders of the Persian Gulf was an activity for another time. He looked up toward the horizon.

The sea to the north was full of ships. Their massive forms left rippling wakes seeming to go on forever in the calm sea. The air above them filled with the smoke from their boilers. They were steaming away from him.

Farad was falling out of the sky to seaward of the Azanian fleet. He had crashed far from shore with the enemy force between him and dry land.

He shrugged in his parachute harness. It was too far to swim, anyway.

Remembering his training, Farad took off his oxygen mask. It hung from his neck by its hose. He inflated the life preservers under his arms. Farad looked up and found the two quick-release handles on the canopy risers. He lifted the covers off and placed his hands on the release switches.

He looked down again to see he was a hundred feet from the surface of the ocean. He forced himself to relax and drifted down beneath his parachute. When his feet touched the water, he jerked the canopy quick-release handles. The parachute drifted free, and Farad sank into the water.

His life preserver floated him back to the surface. The water was warm. The parachute, weightless, fluttered to rest on top of him. Remaining calm, Farad dived under the canopy and came back up a few feet away. The parachute was floating next to him. With a few strokes, he swam away from the canopy to avoid becoming entangled in the parachute lines.

The raft hadn't made it. It was stowed as part of the parachute and designed to deploy when it hit the water. Perhaps it had gone with the primary parachute or was ripped free when he had ejected.

It was a small thing, Farad thought. He could float in the warm water for a long time.

It was quiet. The calm water seemed to absorb sound. The surface reflected glints of sunlight into his eyes. The sun was warm on his scalp.

It was far too pleasant a fate for someone who had barely survived bailing out of a plane a few minutes earlier.

After a few minutes, Farad no longer thought it was pleasant. The hot sun reflected off the water. His eyes burned from the salt and glare. He could feel his skin cooking in the morning sunlight.

As pleasant as it was, he could not hope to survive without shelter and water for more than a day or two.

The clear water began to darken around him. It seemed as if a cloud were forming in the ocean, a dark pool like the inside of a thunderstorm. Farad thought it was a shadow at first, but there was no cloud blocking the sun. Then he wondered if it were a great fish of some kind. Farad didn't know much about sea creatures, but he had heard many tales of monsters which lived in the deep ocean. He paddled slowly away from the shadow.

The cloud ended about half a meter away from him in all directions. A ring of dark water formed around him on all sides.

The ring was slowly closing. The dark cloud drew closer.

Squinting, Farad could see the cloud was made up of tiny, worm-like pseudo-fish. Each was less than 20mm long and half the width of his little finger. When they came near the surface, the pseudo-fish would jump a short distance into the air and Farad could see them. One end was smooth, but the other was a series of circular jaws full of tiny teeth.

Farad tried to swim away from the school of pseudo-fish. When he did, the fish darted through the water toward him. When he saw he could not outrun them, Farad stopped kicking, and the cloud slowed. It seemed they were drawn by movement.

Farad tried to stay still and float. His flight suit was buoyant and would keep his head above water. Perhaps if he didn't move, the current would carry him away, or the fish would lose interest.

The cloud of fish halted in the water, apparently unable to see him. Then, the school started to expand in all directions. The pseudo-fish spread out, searching for him.

The cloud of pseudo-fish became a ring, and the edge of the ring was coming closer. When the edge of the ring came within a few meters, Farad had no choice but to kick away. The pseudo-fish immediately sensed his motion and the whole ring shot toward him as if animated by a single thought. Farad tried to swim as fast as he could, but the school soon caught up and surrounded him.

The cloud of tiny worm-fish closed in around him in a ring of thrashing little jaws. Farad fought off the urge to thrash at the water. Swatting at the small worms in the water only pushed them away. To crush them, he would have to use both his hands, and he didn't want any to reach his skin.

He couldn't get away by swimming. He couldn't get out of the water. Where else could he go? Was there no escape?

With forced slowness, he slid his right hand down to the leg pocket of his flight suit. He found his knife sheath. His fingertips found the button fastening the pocket and worked to undo it. He felt a slimy wriggling string wrapping around his finger. The worm's teeth found the soft skin in the web of his fingers and bit.

Gritting his teeth against the pain, Farad caught the worm in his hand and squeezed as hard as he could. He felt the worm's hard exoskeleton crack under the strength of his grip. Sticky goo came out both ends.

The worm continued to thrash in his grip. Farad pulled the worm apart with his other hand. The head, disembodied, continued to chew into his hand. He had to clap his palms together to smash the last life out of the worm's jaws.

He drew more worms with his movement. The water thrashed with them.

Abandoning stealth, Farad swiped his survival knife free from its leg sheath. He slashed at the life preserver's air bladders under his arms.

Farad let out a long breath. He raised his arms above his head. A few of the worms were already attached to his flight suit and hung thrashing in the air. The worms' segments rotated against each other to counteract the torque of their spinning teeth.

Being eaten alive by tiny worms was not the end Farad had envisioned for himself. Death in battle, yes. Burning to death was a nightmare he had come to terms with, as was falling from a great height. He'd even envisioned being captured and tortured by angry tribesmen in the desert. Never had he thought he would die as worm food. If he were going to die, he would rather risk drowning than be eaten alive.

Farad pitched himself over and dove. His powerful shoulders pulled against the water. Beneath the surface, he kicked with his stout legs.

Something was wrong. Farad was not sinking. He was still floating in the swarm of worms. His thrashing only attracted their attention.

His g-suit! Beneath the legs of his flight suit was a pair of chaps filled with air bladders. They were intended to squeeze his legs during high-speed maneuvers to keep him from passing out in the cockpit from g-forces. Enough air remained in them to keep his legs above the surface.

Farad slashed at his thighs with the knife. He had no time for a delicate cut. Streams of blood mixed with the air bubbles. The worms closed in, seeking the source of the blood.

Knife in hand, Farad dove again. He closed his eyes and pinched his nostrils closed. He could feel the slimy touch of worm-fish over his face. The worms wriggled in his hair. He pulled himself underwater as fast as he could.

He felt jaws attach to his ear. The teeth immediately began boring. They twisted in a circle like a drill. The pain was sharp and immediate. Unlike the Earth-leech, the worm-fish did not need to anesthetize their victims. The more the victim thrashed in pain, the more worms would be drawn into the kill.

More worms attached themselves to his flight suit. Mindlessly, they began chewing through the cloth. The fabric was tight-knit cotton and would take time for them to penetrate.

Down, down he swam. Bubbles streamed from the slashed open flight suit. The worms followed him.

Farad pulled ahead of them. Although aquatic, they were still small and not very fast. He smashed all the worms which had bit him. He saw the rest of the swarm wriggling down from the surface toward him.

He commanded himself not to move, not to draw further attention from the blind worms. They homed in on the movement. If he didn't disturb the water, they would not know he was there.

He sank slowly because the flight suit had emptied itself of air. The worms came to the patch of disturbed water where Farad had crushed their brethren. Farad watched whole worms feed on the thrashing, headless segments of the wounded.

The swarm began to circle in all directions, slowly expanding outward to find their prey again. Farad was sinking faster than the worms were swimming. He was going to escape, but he was escaping in the wrong direction—down.

Farad's lungs began to burn. He looked upward toward the dim sun. The worm-shadows crossed its face. The school of pseudo-fish was between him and the surface.

He faced a choice. He could swim upward to breathe, and the worms would devour him, or he could drown.

Farad had heard drowning was painless. It didn't feel like it.

As when he faced death in the air, Farad did not panic. He gripped his knife tighter.

If I am going to die, thought Farad, *I will not die without a fight.* He kicked his legs and thrashed with his arms. He would kill as many of the mindless worms as he could. It was an unfortunate death, he knew, but he wasn't going to give up.

With his teeth bared, Farad swam up toward the swarm. To his surprise, the worms scattered. They swam away in all directions, and the cloud of tiny worm bodies dissolved into nothing. In a moment, they were gone.

Farad broke the surface and gasped for air. The sunlight burned his eyes. He treaded water to keep his head up.

He looked around. The swarm had dispersed. He was alone.

He was bleeding. He had a dozen cuts where the worms had attacked him, and a slash in his leg from cutting open the g-suit. Blood streamers stained the water. The sea salt burned his wounds.

Why did the worms flee? He didn't know, but he thanked God anyway.

Another shadow grew in the water. It was immense and rising from the ocean beneath him.

Farad knew native life was not the only thing in the ocean. Earth sharks roamed the seas as well. Perhaps the shark had come to chase the worms away and steal their meal.

He gripped his knife again and prepared to fight.

In a moment, it became clear it was too large to be a shark. Farad had heard of the deep ocean predators. Huge native creatures ate anything their maws could grasp. He had never seen one this close to shore. Did the Azanian fleet attract them?

His knife was tiny.

The black shape broke through the surface, not twenty meters away. It was huge, perhaps seventy meters long and ten across. A dorsal fin rose first, followed by a curved body tapering into the water at each end. Farad bobbed up and down in the water from its passage. His head dipped beneath the surface.

When he came up, the creature had risen farther above the surface. It was black, curved, and...metallic?

From the top of the fin, a hatch opened. Two men climbed up on top and cried down to him.

Farad was dumbfounded. He was too surprised to wave.

One of the men called down to the deck. Another hatch opened, and two sailors climbed out. One threw a line attached to a life preserver.

Farad regained his senses and swam toward the life ring. He was tired and getting weak from blood loss. Safety was in sight, but his strength was leaving him.

When he reached the life ring, it took all his remaining strength to grab on. He locked his elbow through the ring and held on. The sailors on deck dragged him toward them.

Farad had to crawl up the slippery metal sides of the submarine. He stood before the two men at the forward hatch could assist him and then climbed down the ladder into the submarine.

Twenty-three

Farad was on board the New Persian submarine *Yunes*. She had been observing the air battle through her periscopes and had spotted his parachute. Armed sailors had been on deck in case he had been an Azanian.

When the sailors saw the Nine-Pointed-Star patch on his suit, they had relaxed. Farad could only lie on the curved deck of the submarine and gasp. He was lowered down the ladder quickly, and roughly so the trunk hatches could be closed above him.

The submarine dived immediately after. The diving alarm sounded, and Farad felt the motors hum through the deck. He was helped to his feet by two sailors. Water fell off him onto the deck.

He found himself in the engine room of the submarine. It was sweltering. The diesel engines had been charging batteries. Farad began to add his sweat to the seawater dripping off his skin.

The deck was steel grating. It hurt his hands as Farad pushed himself up to stand.

The first breath Farad took stunned him with the smell. It was a combination of unwashed men, diesel fumes, cigarettes, and mold. He coughed.

"He's alive, all right," said one of the sailors.

"Enjoying the fresh air?" asked the other.

"Are you enjoying the fresh air, *sir*." Another sailor in a khaki uniform and officer's insignia corrected him.

"Yes, sir," said the sailor.

"He's a pilot, Seaman, and he's been through it. Get him to the wardroom after he dries off."

"Aye, sir."

The officer left Farad with the two sailors, who produced a towel and began to dry him off, roughly. Seawater soaked his flight suit, and he exchanged it for a set of ill-fitting khakis.

The eight-cylinder diesel engine filled the other side of the engine room. There was another engine on the other side of the passage.

More water trickled down from the aft trunk. The air was humid, and Farad could smell mold.

After drying off as much as he could, Farad followed the two sailors through a hatch and a soundproof door. They entered a room full of the smell of food and tobacco. There were four tables, and two dozen sailors were eating and conversing over what must have been lunch. They all stopped to watch when Farad came in. He felt like a new kid at school. Farad waved at them.

"Hey," one sailor asked from his seat, "are you a pilot?"

"Yes," Farad said.

"You shoot down any Azanians?" the same sailor asked in a tone close to a jeer.

"Yes," said Farad, "four."

"That's all?" The sailor said, trying to keep on top of the conversation.

"Today," said Farad evenly. "There have been seven others."

The room was quiet.

The sailors with him led him to a ladder leading up. Farad climbed it and got off on the next deck. Gray paint coated the lower deck, but this deck had carpet. Wood paneling covered the bulkheads.

He was met by three naval officers who led him the short distance to the wardroom. They seemed just as curious about him as the sailors below. Farad reflected it must be monotonous on a submarine, staring at the same faces day after day.

He sat on a bench cushion along the bulkhead. Maps festooned the walls. A radio in the corner murmured music.

Farad could hear activity all around. There were dozens of men going about their daily business all over the boat. He knew how crowded all ships were, but especially submarines.

A bronze plaque on the bulkhead proclaimed that the boat was built by the Bandar shipyard.

The three officers wore shipboard coveralls with their ranks emblazoned on their collars. They looked the same as the other sailors otherwise. Farad looked out of place in the borrowed khakis.

"Commander Azeri," the oldest man introduced himself. He was the equivalent rank as Farad, but the naval rank had a different title.

"Wing Leader Hashemi," Farad said.

"You've had a tough day, Wing Leader," Azeri said.

"It was worse for others," Farad said.

"I suppose," Azeri said. "Did your attack succeed?"

"I was the fighter leader," Farad said. "The torpedo bombers were successful. They hit all the Azanian aircraft carriers. I believe they are all sunk or disabled."

"Did you see them?" Azeri asked.

"Yes," Farad replied.

"It makes it easier," Azeri said. "We let them go last night."

Farad raised an eyebrow.

"Orders," Azeri said. "We are to observe and report. We had the carriers in our sights," Azeri said ruefully. "We let them go and radioed their course and speed."

"We found them," Farad said. "The *Shahins* attacked and hit them all." Farad described the torpedo bomber attack.

"Nice to hear," said Azeri. "Something is going right."

"The war goes poorly," Farad agreed. "I do not know what you have heard, but the Azanians are closing on Persepolis."

"It cannot be," Azeri said. "How did they get so far, so fast?"

"Only God knows," Farad said. "And there is something else."

Farad told Azeri about the Azanian transports he had seen, full of troops.

"Where did you see them?" Azeri said. "Wait, come with me."

Azeri opened a small sliding door and walked into a tight passage. On one side were the beeps and squawk of a radio code. On the other side was a small office. The passage led to another room whose walls were full of switches, dials, and lights. Two periscopes rose from the deck into the overhead.

"Captain in control," one sailor said.

"As you were," said Azeri.

He led Farad between the periscopes to a table covered with charts. "Where did you see those transports?"

Farad looked hard at the charts and closed his eyes. He opened them and asked, "Where are we now?"

Azeri pointed. Farad checked the clock and made some mental calculations.

"Here," Farad said. He pointed at a spot on the chart.

"How fast were they moving?" Azeri asked. He was doubtful Farad would know.

"Not as fast as the carriers," Farad said.

Azeri nodded. "Navigator, plot a course here," he pointed to a spot on the chart. "We'll try to get ahead of them."

The other officer frowned. "We will use a lot of our battery power. Can we snorkel part of the way?"

"I don't see how to avoid it," Azeri said. "They are ahead of us, and they are moving away. We have to play catch up." Both men looked unhappy.

"If we called the transports in, could another air attack be mounted today?"

"No," Farad said at once. "The losses were too heavy. It will take time to reform."

"Then it's up to us," Azeri said. "How long until sunset?"

"Seven hours," the navigator replied. "Run as far as we can on batteries until then?"

"No," Azeri said. "We would have to snorkel on approach and would make too much noise."

"Snorkel now?"

"Not much point," Azeri said. "Tell me, Wing Leader, could you see us underwater?"

Farad remembered the submarine's approach, the vast shadow rising from the depths. "Yes," he said.

"If we snorkel now, the enemy could see us, and if we run on batteries until tonight, we'll be too close for snorkeling." Azeri thought hard.

"Sir," said the navigator. "What if we go deep and creep over here, to the west, behind them," he penciled a line on the chart, "and then charge batteries as soon as the sun goes down. We should be out of their radar coverage if we assume they are heading north. They must be heading here," he pointed. On the chart was the notation, 'Busher Bay.' "The rest of the coast is all rocks and cliffs."

"I agree," said Azeri. "All right, plot the course. Take her down to eight hundred feet, make revolutions for five knots."

"Aye, sir."

The officer of the deck said, "Helmsman, right ten degrees, make your course three-five-zero. Planesman, ten degrees down. Make your depth eight hundred feet."

There was a rushing noise on the other side of the bulkhead as the water was allowed into the ballast tanks. The boat angled downward.

After a few minutes, the submarine leveled off. The hull creaked and popped ominously. Farad saw no one around him was reacting to the sounds. He steadied himself. Being inside a steel tube beneath hundreds of meters below the water didn't bear thinking about. It must require iron nerves to serve like this, following orders and having to trust everyone else on board. Even the sailor steering the boat only did so when commanded. On the other side, the captain had to trust his orders would be carried out. It was all very strange to Farad, who flew his plane alone and expected his squadron mates to fight on their own.

Being a sailor on a submarine was not something Farad would choose to do. Perhaps Basir would have made a good sailor, he thought.

Farad imagined his chess-playing friend, with his methodical and patient mind, would do well in this underwater world. Everything here happened slowly, and there was a plan for everything.

Farad was led back to the wardroom by the sailors, who climbed ladders and stepped over thresholds as if they weren't there. The air was already noticeably colder since the diesel engines had shut down and stopped heating the boat. The whir of a fan from the deck below and the murmur of sailors talking throughout the boat replaced the roar of the engines.

"What will become of me?" Farad asked Azeri.

"You are part of the boat's company now." Azeri smiled. "Temporarily, of course. We will drop you off the next time we make port. Unfortunately, I don't know when that will be."

"How long can you stay out?" Farad asked.

"Two or three months. And we sailed on the first day of the war," Azeri said.

"I see," said Farad. He felt the frustration deep inside of him. What good was it to be rescued if the war could be over before he rejoined it?

"Sorry, Wing Leader, but the needs of the service..." Azeri sympathized. If he had been left on shore, he knew he'd be doing anything he could to get back to sea. This pilot seemed very steady for someone who had just been shot down and rescued from being eaten by carnivorous pseudo-fish. It was too bad he wasn't in the Submarine Service.

Farad had nothing to do. He felt useless on the submarine as he sat alone at the wardroom table. Officers passed through the tiny room on their way to one task or another, occasionally accompanied by an enlisted man on some errand. The mess steward toiled in the small pantry where food for the officers was prepared.

Farad supposed these sailors were specialists, as adept at operating the boat as he was at flying his plane. He remembered the submarine's control room with its hundreds of dials and switches.

If he were going to be here for any length of time, Farad would have to find a way to contribute. It was not his way to shirk his duty even when he was out of his element. Farad knew he could master this new domain, given time. He had his rank as a colonel, and his position could guarantee him a place on the submarine. He had only to assert it.

Farad resolved to find out how far his curiosity and determination could take him in this new world.

Twenty-four

The Azanian Land Force company roared down the highway to Persepolis. The tanks, named after cheetahs, moved like a pack of hungry hunters. Their armor was light, but their powerful engines let them fly down the highway at seventy kilometers an hour. It was exhilarating.

Captain Aran couldn't believe how easy it had been. Once clear of the Siwan border, his tanks had broken through the Persians into the open. No force had been able to stop them. Three times, Persians had put up a fight in villages or natural choke points. Each time, the Azanians had flanked and surrounded the defenders and destroyed them. The Persians would often fight to the death but were slow to react to threats to their flanks. They regularly kept fighting when it was time to retreat.

A delaying strategy had been what the captain had feared most. He was forced to deploy his forces every time the Persians fired at him. If the enemy had made him fight for every kilometer and then retreated to fight again, the Azanian invasion would take forever. As it was, isolated forces spent themselves in hopeless last stands.

It took the same amount of time to chase off a rearguard as to destroy it.

The last stands were not pointless. One of them had consisted of a battery of anti-tank guns dug in a village. They had destroyed two of his tanks before the Azanians had retreated out of range. Aran had called in the Air Force. A half-hour later, two Dumas had dropped napalm canisters and set the whole village ablaze. The captain led his tanks around the blazing ruins. No more enemy fire came from the village. He hoped there hadn't been any civilians in the wreckage, but it wasn't his problem. If the Persians used a village as a fortress, the laws of war allowed him to destroy it. The following infantry would inspect the ash-filled ruins remaining after his guns crushed all resistance.

His orders were to bypass what enemies he could and use firepower to destroy those he could not. His tanks' most important weapon was their treads. Mile after mile passed as the light tank company roared down the highway toward the Persian capital. What awaited them there, Aran didn't know. He hoped it would mean the end of the war.

The captain had been to Persepolis once, between the wars. It had been a beautiful place, with its domed architecture and lush gardens. He hoped the Persians would see reason and surrender before unleashing the destruction of war on such a treasure. He hoped, but he was also determined to see the war to its finish, whatever the cost.

Twenty-five

The *Yunes* sped beneath the waves at a depth of twenty meters. Farad stood in the control room of the submarine. He was an intruder. The officers and crewmen were still curious about him, but they had a job to do, and he was in the way. Worse, he was a senior officer, so they couldn't express their feelings about his useless presence.

Farad knew this, but his curiosity drove him to observe the workings of the submarine. What use was rank if it could not grant him an opportunity like this?

Captain Azeri was the officer of the deck. He took the conn from the normal watch officer for this critical duty. He was ultimately responsible for the outcome of the mission.

Azeri huddled with the navigation officer over the chart table. Dim red lights around the compartment made the interior look sinister. The boat had "rigged for red" a half-hour before in expectation of darkness. The lights reminded everyone it was night outside, even though inside the steel hull there was no way to tell. Only the clocks around the boat offered any other clue as to whether it was day or night.

"Make your depth twenty meters," Azeri instructed. The helmsman and planesman worked their control yokes to bring the boat to the correct depth. The chief of the watch fiddled with the ballast tank controls to compensate for the change in water pressure.

"Bring her to course zero-one-five," Azeri said a moment later. "All ahead two-thirds."

The boat's electric motors in the stern, inaudible this far forward, drew more battery power to spin up the *Yunes'* propeller to the required RPMs.

The navigation officer looked at Azeri with a question in his eyes, but his professionalism prevented him from asking.

"We are going to recharge batteries before we make our approach," Azeri explained, having understood the look. "Prepare to raise snorkel."

Inside the metal sail of the submarine were the periscopes, radio and radar antennas, and a large breathing tube. The tube allowed the sub to gather air for its engines in much the same way as a man could hide underwater while breathing through a reed stuck through the surface. The snorkel was a much more difficult target to spot than the surfaced boat would be.

Farad heard Azeri give the orders for raising the snorkel. There was a series of thumps above him and a whirring noise. Azeri ordered a quartermaster to raise the periscope at the same time. He looked through it one-eyed and spun the periscope around in all directions.

"Clear," he announced after three circuits. "Assume periscope watch."

A junior officer stepped forward to relieve Azeri at the periscope.

"Engage the engines," Azeri said.

Aft, from the engine room where Farad had arrived on the boat, a rumble followed by a roar shook the boat. Farad felt a wave of heat blow through the length of the submarine. On the diving panel, two red lights shone to show the snorkel intake and exhaust were open.

Azeri said to the navigation officer, "Now would be a good time to review your fix."

"Yes, sir. Are there any landmarks?"

"Not yet," Azeri said.

Unhappy with his answer, the navigation officer bent over his slide rule and calculated a position. Behind him, two radio navigation receivers whirred into life. The officer compared the readouts from the radios and his calculations.

Azeri was glad to see the positions matched within a hundred meters but said nothing. He had chosen his navigation officer carefully.

The navigation officer worked himself up to speak again. "Sir, on this course we will be entering—" He interrupted himself and looked around the control room. There were five other men there besides Farad. There are no secrets on a submarine.

"I'm aware," Azeri said. "Are you up to it?"

The navigation officer gulped. He was being asked to do something he would never attempt in peacetime. But this was war.

"Yes, sir."

"Then plot a course," Azeri said. "I want to be through by o-three hundred. We will charge our batteries as we go."

Farad furrowed his brows in puzzlement. He stood on his toes to see over Azeri's shoulder. Farad knew how to read a chart from his navigation training. The markings were strange to him. What did the shaded area on the chart mean?

Farad's eyesight was exceptional, but it was hard to read in the dim light, so he had to squint.

His heart froze when he read the text written over the shaded part of the chart.

Azeri noticed his reaction and smiled. He was enjoying himself, Farad thought. Farad realized Azeri was in his element in the way Farad was when he flew his fighter through the sky.

"We are going where the enemy cannot follow us," Azeri said. "And where they won't expect us to go."

Azeri, Farad saw, was intentionally leading them all into a minefield.

"Call action stations," the captain said.

A junior officer pulled an overhead switch, and sailors all over the ship dropped what they were doing to run to their battle stations.

It took two minutes. Only one man in control left to be replaced by another.

Farad hoped the captain knew what he was doing. He made his muscles unclench. He was forced to trust these men the way he trusted his *Qaher* jet. Farad not only had to believe in them, but he had to accept he could do nothing but watch. The realization came hard to the fighter pilot. Pilots were part of a team but fought as individuals. The submarine crew was a team but fought as an extension of Captain Azeri's will. In a way, he was the only person there. The rest of the crew and all the machinery around him existed to do Azeri's bidding.

The navigation officer sweated. All the men in control did, except Azeri. The heat from the diesel engines cooked the air inside the submarine, already warm, to oven hot. Farad had grown used to the stink of unwashed men, but the smell became stronger by the minute. Sweat and grease ran down the greasy bristles of the men's beards and dripped on the sodden collars of their cotton uniforms.

The navigation officer's pencil marks inched closer to the shaded part of the chart denoting the minefield. Upon closer examination, Farad could see a narrow path passed through the minefield to the other side. The *Yunes* was heading for the entrance to the gap.

"Right five degrees rudder. Come to course zero-two-zero," the navigator said. Azeri gave the command, and the helmsman executed it perfectly, like a machine.

The new course lined the submarine up with the straight path through the minefield.

"I hope they knew what they were doing when they laid this field," the navigation officer mumbled. Everyone in the room silently agreed.

Farad thought about the tactic Azeri was using. They were running near the surface with the snorkel deployed. No ship could come close without endangering itself in the minefield. If the Azanians didn't know about the mines, they would as soon as one of their vessels hit one. And they had no way of knowing about the path through the field.

An aircraft could fly overhead, but Farad's bombers had sent the Azanian aviation ships to the bottom. Going through the minefield was an excellent way to approach the landing beach without being detected. If someone had made a mistake in placing a mine, or if the navigation officer made a mistake, they would never know.

They would all die in an instant, Farad thought. Fate. It would be, as everything was, as God willed it to be.

The diesel engines made a tremendous noise, but there was no one around to hear it. Inside the minefield, the submarine was safe from the Azanians and could charge batteries for later use. When they exited the field, the *Yunes* would be fully ready for combat. It was a courageous move by Azeri if it worked. If it didn't, he would lose the boat with all its crew. The whole war was a risk.

Farad calmed himself. It really would be as God willed, as it had been His will to rescue him with this steel whale. Like Jonah, he was saved from the ocean by Leviathan.

The boat ran through the field in an hour. The control room was tense, but no one showed any fear. Even the junior crewmen were silent and exuded confidence in their boat and their captain.

When Azeri was sure they were approaching the other end of the minefield, he ordered the diesel engines shut off, and the snorkel retracted. There was a blast of air like a cleansing wind as the diesel engines shut down. At the last gasp, the engines sucked down fresh air for the crew to breathe and expelled the stale air of the previous day.

The waves of heat from the engine room ceased, and the rumble of the diesel engines died away. The electric motors still ran, but Azeri reduced the speed of the boat to preserve their stored battery power.

After a last check of the periscope, it was retracted. Azeri ordered the boat deep for the approach to the Azanian fleet.

Although faced with imminent action, the control crew was visibly relaxed. Combat was something for which they had trained. Being sent to a watery death by a mine had been hard to accept, even for these underwater automatons. Farad was glad they were still human.

"Conn, sonar," called a voice from below. The sonar room, where sailors listened for the sounds of the enemy, was located on the middle deck at the base of the ladder.

"Go ahead," Azeri called.

"Engine noise at zero-eight-nine. I can't distinguish between targets. Multiple sources near zero-eight-nine."

"Very well," Azeri said. "Make our course zero-seven-zero." Azeri was taking the submarine to a spot ahead of the noise in the water.

Azeri flipped a switch and played what the sonar hydrophones were hearing on an overhead speaker for the benefit of the control-room crew. Farad thought it sounded like a dozen locomotive engines chugging past.

"The thundering herd," Azeri said. He checked to make sure the new sonar bearing was plotted correctly on the sonar chart.

Everything happened so slowly. This submarine's course changes did not feel like the instinctive movements of a jet fighter in the hands of its pilot. The crew planned everything they did. One thing he recognized was the boredom, mixed with fear, while waiting for action.

Farad watched the men move to every task with fluid purpose. There were no wasted movements, and everyone focused on what they were doing. The crewmen moved around each other like gears in a machine.

Farad understood little of what he saw. Two large machines full of dials and knobs seemed to be aiming the torpedoes. He watched the fire-control crew spin the knob each time there was new information from the sonar room downstairs.

"These machines aim the weapons for you?" Farad asked one of the crewmen.

"No, sir," the crewman said. "They do some of the math for us."

Farad raised his eyebrows. A machine that could calculate? How odd. He wondered if such a thing would ever be useful outside of a submarine.

Azeri brought the boat back up to twenty meters' depth to use the periscope again. He spun the tube around once before aiming it to port.

"They are right where you said, sonar," he said, before dropping the scope back down to the floor. "Good job."

Azeri had saved the bearings to the targets by clicking a button on the periscope. By using the periscope rangefinder, he had calculated a better range estimate than the sonar could provide. Fire-control entered the range and bearing into the mechanical calculators lining the starboard bulkhead.

The fire-control crew estimated the speed the target was moving and registered the speed of the *Yunes*. They calculated the angle the *Yunes* would have to aim the torpedoes so the weapons' courses would intersect the targets' courses. The result was a best-guess firing solution.

"Range is eight thousand meters," Azeri said. "Too far."

Farad didn't think it was too far to shoot. He wanted the waiting to end. Patience was a virtue for a sailor even more than it was for a pilot.

On Azeri's command, the submarine slowed its motors. Farad couldn't tell except by looking at the gauges. The *Yunes* was creeping toward the Azanians, who, according to sonar, had reduced speed.

"They don't want to run aground in the dark," Azeri said. "Their charts are bad. They'll wait until Shaitan-light before moving the last few miles toward the beach. They need shore landmarks to navigate."

The second sun was due to rise within the hour. It would light the shoreline with the equivalent of twilight from the First Sun, which was more than enough to steer by.

"We don't have much time," said one of the officers.

"We have enough," said Azeri.

After a short run at low speed, Azeri ordered the periscope up again. He caught the handles near the deck and duck-walked around the tube as he peered through the scope. The periscope's head was only a foot above the waves and would be almost impossible to see. Azeri was taking no chances. If the *Yunes* was running slow and silent, so could an Azanian ship. He didn't want to find himself beneath an Azanian destroyer.

No Azanians were visible, so he let the periscope tube slide upward until he was standing.

"Words of God," he said. He spun the scope back and forth and clicked the rangefinder on different bearings, one after another. The attack-center crew ignored his remark but took note of the range of each target as the numbers appeared on the calculator dials.

Azeri lowered the periscope and ordered the submarine to halt in the water. He took a step to the sonar plot and checked the range and bearings to the targets he had seen in the periscope. Farad looked over his shoulder at the pencil marks on the paper plot. There seemed to be ten ships, barely moving, all within ten thousand meters.

It was a perfect opportunity. A submarine captain could serve an entire career without ever firing a weapon. Or, he could be sent to the bottom without warning before he could fire a shot. Few men indeed ever saw the profusion of targets Azeri had in his sights. This was a chance that would likely never come again, and Azeri knew it.

Azeri showed no emotion on his face. Whatever eagerness he felt was hidden behind a professional mask. Farad thought of himself and his fellow pilots, who were no amateurs, whooping out their contact reports over the radio. These sailors worked in silence as if playing chess.

The men at the calculators whirred the calculator dials with their hands and wrote down the results on clipboards. After an agonizing few minutes, they had their answers.

"We have firing solutions," said the weapons officer.

"Prepare tubes one through six for firing," Azeri said. "One, two, three, four, five, and six," he repeated.

Crewmen repeated his orders, and the fire-control men flipped a different set of switches. Farad heard a whirring noise forward, followed by the sound of running water.

"All tubes flooded, sir."

Azeri nodded and ordered, "Up, scope."

The periscope slid upward, and once more, the captain caught it near the floor. Again, he squatted and walked the periscope up to its full height. He glanced down to read the target bearings from the dial ringing the periscope. The fire-control crew corrected their solutions by furious scribblings.

Azeri gave the final rudder and course corrections.

"Math bearings, and shoot!" he said, emotion for the first time entering his voice. "Fire one through six!"

The boat shuddered. Farad heard rushing air and water through the forward bulkhead. It sounded like toilets flushing. He heard six flushes.

The boat's bow came up as the torpedoes fired, and the front of the boat lost twelve tons of weight. The chief of the watch immediately attended to the trim and compensated by pumping water to the bow tanks. Between shots, Azeri issued minor course corrections to keep the bow steady and pointed at the targets.

Azeri gave himself only a moment to watch the beginning of the torpedoes' run. The weapons were unguided and, once fired, would run their course. The result of their attack was in the hands of Fate. He brought down the scope and gave orders to dive the boat to two hundred meters.

On the navigation chart, Farad saw the land there dropped away into the ocean like a cliff. Azeri was taking advantage of the underwater geography to dive deep.

"Reload tubes one through six with torpedoes," Azeri gave the unnecessary order. The tubes were already being pumped dry to make way for the reloads.

The weapon officer's eyes locked on a stopwatch he held in his hand. In the quiet control room, Farad could hear the seconds tick away.

A thousand meters a minute. Farad remembered the speed of the air-launched torpedoes. They would soon know whether the weapons hit or missed their targets.

How loud was an explosion underwater? Would he even know what happened?

The first explosion was close enough to hear a rumbling through the hull. One crewman began a cheer, but the elbow of the man next to him silenced it. The nearest officer looked daggers at him, and the crewman composed himself.

They heard three more explosions. Farad wondered if it was good shooting or bad. The Weapons Officer's stopwatch ran past the time for the last two targets, and they heard nothing more. Two misses and perhaps more than one torpedo had found a single target.

Azeri had power few men ever had to bear, Farad thought. Though equivalent in rank to Azeri, Farad's responsibility had limits. He was first and foremost an individual warrior in a way harkening back to the old days when men fought with horses and swords. Honor still existed in the skies.

Azeri's way of war was technology. The *Yunes* was a weapon made by shipyard workers to be wielded indiscriminately at targets Azeri would never see. Farad could see the Azanian pilots he engaged in his gunsights. Inside this steel tube, Azeri would never see the men he sent to drown beneath the waves. He must know they were men like himself, doing a job not much different than his own. Sailors were a brotherhood against the cruel sea, and only war broke the bond.

Azeri let no emotion show on his face. "Sonar, conn, report all contacts."

"Yes, sir," came the call from below. "Explosion effects, sir. Can't hear anything over the reverberations."

Azeri nodded.

A moment later, sonar called out, "High-speed screws! Bearing zero-one-five, bearing is constant!"

A fast enemy ship was heading right for them. They had seen the torpedoes or had heard the *Yunes'* propeller churning the water.

Azeri ordered, "Left full rudder, all ahead two thirds!"

The helmsman responded immediately and turned the yoke in his hand all the way to the left.

"Come to course two-seven-zero," Azeri said.

In a minute, the submarine was heading due west. Azeri's eyes scanned the battery gauge and frowned. Although the *Yunes* was the best submarine ever built, its battery capacity limited the time it could submerge. Eventually, the power stored in the batteries would run out, and the sub would have to go to the surface and snorkel again. Moving at a higher speed underwater depleted the cells more quickly.

Ping.

Farad's head jerked up involuntarily. The submarine crewmen stood still as if nailed down. The sound resonated like a tuning fork throughout the steel hull.

"They are looking for us," Azeri explained. He did not seem bothered by Farad's presence at all. "That is their sonar signal."

"Did they find us?" Farad asked. He kept his voice calm. Azeri's poise was infectious.

"I do not think so," Azeri said. "I believe we moved away too quickly. We built this boat for speed."

Farad remembered the curved shape of the hull on the surface and how it had looked like a whale. The lines of the boat streamlined it underwater as the smooth surface of an aircraft allowed it to pass through the air more quickly.

The boat shook. The sound of explosions rumbled through the steel skin of the submarine.

Farad's eyes widened.

"Those are not close," Azeri assured him.

How does he know? Farad wondered.

As if to answer his thoughts, Azeri said, "When it is close, you will know." He smiled wickedly.

"Come right to three-two-zero," Azeri said. He was turning back toward the Azanian ships. "How long until you reload the tubes?"

"Tube one in one-five minutes," the fire-control officer answered. "Ten-minute intervals after that."

Azeri grunted. Torpedoes took a long time to reload. Forward, his torpedo-men were working hydraulic presses to shove the two-ton weapons into their tubes, one after another.

He rechecked the battery level and didn't like what he saw. The charge indicator was dropping too quickly.

"Navigation, prepare a course to come at the enemy transports from the west. I want another shot before—"

Azeri was interrupted by the blast of Azanian depth charges. Farad was knocked over and hit the deck hard. The overhead lights went out. The red emergency lights flickered into life a few seconds later.

Men around the compartment staggered to their feet. In their eyes was the first hint of fear. Farad was afraid, too.

As soon as everyone was back on their feet, the boat shook again. This time the entire hull rolled to the side. The motion tossed men like dice in a cup. The lights went out again, and Farad heard the cries of panic in the darkness.

"Silence!" came the voice of the chief of the boat.

"Status!" said Azeri in a clear voice recognizable in the dark, colored only by disgust.

"Short circuit," someone said in the dark. "We've lost main and backup power. Sir."

The incipient panic ended immediately. Men reported from their stations in voices reflecting their struggle at self-control. No one ran, and no one failed to answer.

Farad's fear threatened to strangle him. Here he was, underwater, in a steel pipe with no power, destined to fall ever deeper until the weight of the water outside crushed him like a bug. There would be no grave for him. No one would ever know what had happened.

He fought down the fear with disgust. How could he, Farad Hashemi, listen to fear, which he had ever before held in contempt? No matter he was underwater in darkness instead of in the sunlight high above the clouds. Death cared not where it found him. He had only the time he was given, no more, and the fate God ordained would be his. If it were his time to die, he would refuse to die in a panic. He could do better.

Fortified, he pulled himself to his feet. He leaned against a piece of equipment bolted to the wall. The floor was at a steep angle, and his feet slid sideways when he tried to walk on the deck.

Not a single light broke the cave-like darkness. None of the indicator lights on the equipment worked.

A battle lantern switched on and played a yellow beam of light across the dark room.

"What is our depth?" Azeri demanded.

"I don't know, sir," said the helmsman. "The gauge stopped at two-hundred-five meters."

"We could be sinking," said a wavering voice.

The beam of the lantern swiveled to lock onto the sailor who had spoken.

"Secure that," said the chief.

"You," said Azeri, pointing at the man. "Go aft to maneuvering room. They do not answer the sound-powered phone. Find out what has happened and come back to report. Now!"

The man leaped down the ladder into the compartment below.

The emergency lights flickered. Farad held his breath. The lights stopped flashing and glowed steadily. With a loud click, the equipment around the room came back to life. The lights came back on, and the dials worked again. Fans began running around the room.

Azeri's eyes went immediately to the depth gauge. It spun quickly to three hundred meters before slowing down. They were still falling toward the bottom.

"Navigator, what is the depth here?" Azeri asked.

The man looked at the chart to make sure before answering, "Six hundred meters."

Azeri grunted. The bottom here was deeper than the crush depth of the submarine. The boat would implode before reaching the bottom.

The hull creaked like a block of metal crushed in a vise.

"Chief?" Azeri asked.

The chief of the watch had rushed to the ballast controls as soon as they had reactivated.

"Number two ballast is flooded. I'm blowing all the trim tanks on the starboard side. I'll have to compensate with flooding on the port side to right the boat. We have a list of twenty degrees." In response to the captain's unasked question, he said, "I don't know if we have enough air to maintain depth."

Azeri nodded.

Farad remained silent. It was not his place to voice his feelings. Azeri had to think about how to save them all from death.

Azeri tried the phone again. This time someone answered. He spoke rapidly into the receiver. Curt questions followed short answers. Farad didn't understand what he was talking about and did not ask.

The boat righted itself on its keel, but the depth gauge still spun downward. Four hundred meters.

The crewman Azeri had sent away returned up the ladder from below.

"Sir," he said, "maneuvering room reports the main battery shunt in slot two is cut, and there is no power to the motors. They are bridging the gap now. If they succeed, they will have full voltage from slot one, but nothing from two."

"Thank you," Azeri said.

He looked at the chief, who glanced at two large switches on the bulkhead next to the diving panel.

"Not yet," Azeri said.

The chief nodded.

Farad had asked about the two switches earlier in the day. They were for emergency use and would blow all the ballast tanks at once, driving the boat to the surface. The boat would have no control over its depth once the chief threw the switches. The boat would only surface if enough reserve air remained in the air tanks.

They would break the surface, and Azanian warships bent on revenge would surround them immediately. The *Yunes* was designed to travel under the surface of the ocean, not on it. The streamlined hull shape that allowed her to move quickly beneath the waves hindered her performance on the surface.

Farad understood Azeri's choice. He could order the chief to blow all the ballast, and the boat would rise to the surface. Once surfaced, the only course would be to surrender to the Azanians. Or Azeri could hope the engineers could repair the battery shunt before the weight of the water above crushed the boat.

"Can you stabilize our depth?" Azeri asked.

"Not with number two ballast tank flooded," the chief said. "If we blow all the air we have, it might get us shallow enough for the pumps to overcome the pressure. I don't know how big the leak in the ballast tank is."

Azeri grimaced. The depth gauge rolled to four hundred fifty meters.

The hull groaned. It sounded like a colossal beast screeching in pain. Metallic creaking ran down either side of the boat.

"How deep?" Farad asked before he could stop himself.

"According to the builders, the maximum test depth for this submarine is three hundred fifty meters," Azeri said. "The shipyard was wrong." He pointed. The depth gauge read four hundred and sixty meters.

Farad gulped.

He heard a crack like a gunshot from downstairs. Azeri was at the top of the ladder in an instant.

"Flooding in the torpedo room!" came the call from below.

Without being ordered, the chief had already turned on the forward pumps. Men ran over the deck below toward the bow. Seawater sloshed under their feet.

Azeri picked up the sound-powered phone and called maneuvering again. "Status!" he demanded.

He gritted his teeth at the answer.

Above them, more explosions in the water shook the boat. The depth gauge accelerated its descent.

Four hundred eighty meters.

Azeri closed his eyes and nodded to himself. "Chief," he said, and began to point to the emergency ballast switches.

The sound-powered phone growled. Azeri snatched it up. "Status!"

"How?" he asked. Then, "No matter." He hung up the phone and gave the order, "All ahead flank! All rise on the planes!"

The helmsman and planesman leaned into their yokes to raise the control planes at the bow and stern to their maximum up-angle of fifteen degrees. Aft, the two electric motors spun to life, and the *Yunes'* single propeller spun up to its maximum RPM.

The depth gauge slowed its descent. It stopped at five hundred meters. It sat steady for a moment, before rolling upward.

The control room crew exhaled.

The boat clawed upward through the water.

"The pumps are holding the flooding forward," came the report from below. "Number two ballast tank has a blown valve. If we replace it, we can use it again."

"What of the batteries?" Azeri asked.

"We can't use slot two. We have the charge left in slot one. At full power, less than fifteen minutes."

Azeri frowned. If they ran out of battery power, the sub would begin sinking again. "We need the ballast tank. Send everyone you need to fix it. Everything else is secondary."

There was a loud ping against the hull, like a hammer striking a block of ice. The Azanians were back.

"They must have heard us," said the navigation officer.

"All stop," said Azeri. The officer of the deck twisted the annunciator handle, and the motors stopped. The depth gauge rolled a few meters upward before stopping. Slowly, it rotated downward again.

Tension reentered the room. Farad was an observer only, which made it much more difficult for him. He had flown a disintegrating fighter back home to base. It had been different because he had been too busy to think about what was happening. Trapped, he had nothing to do but be afraid. Again, he fought his fear.

More explosions from above shook the boat. Farad slipped and fell against the main gyrocompass. He felt his ribs compress and grunted in pain.

"Steady!" said the chief. "The Azanians missed us."

As bad as being shaken by the explosions was, the depth-charges exploded too far above to damage the boat. Azeri had halted their ascent in time.

Farad pulled himself up and cradled his side. The fall had knocked the breath out of him.

Azeri ordered the boat to dive. The Azanian depth charges overhead formed an impenetrable ceiling trapping the *Yunes* beneath it.

"Hold down," said the navigation officer.

Azeri grunted. The Azanian escorts were keeping the *Yunes* from going near the surface and waiting until the submarine depleted its batteries. The diesel engines needed air to run so they could produce electricity for the batteries and electric motors. Once the battery cells emptied of their stored charge, the boat would become immobile. With the damaged ballast tank, they would not be able to maintain their depth and would slowly sink until water pressure crushed the boat.

The one useable battery slot was three quarters expended. The other slot was useless because of damage. The *Yunes* didn't have much time left. Soon, the submarine would have to surface or die.

"We need that ballast tank, chief," Azeri said.

"Yes, sir," he replied.

"When the ballast tank is fixed, I want to know immediately," Azeri said.

"Yes, sir," the chief replied.

"And the battery," Azeri said.

"Yes, sir," said the chief.

The submarine hovered above crush depth. The electric motors drained the battery as the screw labored to keep the weight of the sub from pulling them down to destruction. Everyone in the control room was quiet. Men locked their eyes on their instruments. No one spared a glance for the ballast panel or the emergency switches.

Farad admired the courage and discipline of the crew. He had never seen anything like it.

Above them, the depth charges blasted the water. The sound was like thunder. The *Yunes* was too deep for the explosions to damage the boat, but the sound of the depth charges frayed nerves to the breaking point.

"Battery at ten percent," the chief reported.

Azeri nodded in reply. He leaned on the periscope with one arm. His bearded face looked sinister in the dim red emergency lights.

A light on the ballast panel switched from red to green. The sound-powered phone hanging on the overhead buzzed. Azeri casually picked it up from its holder.

"Control," he answered in a voice as calm as still water. He listened for a minute. "Thank you," he said and replaced the phone.

"Ballast tank status is green," said the chief.

"Thank you, chief," Azeri said. "All stop."

"All stop," said the officer of the watch as he turned the annunciator lever.

"Make your depth four hundred fifty meters," Azeri said.

The boat went completely quiet. Farad held his breath.

The depth gauge unrolled at an increasing speed as the electric motors holding them up spun down.

The chief of the watch manipulated the switches on the ballast control panel. The boat creaked and groaned more loudly than Farad had heard it do before. Air rushed into the ballast tanks. It sounded like rushing water.

The depth gauge slowed, steadied, and stopped at four-hundred-fifty-one meters.

"You are slipping, Chief," Azeri said.

"Sorry, sir," the chief said. He worked the trim tanks to stabilize the boat at the requested depth of four-hundred-fifty meters.

The boat creaked. The *Yunes* was still below its design depth. Farad and everyone aboard the *Yunes*, in their prayers, thanked the shipbuilders of Abbas for their skill. How long could the boat stay so deep?

Above them, a new sound carried through the water and echoed through the steel hull.

Ping.

"Conn, sonar," an excited voice from downstairs cried. "High-speed screws! Torpedo in the water!"

"All ahead full," Azeri ordered.

Above them, the Azanian antisubmarine torpedo activated its terminal active sonar guidance. One ping after another lashed the *Yunes* with sound energy.

"Sonar, range to torpedo contact?" Azeri asked.

"Conn, unknown, but close. Torpedo bearing is one-zero-zero."

"Why didn't you hear it before?" Azeri asked in a low voice.

"Too much noise from the explosion effects, Conn," the sonarman said. "And we are deep, so cavitation is suppressed by the water pressure."

"Very well," Azeri said. "It is a small thing."

The vibration of the submarine's electric motors reached the control room. In the stern of the boat, the motors spun up to their maximum RPM. The propeller shaft churned the water with the single wide screw.

The boat accelerated quickly. The speed gauge next to the helmsman rose steadily to forty kilometers an hour.

The pinging from the torpedo continued. Farad thought he could hear the sonar pings growing louder. The pulses came more rapidly. At the edge of his hearing, he thought he could hear the whine of a propeller blade in the water before flow noise from the submarine blotted it out.

"Conn, sonar, torpedo contact bearing is changing. The new bearing is zero-nine-zero."

Azeri nodded. "Range to torpedo?"

"Still closing, Conn."

Azeri closed his eyes. Farad could see his lips moving beneath his mustache whiskers. He was muttering softly. Every sailor in the control room kept his eyes locked upon his station.

"Babr," Azeri said, addressing the navigator.

The officer blinked, surprised at Azeri using his first name. "Yes, sir?"

"Babr," Azeri continued. "What is the top speed of the Azanian Type Forty-four torpedo?"

"Fifty-six kilometers an hour," the navigator said.

"And its range at that speed?" Azeri asked.

"Five and a half kilometers."

"I thought so," Azeri paused, pursing his lips.

Farad followed Azeri's eyes to the battery charge gauge, and the pilot's anxiety grew.

At full speed, the battery drained in minutes. Farad could see the charge indicator dropping before his eyes. They would soon be helpless and drifting. The torpedo was still chasing them. The pings echoed through the hull, one after another, each new sound pulse fraying Farad's nerves. The weapon was faster than the submarine, but perhaps not fast enough to catch them before its battery-powered motor ran out of charge. Farad looked at the sonar plot, but the scribble of lines and numbers was meaningless to him.

Azeri took three steps from the sonar plot to call downstairs to the sonar room. "Distance to torpedo?"

"Closing, conn," the sonarman said. He ducked inside the room, and Azeri listened to the sound of a slide rule scratching on paper. The sonarman stuck his head out the doorway. "From its echo interval, I believe the range is one thousand meters."

"It can catch us," the navigator said.

"We shall see," Azeri said.

"Four minutes to torpedo impact," the sonarman said.

"Thank you," said Azeri. From his pocket, he removed a worn stopwatch. He flipped open the cover and carefully set the stopwatch. With a click, the hands began to tick the seconds away.

Azeri called to the room, "Status of all systems!"

Each sailor in the control room reported. Nothing had changed, but by the time the last man spoke, a minute had passed.

"Sonar, report all contacts."

"Conn, my only contact is a torpedo at zero-nine-zero. Target is closing. Impact in—"

"Thank you, Sonar," Azeri said.

The room went silent but for the vibration of the electric motors, the swish of water outside, and the ever-increasing volume of the torpedo's pings.

Azeri kept his eyes locked on the gyrocompass repeater on the floor. He didn't look at the stopwatch for what seemed like an eternity. The seconds seemed to fly by. Farad wanted time to stop, but he felt as if he were in an hourglass whose spout grew wider and wider with every second.

Finally, Azeri looked down at his stopwatch. He nodded.

"On my mark, helmsman, right full rudder. Planesman, full rise on the planes. Make depth three hundred meters." He picked up a handset and called, "Maneuvering."

"Maneuvering, aye," crackled the speaker.

"Release two torpedo countermeasures."

"Countermeasures, aye!" the speaker said. After a moment, "Countermeasures away!"

"Now!" Azeri said, "Right full rudder! Full rise on planes!"

As the helmsman and planesman forced their yokes to the stops, Farad grabbed a railing to keep his feet. The boat pitched upward.

Behind the submarine, the two countermeasures deployed. Each was a tube one meter long and 40mm wide. Fired from an ejector within the submarine's stern, each barely cleared the stern planes before cracking open. When exposed to seawater, the countermeasures reacted by emitting hydrogen gas. The gas formed a cloud of bubbles thick enough to block sound pulses.

Farad was too preoccupied with keeping his footing to notice when the pings from the torpedo stopped lashing the hull.

"We lost it!" One sailor, unable to contain himself, cried.

Azeri looked askance at the man. "We shall see," he said. Watching the depth gauge roll up past three hundred meters, he said, "Make your depth two-hundred-fifty."

"Two-hundred-fifty, aye," said the diving officer.

"All ahead one-third," Azeri added.

"One-third, aye."

The submarine slowed and leveled off.

"Sonar, report torpedo contact."

"Conn, torpedo is pinging to the west. Torpedo has lost contact!"

Farad exhaled loudly. He shut his mouth, embarrassed, but everyone else in the room had done the same thing. Except for Azeri, who stood leaning on one foot in the middle of the control room. The stopwatch in his hand stopped ticking.

"Thank you, Sonar," Azeri said. "All stop."

It was too late. The battery charge gauge was pegged barely above zero. The motors kept turning for a few seconds, then stopped. The sound-powered phone buzzed.

The captain answered the phone. "Understood," Azeri said and hung up.

The boat drifted in silence. The chief of the watch moved air from one tank to another, flipping switches, in a struggle to maintain depth without the use of the diving planes.

More depth charges rocked the boat. They seemed closer than the first attack.

"Sonar, conn," Azeri called on the phone. He flipped on the speaker so everyone could hear.

"Sonar," came the crackling voice on the speaker.

"Is there a pattern to the depth charges?" Azeri asked.

A long silence, then, "Yes, sir. They are in a spiral with our old position at the center. Like they are circling out from where we were."

"Thank you," Azeri said and flipped off the speaker.

Farad thought about it. If the Azanians were dropping depth charges in a spiral pattern around their old position, the charges would first grow farther away, then closer.

"Should I change depth?" the officer of the watch suggested.

"No," Azeri said. "Their active sonar will pick us up. There's no thermocline here because of the river runoff. If we rise above the depth charging, they'll see us." The water temperature was constant, and it would not refract the sound beam from an active sonar set.

The next depth charge pattern was farther away. Farad winced. Instead of good news, it meant the Azanians were following the trend. Farad felt worse knowing what was going to happen, not better. It was only a matter of time before the boat shook again from the pounding of the explosions.

"How many depth charges can they have?" the navigation officer complained.

Azeri's look silenced him. "Be glad they don't launch another torpedo. We cannot run."

Everyone in the room silently agreed.

The *Yunes* drifted in silence and listened to the next two depth charges to the east and southeast. They were coming closer.

Farad saw Azeri was facing away from both the battery indicator and the sound-powered phone. His eyes scanned the rest of the compartment, focusing on the men at their stations.

The boat shook as charges exploded to the south. The next pattern would be on them.

Azeri reluctantly gave an order, "Make your depth two hundred meters." He was bringing the boat up to throw off the aim of the depth charges. It would also bring them in range of the Azanian sonar beams.

The phone buzzed.

Azeri answered it as casually as he had before.

"Thank you," he said, after listening for a few seconds. He replaced the receiver with a shaking hand.

Farad pretended not to notice Azeri's nerves.

"All ahead full," Azeri ordered in a steady voice.

The battery charge indicator rose back to thirty percent. The damaged battery slot was back online. "Turn off all unnecessary equipment," Azeri ordered as an afterthought.

"Already done, sir," said the officer of the watch.

"Thank you," said Azeri.

The boat shot forward and reached a speed of thirty-three kilometers an hour before the next depth charge barrage detonated astern of them. The boat shook again. It was terrifying, but Farad felt better knowing the boat was under power, and they could do something about it.

"Come to new course three-two-zero!" Azeri commanded over the thunder of the charges.

The helmsman followed the orders relayed by the officer of the watch.

The sub turned north. The course Azeri ordered would take them as far from the spiral pattern the Azanians were using to aim their charges as possible before the enemy destroyers came around again. The next barrage was loud but further away.

Farad began to relax. He realized he couldn't stay keyed up any longer. His body's endurance was tested in a way it had never been. Air combat was inhumanly intense but quickly resolved in either death or glory. Boredom while flying was the norm. A four-hour mission could have five minutes of fighting if there were any at all. He had never experienced the hours-long tension he had witnessed today.

The rest of the crew was coming down from the ordeal. Farad saw them relax. Their shoulders slumped, and they began to look at each other in wonder at being alive.

Azeri noticed the change, too, and brought everyone back to attention by asking the status of all systems. It was no time to relax.

Azeri ran the submarine for five minutes before shutting down the motors again. They had traveled about four kilometers since beginning their sprint. The *Yunes'* speed was more than the Azanians suspected, and Azeri used the advantage to the fullest.

When the engines cut off, they drifted and listened to the charges fade away to the southeast.

An hour later, Azeri secured them from battle stations, and the sweat-stained crew left their stations for the watchstanders. Some went on watch, and others collapsed into their racks to sleep. No one went to get anything to eat. For many, it was their first taste of combat, and it was not something to feed an appetite.

Twenty-six

Captain Aran of the Azanian Land Force was tired. He'd been awake for a day and a half and had only snatched a few hours of sleep inside a farmstead during a brief halt before climbing onto his tank and moving out again. The Persian terrain crawled by monotonously as he tried to keep his head up and looking for threats. The afternoon sun beat down on his wide-brimmed hat, and sand clogged his nostrils.

His ten *Mbwas* were now seven. Two had broken down and been left behind with their crews. It was vexing to lose a fifth of his strength to preventable breakdowns. The tracks had been running flat-out for five days. It was inevitable that something would break. Even so, Aran had been so sure his emphasis on maintenance back in barracks would prevent non-battle losses, at least until they were deep inside Persia.

A Persian mine had destroyed the other tank. The mine had blown his first platoon leader out of his hatch and into the sky before the tank flipped over and burned next to a culvert. Aran had leaped into action and deployed his company to face the expected ambush, but there had been none. There had only been the single mine laid in the road. No Persian soldiers had been nearby to take advantage of the chaos, which was fortunate, but puzzling.

The other two members of the tank's crew were severely burned. Aran had arranged to have them sent by ambulance back down the highway toward Siwa. He'd managed to have his platoon leader's corpse sent back with them. It was a much surer way to get his body home than depending on a passing grave detail to do it.

With his eight remaining tanks, the company rolled forward into New Persia. They moved with restraint. The leading elements of the Land Force had gotten so far ahead of the rest, the brigade commander had ordered them to halt, and when they'd started moving again, they kept to under forty kilometers an hour. The highway they were advancing down could only allow so many vehicles on it to move east at the same time. Most of those would be trucks. Trucks carrying fuel, ammunition, and everything the invading force needed would be packing the road back through Siwa to the Azanian border. Trucks were slow, and traffic jams endless.

It would be a perfect target for air attack, Aran knew. All of those closely-packed vehicles full of supplies and fuel were an attack pilot's dream. However, there were no Persian planes to be seen. Only the Azanian Air Force could be heard passing overhead, the deep boom of turbojets announcing their presence.

The air force had done it. They had claimed to have a plan to destroy the Persian Air Corps on the ground, and it had worked. They would be insufferable now, having smashed their opponents before the land force had crossed the border.

Aran looked down at the map section laid out on the top of his turret. He wiped away the dust and studied the symbols with bleary eyes. He tried to remember what he was supposed to be looking for.

There. He saw the town on the map. Khorasar. It was a medium-sized town of ten thousand in peacetime. He couldn't go around it because the highway ran through the center. Driving through the town would be dangerous, and he'd have to plot a path off-road to curve around it to the north. His orders were to bypass population centers and leave them to be pacified by follow-up forces. Behind him were track- and truck-mounted infantry who had the numbers and training to clear a town. His light tanks were the exact wrong tool for the job. The tanks were vulnerable to almost any weapon more powerful than a machine gun, and inside a town, they would lose their ability to maneuver. A single anti-tank gun firing down a road could knock out half his tanks before he knew it was there. Worse, Persian infantry could get close to his tanks and attack them with satchel charges. Aran would make sure to stay in the open where his tankers could see any threat coming from far away.

He adjusted his headset. It was about time to call a halt and lay out the plan for bypassing the town. Khorasar was the final obstacle before his tanks reached their objective, the Sheban Passes. Once through the Sheban Passes, there was no natural barrier between the Azanian Land Force and their goal: Persepolis, on the Karun River.

After meeting with his three platoon leaders in the shade of an olive tree, Aran felt they understood his objectives. The company would split into two parts. Aran's tank and one platoon of three tanks would drive around Khorasar to the north on an unmapped track which one of his tank commanders had spotted when they arrived. It seemed to run east along a dry streambed lined with dead trees. It was a risk because Aran had no guarantee the track would take them anywhere close to where he wanted to go. However, he commanded a reconnaissance company, and his job was to reconnoiter. If there was a way around the town to the north, he had better find it before the enemy used it to attack the flank of the Azanian Land Force units following his tanks.

The other two platoons, down to two tanks each, would skirt the town to the south. Aran knew there was a clear path there. The Persians knew it, too, of course. He ordered the two platoon leaders to engage the enemy only if they could destroy him quickly. Otherwise, they were to withdraw and report.

Aran fretted inwardly at having no reserve to send either of his forces if they got into trouble. He needed another platoon and dearly missed his three lost tanks. On the other hand, his company was too small to conduct an assault against any organized resistance. A single anti-tank gun and a platoon of infantry could put a stop to either of his probes. He couldn't afford the time to shift his entire force to find another way around the town, so splitting his strength made sense. His battalion colonel had made it clear speed was the priority.

"Don't get tied down fighting," he had said. "Keep moving at all costs."

Another advantage to the two probes was if one of them ran into an ambush, he wouldn't lose his entire command. There was no telling what Persian forces defended the road to their capital city. Even an isolated platoon of *Karar* tanks could destroy his little company in minutes.

Aran mounted his *Mbwa* and ordered his driver to move out. The tank jumped and puffed diesel smoke as the driver put the light tank into gear.

Brush covered the hills north of Khorasar, Aran saw through his binoculars. It was hard to keep his eyes focused on the lenses of his binoculars while the tank bumped his midsection against the commander's hatch opening as he stood. He was permanently bruised from being bashed into the hatch rim by the motion of the tank.

Ahead of them, the ground spouted dirt as if from a small geyser. The sound of the explosion reached Aran a second later. He reflexively ducked inside his turret and slammed the hatch above his head. He was on the radio in moments.

"SHELLREP," he began and gave the position of the impact relative to the moving tank column.

As he warned his tanks to button up against the shell fragments, he wondered what to do next. The shell impacts were small, and although they were in his path, hitting a moving tank with a shell was more a matter of luck than skill. If his tanks cleared the beaten zone quickly, it was unlikely they would be hit.

"Advance," he ordered and gave a set of map coordinates half a kilometer ahead for the northern group. The southern probe would continue as planned.

His *Mbwa* revved its engine and darted forward. The first jump of acceleration always seemed to catch Aran unawares and jammed his side into the turret ring. He cursed and braced himself for the next gear change when he would be cast forward into his stomach.

Being a tank commander was supposed to be glamorous, but Aran had found it was mostly painful. He thought the most useful attribute for a tanker was the ability to endure pain and fatigue.

The four tanks of the northern probe drove on the dirt path into the hills. The commanders stayed unbuttoned, so they could stand up in their hatches and see the terrain around them. One tank took point fifty meters ahead. Aran saw it was his First Platoon leader. It was good to lead from the front, but he didn't want to lose his lieutenant to the first shot of an ambush. Aran considered calling him back but decided against it.

Within fifteen minutes, the little armored column came to a steep hill. The tank engines whined and strained to pull the thirteen-ton vehicles to the top. Treads slipped and shot gravel behind the tanks like bullets. Aran ordered his tank to the side of the tank in front of him to avoid the bombardment of dust and rocks. Dark puffs of diesel exhaust clouded the air as the tanks downshifted to their lowest gear.

Ahead, the first tank crested the hill. Aran couldn't see it, but he heard the sound of a machine gun firing. A short burst, then another. He couldn't see what was happening because his tank was still climbing the hill. He keyed his radio to listen. Hearing nothing, he transmitted on the company net.

"THIS IS FOX TWO ZERO. FOX ONE ONE, REPORT STATUS."

The machine gun kept firing. Aran imagined the platoon leader, who was also the tank commander, was firing the top-mounted machine gun and couldn't hear his radio call.

The other tanks were still climbing the hill. Soon they would reach the top and be exposed to whatever enemy Fox One One was engaging.

Aran thought about what to do. He could halt the other tanks and wait for One One's report, or he could let them climb the hill and assist the first tank.

He decided to let the tanks go. If One One were in real trouble, his platoon leader would be backing down the hill as fast as he could go. Whatever he was firing at, it wasn't a tank because his main gun was silent.

One by one, the tanks clambered up the hill to the top. As each reached the crest and leveled off, their machine guns came to life. Short bursts of fire spat from each tank. They formed a line to either side of One One.

Aran's tank finally reached the top, and he could see what was happening. The line of tanks sat above a bare slope, looking down on a shattered complex of buildings two hundred meters away. There were two large bomb craters in the roof of the center building, and two smaller buildings had been shot up with aircraft cannon. There was a fence around the three buildings and a road that led to a gate.

Below, in the ruins, dozens of men in uniform ran in all directions like ants whose nest had been disturbed. The tanks were shooting at them as they ran. Some ran in circles in the open. Others seemed to be rushing for cover. Aran saw one man sitting down, holding his head and rocking. A burst of gunfire knocked him over and left him twitching, bleeding from a half-dozen wounds.

Something was wrong. Aran knew it before he could understand what it was.

No one was firing back. All of the gunfire was coming from his tanks. The men below were helpless.

"ALL FOX ELEMENTS, CEASE FIRE," Aran shouted into the radio. The gunfire continued. Now the main guns were rotating right and left as the gunners aimed their coaxial machine guns into the crowd of men below. The shots were so easy, and the Azanian gunners so absorbed in their work they were reluctant to stop.

Aran repeated his call until three of the tanks stopped. The fourth, One Four, wouldn't cease fire until Aran jumped out of his tank and ran over to hit the tank commander over his helmet with his hand.

"Cease fire, damnit!" he screamed.

The guns were silent. When his ears stopped ringing, Aran could hear voices. From below came screams, sobs, and wails. There was something wrong about the sound. Aran had heard men in combat before. He knew the sound of wounded men screaming in agony. There were a few of those, but the other noises barely sounded human.

Aran made sure his pistol was holstered and ran down the hill alone. In his mind, fear was growing, a different kind of fear than the fear of combat. This was the fear of having done something wrong—the fear of guilt.

Aran approached the buildings. His tanks sat silent above as their company commander ran down the hill. He came to the fence. It was barbed wire, but there was a downed section allowing him to enter a courtyard.

A man suddenly stood in front of him. Aran reached for his pistol. Before he could draw it, the man ran straight at him. Aran felt panic as his gun caught on his web belt. He couldn't free it before the man reached him.

Aran realized he was between the man and the tanks behind him, so none of them could fire a machine gun without risking hitting their commander.

The man stopped ten feet away. Aran saw him clearly. He wore a blue smock covered in dust, making it appear to be a khaki uniform like the Persian Army wore. The smock had no buttons but was meant to be pulled on. His trousers were held up with a drawstring. He had no belt. Slippers covered his feet.

It was his face which confirmed Aran's fears. The man smiled at him. He opened his mouth, and instead of speech, an inarticulate moan escaped his drooling lips.

Aran's hand fell limply away from his weapon. A cold hand wrapped around his heart.

What had he done?

He stood paralyzed for a minute or more. He watched the slouching disabled people run, shuffle, and windmill their arms. His ears, having grown used to the whine of the diesel engines and the ripping of machine-gun fire, adjusted to the relative silence. He could hear cries and sobs coming from the rubble.

Aran's wits returned. If he was to do anything, he couldn't do it alone. He awkwardly waved goodbye to the man who was still examining him. The man waved back.

"I'll return," Aran said. He looked away from the scene and ran back up the hill to his waiting tanks.

He climbed up his tank, clambered into the turret, and turned on the radio he had set on the battalion net frequency. He had been part of a reconnaissance battalion, but losses at the Sheban pass had caused brigade to break the survivors up into companies attached to land force tank battalions. As an independent scout company, Aran's light tanks were attached to the 1st Battalion of the 8th Armored Regiment, which was heading the offensive. He was expected to operate ahead of the rest of the battalion, but not too far, so the more massive tanks of the armored battalion could take on enemy resistance too heavy for the scouts to handle.

After three tries, he reached a radiotelephone operator who told Aran the battalion commander wasn't available. Aran hadn't expected him to be—colonels were busy. Could he speak to a staff officer?

The radiotelephone operator was new and didn't seem to understand the radio procedures. He suddenly demanded Aran authenticate his identity to prove he belonged on the radio net. Aran did this using the code cards issued to every commander. Then he had to do it again when the operator misunderstood him.

Ten minutes had passed. Aran watched the escaped asylum inmates milling around the blasted building. Some were injured and needed medical help, fast.

Frustrated, he tried to get the radiotelephone operator to understand the urgency of the situation, but the man was unmoved. No members of the brigade staff were available for anything that was not a high priority item. Enemy civilians weren't a top priority.

Aran stared at the transmitter in his hand. This was ridiculous. He wasn't being ordered to ignore a humanitarian emergency but was being obstructed by a low-level idiot who was making a decision he had no right to make.

Meanwhile, his radio tuned to the company net came to life.

"CONTACT REPORT," said the first platoon leader, "TWO ENEMY TANKS, K-TYPE, NORTH-NORTHEAST," and gave the grid coordinates.

Aran took up his binoculars and looked. On the other side of the valley, two kilometers away, the tanks were raising dust as they moved quickly down the hill. The Persians were coming.

He immediately ordered his tanks off the crest upon which they were sitting. The tanks backed carefully down the hill behind them and out of sight.

Aran couldn't believe this was happening. He had a dilemma.

The Persian force, so far, was just small enough to fight. He could split his larger force and set up flanking shots on either side of the approaching tanks. In a running meeting engagement, his light tanks were capable of getting side shots on the big Persian tanks and penetrating their armor. They were undoubtedly a probe, just like he was, and destroying them would force the Persian commander to send a larger force, which would take time.

Moreover, the blasted mental asylum would be in the middle of the crossfire.

He could retreat, leaving the Persians to deal with the civilians. His mission was to find a route around Khorasar to the north, if possible, and he could easily back off and declare the way closed. He could direct the forces following his scout company to the south of the town and leave the Persians alone.

Aran called the second and third platoon leaders. They reported no opposition south of the town. He sighed inwardly with relief. It wasn't his responsibility. Aran felt momentary guilt, but the military necessity, in this case, overrode the demands of humanitarian aid. He could withdraw behind the hill and let the Persians handle the situation while his scouts directed the Azanian Land Force battalion to the south.

"FOX TWO ZERO, FOX THREE ONE. SIGHTING REPORT," said the third platoon leader. "ELEVEN, ONE-ONE, K-TYPE TANKS, AND FOUR ARMORED CARRIERS MOVING SOUTHWEST FROM K-TOWN."

The Persians were moving in company strength. Aran checked his map. The four tanks remaining in second and third platoons were south of Khorasar. The Persians were moving southwest from the town and would cut off the scouts from the Azanian units moving east along Route One.

Engaging the Persians wasn't an option. They outnumbered the first and second platoons, and in the open country, they would blow apart the Azanians with the long-range guns on the Persian *Karar* tanks.

If the Persians could take the time to set up a defensive position, they stood a good chance of stopping the entire battalion following Aran's company. One thing the Azanians had learned was the futility of trying to attack the *Karar* tank from the front at a long range.

Aran had to report this, of course. First, he ordered the second and third platoons to break contact to the south. There were many miles of open desert between Route One and the Persian Gulf. With their high speed, the *Mbwas* would be able to stay out of range of the Persians and hopefully draw some of them away from the highway.

When he called in his sighting report to battalion, he got the same radiotelephone operator. Aran took a deep breath before carefully listing the number and type of Persian vehicles and their position south of Khorasar. He had the operator repeat the message back, which he did, incorrectly.

Aran struggled not to lose his patience. He entertained the possibility of driving his tank back to battalion HQ and delivering his message personally, backed by his fists. This was too important for the third-rate moron on the other end of the radio to mess up.

"NEGATIVE," he said into the radio and spoke the message even more slowly and carefully.

"FOX TWO ZERO, AUTHENTICATE," the operator demanded.

Aran couldn't take any more. He unkeyed the radio transmitter and swore for thirty seconds. His crew watched with amusement as he went through his entire litany of swear words one by one, peppered with suggestions of what he was going to do to the radiotelephone operator if he ever met him.

First platoon reported in. The Persians, seeing the Azanian tanks fleeing to the south, had failed to pursue them. They had left a platoon to guard against their return, but the other tanks and infantry were deploying north and south of the highway. It was clear they were preparing to fight the battalion as it drove in a column to the east.

Finally, taking a deep breath, he keyed the transmitter.

"THIS IS FOX TWO ZERO. ENEMY FORCE IN COMPANY STRENGTH SOUTH OF KHORASAR. YOUR FORCE IS HEADED INTO AN AMBUSH."

"FOX TWO ZERO, AUTHENTICATE," was the only reply.

Aran closed his eyes, reached for the code cards, and carefully modulated his voice as he read the proper responses. He wanted to scream.

Halfway through his authentication, he was interrupted.

"FOX TWO ZERO, THIS IS ZULU SIX ACTUAL, PLEASE REPEAT."

Aran blinked. Somehow, the commander of the 1st of the 8th had gotten on the net. Aran began authenticating again, but he was interrupted again.

"NEGATIVE, FOX TWO ZERO, JUST TELL ME ABOUT THE PERSIANS SOUTH OF K-TOWN."

With relief, Aran passed on his report of the Persian company preparing to fight south of Khorasan.

"FOX TWO ZERO, WHAT IS THE SITUATION NORTH OF K-TOWN?"

Aran was silent. His mind ran ahead of him, playing out what was going to happen, and he didn't like it.

"FOX TWO ZERO, REPEAT, WHAT IS THE SITUATION NORTH OF TOWN?"

Aran took a deep breath. "NORTH OF TOWN IS A LARGE CONCENTRATION OF CIVILIAN NONCOMBATANTS IN THE

BATTLE AREA. I DO NOT RECOMMEND USING NORTHERN ROUTE AS IT WOULD ENDANGER CIVILIANS."

The radio was silent for a minute.

"FOX TWO ZERO, REPEAT AND EXPAND YOUR LAST."

Aran could feel the confusion and indignation in the reply. Company commanders weren't supposed to make recommendations to colonels.

He keyed the radio and gave the grid coordinates of the bombed asylum. "AT LEAST ONE ZERO ZERO NONCOMBATANTS IN THE OPEN AND UNABLE TO CLEAR THE AREA."

"FOX TWO ZERO, FIRE SOME GUNS IN THE AIR AND MOVE THEM OUT." He could hear the exasperation in the voice. "WHAT IS THE ENEMY SITUATION?"

"NEGATIVE. CIVILIANS ARE ESCAPED ASYLUM INMATES. THEY ARE CRAZY PEOPLE AND DON'T UNDERSTAND WHAT IS HAPPENING. THEY NEED MEDICAL ASSISTANCE. OVER."

"FOX TWO ZERO, WAIT ONE."

While Aran waited, his first platoon leader walked over to his tank and spoke up to his company commander sitting in the turret.

"Sir, the Persians have stopped outside the walls."

Aran directed his gunner to answer the radio and jumped down. He scurried up the slope and crouched beneath the crest to minimize his outline. Taking out his binoculars, he peered down into the valley.

The two Persian tanks had stopped, and Aran could see one of the vehicle commanders climb down the side of his tank. One of the inmates approached him and seemed as confused as Aran had been earlier.

His gunner called from behind, and Aran trotted back to his radio.

"FOX TWO ZERO, REPORT ENEMY UNITS ON NORTHERN ROUTE."

Aran did as he was told and reported the two *Karar* tanks.

"REPORT YOUR STATUS."

"FOUR TRACKS ON HILL SOUTH OF CIVILIAN CONCENTRATION," Aran said.

The radio was silent.

"FOX TWO ZERO, NEUTRALIZE THE ENEMY AND CONTINUE ON MISSION. YOUR OBJECTIVE IS HILL ONE-TWO-FOUR NORTH OF K-TOWN. SECURE A ROUTE FOR FOLLOW-ON FORCES. ACKNOWLEDGE."

"Damnit!" Aran said to himself. He didn't want to fight the Persians. Not now.

He wanted to object to the order. If he did, he knew he'd be risking the wrath of a colonel who labored under a timetable which couldn't be altered. The success of the entire Azanian offensive rested on how fast the armored columns could push down the highway toward Persepolis. Any delay was time lost, and time lost by the Azanians was a gift to the enemy. Halting here could have consequences far beyond the lives of a few dozen civilians.

It wasn't his decision to make. He was a captain of a half-strength scout company. He could follow orders with a clear conscience. Already in his mind, he had a plan. Two tanks could move east behind the valley crest while the other two remained here, ready to climb the slope and engage the two Persian tanks. Perhaps he could neutralize them quickly, and the Azanian follow-up forces could seize the area and care for the inmates?

He knew that was unlikely. The Azanians would be routing combat forces through the northern route as fast as they could, and the paths Aran had scouted could only hold so many vehicles. To bypass Khorasar, the bulk of the 1st of the 8th would have to pass through, and it would take hours.

Orders were orders. Aran could feel the pressure to comply. He wanted to comply. He knew the war could depend on it. Another part of him knew it was wrong.

So, whose orders applied? The colonel's?

Or God's?

Why was he thinking of this now? He was a soldier. He was already responsible for the deaths of many men, from the Siwan border, through the Sheban pass, all the way to this valley north of Khorasar, a Persian town he had never heard of before. Why did the lives of a hundred disabled people matter more than those he had already killed? How many of his fellow soldiers would die if he delayed?

Was this about his conscience? If so, what arrogance to impose his precious morals on a conflict between nations? He was a cog in a machine. He didn't matter. He was no one. He was a soldier, and it was part of his trade to accept the horrors of war and carry on. His conscience was another sacrifice on the altar of victory. Whether he could sleep at night was his problem. It was monumental self-importance to make this about his ideas of right and wrong.

It wasn't about him.

However, had he grown up listening to the Gospels, the old and new, from Earth and First Landing, only to reject them when the time came? Had Jesus come twice to Earth and a third time to Azania so His Message could be ignored?

Whether he could live with himself didn't matter. God's will had to be done.

He keyed the microphone. "ZULU SIX, FOX TWO ONE. NEGATIVE. COMBAT IN THIS AREA IS NOT PERMISSIBLE UNDER THE ZANZIBAR CONVENTION REGARDING THE TREATMENT OF NONCOMBATANTS."

There goes my career, Aran thought. *At the very least.*

The radio erupted into orders and accusations and threats. Aran hooked the transmitter back onto its holster and removed his headset. He told the gunner to stay put and climbed out of the turret. He clambered over the outside of the tank until he reached his duffel bag. Rummaging inside, he found what he was looking for.

His crew stared at him. None knew what to do. Aran could see the confusion caused by the enlisted men's trust in the chain of command breaking. Aran wasn't following orders, so what could he expect of them?

"I'm going down into the valley," Aran said to them. "Lieutenant Zuberi is in command until I return. Zuberi," Aran locked eyes with the lieutenant, "I cannot order you to disobey the battalion commander. I will understand if you engage the enemy here. I only ask, as a personal favor, to give me fifteen minutes."

Zuberi saluted, and Aran returned the salute. Then the company commander did an about-face and strode up the slope and over the top into the valley.

The bombed asylum was still full of wandering people. Aran, picking up his pace on the downhill run, stood out as the only figure moving with purpose in a straight line. Perhaps this drew the attention of the Persians, who had driven their tanks to the edge of the asylum grounds on the other side.

Aran saw the tank turret come to life and aim its cannon directly at him. It was a different feeling than being shot at while within his *Mbwa*. It seemed much more personal. He thought he could see down the long gun barrel into a pool of darkness as black as death.

Aran stopped and raised the white shirt he had taken from his duffel bag. He wanted to close his eyes. He didn't want to see the flash of the gun in the instant before the round arrived to end his life, but he found he couldn't even blink. His eyes burned as he watched the dismounted tank commander wave at the tank and call something in Persian. Then the officer strode toward Aran and covered the distance in a minute. Aran remained motionless, his arm holding the shirt above his head.

When the Persian officer approached, Aran lowered the shirt. He watched the Persian, who was a tall, thin man with a mustache. His uniform carried the rank of captain. Aran decided to salute first, as he had initiated the parlay.

"*Salom*," Aran said. Then he realized he had a problem. How would they speak to each other? Persian and Swahili were not mutually intelligible, although both carried many Arabic loan words.

The other officer returned the salute and then replied in Swahili, "I accept your request to parley. I am Captain Pahlavi of the Persian Army."

Aran was grateful for the other officer's knowledge of his language. "I am Captain Aran of the Azanian Land Force. I request a cease-fire for the evacuation and care of these people," he waved at the crowd of inmates all around.

"Were you responsible for this?" Pahlavi asked.

"No," Aran said, "not the bombing. I don't know what happened. I am responsible for my men opening fire on the inmates when we arrived. They mistook them for soldiers. The uniforms..." Aran trailed off. "Those who were shot are my responsibility."

"I see," Pahlavi said, his voice cold. "I will have to report your name for later investigation for violation of the laws of land warfare."

"I understand," Aran said. "I request a six-hour cease-fire in place to allow medical units from each side to assist these people."

"We will need longer than that," Pahlavi said.

"I cannot offer any more time because it is beyond my authority," Aran said. Also, I doubt I'll be in command of my company in six hours, he thought.

"Who is your superior, then?" Pahlavi asked. "I should speak to him."

"He is not available," Aran said.

"This is irregular," Pahlavi said.

Aran made a decision. "Honestly, my superior would not approve a truce. I am taking a risk being here without orders."

"I see," Pahlavi said. "How can I trust a truce when your chain of command will not honor it?"

"They will not break a truce, once made," Aran said. "It would look very bad."

"You already broke a truce when you attacked our country," Pahlavi said.

"The president and council ordered us to attack. It is not the same thing," Aran said. "And it is beyond my responsibility to decide matters of war and peace."

"Your side will honor a truce?" Pahlavi said.

"For six hours," Aran said. "No more."

"Where is this truce in effect? For Khorasar and the environs?"

"No," said Aran, "Only this valley and the asylum. Not for the whole town or to the south of the town."

"Where your forces will attack," Pahlavi said.

"I cannot answer that," Aran said.

"Very well," Pahlavi said. "I could waste more time in negotiations, but these people need help, and it sounds as if you won't be able to honor anything beyond what you have offered."

"No," said Aran.

"I have already sent for the Red Star and our medical unit," Pahlavi said. "Can we expect any assistance from your side?"

"I will request it, but I do not know what is available or—"

"Or whether your superiors will authorize it. I see," Pahlavi said. "We should get moving. My forces, save medical units, will freeze in place for six hours. Will you do the same?"

"Yes," Aran said.

"Then it is done," Pahlavi said. He saluted.

Aran returned the salute. Both men did an about-face away from each other and marched back to their vehicles.

When he returned, Zuberi asked him what had happened.

"I made a truce for six hours," Aran said.

"Can you do that?" Zuberi asked. The eyes of all the tank crewmen were on them.

"I did," Aran said. He reached into his pocket and withdrew a cigarette. Lighting it, he said, "It is probably the last order I will give."

He climbed back into his tank, put on his headset, and keyed his radio microphone. He had some explaining to do.

Twenty-seven

Suri showed her identity badge to the guard. The man scrutinized it and Suri, matching the face to the picture on the badge. Reluctantly, he returned the badge and pressed a button. Suri clipped the badge back onto her uniform blouse pocket. A low buzz signaled the door leading inside was unlocked. Suri opened the heavy metal door and left the guard shack to enter the site.

The site was inside an old run-down government building that had once housed the archives for the Ministry of the Interior. Tax records, mostly. Now the old, ornate façade concealed a hive of new additions and cross-dividers. Suri made her way through a maze of hallways and open offices inhabited by hundreds of men and women doing the paperwork necessary for any government endeavor. Typewriters and teleprinters punched paper. Old-style incandescent lamps hung from a high ceiling.

Suri showed her badge again at another waystation. This time the door opened onto a stairway leading down into the building's basement. The air was cool, damp, and musty. The stairway was long and poorly lit. The stairs were narrow, and it was clear they had never been intended for use by anyone other than the maintenance staff.

Down she went anyway. The stairs wound around a landing before ending at another door. This time the guard was on the other side and saw Suri through a barred window. He pushed a buzzer and opened the door. Behind the guard was another guard standing ten feet away holding a submachine gun. It wasn't quite pointed at Suri.

Suri tried to remain nonplussed.

Was she in the right place? She'd memorized her instructions and the guards had let her in. She had a terrible thought. What if she'd been admitted by mistake and the guards discovered their error?

Suri suppressed a gulp and said, "My name is Suri Pahlavi, and I'm to report to Major Jahan."

The first guard checked a clipboard. He scowled. The other guard said nothing and moved nothing but his eyes.

The first guard set down the clipboard and called out, "You there! We need an escort."

Behind him was a crowd of women doing something Suri didn't understand. They seemed to be fussing over a machine. Suri didn't have time to study it. One woman trotted over and said, "All right."

Suri read her insignia. She outranked the guard, but it didn't seem that way. The guard grunted, and the woman said, "Come this way," before turning and walking away.

Suri blinked and followed. The woman she was following was older than Suri. She was squat with heavy arms and a square face.

The woman stopped suddenly and turned to Suri. "You are sure you are cleared?"

Suri's eyes went wide, but she said, "Yes." She sensed any equivocation would be pounced upon. She didn't want to be thrown out, or worse.

The woman stared hard at Suri's badge before continuing.

The basement opened into a large space. It was divided into corridors by large, whirring machines, which reminded Suri of looms. She'd visited a textile mill once. She wondered what these machines were doing.

Each machine was about six feet tall. On the front side, they had four rows of exposed wheels, each two inches across, and the wheels spun slowly by increments. Each wheel clicked as it spun to the next setting, like the hand of a clock. Some of the wheels had stopped while others still turned.

The rear of the machines was a nest of cables and wires. Behind one device, a *Bar Basij* woman unplugged one set of cables and plugged in another.

Suri thought this was very strange.

The woman she was following looked backward with disapproval and Suri directed her eyes away from the machines and toward where they were headed.

They came to a row of red-painted metal doors along the far wall of the basement. The offices, instead of being walled off with thin dividers like the upstairs rooms, were built of concrete walls. Suri could hear nothing from within over the machine noise, which she suspected was the point.

Her guide halted at the last office door in the basement corner. The thickset woman extended a short finger and pushed a ringer button. It made no noise Suri could hear. However, after a second, there was a loud click from the door, accompanied by a low buzz. The woman reached for the handle and pulled the door open with practiced ease. Suri saw the door was an inch thick.

Inside was a large metal desk, several filing cabinets, a typewriter, piles of paper overflowing from wire baskets, and a chair with a man sitting in it. He didn't look up from his work. He was balding, and his uniform was too large and hung on him. His sleeves were open and dragged on the papers spread on his desk, threatening to spill them onto the floor. He wore the rank of major on his collar. The walls were half-covered in soundproofing, more to reduce the echo inside the room than to prevent any sound from escaping through the concrete.

Suri nervously stood in the threshold, unsure what to do. Her guide waved Suri in without saying anything while giving the impression Suri should have figured this out for herself. Taking a deep breath, Suri stepped inside.

The guide released the door handle. The heavy door swung shut behind Suri and closed with a clang. Suri jumped from the sound and the pulse of air which pressed on her backside.

The room air was stale and smelled of cigarettes. There was one small vent in the ceiling, but no air seemed to pass through it. The room was cool and clammy.

The spectacled man looked up from his desk at her. His eyes were watery and seemed too large for his face.

"I'm sorry," he said in a reedy voice, "but there's no place for you to sit. I'm afraid regulations prohibit chairs."

Suri didn't know what to say. In awkward situations, she had learned it was best to follow protocol.

"Lieutenant Pahlavi, reporting," she said and saluted.

"Yes, quite," the man said, waving his hand at her. "Yes, I know. I've been expecting you. I am Major Jahan."

Suri had nothing to say in reply, so she remained silent.

Major Jahan looked her up and down. It made Suri uncomfortable. Finally, Jahan said, "I'm afraid to disappoint you," he said, "but you are too short."

Suri was so confused she blurted out, "What? Too short for what?" She forgot to say, "sir."

Major Jahan looked at her as if surprised she didn't understand a simple statement of fact. He didn't seem to notice Suri's lack of honorific.

"Too short for the machines," he said. "To work on the machines, you must be a certain height, some number of centimeters, it escapes me at the moment, but you clearly do not reach the required height," he spoke the words without emphasis as a long run-on sentence.

"I don't understand," Suri said. "Sir," she added.

"It's a simple matter of reach," Major Jahan said, "your arms won't reach the upper row of wheels while you are standing on the floor."

"I mean, sir," Suri said, "why would I be working on a machine?"

The major blinked and leaned back. He stared at her as if she were a child asking an awkward question. "Of course," he said, to himself, "they wouldn't tell you. And I won't either, especially because you are too short."

Suri felt as if she were losing her mind. She was trapped in a windowless underground bunker full of mildew and paranoia.

"Very well, I'm too short," Suri said. "Surely, there's something else to do here than turn wheels on a machine."

The major looked surprised. "Why else would you be here?" His brow furrowed. "You don't have advanced training in mathematics, do you?"

"No," Suri said. "I study history—"

"Or logic problems? Ancient languages?" Jahan winced, "Oh, no, forget I said it. Giving too much away."

Suri said, "No, I don't know anything about any of those things. I study history."

"But not ancient history?" Jahan looked hopeful. Before she could answer, he said, "Do you know what a 'computer' was?"

"No!" Suri said, growing irritated. "I know none of those things."

"So explain to me," Major Jahan said, "why you were sent here if you have no specialized knowledge which would be helpful to our task, and are also too short to tend a machine."

"I have no idea," Suri said.

"It doesn't matter," he said. "If you have no useful skills, there's nothing to be done with you. You'll have to leave."

"Leave?" Suri asked, amazed.

"Yes, leave. Depart forthwith. Go, ye, and serve the war effort in another capacity. Begone. Darken not my doorstep again."

"I will not!" Suri said.

"I'm sorry, what did you say?" Major Jahan said. There was no anger in his voice. He sounded bemused. "I was under the impression this was a military hierarchy, and you had to do what I say. Orders, chain of command, that sort of thing."

"That may be, sir," Suri said. "But I will not be let go like this. Not because I don't know ancient languages and absolutely not because I am *too short!*" She drew herself up. Even with her garrison cap, she was barely taller than the major, who was seated.

"I'm afraid you will have to live with it. We do vital work here, and not everyone is suited for it." He reached for a buzzer on his desk. The door clicked behind Suri.

Suri was furious. She sputtered, struggling to find something to say. Finally, she managed, "General Avesta will hear about this."

"Oh?" Jahan said, sounding curious. "You know him?"

"I do!" Suri said. "I am very close to his daughter."

"Who's that? I wasn't aware the general had any children."

Suri was amazed. It was the first time she had met someone in Persepolis who didn't know who Nasrin was.

"I have orders," Suri said, "signed by General Avesta, Commander in Chief West, to report here immediately. This I have done and I won't be sent away by some major living in a sewer!"

Suri stopped. She covered her mouth with her hand, horrified at what she had said. She was hugely indignant, but she had gone too far. It was the military, and she'd stepped far beyond the limits of protocol.

Major Jahan was silent. Suri felt his stare upon her as a burning sensation on her skin. He was quiet for half a minute before speaking again.

Quietly, he said, "It was a sewer. The basement was full of pipes before we arrived. We had to divert them to create this space. It still leaks and the smell—"

Suri stood motionless.

"Very well," he said. "There is an open post, but I doubt you have the skills for it, being a woman. I don't suppose you can drive?"

Twenty-eight

Suri Pahlavi carried a briefcase from Major Jahan's office past the whirring machines and up the basement stairs. At the top of the stairs, two guards were waiting to meet her. She checked their ID badges, and they examined hers. All three passed a clipboard between them with a signed statement that confirmed their receipt of the case.

They left the building through the back entrance. Suri presented the back door guard with the clipboard, and the guard signed the paper without opening the briefcase. Outside, it was a sunny morning, and the air was dry. Smoke rose from the airbase to the northwest, perhaps from a crashed plane or another Azanian attack. There was an official car waiting for them in the motor pool.

The driver stepped out of the black-painted car and handed another clipboard to Suri. Suri signed for the car and got in the driver's seat. Her two guards sat in the capacious back seat. Suri had never gone in for cars like this. They were too big, too comfortable, and couldn't turn worth a damn.

She didn't feel any safer with the guards in the car, either. They were there for reasons other than protecting her. Suri knew they were there to safeguard the information in the briefcase, not her. There were two of them so they could keep an eye on each other, both out of official paranoia and because in New Persia men and women were never left alone together even in an official capacity. Suri would have preferred two women, but women weren't allowed under arms in the Army, and the *Bar Basij* was unarmed.

Her status as an officer tended to stifle conversation between the guards in the back seat. It was odd for an officer to be driving two enlisted grunts around Persepolis, but men who could drive were needed closer to the front. More and more women were driving trucks in the rear areas of the front. There were a surprising number of them, Suri thought. She wondered what other jobs women would be doing before the war was over. It was a useful excuse for Suri. For whatever reason, couriers of the information she carried were required to drive themselves if necessary, and Suri wasn't about to relinquish the wheel of any vehicle she was in.

She drove through the gate of the motor pool after being checked by yet another guard, who also signed off on the clipboard. Once out on the street, Suri drove the sleepy, powerful car carefully into the light traffic on the main boulevards. Civilian cars were still banned from travel on the roads, and military cargo almost always moved at night to avoid air attack. Suri hoped her single car driving alone wasn't enough to draw a strafing run from a marauding Azanian fighter.

As she drove, she passed more anti-aircraft guns than she remembered ever seeing before. Barrage balloons rose from parks and plazas on cables to obstruct low-flying planes. Persepolis was adjusting to war.

She was stopped once by a military policeman on a motorcycle and presented her pass and the clipboard. The enlisted man checked her paperwork, saluted, and released her. Suri sighed. She'd be late as a result.

Or...perhaps not. She peered down the boulevard. It was straight all the way to her destination. There was barely any traffic. The information she was carrying was time-sensitive. Suri accelerated, startling the guards in the backseat.

The car was no racer, but the engine was powerful and the rear wheels spun. When the wheels caught, the sedan catapulted forward. The acceleration pressed Suri into the back of her seat and she smiled, listening to the complaints of the guards in the back. The car went faster and faster, whirring as Suri shifted gears.

As she approached her destination, Suri didn't slow. She waited until the last possible second and then flipped the wheel to the right. The car skidded, and two wheels threatened to rise from the ground. Suri hit the accelerator and pulled the car out of the skid before hitting the brakes and stopping in front of the gate to the palace.

The surprised gate guards had reached for their weapons. Suri hid her smile as they approached the car. They grumbled about her approach, but her paperwork was in order, and the clipboard, which they signed, gave her a certain power to do as she wished.

Her two guards gratefully left the car in the custody of the motor pool and escorted her inside the building. More guards, checkpoints, and heavy doors led to the innards of the palace. Suri finally presented the clipboard to the final recipient of the briefcase, another woman in a *Bar Basij* uniform, who signed for it and took custody while being witnessed by Suri's guards and two of her own.

Suri saluted and then left the building by the same route. The car was waiting, and the two guards reluctantly climbed in. Suri smiled as she sat and took the wheel. This job wasn't so bad, she thought.

Twenty-nine

Suri woke up to the phone ringing in her quarters. She answered it automatically, and it was Major Jahan. Suri knew immediately something was wrong. She wouldn't be contacted directly by the office, and she'd expect it to be through an intermediary, usually a secretary. A direct call from a major was unusual, especially at this hour.

"Lieutenant Pahlavi, your presence is required at the office immediately," is all he said.

Suri, fully awake, answered, "Yes, sir," and the major hung up.

She went through the motions of getting into her uniform while being careful not to disturb her roommate any further. The phone call had already caused her to grumble half-asleep, and Suri didn't want to explain what it was about. She slipped out of her room within a minute, fully dressed.

She would have to deal with the CQ desk next. It wasn't normal for females to leave the building this early in the morning. The enlisted man guarding the building door would be polite but firm about letting her leave. She didn't have any written orders, and she doubted Major Jahan had thought to call ahead to let her go. He wasn't a detail person.

Suri was thinking of what to say when the problem was solved for her. The air-raid siren began to sound. Its wail pierced the walls of the building. She ran the last stretch of hallway and without so much as a salute, went out the door. The guard at the CQ desk was on the phone and didn't have time to stop her.

In the twilight outside, the wail was deafening. Shaitan was still up, and Suri used the Second Star's light to find her car in the motor pool. All around, people were scrambling, either to the bomb shelters or to man searchlights and anti-aircraft guns.

Suri briefly considered running to a shelter, but she knew if she did, it could be hours before she would be able to leave. "Immediately" didn't leave room for excuses. Of course, she wasn't the only courier. Jahan could find someone else, and the air raid was a good reason not to risk her life driving across the city.

Suri didn't want Jahan to find someone else. Whatever he needed, it seemed important. Suri wanted to be part of something important. She didn't want to be the person who missed out.

She knew that was an excuse. The real reason was she never wanted to be trapped in a basement shelter ever again. Her first time had been ordeal enough.

So instead of running for the building's shelter entrance, she ran the other way to the motor pool. She was confronted with a sergeant running the opposite way, who demanded to know what she was doing.

"I need a vehicle," Suri said.

"You need to go inside!" he said, forgetting protocol. "The bombs will be falling soon!"

"I'll worry about that, Sergeant," she said. "You go inside!"

With a shake of his head, the sergeant left her alone. Suri decided the air raid was making everything so much easier. She didn't have to spend much time explaining herself.

Upon arrival at the abandoned motor pool, Suri realized she had her pick of vehicles. Her own car was in storage, personal vehicles not being allowed to junior officers living on base. A senior officer had seen her with it and disapproved, so Suri had reluctantly hidden it away in a warehouse on the other side of the base.

There was a staff car belonging to some higher-ranking officer. Best to leave it alone, she thought. Six trucks sat in a row. Suri could drive a truck, but it didn't seem fast enough for this assignment. Looking around in the twilight, she spotted an alternative.

Parked on its kickstand at the end of the row of vehicles, the green-painted machine beckoned to her. Suri ran over and stopped to examine it. She recognized the controls because it was a civilian model converted for military use.

She wasn't overly familiar with motorcycles. She'd had a bad experience trying to ride one as a girl. The small 50cc bike she had fallen off had been much smaller than this monster she was eyeing. It was big enough for a tall man to ride, and she guessed it had a 750cc engine.

Suri wasn't sure what to do. She could certainly take one of the trucks, but they were slow, and she didn't want to be out in the open with falling bombs any longer than she had to be.

As if to encourage her to make up her mind, a flash of light from the other end of the base lit up the lot like lightning. A thunderous BOOM followed a second later. The shock wave almost pushed her over. The air was ripped from her lungs and left her gasping.

Above her head, Suri heard the hiss of bomb case fragments cutting through the air. As she stood, stunned by the blast, pieces of dirt and rubble began falling from the sky. Through the twilight, she saw a plume of smoke and flame rising from the base post office, barely five hundred meters away.

A smoking brick crashed into the pavement next to her foot and made a crater in the asphalt. It made up her mind.

Suri leaped onto the big cycle and gripped the throttle. Her foot could barely reach the clutch. She sat as best she could and opened the choke on the handlebar. She kicked the starter, and nothing happened. Her leg could barely extend far enough to turn the engine over, and the engine gave only a slight cough.

Another explosion shook the air around her.

Suri took a deep breath and prayed the bike would start. She leaned over as far as she dared, opened the choke further, and jumped on one leg to force the starter down. The engine coughed again then caught. Suri forced herself to wait to make sure the carburetor had caught and turned up the idle. Sand and masonry rained down, coating her uniform with white dust. Her eyes stung with it, so she reached into her coat pocket and removed her goggles and earplugs. She put them on and took the handlebars in both hands. She carefully squeezed the throttle lever, and the bike shot forward, engine revving.

The bike jerked when Suri tried to add more throttle, and she realized she needed to shift gears. On this monster, the gear shift was on the cycle body to her left in front of her leg. She had to let go of the handlebar to pull the shifter back. She remembered to push in the foot clutch at the last second. The bike wobbled, and she nearly fell off.

"This is a poor time to learn to ride!" Suri said to herself. The gear caught and the bike accelerated toward the end of the motor pool. Unfortunately, the lot ended in a brick wall. Suri, nearly panicking, turned the bike left as far as she dared and hit the brake. The bike slid to a stop. The engine coughed and Suri's heart rose in her throat as she pondered not being able to start the bike again. She remembered the foot clutch and kept the engine from stalling out. Suri downshifted again, slowly released the clutch and turned the bike around. She pointed herself at the entrance, released the clutch, and smoothly shifted gears as she left the motor pool behind.

A string of bomb explosions flashed on the horizon like chain lightning. Thunder roared in her ears and the ground shook. The feel of the bike's engine and the vibrations from the ground blended together. The explosions rumbled dully through her earplugs. Suri could feel the blast waves in the air more than she could hear them.

She dodged the bigger pieces of concrete and brick which had fallen onto the roads leading to the west gate. From the sky, burning pieces of paper were falling. The post office had been hit, and the pulverized, burning mail was falling to earth. It was like a man-made seed storm, Suri thought, as the smoking remains of letters fluttered around her and burned to ash on the ground.

The gate had been blown open by a nearby explosion, and the guards had abandoned the area for shelter. Suri aimed her bike at the gate, dodging a smoking crater on the way.

High above, anti-aircraft fire followed the beams of searchlights sweeping the sky. The huge beams crossed over an unlucky Azanian bomber. Suri saw the plane caught in the beams, weaving desperately to escape as exploding shells bracketed it. She clenched her teeth into a smile. At least they were getting back some of the terror they were inflicting on her and her fellow Persians.

Once out of the gate and past the cleared area around the base perimeter, Suri entered Persepolis. Everything looked strange to her. The imposed blackout made every building look abandoned, a perception reinforced by the boarded and shuttered windows. Broken glass from bomb blasts crunched under the bike's wheels.

Suri saw a few people scurrying around in the twilight. She imagined they were trying to get to their home shelters rather than cower with strangers in whatever place they happened to be when the air raid siren sounded. No one liked to be trapped far from home, and it was very hard to make civilians understand they needed to get to shelter immediately wherever they were when the bombs came.

The road looked unfamiliar in the twilight and bomb flashes. Suri had to think twice to trace her route to the Ministry building.

The bomb blasts pulsed through the air. As she watched, the hollowed-out walls of a roofless three-story stone building leaned inward. The highest blocks rained downward and crashed through the floors inside. Windows cracked and falling shards of glass cut the air like knives. A woman and her daughter cowered against the wall and held their arms over their heads to ward off the falling debris.

The third-floor wall collapsed into the building. The air filled with the crash of masonry pummeling the second floor. The floor held for a moment, but the outer wall bowed outward under the weight of the fallen stones. It threatened to crush the two people huddling beneath.

Without a thought, Suri opened her throttle and raced into the shadow of the falling wall. She slammed the brake and skidded to a stop beside the distressed couple. She tried to scream over the sound of the collapsing building, but her words were lost in the tumult. Her proffered arm and gloved hand spoke for her.

The woman didn't seem to understand what was happening. She stood dumbly, frozen beneath the falling wall. Her daughter acted for her. She broke free of her mother and gripped Suri's arm like a drowning person. Suri scooped her up into her lap, surprised at her strength. Both stared at the woman and cried for her to get onto the bike.

The wall began to fall. It broke on one end and collapsed toward them like a cresting wave. The woman still stood frozen in place.

Suri could wait no longer. She gunned the engine and pulled away from the curb with the girl in her lap.

The collapse displaced the air inside the building and created a wind blowing dust in all directions. Suri's bike was engulfed by the cloud, and she was blinded. She tried to keep the bike pointed away from the falling building. She looked back to see what was happening.

Out of the dust, an arm appeared. The woman leaped out of the path of a falling block and reached desperately for the rear seat of the motorcycle. She clutched at it and held on. Suri had no time to stop. The bike dragged the woman through the street as Suri struggled to keep the bike upright. She could see nothing at all. Bricks and other debris flew past as if blown by a tornado. The freight train roar of the building's collapse chased them like an angry beast. Suri didn't dare stop the bike despite the woman dragging behind.

Finally, the wind ceased, and Suri stopped the bike. She looked back, and the woman was gone. Suri stared with horror into the dust cloud. She had felt the pull of the woman's arms at the end of the bike a moment before. Where had she gone?

Over the ringing in her ears, she heard the girl screaming in her lap.

Suri turned the bike around to shine the headlamp into the dust cloud. Out of the darkness, a shape emerged.

The woman staggered into view. Suri got off the bike to help her. She was crying, not for herself but for her daughter. Suri could understand none of the words but saw them embrace.

More thunder sounded, and flashes filled the dusty air around them. Suri beckoned for both to get on the bike. She couldn't leave them to the mercies of the Azanian bombardment. She succeeded in getting all three of them mounted unsteadily on the bike. More cautiously than before, Suri nosed the bike through the dust cloud toward the nearest intersection.

The dust settled, and she could see again. From the street signs and landmarks, she knew where she was. The temple spire was visible above everything else. It was untouched. Suri wondered if its roof of ancient, unbreakable metal was proof against falling bombs. The bike labored under its heavy burden but carried all three toward the city center.

The bombardment was lifting as they arrived at the Archive building. With gestures, because their ears were still deafened, Suri directed the pair to the government shelter in the basement. She had to leave them to carry on with her assignment. She would never know their names.

Suri climbed the steps of the still-intact Archive building and wondered why she wasn't terrified. She felt no fear, even in retrospect, but a sense of exhilaration at being alive. Her ears still rang, and her eyes stung with sweat and dust, but she was alive! She reached the top of the steps and jumped into the air. The street was deserted, and there was no one to see. She went inside.

The guards at the top of the stairs leading to the basement were still at their posts, which Suri regarded as commendable. Suri removed her goggles and brushed at the dust covering her uniform coat. The guards waited until she presented her badge and checked the photo against her dirty face. With a grunt, a guard opened the door to the basement.

Suri repressed her desire to run down the stairs. Upon reaching the floor, she was aware of the normal whirring and clicking of the mystery machines. The *Bar Basij* women minded the knobs and wires on each one. No one seemed particularly concerned by the recent air raid. Other than a light coat of fallen dust and plaster on the floor, nothing had changed since her last visit.

Major Jahan answered his door and welcomed her into his office. He seemed not to notice her dirty uniform and rumpled hair. Suri didn't call attention to them or mention the air raid.

"Ah, Lieutenant Pahlavi, good to see you. We have a problem," he said.

"Yes, sir," she said.

"I require your services to bear an extremely high-priority communication to the front. I am aware this is highly irregular, but the phone lines have been cut, and we cannot risk using the radio because the Azanians could intercept the message. As you may have heard, radio codes can be broken," he smiled stiffly.

Suri crinkled her brow. What could this mean? What message could be so important it had to be delivered by hand?

"This is a dangerous mission, and I cannot, in good conscience, order you to perform it," he said.

Suri waited for him to say more, but when he didn't, she realized what he was saying.

"You are asking me to volunteer, sir?"

"Yes," Jahan said.

Suri's heart leaped inside her. Her mind was worried, extremely worried.

"Would you ask a man to volunteer, sir?" she asked.

Jahan was taken aback. "Yes, I would," he said.

"I see," Suri said. "Can I ask for more details?"

"No," Jahan said, "I'm afraid not."

She took a deep breath. Suri felt her caution and anticipation war within her. She gave in.

"Yes," she said, "I'll do it, sir." She exhaled.

"Outstanding," Jahan said. He went to his desk and unfurled a map. "You'll be going here," he pointed.

It was a spot in the Karun Delta southeast of Persepolis.

Suri waited a moment to make sure Jahan realized where he was pointing.

"Sir, that's east of the city. To the rear, not the front."

"Not for long, I'm afraid," Jahan said. "Which is why you need to deliver this message as soon as you can."

"I see," Suri said. "What's going to happen?"

"I'm afraid I can't divulge that information," Jahan said.

Suri nodded. She had learned Security was a false god who demanded sacrifices for which mortals could not understand the need. It was stupid, but she was accustomed to people being stupid.

"How will I get there?" Suri asked.

"You'll be part of a convoy leaving," Jahan looked at his watch, "in an hour. You'll be well-protected."

Suri suppressed a desire to roll her eyes. After what she'd gone through to get there, she felt very brave.

The convoy was late. It consisted of three trucks full of hard-bitten soldiers, a truck with an anti-aircraft gun mounted on the back and a staff car. The car came with a captain assigned to command the convoy and, to Suri's disappointment, a driver.

To her surprise, someone else emerged from the car when it stopped.

"Nasrin!" Suri cried. "What are you doing here?"

Nasrin smiled in greeting. "I'm going with you," she said. The two friends embraced.

"Really? Why?" Suri was confused.

"My father decided to have me whisked away from the city," she said, "for my safety, of course." She rolled her eyes. "Now he is head of the Western Theater and Capital Corps, it's gone to his head. I decided not to go the way he wanted. If I'm going to leave Persepolis, I'll go with my friend."

"How did you find out I was leaving?" Suri asked. "I thought this was secret."

"Not secret to the man who cuts the orders, who happens to be a big fan of mine," Nasrin said.

"It's a good thing you don't work for the Azanians," Suri said.

"It is," Nasrin said, "but now we are both here, where exactly are you going? My friend couldn't tell me."

Suri said, "I'm afraid I can't talk about it."

"No secrets between friends!" Nasrin cried.

"I'm afraid so," Suri said.

"Oh, no, the uniform has gone to your head as well," Nasrin said. "Damn the war, all these insufferable people in uniform." She glanced at the captain. "At least I'll have someone to talk to during the trip."

Thirty

Zafir waited in the cistern for the storm to abate. He cracked the lid every few minutes to look outside into the fiery maelstrom. Choking smoke would rush in if he left the lid open too long. He grew concerned the air inside the cistern would go bad, and he'd be unable to breathe. He considered his options. Outside was a fiery death. Inside was a slow, smothering one.

Zafir chose to let Fate decide. He would stay immersed in the water until he could bear it no more, and the fire outside would be burning, or it would not. Shrugging, he passed the decision of whether he would live or die into the hands of God.

The water grew warm as the fire outside heated it. Zafir had the unpleasant thought he would be boiled alive. If the water grew too hot, he would contend with the smoke and fire outside.

Satisfied with his decisions, Zafir made himself think of other things. It had been a dry year, and the crops had withered despite the irrigation. His cows had been hungry, which had led him to trespass on a neighbor's land. The transgression had led him to the courthouse and a short jail sentence. It was inconvenient, but he held nothing against his neighbor. He was only doing what he had to do, as Zafir had done what he had to do. Life was hard, and Fate had decided he would be caught.

Then the war had come, and his cousin had died at the hands of the Azanians. When the militia officer had offered him a chance at revenge, Zafir had leaped to take it. So had many other men, some who were jailed for serious crimes and would earn their freedom or die trying.

Fate had chosen their deaths, all of them. Except for Zafir. He wondered what this meant. He had been chosen to be caught by his neighbor, jailed, and then God's Fate had killed his cousin and chosen Zafir as the instrument of revenge. Setting fire to the fuel tanks at airfield K-2 had been decisive to the victory, he had heard. The militia had wanted to shower him with rewards. Zafir had refused them as charitably as he could. He had escaped with his life, and Zafir knew that to accept the reward owed to God and Fate would be blasphemous.

Again he had been chosen, this time to find the councilman's family. It was not going well, Zafir thought, trapped in the cistern.

He admonished himself not to doubt. He would have faith that this was only a trial and not the end of his story.

The sound of wind rushing outside rose. The water grew hotter. The sides of the cistern grew too hot to touch. Zafir did not dare to crack the lid. Outside was an inferno.

Thoughts came to him unbidden. Perhaps his fate was to be punished for his transgressions by boiling in this hell of a cistern. Had he done anything to deserve such an end? Zafir had to admit he had done many things and failed to do many things which would rightly earn him the wrath of God.

A peculiar calm came over him. If this were his end, he would accept it.

After a long time, which Zafir could not measure, the rushing air outside faded. The cistern walls began to cool. Zafir realized this was not his time to die.

He lifted one edge of the heavy stone lid. There was light outside. Everything he saw was blackened, burnt, and covered in soot. But the flames had passed him by.

Zafir was careful to give thanks to God before pushing the lid onto the ground. He stepped out, soaked, into the hot, dry air. Tendrils of evaporation poured off him like steam.

The landscape was utterly, horribly, changed. Where houses had stood, there were skeletons. Fallen walls and collapsed roofs buried half the courtyard. The street outside was blocked by a collapsed building. Zafir climbed over the rubble and made his way to where his memory placed the Kermani home.

He recognized nothing in the blackened husks of homes that had taken years to build. All of the townspeople's efforts to contain the fire had failed. Nothing remained alive anywhere he looked.

Smoking seedpods littered the ground, and Zafir stomped the nearest, smearing the inside over the blackened earth.

He took a careful look at the remains of the buildings and guessed at his location. The sky was full of smoke, and he could not see far. It seemed unlikely he could find anything or anyone alive in the destroyed neighborhood.

He searched for an hour in the ruins and found nothing. It pained him to see so many homes reduced to ash. He would occasionally find small items untouched by the flames, like a pot or a pan. Once, he found a singed family portrait still hanging on a lonely wall in a collapsed house.

The wind began to blow from the south. It pulled the ash and soot into the air and raised it into clouds of smoke. Zafir coughed and covered his eyes.

He came to an intersection in the road and could see north. There, to his horror, stood a wall of flames not a kilometer away. The flames curled into the sky beneath a rising thunderhead of smoke. The fire was so hot, so powerful, it pulled the winds to itself to feed its hunger. Zafir realized this was the worst possible sight, a firestorm. It was moving south and would consume everything the early fires had spared and left nothing in its wake.

At that moment, Zafir knew he had failed. He had to run as he had never run before only to save himself. He had not found the Kermani family. If they still lived, he knew not where, and he had only the hope they had already fled or failing that, had died quickly.

The wind began to rush past, blowing to the north to feed the monster firestorm. Zafir turned into the wind and ran south away from the flames.

He had taken only a few steps when he heard a noise. He did not stop. He thought it could only be the wind blowing through a small opening. But the noise came again, and he could not deceive himself. It was the cry of a child.

Zafir turned back toward the wall of flames and listened. The sound came again, from the north.

He ran to it as fast as he could. The wind chased him from behind, pushing him, encouraging him to run to the firestorm and his doom.

The cries led Zafir to a cellar door. It was half-buried by heavy roof tiles. He grasped the largest and pulled with all his strength. The tile barely slid. He tried again, and the stone would not budge. The wind rose around him. He dared not look north to see how close the flames had come.

He knew then Fate had chosen him, after all, and with this knowledge, he knew he would be able to open the door. There had to be a way, and Fate meant for him to find it.

He cast around for any instrument which could help him. He found it in seconds. The end of a fallen wooden beam peeked through the rubble. Zafir ran to it and extracted it. It had been severed at a length of four feet when the roof had given way, perfectly for his purpose.

Zafir shoved one end of the beam beneath the heavy roof tile. It would fit, but he needed a fulcrum. He found a stone block from one of the walls and, straining, rolled it end-over-end to the cellar door. He braced the beam on the stone and pushed down with his full weight.

The tile lifted. With a thump, it fell over onto the floor next to the cellar door. Zafir rushed over, cleared the remaining debris from the door, and lifted the handle. The door opened.

From the darkness inside appeared the soot-blackened faces of six women, a large man, and a small child.

"Are you the Kermanis?" Zafir asked, knowing they must be.

One of the women, an older woman Zafir knew must be the councilman's wife, spoke, "Yes, and this man and woman are with us."

"We must go, now," Zafir said. "The fire comes."

"We have a small child and five women," Narda said, not including herself. "We must wait here for the fire to pass."

"You cannot hide from this fire," Zafir said. He reached for Narda's hand and pulled her up. He pointed to the north.

Narda understood immediately.

"We must leave now!" she cried over the rising wind. "There is a firestorm!"

The women inside jumped out, followed by the boilermaker carrying the child in his arms.

Zafir said, "Follow me," and led the little group away from the flames. He moved as fast as he thought they would be able to follow. The burned and blasted landscape was unrecognizable, but the rising wind gave him all the direction he needed. He must lead them away from the storm, and the wind was blowing straight into it. He would face the direction of the wind, and it would show him the way.

The soot and ash rose from the ground and blinded them. The sky was completely dark, and the sun went out, blocked by ash. Zafir commanded the line of survivors to hold hands so none would become lost. The human chain stumbled into the night.

Zafir was unsure they could move quickly enough to escape the firestorm. He knew he could run faster alone, but he was also sure if he did such a low thing, it would not save him. If his fate were to die in the storm, it had already been written.

The wind screamed past. One of the women cried out, and Narda comforted her. The child wailed, but his cries were blown into the darkness.

Zafir kept on, forcing himself to ignore the tendency to bear off from the wind blowing directly into his face. Embers flew onto his robes. One scalded his cheek before he could swat it away. The air was stale, and his chest heaved with the effort to breathe.

They hung on to each other against the wind and the rising heat behind them. Zafir pulled them forward as much with his force of will as his strong arms.

The heat was growing all around. The wind blew harder. The storm was coming. Zafir's faith was shaken. Surely, they would die soon.

The women were faltering. Fatigued by fear and the stale air, they would stop to cough the soot from their lungs. Zafir and Narda yelled encouragements and threats to keep them moving.

The wind shifted. Zafir took a while to notice, but even in the dark, his sense of direction was honed by years of smuggling runs and cattle raids. The wind was clearly shifting from the south to the east.

He looked back at the storm and felt the heat coming from the north. The storm was still in the same direction. It had not curled around to the west to come at them from a new direction. This must be a normal wind, not caused by the firestorm.

Normal or not, it would blow the flames in a new direction. West, away from Zafir and his little band.

"We must keep going!" he cried to the exhausted women. "We will escape! But we must not stop!"

The east wind grew in strength until it was blowing harder than the winds driven by the firestorm.

A rumble sounded above them from the black clouds. A flash and the crash of thunder.

Zafir stopped for a moment to look up in amazement.

All around them, black rain began to fall. Huge raindrops washed the soot and ash from the air and splattered the mess everywhere they landed. Soon all of them were covered in the gooey mess.

They stepped into the caked, wet soot which clung to their feet and threatened to hold them in place. It seemed like a new, hellish trial they could not escape.

Zafir felt hope instead. The wind would blow the flames away. The black rain would cool the air.

The rain grew in strength. Sheets of water fell from the sky. Soon, the air was cleansed, and Zafir could see through the air to the south.

Ahead, the metal dome of the temple rose up to the clouds. Lightning flashes reflected from its surface. Zafir could no longer get lost. The way was clear. They were saved.

"Thanks be to God," he said to the others. They all knelt in the ash mud and broke into prayers of thanks.

Thirty-one

The *Yunes* sailed into the port of Bandar early in the morning. She glided in on the surface with Captain Azeri and two watchstanders manning the bridge. He had commanded that a broom be lashed to the sail, an ancient custom meaning the boat had swept the enemy from the seas. Azeri felt the crew deserved the honor after what they had been through.

She had arrived safely in port after evading a determined hunt by Azanian destroyers. Azeri had skillfully led them away from danger but had been driven away from the Azanian formations. After a day of trying to regain contact with the Azanian fleet, it was time to give up. The submarine did not possess the sustained speed to catch the Azanians, even the slower transports. While fast in bursts, the submarine could sustain a speed of only 30 kilometers an hour by snorkeling, and to snorkel near patrolling destroyers and, especially, aircraft was suicidal.

The *Yunes* had fired many of its torpedoes and had suffered damage from the depth charge attacks. Many of the repairs to the boats' systems were temporary, and he did not want to test them in another round of combat. Azeri knew they had done their part, and while eager to get back to the fight, he knew the boat needed to break off and return to port.

Azeri guided the boat to a dock and, without assistance from a tug, expertly brought the *Yunes* to a stop. The sailors on the deck and the dockworkers moored the boat. A gangway was brought over.

Azeri called his crew to formation on the deck of the boat. Farad, not having duties to perform, stood with the submarine officers. He could see the sprawling port and shipyard of Bandar and the smoke rising from the many foundries and mills in the city. Ships of all kinds, many of them damaged, were docked all around.

Azeri thanked the crew for their hard work, admonished them more was to come and then released them by shifts to shore liberty. The first lucky shift rushed down the gangplank to freedom.

Farad went to Azeri and saluted.

"It is goodbye to our brave pilot," Azeri said.

"Yes, I must go," said Farad.

"I am sad to see you leave us," Azeri said. "You would make a fine submarine officer."

Farad laughed. "I need to see the sky," he said.

The two men embraced, and Farad followed the sailors down the gangplank and onto the dock. His presence had been announced by radio to the local fleet headquarters, but Farad doubted the Air Corps had been informed of his arrival. So it always was with the military. He'd have to find his own way to the nearest airfield and find a flight back to Persepolis. He would get there, one way or another.

Thirty-two

Basir Turani bounced around inside his command carrier, grateful for his helmet as his head careened off the steel roof of the vehicle for the hundredth time. The ride inside the steel box on treads was awful. It was impossible to relax, even if he had time, and doing the work of guiding the road march of an entire mechanized regiment was proving equally difficult. Unfolding a map was hard. Reading it while bouncing up and down was an exercise in frustration.

They were moving, though. Basir had anticipated the order, which finally arrived from General Avesta in the early afternoon. Every one of his battalions and companies was already inspected and prepared for a road march. The trucks were loaded, and the vehicles fueled. He'd already given them a warning order. All he needed was the time to move out, and it finally came. They'd left at dusk, the entire regiment minus the heavy tank company, and went as fast as they could during the darkness before Shaitan rose. A platoon of Captain Pahlavi's scouts led them along the route they had found the day before and military police from corps, briefed on the route, provided traffic control. General Avesta had planned ahead, Basir was happy to see.

They would have to keep moving during the twilight of Shaitan-light despite the danger of discovery and attack by Azanian planes. Basir was extremely unhappy about moving while enemy planes were overhead. He knew war required risks, but his regiment would be driving on roads and exposed to air attack until they reached the safety of the Gerdkooh hills. The only positive development was the low overcast, which shielded his men from above like a protective blanket.

One of the radios crackled. A scared voice blared from the speaker, "Enemy aircraft!"

Basir, annoyed, was gratified when an angry net controller demanded a call sign, position, and proper spotting report. When these were forthcoming, the unit involved broke column and spread out on either side of their section of road in a "herringbone," with each vehicle pulling off at an angle, alternating on each side of the road. The preceding and succeeding units did the same, and soon Basir's own track rumbled off the pavement and stopped. He took the opportunity to open the rear hatch and exit. They were parked near a stand of pistachio trees. Basir noted a nearby irrigation ditch to dive into should the need arise.

Sky guards manned their machine guns and peered into the air.

Soon the source of the alert flew into sight. Two aircraft roared overhead at treetop height beneath the overcast. They were fighters with swept wings but carried no bombs.

Basir ducked at the sound but not before he noted the Nine-Pointed-Star insignia on the underside of the wings.

Many of the soldiers around him didn't notice. Machine guns opened up and spat at the air up and down the road.

"They're ours!" he yelled. Only his own carrier's gunner could hear him.

He crawled back into the command carrier and got on the radio, "ALL KILO UNITS, THIS IS KILO SIX ONE, AIRCRAFT OVERHEAD ARE FRIENDLY, REPEAT, FRIENDLY. DO NOT FIRE ON THEM."

The order was passed down the chain of command, and within a minute, the firing had stopped. Basir made another transmission, ordering all of his troops to check their targets before firing. There was no point in recriminations. To this point in the war, all the planes any of his soldiers had seen were enemies. He was glad the Persian Air Corps had finally appeared, and he didn't want to shoot down a friendly plane.

Within five minutes, the regiment was back on the road and heading west.

Thirty-three

Suri and Nasrin traveled in relative comfort in the back seat of the staff car headed east. They watched the river-delta country pass by on either side. It was lush from irrigation, and many trees and crops grew. The low overcast hid the sky above. Water drizzled onto the windows and windshield. Ahead and behind were the trucks of their escorts. Occasionally, a convoy would pass going the other direction.

The slow speed of the trucks was frustrating.

"If they had let me go alone, I would be there already," Suri said.

"Yes, but would you have made it?" Nasrin asked.

"Of course, I would," Suri said. "I can take care of myself. I've done it before."

The truck ahead stopped. Suri sighed. Convoys stopped all the time for reasons she could not fathom. They never knew how long a stop would last.

"I'm getting out," Suri said and opened the door.

"We need to move at a moment's notice," said the captain, their minder, from the front seat.

"I'm sure you won't leave without me," Suri said and took the briefcase with the message with her.

"I'll come with you," Nasrin said, ignoring the captain's scowl.

The two women found the ground beyond the pavement to be soft. Recent rain had soaked the soil and made it into mud. Suri took a few steps before giving up when her boots sunk to her ankles.

Nasrin watched with distaste from the road.

"I'm not going out there," she said.

"I'm coming back," Suri said. She struggled back to the road. The mud almost sucked off one of her boots.

The two women stood on the road next to the car and watched. The trucks around them slowly emptied of soldiers eager to use the chance to relieve themselves. They ignored Suri and Nasrin, who dutifully looked away.

From above came a rumbling sound.

"What is that?" Suri asked.

"It's not thunder," Nasrin said.

"Is it a plane?"

More rumbling seemed to come from the south. They peered at the overcast but saw nothing.

Suri decided to ask the captain.

"What's going on?"

"I don't know," he said, looking confused.

Suri reached into the car and took the binoculars from the glove compartment over the captain's objections. She ignored him and looked up.

From the low overcast above, parachutes were blossoming. They were falling slowly like flower petals all around.

"Oh, my God," she said. "Paratroops!"

"What?" said the captain.

"Enemy parachutists! They are going to land all around us!"

"What?"

"We need to shoot them! Order your men to start firing!"

The captain got out of the car, and Suri thrust the binoculars at him so he could see for himself.

"This isn't part of the plan," he said. "We need to radio for orders."

"What?" Suri said, astounded. "By all means, report it, but we need to do something right away! What's ahead on the road?"

"I'm sorry, what?"

"They are dropping on something, something important. They must be. What's ahead?"

The captain, confused, said, "Only the Karun Delta bridge."

"The bridge! That must be it!" Suri cried.

"What?" said the captain.

"Damn you!" Suri cried. "Get your men together. The Azanians are going to seize the bridge!"

"Why?" he asked.

"I don't know! But it must be important," Suri said.

The captain went to the nearest truck. Suri was expecting him to order the men to grab their weapons, but he got on the radio instead. Suri looked up to see the parachutes falling in greater numbers. Many other soldiers had noticed them and were peering upward.

"Oh, damn, damn, damn," Suri said.

"I believe it's time to earn your officer pay," Nasrin, who had been watching the whole conversation, said.

Suri ran to the truck behind them. It had a heavy dual-barreled anti-aircraft gun mounted on a flatbed.

"Those are Azanians!" She pointed at the parachutes in the sky. "Fire at them!"

The gun crew looked at her in bewilderment. "What?" the gun sergeant said.

Suri drew herself up to her full height and put all of her determination into her voice. "Sergeant, fire your weapon at the enemy. I order you!"

"But—" he stammered.

"I am Lieutenant Pahlavi of the Persian *Bar Basij*, and those are the enemy you are failing to engage! If you don't get off your worthless ass and fire your weapon, I'll have you flayed!" Suri tried to yell without shrieking. "Now, Sergeant!"

The sergeant decided he didn't know what was going on or who this woman was who was giving him orders, but they were orders he understood.

"Lay the gun!" he said, and the two privates with him unhitched the weapon and pointed it skyward.

Suri took Nasrin's arm and led her away before the guns could fire.

CHUNK CHUNK CHUNK CHUNK CHUNK.

The twin barrels spat fire into the sky and sprayed brass cartridges into the mud by the road. The gun crew loaded two new five-round clips into the breaches and fired again.

Suri and Nasrin held their ears against the noise.

"We need to get the men deployed!" Suri yelled.

"What does that mean?" Nasrin said.

"Out of the trucks and ready to fight!"

Suri ran to the nearest truck and roughly ordered the squad sergeant to get his men out. This time, he obeyed, and Persian soldiers with rifles spilled out into the mud on either side of the road.

She ran down the line of trucks, bellowing orders.

"Get out and get ready!"

The captain in charge of the escort force noticed what Suri was doing. He put down the unresponsive radio receiver and stormed over.

"Lieutenant, I am in charge here!" he said.

"Take charge, then!" Suri said.

The captain's face darkened. "I have been more than forgiving of your insubordination, Lieutenant, but I will not let the fact of your being a woman infringe on military discipline!".

Suri felt the heat build inside of her. She knew something had to be done immediately, and she had a good idea of what needed doing. She also knew *Bar Basij* were not in the normal Army chain of command, and she was outranked by the captain. She had no formal authority there. Suri also realized the last thing that was needed then was an open breach in the chain of command while enemy soldiers were falling from the sky.

Suri controlled her emotions and took a deep breath. "Yes, sir," she said.

Nasrin watched impassively and studied both of their faces.

"Very well, Lieutenant. Your mission is to carry the message you bear. Mine is to make sure you get where you are going. That is all. Now, get in the car and stay there until you are summoned."

Suri had to bite her lip to keep her thoughts from spilling out. It was one of the hardest things she had ever done.

"Dismissed!" the captain said.

Suri saluted and walked over to the car. She opened the door, sat down, and slammed the door behind her.

Nasrin entered through the other side.

"I've never seen you back down like that," she said.

"Damnit!" Suri said. "He's an idiot. I know what to do!"

In front and behind, Suri saw the captain giving orders for the soldiers to get back on the trucks.

Suri seethed.

"I don't mean it as an insult," Nasrin said. "It takes a lot of self-control to swallow your pride."

"I hate having to defer to every idiot I meet because they are a man, and I'm not!" Suri said.

"But you didn't this time," Nasrin said. "He does outrank you, and you are in the Army now."

"That's the only reason I didn't, oh, I don't know!" Suri said.

"Shoot him?" Nasrin smiled. "If only."

Their driver returned to the car, but the captain did not. He directed the trucks to start moving forward by pulling into the opposite lane and passing the convoy ahead of them. The trucks' diesel engines whined and coughed smoke. The little convoy was moving again to the east.

Outside, the parachutes were landing in the fields to the north and south. Suri could do nothing but watch as the Azanian soldiers hit the ground, rolled, and then stood. Each man would detach his parachute and then grab his weapon. Persian soldiers from the roadway were shooting at the Azanians, but not in any organized way. A few of the enemy were hit, but most were able to get up and move to the nearest cover. Suri could only seethe with the thought of a platoon of men engaging the Azanians as they landed with rifles, machine guns, and the anti-aircraft cannon, which was stowed in its travel position, unable to fire.

The convoy nosed forward a few hundred meters before it stopped again. Suri couldn't see anything to the north because of a stopped truck next to the car. To the south, there was a grove of trees coming up to the road.

Suri and Nasrin sat in the car for a minute before anything happened.

Then the whole car seemed to explode. The windows shattered, and holes instantaneously appeared in the car doors. Bullets cracked through the air and thudded into the seat cushions. The metal car frame sparked from a dozen bullet hits.

Suri and Nasrin ducked in the back seat. The soldier driving the car could not and was hit by a stream of bullets. Blood sprayed over the shattered windshield.

Suri, directly behind him, was saved by the driver's body blocking the rounds aimed at her. She could hear the thuds of the bullet impacts and see the indentations in the seat in front of her from the spent bullets.

"Oh, my God!" Suri yelled.

More bullets cut through the car. The bullet trails passed directly over Suri's head. She could see the wave of air left in their wake.

"Get out!" Nasrin said and lifted the door handle. She kicked the door open and rolled out onto the roadside. Suri reached up for the door handle on her side of the car, but a bullet smashed the door above her hand, and she jerked it away. She laid down on the floorboard as low as she could.

She saw Nasrin through the open door on the other side. Her friend had rolled off the road and was running for the trees nearby. Suri decided to follow her. She scooted along the floorboard to the open door and fell out onto her bottom. Suri sprung to her feet faster than she ever had in her life and ran for the trees.

The machine gun which had raked the car turned on the two running women. Nasrin seemed to sense the incoming bullets and fell face-first into the mud just in time. The bullet stream passed over her. Suri, remembering something she had read, tried suddenly changing direction, and zigzagged to the nearest tree. The bullets cut the air in front of her, and she reached the tree line unhurt. She, too, dropped to the ground.

The machine gun lost interest in Suri and Nasrin and turned its attention to the parked trucks. The soldiers inside were starting to get out, but it was too late. Suri watched green tracers cut the air and riddle the trucks lengthwise. Soldiers were hit and screamed where they fell. Panicked, they ran in all directions to escape the ambush.

The two women lay in the mud, burying their faces and covering their ears against the horrible sounds of combat.

Suri recovered first. She had been through air attacks before, but this was different. It was much more personal. Someone was pointing a gun at her, Suri Pahlavi. Not a car or a blur on the ground. Her.

The thought made her more afraid than she'd ever been. This didn't feel like a game, and she didn't feel the exhilaration she'd experienced during the air raid. Cowering in the mud from an unseen enemy, Suri was terrified.

The guns kept firing, and the screams continued. Suri couldn't make it stop.

Nasrin crawled over to her.

"Suri," she said, over the gunfire, "Suri, you need to do something!"

Suri heard her as if at the bottom of a deep well. Do something? What?

She felt helpless and alone and guilty at the same time. She really wasn't any good at this, and she was resentful of Nasrin for pointing it out.

She hated everything happening to her. The guns, the screams, the mud, and, most of all, her fear.

She hated it. She hated the Azanians for doing this to her.

Anger began to grow inside Suri Pahlavi.

"Suri!" Nasrin cried again.

"Damnit, I know!" Suri said.

She raised her head from the mud and looked around for the first time. The pair of women were lying in a small defile below the roadway to their north. It wasn't quite a ditch, more of a low spot where the water ran next to the road. To the south, the trees offered safety in the shadows under their eaves. Suri thought she could run away into the trees and be safe.

She stifled the thought. Safe until some Azanian with a gun found her. Then what?

And she couldn't run away. Not now. The lieutenant's bars on her collar weighed heavily on her.

She brought herself up to a crouch and forced herself to look east toward the gunfire.

She could see the indistinct shapes of men in camouflage moving in the shadows. Not many men, she judged. She flopped back down into the mud before she made herself a target.

"All right," she said to herself. "There aren't that many."

"What?" said Nasrin.

"Come with me," Suri said. "We have to gather some men."

Nasrin nodded agreement.

The two women half-walked, half-crawled back toward the road.

The gunfire stopped. A part of Suri's brain told her the machine gun must have finished firing a belt of cartridges, and the crew was reloading. Instead of the continuous stream of bullets, short bursts or single shots whizzed by overhead.

Suri took the opportunity to get up and sprint to the nearest truck.

It was awful there. Dead and wounded men were all over the pavement. Suri shut down her feelings, knowing she'd feel them later. The dead were beyond her help, and the wounded would not be safe unless she could silence the machine gun.

She saw the survivors of the ambush spread out in the muddy field to the north of the road. She recognized one of them.

"Sergeant," she called. "Get your men firing!"

He didn't answer her but seemed to bury himself more deeply in the mud.

"Men, fire your weapons!" Suri called.

The fear was too strong. A bullet whizzed by Suri. She ignored it.

Nasrin watched Suri screaming at the pinned soldiers and came to a decision. She reached down to one of the wounded men on the pavement and pried the rifle from his cold hands. She wiped the blood from the charging handle before pulling it back and chambering a round. She lifted the rifle to her shoulder. It was a heavy weapon for her slender form, and she held it unsteadily. She took aim at the sounds and flashes down the road and fired.

It was the first return fire from the Persians.

Nasrin pulled the trigger again, and the rifle barked. She had no target in her sights and had no idea where the bullets she fired were going. She only stood and fired back. Again and again she pulled the trigger, and the rifle's mechanism loaded a round for the next shot.

Suri saw Nasrin's example and snatched another rifle from the shattered truck bed. She aimed the weapon down the road and began firing.

"Up and at 'em!" she yelled. "Death to the Azanians!"

Return fire came in individual shots from the Azanians down the road. Bullets cut the air around Nasrin and Suri. Suri saw flashes through the drizzling mist and fired at them. Nasrin fired in a steady cadence that steadied Suri's nerves.

The men scattered in the field put up their heads and saw the two women shooting back. A few of them shouldered their weapons and began firing, too.

Suri's rifle clicked on an empty chamber. The magazine was empty. She ducked behind a truck and listened to the gunfire. She could hear New Persian rifles cracking as the men in the field shot back. That was good, but it wasn't enough. The Azanians were in the trees and in cover while her men were in an open field. She had to do something more.

Her eyes found the anti-aircraft gun.

Before she could do anything else, bullets began whirring through the air. The machine gun was firing again, and it was aimed at Nasrin.

Suri reached out for Nasrin's thin ankle and clasped her fingers around it. She jerked as hard as she could and pulled Nasrin's leg out from under her. Nasrin fell onto the pavement right as a stream of tracers blasted through the air where she had stood.

"Ow!" Nasrin said.

"Thank me later!" Suri said. "We need to get the gun working!" Suri pointed at the anti-aircraft gun.

"How?" Nasrin said. The two women hid behind the truck, and bullets thudded into the pavement around them.

"We need the gun crew if there are any left. I don't know how to operate the gun."

"How will they get up here?" Nasrin asked.

Suri didn't know. To get back to the truck, the men in the field would have to cross open ground and would be cut down by the Azanian fire.

Her eyes fell onto the wounded men. She wanted to help them, but the rest of the soldiers needed her if they weren't going to end up dead or wounded. As her eyes played over the bloody bodies around the truck, she noticed an odd can-shaped object on one of the dead soldier's web gear.

It was a grenade. On it, the flowing Persian script said, "TYPE 18 SMOKE." She remembered part of the story of Basir's capture of Airfield K-2. He had used the smoke from burning fuel tanks to cover the advance of his tanks from behind the Azanian lines.

A plan formed in Suri's mind.

"Sergeant!" she called to the men in the muddy field to her north.

"Yes, Lieutenant?" replied the noncom, between gunshots.

"I want you to crew the gun," Suri pointed at the gun truck, "when I say go."

Suri could barely see the sergeant's face through the mud covering it, but his body tensed. He was not a happy man.

"I have a plan!" Suri tried to sound reassuring. It didn't work.

When she saw the Azanian machine gun firing across the field to the north, keeping the Persians there pinned to the ground, Suri reached for the smoke grenade. She pried it loose and looked for more. She found three and narrowly avoided being shot while detaching the last one from its harness on a dead Persian soldier.

She looked around and judged the wind.

"Here," Suri said and gave Nasrin a smoke grenade. "When I say, pull this pin and throw it over there," she pointed at a patch of ground on the other side of the truck.

Nasrin nodded.

"Cover me!" Suri yelled, and the Persians in the field started firing their rifles toward the Azanians.

Suri wrapped her finger around the grenade pin and pulled. The grenade immediately began to sputter. She threw it as hard as she could toward the Azanians.

"Throw it, Nasrin!" she called.

Nasrin threw her grenade. Suri took the last smoke cannister and threw it between the other two.

Smoke billowed from the three cans and streamed slowly downwind. When it thickened enough to block sight, Suri yelled, "Now, Sergeant! Man the gun!"

The gun sergeant yelled his own orders, and three men rose with him. One didn't make it. The Azanian machine gunner fired a long burst sideways at waist height and shot him through the smoke. The other three men sprinted to the gun trailer and climbed onto the gun mount.

Hurriedly, the gun crew readied the weapon. They released the travel hooks and deployed the sights. The loader filled each breach with a five-round ammunition clip. Before the smoke dissipated, the gun was ready to fire.

The Azanian machine gun fired again, and its green tracers swept across the field. The sergeant aiming the anti-aircraft gun pointed both 20mm barrels at the source of the shooting.

CHUNK CHUNK CHUNK CHUNK CHUNK.

The twin barrels spewed ten shells at the machine gun position. The shells exploded on impact and filled the air with mud and shrapnel. The machine gun never fired again.

The gun crew traversed the weapon and methodically fired short bursts along the line of suspected Azanian positions. Soon, Suri was able to order the men in the field to advance under cover of the gun's fire. They took the Azanian line and killed or drove away the squad of enemy soldiers who had been tormenting them. The firing slowed, then stopped, and there was no more shooting.

Suri gathered the remaining soldiers. There were twenty men left who could fight. Ten were dead, and another ten wounded. Suri directed the wounded be placed in the one remaining operational truck. The medic was dead, so she assigned three men to drive the truck and tend to the wounded and ordered them back the way they had come. There had been Azanians parachuting all over the area, but Suri guessed there would be more where they were going than where they'd come from. The others had probably been dropped in the wrong place because of the heavy overcast.

The gun truck was a problem. All the tires had been shot out. Suri badly wanted the guns' firepower.

"Can we change the tires?" Suri asked the sergeant.

"Yes, ma'am," he said, "It will take an hour. We don't have an air hammer."

"Damn," Suri said. She needed the gun, but she suspected time would run out if they didn't get moving.

"What do we have for weapons?" Suri asked.

Everyone had their personal weapons, and there was one belt-fed machine gun they recovered from a truck.

"Can we use the Azanian machine gun?"

"No, ma'am," one of the private soldiers answered, "The gun blew it to hell."

Suri pondered. She could find a good place to hole up and wait for friendly forces to find them. She had no idea how long it would be.

Suri went looking for a radio. She found the captain, dead, still holding a radio receiver. Suri put the headset on and listened. She could barely understand the call signs and military abbreviations, but she caught a few words.

"It's the bridge," Suri said. "The Azanians are trying to take the Delta Highway bridge." Suri looked for the transmitter, but it had been shot away. She couldn't talk on the radio, only listen.

"We've got to help," Suri said. She took the dead captain's map case and oriented herself with her compass. "We're two kilometers away from the bridge," Suri said. "We can get there."

"And do what?" asked the sergeant.

"The Azanians want the bridge," Suri said. "If they want it, it must be good for them, and that's bad for us."

The sergeant nodded.

"Get the men together, and we'll march to the bridge. You know your business, Sergeant, so I'll let you organize them in the best way to get us there without walking into an ambush."

The sergeant nodded and gave orders. The men formed into a wedge with one man fifty meters in front, and the formation marched east.

Suri found Nasrin, who had been leaning on one of the trucks. Her clothes were caked with mud and blood.

"I thought you'd be going with the wounded," Suri said.

"I'm not a doctor," Nasrin said. "I don't have any idea how to tend to wounds. And it makes me sick," she admitted.

"You aren't a soldier," Suri said.

"Neither are you," Nasrin said, "not really."

"Today I am," Suri said.

"And today I am your friend, so I go with you," Nasrin said.

The two women followed the infantry half-platoon east toward the Delta Bridge.

Thirty-four

The prince arrived for an unannounced visit to the war room. The staff, surprised, saluted, and the *Bar-Basijis*, as they had been ordered, kept at their tasks. Their ears glued to radio headsets, they pushed wooden blocks across a large map in the center of the room.

Two of the women walked to the other side of the map. Their headset cords barely reached. They placed red blocks to represent Azanian units onto the map, east of Persepolis on the coast.

"What is this?" the prince asked. He recognized the woman he had spoken to during his earlier visit.

"There are unconfirmed reports of Azanian marines landing in the delta, sir," she said.

"Unconfirmed?" the prince said.

"Unconfirmed but credible," a voice behind him said.

The prince turned to see General Avesta. He seemed overly cheerful for such a grim time.

"The Air Corps passed on an unconfirmed sighting of sea transports during the attack yesterday, and now there is an unconfirmed report of a troop landing. Two unconfirmed reports equal one confirmation. Especially when it's the last thing I want to hear," Avesta said. "There's 'Force C,' Your Highness."

"They were not supposed to land for another day," the prince said. "The—"

"I'm required to remind you this room is not secure, Your Highness," Avesta said. He wasn't privy to special intelligence except as it pertained to the Western Theater. He'd been briefed on a possible Azanian landing on the coast, but the exact location had been vague.

The prince, annoyed but understanding Avesta was correct, changed his tack.

"They are attacking Persepolis from the rear," the prince said. "What do we have to stop them?"

"There are many mobilization units in the area on the way to the Western front," Avesta said. "We have redirected them to face this new threat."

"Will they be enough?"

"I believe so. If we can catch them on the beach before they can deploy," Avesta said. "It depends on how fast they can move."

"In my experience, General," the prince said, "the Azanians always move too fast."

"Indeed," Avesta agreed. "In this case, it depends on a bridge," he pointed at the map.

The prince looked more closely at the map. "The Delta Highway bridge?"

"Yes," Avesta said. "If we can hold it, or blow it up, the Azanians will be trapped on the wrong side of the river and will not be able to reach Persepolis."

Another *Bar Basiji* came around the map table. "Excuse me, sir," she said, and the prince stepped out of her way. She placed a red block squarely on the bridge.

"What's this?" the prince asked.

"There is an unconfirmed report of a parachute landing near the bridge," she said.

General Avesta frowned. "Too fast, indeed," he said.

"If they have the bridge..." the prince said and looked at the eastern approaches of Persepolis. They were empty of friendly units.

"We may have visitors soon," Avesta said.

"Where has the Capital Corps gone?" the prince asked.

Avesta pointed northwest of the city. "To the Gerdkooh hills, Your Highness."

"You stripped the city defenses? Why?" The prince was incredulous.

"To win the war," Avesta said calmly.

"You seem to have lost it, instead." The prince pointed at the Delta Highway bridge.

"We shall see," Avesta said. "We'll know more in an hour."

"We shall know if you will keep your head, General," the prince said. "You should recall the Capital Corps immediately."

A quiet fell upon the room. The nearby staffers looked dutifully away. The *Bar Basij* women looked at the map more intently.

"Your Highness," General Avesta said quietly, "Am I to continue serving as your Western Theater Commander?"

"You offer your resignation to escape responsibility for this?" the prince said.

"No, Your Highness," Avesta continued, his voice tightly controlled. "I wish to continue serving you. However, I believe in the unity of command. I must be free to carry out operations as I see fit."

"Or I can find someone else. Is that it?"

"If you don't agree with my course of action, I believe you should replace me with a commander more to your liking, yes," Avesta said.

"How long will it take these Azanian forces which have landed in the Delta to reach Persepolis?"

"A day, perhaps two, if they are not stopped," Avesta said.

"So there is no time to lose," the prince said.

"I believe we can prevail if the offensive by the Capital Corps can continue as scheduled. The Azanian landing can be contained by the units already present or arriving in the next twenty-four hours," Avesta said.

"What about this report of an airborne landing on the Delta Bridge?"

"Airborne operations are notoriously chancy undertakings."

"The Azanians seem unusually lucky when they try them," the prince retorted.

"So far, yes," Avesta agreed. "I don't believe luck lasts forever."

"You were known as a lucky commander, General. Perhaps it's your luck which has run out."

"As I said, Your Highness, I serve at your sufferance," General Avesta said. "I believe our strategy is the best chance to drive the enemy from our territory and win the war. I believe recalling the Capital Corps and relinquishing the initiative to the enemy will lead to ultimate defeat. We cannot keep reacting to the Azanian moves. We must seize the initiative and that requires taking a risk."

"You are risking the capital city of the empire!" the prince said.

"If we don't counterattack now, the Azanians will surround Persepolis and besiege it. We will be forced to turn the city into a battleground, and with the Azanian control of the sea and air, we will not prevail. War is risk, Your Highness."

"Don't lecture me about war, General. But you are correct about one thing. We cannot allow the Azanians to dictate our every move. Can you return part of the Capital Corps to the city as a precaution?"

"No, Your Highness," Avesta said steadfastly. "It would only weaken our offensive."

"Very well. I see you are serious about resigning. I may accept your offer, but not yet."

"Thank you, Your Highness," Avesta said evenly.

"I will leave you to your business," the prince said.

General Avesta saluted as the prince left the room.

Avesta studied the map. "I hope I am right about the Delta Bridge," he said to himself.

Thirty-five

In the forest of the Gerdkooh hills, Colonel Basir Turani inspected the deployments of his 1st Battalion. Major Ormuz had commanded the regiment's scout company until very recently, but he seemed to understand tanks as well. His positioning of the three tank companies under his command was better than anything Basir could have come up with. They were well hidden and well placed to counter any Azanian attack from the south or west.

"When do we move out, sir?" Ormuz asked.

"Soon," Basir said. "I haven't received a warning order yet, but you can tell your men it will be soon. I would expect by tonight."

"A night attack, sir?" Ormuz was surprised.

"It's the damn airplanes," Basir said. "Even with damned Shaitan, we are much harder to see if we move at night. And in the dim light, we can get closer to the Azanians before they see us."

"Will we have fuel? I haven't received a fuel convoy since we moved out of Persepolis," Ormuz said, concern in his voice.

"It's being worked on," Basir said. "A convoy is on its way now."

"In the daylight?" Ormuz was surprised. "What about—"

"The damned Azanian planes, yes," Basir agreed. "That's being worked on, too."

"I hope so," Ormuz said, skeptically.

"Me, too," Basir said. "We'll be in before the storm, at least."

~ * ~

Farad Hashemi flew with a full wing of *Qaher* fighters high over the Gerdkooh. The hills rose and fell like the crests of waves in the ocean. Trees, real Earth trees, covered their slopes and hid everything beneath.

To the north, at the horizon's edge, was a wall of sand and smoke. The Seed Storm was coming down the Karun Valley, burning everything in its path. The kilometers-high wall of dust and ash bore down on the lands around Persepolis like a hungry monster. Farad was reminded of the swarm of pseudo-fish in the ocean and shuddered. The storm would arrive in a matter of days and put an end to all fighting around Persepolis.

All around him were dozens of Persian fighters. The Air Corps had scraped together the survivors from the attack on the Azanian fleet and all the planes which had fled to East Province after the initial Azanian surprise attack on the border airfields. Far beyond the range of the Azanian Air Force, the Persians had consolidated their survivors into new squadrons. The aircraft assigned to patrol duty in the east and north provinces had been recalled for the war with Azania. Together they had been kept in reserve, waiting for the right moment.

The moment had arrived.

Hashemi commanded the largest force of fighters yet fielded in the war. His mission was to gain total air superiority over the Gerdkooh hills. He had no idea why, but he knew it must be important. And he relished the mission. Without any bombers to escort, his fighters would be free to range at will, attacking any Azanians who dared oppose him.

Above and below, the fighter planes were stacked in finger-four formations from twenty thousand down to ten thousand feet. Farad's flight led them all.

"Enemy aircraft, bearing two-six-five, forty kilometers, twenty thousand," said the radio. "At least five," the controller added. A mobile ground radar brought up to the Gerdkooh was directing the Persian fighters.

"First squadron, intercept new contact," Farad transmitted.

Three of the finger-four formations accelerated and flew off to the west. The radar fed information to the fighters, but it was the fighter squadron leaders and wing commander who made tactical decisions in the Air Corps.

"Enemy aircraft, bearing two-six-zero, fifty kilometers, fifteen thousand, ten contacts," said the radio.

It was beginning, Farad thought. The Azanians had radar, too, and they couldn't miss so many Persian planes in the air. All over the eastern airfields of Azania and Siwa, the Azanian pilots would be scrambling to get their airplanes in the air.

Good, Farad thought, make them run for a change.

Farad directed a squadron to the new contacts and kept one eye on his map and the other on his fuel gauge. The Persian planes were flying out of the nearby airfields around Persepolis. They didn't have to go far to reach the front line. The Azanians had much further to fly and would not be able to stay over the battlefield for long. Farad intended to keep his planes over the Gerdkooh and draw the Azanians to him. His fighters would be able to fight longer, which would effectively increase his numbers over the battlefield.

The rest would be up to his pilots. They were motivated. All shared his rage at the arrogant Azanians, who had surprised their planes on the ground on the first day of the war. Many of their comrades were dead, having been killed on the ground, often in their sleep. It was no way for a pilot to die.

More contact reports came in from the ground radar controller. Farad gave his final deployments before the two air forces met in battle. Soon he would be very busy flying his own plane.

He saw the first Azanian fighters, their bare-metal finish glinting in the sun to the west. A formation of *Qaher*s dove at them, and the two groups broke up into a dogfight as pilots fought for their lives.

One by one, his squadrons engaged the enemy until Farad's was the only one left. He had stayed high so he could see the whole air battle and choose to fight where he was most needed.

"It will be as God wills," he said, as he opened the throttle of his *Qaher* and accelerated toward a wing of Azanian fighters. "Heaven awaits!"

~ * ~

Colonel Turani looked up through the trees to watch the maze of contrails overhead. He had never seen so many planes in the sky. He couldn't tell one side from the other, but he could see the explosion when a plane blew up, and the dark smoke of damaged or dying aircraft plummeting to the ground. Sometimes, a parachute would bloom, and a pilot would fall slowly back to the ground.

"We can't say the Air Corps failed to appear this time," he said to Shirazi.

"About time," Shirazi said. "Where have they been all this time?"

"I don't know," Basir said, "but I'm glad they are here now."

He wondered if Farad were up there. He hadn't heard anything about his friend since he'd arrived in Persepolis. He had no idea if Farad were alive or dead. If he were alive, Basir believed he would never miss the air battle he was watching right now.

"We need to make use of this," Basir said. "Find Captain Pahlavi. It's time to start moving. The Azanians won't notice with the air battle going on. If we can get a jump on our movement orders, we'll be closer to our objectives."

"Yes, sir," Shirazi said.

In a moment, Javad Pahlavi appeared.

"Get your scouts moving. I want a route for our road march to the starting line. We're moving out early."

"Yes, sir," said Javad. "May I make a suggestion?"

"Yes," Basir said.

"Can the First Battalion move out behind us? If we run into the enemy, we may have to fight a superior force."

"I don't want to trigger the plan too early," Basir said.

"But if we have to run for it, the enemy is going to run right into the regiment anyway," Javad said. "When have the Azanians failed to pursue?"

Basir nodded. One thing you could count on with the Azanians was aggression.

"We could set up an ambush in case it happens," Basir said, "but we are on the strategic offensive, and a fight in the Gerdkooh isn't what we want. I'll send the First Battalion with you. Don't get spotted and don't engage the enemy if you can help it. It's much better to maintain surprise."

"I understand," said Javad.

"Get moving," Basir said. "I'll tell Ormuz to follow you."

Thirty-six

Suri's little platoon approached the Delta Bridge from the west. She could see the metal and concrete structure rising from the river banks a kilometer away. The sound of firing and the streams of tracers came from the bridge. From where she was, Suri couldn't tell who was fighting whom or where they were.

A stream of soldiers appeared through the trees a hundred meters away. All her men dropped onto the ground, and the sergeant yelled a challenge. The other soldiers yelled in many voices not to shoot. There was no password challenge the different units shared, so the Persian accents and uniforms had to be enough. As they approached, Suri hoped they weren't Azanians in disguise.

It turned out they were part of an engineer unit whose officers had been killed by an air attack. Azanian paratroops had fallen from the sky immediately after, and the rest of the unit had fled.

Suri ordered them to join her platoon. Half of them, ten men, did. The rest insisted on continuing to the west. Suri had no desire to point guns at Persians, so she let them go. Perhaps it was a mistake, she thought, but she suspected that kind of discipline was not what was needed.

"You're crazy to fight them," one soldier said. "There's too many!"

"We'll see," Suri said.

Nasrin stood and watched the men retreating to the west. Holding her oversized rifle, she gazed at them with contempt. Two of them, unable to bear her look, changed their minds and came back.

The engineers brought with them their personal weapons and a few satchel charges full of explosives. Suri thought she may need those later.

Suri and Nasrin met another two shattered units retreating to the west and gathered those who were willing to fight into their force. After an hour, they had almost fifty men. It would have to be enough, Suri thought.

They heard a new sound. From the south came the crash of thunder. Artillery fire.

"There's fighting to the south," Suri said to Nasrin and her sergeant. "The Azanians must be coming from there. We need to take the bridge before they get here."

"What good is taking the bridge if we can't hold it?" the sergeant asked.

"We don't have to hold it if we can destroy it," Suri said. She called one of the engineers over. "Can you destroy the bridge?" she asked.

"I don't have enough explosives to do that," he said. "Ma'am."

"We'll have to figure it out later," Suri said. "Sergeant, how do we take a bridge?"

Fifteen minutes later, Suri, Nasrin, and the sergeant had crawled to the edge of the trees on the west bank of the river. The river was wide in the delta, here at least two hundred meters wide. The bridge was longer than that, and its ramps rose above each bank. They could see the span clearly and Azanian soldiers digging foxholes around the west ramp. There were disabled Persian vehicles all over the span.

"How many do you see, Sergeant," Suri asked.

He sucked in a breath between his teeth. "Maybe twenty, ma'am. And they are digging in. They've got a machine gun, too."

"Where?" Suri asked, and the sergeant pointed it out. It was hidden behind some rocks, and the crew was covering the position with branches cut from a tree.

Suri thought about it. She'd seen what a machine gun could do first-hand. It didn't matter how many men she had if the machine gun were active.

"We need to kill the gun," she said. The sergeant agreed. "Ideas?"

"Fire and maneuver," the sergeant said, and explained, "Take the enemy under fire with one force, then move another to flank him."

Suri looked around. "I think we can get within rifle range in the trees over there," she pointed to the north, "and perhaps if another force moved toward the bridge from where we are now—"

They spoke for a few minutes. "I think it's the best plan we have," Suri said. "How long will it take to get ready?"

"A half-hour," said the sergeant. "It's not complicated. Gonna be really hard to get the machine gun, where they have it."

Suri nodded.

Nasrin had been listening and watching. She waited for a break in the conversation and said, "Look at the bridge supports."

Suri did. She saw bundles of blocks connected to wires attached to the columns of concrete supporting the span.

"It's wired to blow," Suri said.

"Yes," Nasrin said. "The explosives are still there."

"If we can take the bridge before they disarm those..." Suri said.

"Yes," said Nasrin.

"Sergeant, get moving. We have an objective," Suri said.

The three carefully snuck back into the trees and found their ragtag platoon. Suri decided the covering force, who would first engage the enemy to fix them in place, would be the remnants of the units she had gathered along the way. The men were a mix of different units and couldn't be expected to advance under fire. They would take the machine gun and use it to suppress the Azanians.

The other group, who would maneuver to take the Azanians in the flank, would be the men of the escort force. Suri took some satchel charges from the engineers and gave them to some of her men.

It was time to go. Suri felt like this was when characters in stories would give a speech to incite the men to bravery and great deeds. She couldn't think of anything to say, and there was no time. She thought everyone understood the plan, so it would have to be enough.

"Let's go," she said.

The two forces split, one to the tree line to the north and the other south to the bridge approach. Suri checked her watch. Firing would begin in ten minutes.

"I hope you know what you're doing," Nasrin said and smiled.

"Me, too!" Suri said. "But don't let the men hear."

"They follow you," Nasrin said.

Suri considered it, and it was amazing that men whom she did not know were willing to take her orders. All because of the officer's tabs on her collar.

Reading her mind, Nasrin said, "It's more than the uniform, Suri. You've shown them."

Suri nodded, unsure of herself. "We'll find out if I can show them again."

Suri thought for a moment and said, "I want you to go with the other group."

"Why?" said Nasrin.

"We shouldn't both be in the same place. It would be a pity if both Farad and Basir lost their girlfriends on the same day."

"Nonsense!" said Nasrin. "Anyway, they could both be dead already."

"Happy thought, Nasrin," Suri said. "Seriously, I wish you would go with the other group. We will be depending on them, and I don't want them to run away."

"How am I supposed to keep them from running? I'm not an officer, like you. I can't give orders."

"No, but you can be you," Suri said.

"What do you mean?" Nasrin said.

"No man is going to run when you are around," Suri said.

"I think you underestimate—"

Suri cut her off, "Please, Nasrin, it would mean a lot."

Nasrin nodded. She hugged her friend and went to join the other element.

The remaining time until the attack passed in silence. Suri checked her watch every thirty seconds. She sweated despite the cold air and wet ground. Thoughts raced through her head. Doubts grew. What had she missed? Would she get more men killed? What if they failed? Her stomach contracted into a heavy stone.

Suri stared at her watch for the last minute. For the first thirty seconds, her fear built up to near panic. She wanted nothing more than to run away. Only her pride and the presence of the sergeant prevented her from following her impulse to flee.

When the fear reached a crescendo, and her heart felt as if it would burst from her chest, Suri felt a calm descend on her emotions. The air seemed to clear. Everything around her took on a crisp appearance. The colors were brighter. She could breathe deeply.

Suri was surprised when the firing began a few seconds early. A soldier who couldn't bear the waiting anymore had opened fire to the north.

The northern group formed a base of fire. The Persian machine gun opened up and sprayed the Azanian positions. The Azanians, reacting quickly, ducked in their holes. Their heads reappeared, and they raised their weapons to return fire. The individual pops of personal weapon fire punctuated the long hammering bursts of the machine gun.

The Azanian machine gun crew traversed their weapon on its tripod and fired to the north. Its barrel spat fire, and dust shook off the branches concealing its position. Suri had been watching for it, and when it fired, she gave her order.

With an even voice, Suri said, "Sergeant, move out!"

The maneuver element, half the platoon, broke cover and ran forward toward the bridge span. They closed the range by fifty meters before an Azanian saw them and began firing his rifle. Suri, not the fastest woman, fell behind her troops and could see the bullet impacts in the mud.

One rifle was not enough to stop twenty men. Even after one soldier was shot and fell, the rest kept going out of momentum. It was only when the machine gun turned its attention to the new threat that the advance stopped.

BRRRRRT came the sound of the machine-gun burst. A stream of tracers tore through the air toward Suri.

"Get down!" came a cry from the sergeant. The whole body of men dropped into the mud. One man was too slow and was shot twice. He fell in a bloody heap. The gun kept firing, traversing back and forth over their heads, hitting one man who was more exposed than the others. He screamed.

"Damn it!" Suri said. They'd covered half the distance to the Azanians. Only a hundred meters of muddy ground separated them from the nearest enemy. With the machine gun firing, it could have been a kilometer.

It was too far for grenades, and her earlier smoke trick wouldn't work because she had no more smoke grenades. If any of her men tried to fire, the Azanians would kill him in seconds.

It all depended on the fire element keeping the Azanians pinned. If they couldn't keep accurate fire raining on the Azanians, Suri's little group would be pinned and eventually killed.

The shifting of the Azanian machine gun's target was noticed. The fire coming from the tree line increased. The friendly machine gun found the range and walked its bursts into the Azanian positions. Individual soldiers, freed of the need to duck from the murderous machine-gun fire, squinted down their sights and fired at Azanians barely glimpsed at two hundred meters.

The Azanian machine gun stopped firing. Suri didn't know if it had run out of ammunition and had to change belts, or if its barrel had overheated and needed changing. Perhaps the crew was pinned by the Persian machine gun. She didn't know, and it didn't matter. Now was their chance.

"Get the satchel!" Suri cried.

"Cover me!" one of the soldiers yelled. He rose to his feet with a satchel charge in his hand. He sprinted for the machine gun nest.

The other soldiers lifted their rifles and sprayed bullets at anything they guessed could hide an Azanian.

The soldier made it fifty meters before an Azanian rifle bullet struck him in the chest. He took two steps before falling forward into the mud.

Suri watched him fall and felt as if she'd walked off a cliff. She'd ordered him to his death.

Shut up, Suri! A voice inside her cried. *Not now!*

"First squad, advance!" She yelled and rose to her feet. "Second squad, cover us!"

Half the remaining men got up out of the mud and ran forward. The others stayed down and continued firing their rifles.

Suri slogged forward, up to her ankles in mud. She felt as if she were barely moving. The men, while faster, still seemed to be crawling forward. One was shot, then another. Gunfire cracked all around her, from the Azanians ahead and the Persians covering her from behind. At any moment she expected to be shot herself. She found herself wondering what it would feel like.

One of the soldiers ahead picked up the satchel and carried it forward ten meters before being shot. The next soldier behind him scooped it up and took a few strides before he, too, was shot. This time, the Azanian who shot him was spotted and went down in a pummeling hail of bullets.

Suri plodded forward as fast as she could. She heard herself screaming, but no words came out.

The third man picked up the satchel, and Suri realized it was the sergeant. He ran forward to the machine gun nest and pulled a cord. He heaved the five-kilo charge into the air. With his burden released, he ducked for the ground.

At that moment, the machine gun fired one last time. The crew must have finished reloading, Suri thought. The gun fired a long killing burst into the sergeant. He fell backward, bleeding from a dozen wounds.

The charge landed inside the machine gunners' hole. The five kilograms of explosives detonated a second later.

The blast was channeled upward by the foxhole. Pieces of the gun, tripod, and the three Azanian soldiers flew into the air as if launched by a rocket. The bits fell in a grisly rain of death.

"Sergeant!" Suri cried, and realized she'd never known the man's name.

The destruction of the machine gun seemed to light a fire in the remaining men. With a cry of rage, they charged forward into the Azanian positions. The covering squad rose out of the mud to follow them.

A desperate close-range struggle ensued. Men charged foxholes and bayoneted the occupants. They threw grenades and ducked to avoid return fire. Suri saw two men dueling with bayonets before a third man shot one of the duelists. Both were covered with mud, and with the mist, she couldn't tell which side they were on.

Her own run brought her to the destroyed machine gun. She found the sergeant's body nearby and fell to her knees next to it.

He was dead. There was nothing she could do for him. Tears of sorrow and rage fell down her cheeks.

The covering squad arrived, and Suri got back to her feet. To the west, the covering element ceased fire because the Persians and Azanians were intermixed in a desperate fight to the death. Half of them were advancing at a run to support their brethren.

Suri took little part in the final combat. It was over quickly, and she was slower than the men. Once, she aimed her heavy service rifle at an Azanian, but someone else shot him before she could pull the trigger.

By the time the second element arrived, it was all over. The Azanians were dead except for two prisoners who had surrendered before they could be killed. Fortunately for them, they hadn't been seen firing before they surrendered. Suri doubted they would have survived otherwise. The Persian soldiers were enraged. So was she.

What remained of her command gathered at the west ramp of the bridge. The bridge rose up in an arch toward the east bank, and she could only see fifty meters across. Suri didn't know what was on the other side, but she knew what she would do if she were in charge of the Azanian force.

"Take positions to fire onto the bridge!" she ordered. "They'll be coming! Set up the machine gun!"

The Persians re-oriented themselves just in time. Over the bridge came two squads of Azanians running flat out for the west bank. The Persians poured fire into the mass of men, and they fell in groups of twos and threes. The Azanians, exposed, could not fire back effectively and turned to flee.

The Persians kept firing until no more living Azanians could be seen.

Silence fell on the platoon of soldiers holding the west bank of the bridge span. Suri did a count and was dismayed. Over a third of her force was missing. Thirteen men were dead or wounded, and another five were tending to them. She couldn't lose many more men before there were no more.

"Check ammo!" Suri ordered. "Redistribute it to the men who need it." When the men were done, she found out they were down to forty rounds each, with only one two-hundred-round belt for the machine gun. They had only one fight left in them before they were out of ammunition. Suri ordered her men to scavenge for Azanian weapons, but it wouldn't be enough.

Two things happened which offered her relief from her anxiety. The first was Nasrin's arrival.

"You made it!" Suri said, embracing her friend.

"Of course," Nasrin said. "All I had to do was hide behind a tree."

"The second element's base of fire saved us," Suri said. "They didn't run."

"It was not my doing," Nasrin insisted. Louder, she said, "The men fought well."

Several nearby soldiers nodded their heads.

The second thing was Suri's discovery of the engineer she had spoken to earlier. He was alive and unwounded.

"Can you blow the bridge?" Suri asked.

"If I can rewire the charges, yes," he said. "But I have to get to the supports."

Suri frowned. The supports were underneath the span, and getting there would require crossing the first third of the bridge span, totally exposed.

"But you can do it if we can get you there?"

"Yes," he said.

Suri nodded. She needed to think. All around was the detritus of war. Dead bodies, abandoned equipment, and the husks of burnt vehicles lost to the Azanian's initial attack on the bridge. The smell of smoke and death was in the air. Nasrin saw her friend ruminating.

"You better think fast," Nasrin said. "It's getting dark. The Azanians will try to cross in the dark."

"I would," Suri said. "We can't hold against another assault. We have to blow the bridge. We need a distraction. Some way to get onto the bridge without getting shot to hell."

"Too bad we don't have one of Basir's tanks," Nasrin said.

"No, we only have a truck—" Suri said, pointing at an abandoned but undamaged five-ton truck parked at the bottom of the ramp.

An idea flashed into her mind. She called the engineer back.

"Do you have any more explosives?"

"Yes, there's more than enough stored here for blowing the bridge," he said.

Suri explained her idea and asked him for details.

Thirty-seven

Captain Aran led his *Mbwa* tanks through the irrigated fields west of Persepolis. The ground was muddy, and he took care to avoid leading his tanks in a quagmire. He wasn't sure any but the lightest armored vehicles would be able to cross this terrain.

The highway to the south was blocked by a Persian tank force, and Aran had been sent to find a way around them. So far, he was having little success. The fields south of the enemy force had been flooded all the way to the Persian Gulf and were impassable to tanks. To the north, the situation wasn't much better. The Persians had chosen a perfect choke point to defend.

If they couldn't get past the Persian blocking force, they'd be stuck in the open when the Seed Storm arrived and put a stop to all combat. Caught without shelter, even armored vehicles were vulnerable to the fires started by the storm. They had to find a way to Persepolis quickly.

Aran came to another dead end. The ground was too wet for even the thirteen-ton *Mbwa* to cross. He turned his unit around and headed southeast. Perhaps there was another way.

As his tanks passed a homestead, miraculously untouched by artillery and aircraft bombs, he saw an old couple watching his tanks drive through their fields. They were old, but stood together, apparently unafraid. Aran almost waved but realized his tanks were ripping up their crops. He felt guilty. It was a strange thing to feel guilty about after all the other things he had done in the war. Perhaps he had killed their son in the fighting to the west. He couldn't know.

He stared back at them for a moment before turning away.

The tanks rolled on. Aran was grateful to still be in command of his company. His brigade commander had saved him from the wrath of the battalion commander he had disobeyed to negotiate the truce at the asylum. How far that mercy extended, Aran didn't know. He doubted he would be promoted again. The truce had held, the inmates had been evacuated, and the fighting resumed soon after. The Persians had been unable to stop them even with the break in the fighting.

After, the Azanian forces had leaped forward to the outskirts of Persepolis. According to the intelligence officer on the battalion staff, aerial reconnaissance had found almost nothing between the Azanian offensive and Persepolis. It was very strange to Aran. Shouldn't the enemy be trying to keep them away from their capital city? Or were they trying to draw the Azanians into a costly city fight? He'd been assured such a fight wasn't in the cards. There was a plan for Persepolis. Aran hoped so, but he didn't believe it. Plans had a way of going awry.

His tanks proceeded east until they encountered a canal running north-south, which wasn't on his map. He couldn't cross it, so he followed it south toward the sounds of battle.

Aran checked the radio and was surprised the fight hadn't moved east. This battle had gone on for a day and a half. Never had the Persians been able to hold the Azanian advance so long.

Another strange thing was the lack of planes in the sky. Aran had no idea where they were.

His tanks crested a hill and he could see the battle to the south.

The Azanians were pushing down Route One from the west on the coastal plain. Aran could see the Persian Gulf on the horizon.

On the road were the twisted, burning wrecks of dozens of tanks and other vehicles.

There the road passed through a small village. All that was left of the village was piles of rubble after a day and a half of artillery and airstrikes. Within, from his vantage point, Aran could see the source of Azanian frustration.

Inside the ruined village were the remains of a company of *Mobarez* heavy tanks. The behemoths were squat, with turrets like turtle shells over their enormous, flattened bodies. The tanks spouted huge puffs of smoke whenever they moved. Within the maze of rubble, the monsters hid until an enemy attack approached, and they came out to fight. The result of the fighting was the smoking hulks of Azanian tanks blown open by the *Mobs'* 120mm gun tubes.

Aran saw another attack happening before his eyes. Artillery pounded the village, but the huge tanks were impervious to anything but a direct hit from a heavy shell. The shell blasts barely rocked the heavy tanks, and the shrapnel did nothing but scratch their paint. The tanks, alerted by the artillery, lumbered to their firing positions.

The Azanians, behind a ragged smoke screen, tried to close with the village to a range where their guns had a chance to penetrate the foot-thick sloped glacis plates of the *Mobarez* tanks. Flank shots were impossible on the narrow coastal plain.

The *Mobs* crawled to their firing slots and waited for gaps in the smoke. When they spotted a tank through the blowing smoke, the *Mobarez* fired. Aran could hear the gun cracks as distinctive, loud booms. The high-velocity shells did not miss often. When they impacted an Azanian tank, the result was catastrophic. No tank in the world could stand up to the heavy 120mm shells fired by the *Mobarez*.

Aran saw the attack collapse into panic as the remaining Azanian tanks turned on their smoke generators and ran away.

From where he sat, he had a perfect view of the village. Any tanks here would be able to drop fire into the village and spot artillery fires. It was a perfect spot to outflank the enemy. His own tanks' 75mm guns were useless even against the side armor of the *Mobarez* tanks, but there were other guns in the Azanian arsenal.

Aran got on the radio and called in to report his status and position.

Thirty-eight

Farad dove his *Qaher* fighter into a formation of Azanian *Duma* fighter planes. The four-ship finger-four split into a high and low pair. Farad and his wingman pursued the two Dumas diving away. Farad directed the second pair in his formation to cover him by pursuing the Azanians breaking high.

It was down to the two pairs of fighters and the individual skills of the pilots. Farad aimed through his gyro gunsight at the trailing *Duma* of the pair. He fired off a short burst from his four 30mm cannons, but the Azanian cut hard to the right, and the rounds missed. With his excess speed from his dive, Farad could not turn hard enough to pursue. He continued his dive and turned it into a vertical scissors maneuver. Farad pointed his nose further down, rotated toward the Azanian, and then pulled his nose up until it pointed near the vertical. He was tracking the Azanian's turn from below. He firewalled the *Qaher*'s engines to maintain his speed.

The Azanian lost sight of him and reversed his turn to roll his aircraft for a look. Farad tracked the move and brought his fighter's nose in line with the pipper on the gunsight. He fired again. The rounds connected, and the *Duma* was blown to pieces. A fireball erupted in the sky and rained debris in a falling arc.

Farad immediately searched for the next threat. On the radio, he heard the top pair of his flight in trouble. He checked his wingman. He was pursuing the remaining Azanian of the first pair. Farad decided not to leave him to save his top pair. There were dozens of Persian and Azanians jets flying and fighting through the air all around. If he abandoned his wingman, he'd likely never find him again, and he'd leave the pilot at the mercy of any enemy fighter which flew past.

"Qabish, I remember," Farad said to himself.

He bracketed his wingman's course and set upon the enemy plane. The Azanian was turning wildly left and right but wasn't moving vertically. Farad pulled up to fly above the weaving pair before diving on top of the Azanian. With another burst of cannon fire, Farad blew off the right wing of the *Duma*. This time, the pilot escaped his spinning aircraft. Farad saw the parachute and was happy the Azanian would live. Perhaps someday they would meet and talk over tea.

Farad commanded himself to pay attention and searched the skies for more enemy planes. The other pair in his flight were still weaving a twisting ball of contrails overhead with the Azanians. Farad and his wingman climbed to assist. He saw similar combats all around as formations broke up into ones and twos. Planes fell in smoking trails, and parachutes bloomed like white flowers.

The "furball" of dogfights drifted downward as the fighter planes maneuvered and lost altitude. Farad's flight was one of the dozens engaged. None of the pilots could tell who was winning the battle.

Down below, on the ground, it didn't matter who was winning. The battle was consuming the full attention of the Azanian Air Force. No recon flights spotted the movement of the Persian tanks in the Gerdkooh. No fighter-bombers could be spared to counter them. The air battle was already a success.

~ * ~

Colonel Basir Turani stood in his mobile command post, three command carriers parked in a triangle covered with camouflage netting sitting beneath a thick canopy of trees. He ordered the final preparations for the attack over the radio and by field telephone. The radio antennas were some distance away, so enemy aircraft could not home in on their transmissions and bomb the command post. A rat's nest of telephone wires snaked in all directions to connect Colonel Turani with the nearest units.

All the battalions were in place. Javad's scouts had led them all to their start lines without encountering any Azanians. The artillery fire plan was drawn up, but the big guns wouldn't fire until the tanks were moving. Basir wanted no indication of his attack to reach the Azanian commanders until it was too late.

The scouts were out ahead, searching for the nearest Azanian units. Once they found them, Basir would order artillery to suppress them so his tanks could close with or bypass them, as appropriate.

The scouts were closing in on Route One, the Western Highway, and still had encountered little in the way of organized resistance. Could it be the Azanians had left their flank exposed? Basir found it incredible. Perhaps they had something planned? Was it a trap? He couldn't know. He hadn't seen an Azanian commander make a mistake like this. Maybe their forces really were stretched thin by the advance on Persepolis, and they simply didn't have enough to cover their north flank.

If it were a trap, he would be the first to know. His regiment of the Capital Corps was the lead unit of the counter-offensive.

He looked at his watch. It was time. He took the radio transmitter and made sure he had the correct frequency.

"ALL UNITS, THIS IS CHARLIE SIX ZERO, THE ORDER IS GO," he said.

All around, tanks started their diesel engines and whined to life. The clank of the *Karars'* treads filled the forest. A hundred tanks began moving south toward the Route One highway, the lifeline of the Azanian assault on Persepolis.

"Let's get ready to move," Basir told Shirazi. "I have a feeling we won't need to stay here for long."

The command post staff began packing up their things and preparing the command carriers to follow the tanks south.

Thirty-nine

Suri and Nasrin watched the truck drive up the bridge ramp toward the main span. The truck had no driver. The engineers had jammed the steering wheel in place and locked the throttle open before releasing the brake and clutch. The engine whined, and the transmission screamed. The truck was stuck in second gear. It made its way up the ramp, and it looked as if the engineers had done a good job aiming the truck down the middle of the road.

After a few more seconds, the truck drifted to the left. Suri held her breath. Would it make it to the middle of the span or get stuck? To her relief, the truck scraped the guardrail but kept moving up the span. Sparks flew as the steel bumper scraped the left guardrail of the bridge.

Behind the truck, a line of cord unraveled from a spool in the truck bed. The cord led to a plunger in the hands of the engineer next to Suri and Nasrin.

The truck crested the middle of the span, and the Azanians opened fire. A barrage of bullets shattered the windshield, perforated the radiator, and flattened the tires. The truck scraped along the left guardrail until its right front tire was shot out, and the wheel rim dug into the pavement and jerked the truck into the middle of the bridge.

More bullets riddled the truck, and it ground to a stop in a cloud of steam from the radiator.

"Hit it!" Suri yelled and covered her ears. The engineer pressed the plunger, and an electrical impulse shot down the wire and triggered the bomb.

One hundred kilos of explosives blew the truck apart in a flash of light. The supersonic blast wave cracked across the span and over the heads of Suri and her companions on the entry ramp. The explosion sent fragments of the truck in all directions, whizzing over Suri's head in a deadly arc. The bomb blew a shallow crater in the bridge span's concrete roadbed, but since the blast was directed upward and outward, it did nothing to compromise the bridge's structural integrity.

"All right, let's go!" Suri cried. "Move out!" Her ears rang from the sound of the blast.

Her little force followed her up the ramp. Within a few seconds, metal fragments from the truck and concrete from the blasted roadbed fell from the sky in a deadly rain. Suri could do nothing but ignore them and hope none fell on her head. She wore no helmet, and her mud-matted hair stuck out at all angles.

Suri crouched unconsciously as she approached the crest of the bridge, where the road flattened out to cross the river. She was exposed to Azanian fire from the other side. None came. The enemy had been killed or stunned by the truck bomb. Shattered bodies lay on the span. Smoke still drifted from the blast.

"Get the charges wired!" Suri ordered.

An engineer with a roll of wire ran to the edge of the road. Another tied a rope to the guardrail. The first man climbed over the rail and slid down the rope, trailing the detonation wire as he went.

Suri decided to push forward a few more yards to cover the engineers. When she had taken ten steps, shots greeted her. Steel-jacketed rounds buzzed past her head like angry insects. She dropped prone onto the pavement. The rest of her men did likewise.

Not knowing what else to do, Suri fired her rifle down the bridge span even though she couldn't see any Azanians. The mist and smoke made it difficult to tell where the shots were coming from.

The man next to her was hit and cried out. Suri turned in surprise. Then another bullet hit the pavement where her head had been. She rolled to the right in fright.

She saw a flash high above as she rolled. An Azanian soldier had climbed into the bridge's metal superstructure arching over the span. Suri cried out and pointed with her rifle. Another bullet smacked the concrete between her legs, and she rolled the other direction.

Suri thought she was doomed. She was pinned, unable to get up and run and spread out on the pavement like an insect, exposed to the sniper far above.

The machine gun fired behind her. A long burst sent rounds sparking in the metal arch until one found its mark. The Azanian mortally wounded, fell from the arch past the road span and plummeted out of sight below to fall in the river.

Suri crawled back to the engineer holding the rope.

"How long?" she asked.

"I don't know," he said. "I can't see him down there." He let out some rope in response to a tug from below.

"Make it fast!" Suri said unnecessarily. She crawled back to the front and directed the machine gun to fire down the span at waist height.

The bridge rumbled with a new sound. Over the sound of gunfire came a clanking and rattling sound. Suri had heard it before.

Out of the mist and smoke came the dim outline of a squat vehicle. The rumbling grew in strength like the growl of an angry beast. The shape came closer, and its lines sharpened as it came into view.

"Tank!" someone cried.

The Azanian tank clambered slowly onto the span. Its turret tracked from side to side, searching for targets.

Suri cursed. It wasn't fair! She had no anti-tank weapons, and her men were trapped on the span at the mercy of the tank's machine guns. The Azanian relief force must have arrived.

A man, terrified by the appearance of the metal monster, got up and ran. The tank spat fire from its coaxial machine gun and cut him down.

Suri felt panic all around her. She sensed the men were about to run. She felt the same impulse. What could she do against the tank?

Nasrin saw the tank and immediately knew what it meant. The tank could clear the entire span of the Persians by driving forward slowly and sweeping the road with its machine guns like a broom. Her mind almost stopped working in a paroxysm of panic, but a thought came to her. She'd seen the Azanian sniper fall from the girders above.

Rising to a crouch, Nasrin hurried over to one of the soldiers. She took a bundle from him before he could object. Running as fast as her long legs could carry her, she reached a metal support. She shouldered the bundle and started climbing up the metal stanchion.

The tank spotted her and fired its machine gun, but the rounds missed behind her. She was behind the metal support before she could be hit.

The tank turned its attention back to the road. Suri tried firing her rifle at the tank's treads, the most vulnerable part, but the bullets did nothing to the steel and rubber links. Another soldier tried throwing a grenade beneath the tank, but it exploded harmlessly on the pavement in front of the machine. Still, the tank came on at a walking pace, clanking on its treads, unstoppable.

Suri rolled to the side of the span and tried to make herself small. She prayed the tank wouldn't see her or think her dead.

Streams of bullets thudded into the pavement all around. Some of the thuds were followed with screams as cowering soldiers were hit.

"It isn't fair!" she cried. "I got them this far, and it isn't fair!"

The tank didn't hear her. The monster kept coming like a juggernaut.

Above, Nasrin scrambled up the metal beam to one of the dual arches holding up the bridge. There was one supporting each side of the roadway. Between them were cross-supports. She climbed up the arch until she reached a crossbeam. It wasn't as thick as the arch, and her arms and legs hung over the sides as she shimmied across.

Below, Azanian soldiers had risen to their feet to follow the tank across the bridge. They stopped to aim at helpless Persians cowering in front of the tank. One happened to look up and saw Nasrin. He raised his rifle and took aim.

The bullet cracked by Nasrin's head and startled her badly enough that she almost fell off the crossbeam. She tried to pull her arms and legs in as far as she could and kept crawling toward the middle of the roadway.

More bullets whizzed by. Other soldiers had noticed her up above. Sparks shot off the steel beam in front of her, and ricochets whizzed overhead.

Nasrin glanced down and tried to judge where she was above the road. The tank appeared to be directly below.

She took the satchel from her shoulder and pulled the wire as she'd seen the other soldiers do. Nothing seemed to happen, but she lowered the satchel by one arm while precariously balancing on the beam. She looked down and lined up the bag with her eye.

An Azanian took careful aim and fired. The bullet hit Nasrin in the right shoulder.

The blow hammered Nasrin so hard she almost lost her hold on the beam. She dropped the satchel, and it fell.

The bomb fell from the crossbeam fifty feet in the air. Everyone who was looking up saw the satchel drop. A dozen pairs of eyes followed its plunge on the rear deck of the tank.

A moment passed, and the firing seemed to stop as everyone waited to see what would happen.

The five kilos of explosives in the satchel charge blew open the engine vent on the top deck of the tank. The fuel lines burst, and a fireball rose into the air. Black smoke poured from the ruined tank.

Suri screamed in triumph and relief. She had no idea who had dropped the bomb. She looked up and saw Nasrin.

Nasrin couldn't move. Her shoulder hadn't started hurting yet, but she was woozy with shock. Her one good arm clung to the steel girder. She tried backtracking while straddling the beam with her legs, but it was slow and painful.

Suri watched Nasrin with concern as she wobbled on the beam and almost fell. Suri ran over to the nearest beam and looked up, ready to climb.

An engineer interrupted her. "The charge is wired!" he said. "It's ready to blow!"

Suri blinked in surprise. In her concern for Nasrin, she had forgotten why they had come.

She took a deep breath. "Get off the bridge. Tell everyone to rally at the base of the ramp. Make sure the wounded aren't left behind."

The engineer looked at her curiously. "What are you doin', ma'am?"

"I'm going to save my friend," Suri said.

The engineer looked up and then back at Suri. "That's a bad idea, ma'am. The Azanians will be coming. They'll shoot you both right off there."

"Do it, Corporal," Suri said and clambered onto the girder.

"Beggin' your pardon, I won't!" he said and grabbed Suri from behind.

"What are you doing!" she screamed. Another soldier ran over, and the two of them bodily removed her from the girder.

"You's coming with us!"

"No! We can't leave Nasrin!" Suri cried.

"She's dead already," the engineer corporal said. "You's alive, and you can thank me later."

Nasrin felt a warm haze overcome her. She laid back down, face-first on the cool steel girder. She could see Suri being carried away and thought it was very funny. She was flying, like Farad. Blood seeped out of her shoulder wound and soaked her shirt. Drops dribbled off the steel beam and fell like rain onto the roadway far below.

"No!" Suri cried. "No!"

The Persians ran east, with one soldier unspooling a thin cable behind him. They ran past the bomb crater and down the ramp. Azanian bullets chased them.

At the base of the ramp, the soldiers gathered. The engineer put Suri down on her feet. She punched him as hard as she could.

"You bastard!" she cried.

"Yes, ma'am," he said.

The soldier unspooling the cord ran to them and connected the cord to a plunger.

"The charges are wired, ma'am!" he said. "We can blow the bridge!"

Suri felt tears coming to her eyes. She couldn't give the order. Nasrin was still up there, helpless, hanging in the girders.

"Ma'am, they're coming this way. They'll cut the wire," the engineer said. He pointed, and she saw Azanian soldiers reaching the crest of the roadway and spreading out.

"No!" Suri said.

"Ma'am, you have to," the engineer said quietly. "We can't save your friend. I lost friends today, too."

"Damnit!" Suri said. "Do it! Do it now! Before I change my mind!"

The soldier with the plunger pushed it down with a click, and the bridge erupted. The charges blew and cut the supports in half. The bridge wobbled for a few seconds, and then the roadway twisted and thrashed like a living thing. Azanian soldiers tried to run but were caught in the collapse. The eastern third of the bridge fell into the river in an avalanche of noise and dust. The water roiled and splashed as the debris fell in.

Suri looked for the crossbeam where Nasrin laid, but it was gone. She was gone.

Forty

Under the Shaitan-twilight in the Gerdkooh hills, Colonel Basir Turani couldn't believe how well things were going. His battalions were driving south as fast as they could go against minimal resistance from the Azanians. His staff had set up their headquarters twice, only to pack up again almost immediately when the front line moved forward again.

He knew he would have to stop his frontline units soon, though. Lack of fuel and ammunition would halt them, even if the enemy could not.

"We need to get to Route One before we stop to rearm and refuel," he said to Shirazi, who nodded. "Pass on to all battalions not to halt before reaching the highway. No one is to stop for daylight, either. Time is our enemy more than Azanian planes."

His three armored battalions were poised to cut the east-west road link supplying all Azanian forces attacking Persepolis.

His first battalion, led by Major Ormuz, reported in. Shirazi dutifully recorded a message, then scribbled a note on the map spread out on a table beneath the camouflage netting.

"Some resistance, sir. He estimates a company of Azanian tanks," Shirazi said.

"Tell Ormuz to fix them in place with one company and bypass them here," he pointed at a valley on the map, "and here. If it turns out to be more than a company, we'll bring up the third battalion and smash them." Basir had kept his third battalion in reserve while the other two pressed forward.

Shirazi nodded and passed on the message. Basir ordered a battery of mobile guns to engage the new enemy unit for good measure. He couldn't afford to be slowed down.

"If they can just keep moving forward until daybreak," he said. "We may pull this off."

The radio buzzed again, and Shirazi answered.

"Scout company reports Route One in sight, sir," he said, his voice full of excitement. "Enemy logistics units in sight."

~ * ~

Captain Javad Pahlavi was more excited than he'd ever been in his life. He rode in the commander's seat of a *Tosan* light tank. Like the Azanian *Mbwa*, the *Tosan* was lighter than the main battle tanks and could go more places more quickly than heavier armor. The price they paid for their mobility was a smaller gun and thin armor. Right now, it wasn't a problem.

Javad's tank sat at the edge of the woods overlooking Route One. Before him, stretching from left to right as far as he could see was a line of vehicles moving west on both lanes of the highway. Trucks carrying stores and fuel, anti-aircraft vehicles, infantry carriers, and prime movers pulling towed artillery drove by. There were no tanks to be seen.

He called in his report to regimental headquarters, trying to contain the excitement in his voice. He wanted to attack right away, but he knew if he got too far ahead of the rest of the regiment, he could bite off more than he could chew.

"You are permitted to engage the enemy," came the call from Shirazi on the radio.

Javad didn't order his units to charge right away. First, he carefully called in an artillery fire mission targeting the road to the east and west. The barrages would cut off this section of the highway from reinforcement from either direction. Only after the first few rounds fell on target did he order his tanks and infantry carriers to advance.

Ten kilometers north, within the forest of the Gerdkooh, two batteries of self-propelled guns aimed their long 150mm cannon into the sky. They fired ranging shots, and Javad watched them impact near the highway. He called in range corrections and the fire direction centers for each battery. A group of men in a nearby infantry carrier, whose job it was to calculate the fall of shot, issued corrections to the guns' aim. When that was accomplished, the guns fired again. This time their shells were on target.

"Fire for effect!" Javad said into his radio.

The batteries fired a special kind of shell. They were variable-time shells programmed to burst above the ground, showering the enemy below with metal fragments. The shells lit up the twilight like lightning, and their bursts sounded like a staccato thunder. The airbursts ripped through the thin-skinned vehicles clogging the highway. Hot shrapnel cut fuel lines and set trucks aflame. One tanker truck, cut open in a dozen places by a shell, exploded into a fireball, spraying burning fuel all over the area.

The two artillery fires cut off a kilometer-long section of road. Onto this section fell the ten *Tosans* of Javad's scout company. The tanks broke out of the woods to the north of the road and rolled forward until they had good firing positions. Then each tank began firing its 75mm main gun and two machine guns.

The results were devastating. Unarmored vehicles exploded into pieces when hit by tank shells. Machine-gun bursts cut down men fleeing from their stalled trucks. Spilled fuel caught fire and added to the holocaust engulfing the trapped Azanians on Route One.

The armored carriers of Captain Pahlavi's company followed the tanks and added their own machine-gun fire to the slaughter. When the smoke from the burning trucks on the highway became too thick, Javad ordered his tanks forward to complete the destruction of the Azanians and to seize the roadway.

Javad's *Tosans* rolled forward, firing their weapons on the move. The Azanians had nothing with which to stop them. A few brave souls fired their personal weapons at him, but he or one of his companion tanks cut them down with short bursts from their machine guns.

In fifteen minutes, it was all over. No Azanians remained to fight. The highway was a clogged ruin of smoking metal and dead soldiers. Javad reported his success to regiment.

~ * ~

In his command post, Basir listened to the reports over a radio speaker. He didn't want Shirazi to have all the fun.

The enemy unit Ormuz had reported had retreated when outflanked to both sides. Ormuz chased it with one company while the other two companies of *Karars* pushed for the road, following the path Captain Pahlavi had scouted.

As day broke, the 1ˢᵗ Regiment of the Capital Corps, The Primes, had straddled the main supply route of the enemy force attacking Persepolis. The Azanians were cut off.

~ * ~

Farad landed his *Qaher* fighter and climbed out of the cockpit, drenched in sweat. His flight suit smelled like a sewer. He'd flown three sorties over the Gerdkooh, returning to airbase P-2 each time only long enough to refuel and rearm. The Persian Air Corps had put out a maximum effort to surge planes over the critical battlefield, whatever the cost.

The cost had been very high. Of the 96 aircraft in Farad's wing, half had been shot down or were too damaged to fly again. Of those shot down, many of the pilots had not yet been found after bailing out over the Gerdkooh. Fortunately, it was friendly territory, and a pilot who was picked up by friendly forces could expect to be back at an airfield within a day.

For the Azanians, the situation was very different. Forced to engage the Persians far from their own bases, the Azanian Air Force had not been able to keep as many planes over the battlefield, as each plane had a limited endurance because of fuel constraints. Less fuel meant less freedom to maneuver and often forced planes to break off instead of following through on attacks. The Azanians, though outnumbering the Persians overall, had fewer planes fighting in the air battle at any moment, and the results showed it. If the kill claims could be believed, and Farad knew *he* never exaggerated *his* kills, over one hundred Azanian planes had been shot down by his wing. Once the gun camera films were examined, his ground crew would be painting four more kill markers beneath his cockpit.

As remarkable as this result was, Farad knew the critical battle would be won or lost on the ground. He'd never admit it, but he knew the air battle had only been a part of the desperate offensive to save Persepolis. Even so, it was a battle his pilots had won decisively.

So it was that Farad was smiling as his feet hit the tarmac, and he walked proudly toward the squadron building, where he'd debrief his men and order them to get some rest before tomorrow's missions.

~ * ~

Captain Aran didn't know what to do. The radio net was chaos, full of conflicting orders, and calls for assistance. The Persian counteroffensive had caught everyone by surprise. The Persians had attacked out of the Gerdkooh, an area judged unsuitable for tanks and left with only a very light screening force to guard it.

Aran believed the Persians must have left their capital virtually unguarded to find the forces to counterattack. It didn't matter, though. With his help, the main offensive column had finally overcome the resistance of the *Mobarez* heavy tanks dug in across the road, but the attack toward Persepolis could not continue without the delivery of enormous amounts of supplies, especially fuel. Without fuel, the Azanian tanks would soon be immobilized and be left as stationary pillboxes along the road.

Aran was left with the task of finding a way out of the mess. There was no apparent escape. He stared at his map. To the north was the Gerdkooh, full of Persians. To the east was Persepolis, their main objective, but they didn't have the supplies to press forward. To the south was the Persian Gulf, and to the west, the road was blocked by Persian tanks.

They could try to break out to the west and break the blockade, and this was, in fact, what the main strike force was doing. They'd turned three brigades of tanks to the west in the hope of breaking through the Persians and restoring the main supply route. Aran had no idea if they would succeed.

He did know throwing his light tanks into a cauldron like that was suicidal. He would do it if ordered but in the meantime—

He glanced at the map and found an odd marking. A port, the map key said. Of course, he thought. If things got even worse, a port would be useful. The Azanian fleet still sailed. Aran radioed his few remaining tanks to follow him and headed for the port of Bandar.

Forty-one

Colonel Turani had boarded his command carrier again and followed his forces to Route One. He had placed his HQ in a small depression near the road and hoped he wouldn't have to move again.

The whole regiment was in defensive positions on the south side of the highway. The north side had been taken by his old unit, the Prince's Own, which had followed the Primes out of the Gerdkooh. Engineers from both regiments were busy digging revetments for the tanks and the infantry was out digging foxholes for themselves.

He'd planned a textbook fixed defense because there were few other options. He could set up a mobile defense or even meet the Azanians charging west by charging east himself. The Azanians tended to be better in that sort of fight, so Basir chose an option his own forces were more comfortable with. His first battalion under Ormuz was a mobile reserve, but the other two were well dug in south of the road. Captain Pahlavi's scouts were out ahead of the line probing to the east, seeking out the Azanian attack. To the west, he'd detached a company of infantry to man a roadblock and cover the road to Siwa just in case.

The first sun was high in the sky before the Azanians appeared. Basir was most concerned about a push to outflank the Prince's Own

Regiment to his left, guarding the northern side of Route One. He deployed his 1st Battalion close to the northern limit of his area of responsibility for this eventuality. If he had to attack a force such as his, dug in and prepared, he'd do his best to outflank it.

As it happened, the first Azanians encountered were to the front. The enemy launched a short preparatory bombardment from their mobile artillery batteries, which caused some casualties but could do little to dug-in *Karar* tanks. Then smoke rounds landed to lay a screen in front of the regiment's positions. Neither the artillery bombardment nor the smoke barrage was as intense as Basir expected. Perhaps the Azanian supply situation was even worse than he imagined.

Aircraft flew overhead, and to Basir's relief, they were Persian. Since the shootout over the Gerdkooh, the Azanian Air Force had become reluctant to appear over the battlefield. Persian aircraft flew over the Azanian lines. Some were on reconnaissance missions, taking pictures to provide ground commanders with up-to-date intelligence on the Azanian forces. Others carried sticks of bombs and dropped them on the advancing enemy. From Basir's command post, the explosions sounded like distant fireworks.

Some of the planes sought out the enemy artillery. One successful strike sent a towering pillar of smoke into the air, fed by exploding munitions.

When the enemy reached the smokescreen, the *Karar* tanks dug in south of the road opened fire. The smoke had allowed the Azanians to advance within half a kilometer of the Persian tanks. Half-visible shapes appearing and disappearing between wind-blown smoke clouds drew the first shells. Within a minute, the Azanian tanks penetrated the screen and ran flat-out toward the Persian lines.

The Persian *Karar* tanks were built for exactly this kind of fight. Heavily armored and mounting a 100mm rapid-fire gun, the *Karar* could fire eight aimed rounds a minute. The crews Basir had inherited were not the equals of those he'd left behind in the Prince's Own Regiment, but they were good enough to hit targets at less than five hundred meters.

The *Karars* were dug in behind dirt revetments where possible. When they were exposed, their thick frontal glacis plates were still more than a match for most hits.

The Azanians employed the *Nyati* medium tank, which was faster than the *Karar*, with a similar gun, but not as well armored. It was best used with the traditional Azanian maneuver and flanking tactics, which had been so successful up to this point of the war. Charging straight into enemy defenses was not what the tank was designed to do.

The *Karar* tanks opened fire first and killed six Azanian *Nyaris*. The Azanian return volley hit many Persian tanks, but the thick armor and deep holes saved most of them from destruction. Only two were destroyed, and another *Karar* damaged. The Azanians fired on the move, reducing their accuracy but closing the range to the Persians.

In this kind of fight, where maneuver counted for little and the outcome was determined by who could put the most steel on target, the Persians came out ahead. The Persian gun crews were just as capable as the Azanians, and fighting from prepared positions with an enemy to their front was an easy test of their skills. A dozen more Azanian tanks were destroyed, and only a few Persian tanks fell victim to their shells.

Basir was concerned about how easy it was. His front-line battalions were going to stop the Azanians cold without him needing to commit his reserves. Was this a feint? If so, where was the real attack? He wracked his brain thinking of possibilities. Another paradrop? An amphibious landing to his rear? What was the Azanian plan?

The Prince's Own Regiment's guns fired to the north, across Route One. Soon, they were as heavily engaged as the Primes. To their north, within the confines of the Gerdkooh, a close-range battle embroiled the tanks and infantry of the Capital Corps against an attempt by the Azanians to outflank the road. The rough hill country did not allow much room for the mechanized Azanian forces to maneuver, and they did not find a flank to turn.

Basir waited, listening to the radio and carefully watching the notations Shirazi made on the map. He also listened to the tempo of the gunfire to the east. When the word came the Azanians were retreating, Basir unleashed his 1st Battalion.

"Tell Major Ormuz to pursue the enemy," he said to Shirazi. "Caution him not to chase them beyond the range of friendly artillery."

The *Karar* tanks of the 1st Battalion broke cover and emerged from their hiding places under trees and camouflage netting. Forming into three company-sized wedges, the three dozen tanks spread out and rolled after the retreating Azanians. The Azanians who had made it back to their own front line stopped and tried to form a defense. Ormuz didn't allow them the time needed to take up defensive positions but kept rolling forward.

The Persian *Karar* tanks caught the Azanians who stood and fought, and destroyed them with direct fire. The 1st Battalion formed up into a line when they reached the Azanian jump-off point, the limit of artillery range from Persian lines. From there, the *Karar* tanks picked off the fleeing Azanian tanks and infantry carriers.

At this point, encouraged by his 1st Battalion's advance, Basir ordered the battered but still deadly 2nd and 3rd Battalions to advance to the 1st Battalion's new positions. He also ordered the artillery to move up as well. Soon, he was watching Shirazi and his staff packing up the command carriers to move the command post yet again.

A quarter-hour later, bouncing around inside of his advancing command carrier, Basir was coordinating his regiment's advance with the movement of the Prince's Own Regiment to his north. He didn't want a gap to open between the two units which the Azanians could exploit. So far, the Azanians seemed unable to stop his counterattack. Proud units that had advanced hundreds of kilometers from the Siwan border to the gates of Persepolis were fleeing from his tanks. Basir wished to keep the pressure on and prevent the Azanian commanders from catching their breath and forming a defense or an effective counterattack. He had a high degree of respect for his opponents and wouldn't give them any chance if he could help it.

Forty-two

Suri Pahlavi watched artillery shells land on the other side of the river. The explosions dredged up chunks of earth and mud and hurled them into the sky. The ruined bridge's eastern third still stood, but the rest was a wreck of twisted metal and concrete dragging in the river current. It was raining heavily and the ground was liquid mud.

Her little force had been relieved by the 743rd Motorized Infantry Regiment, a reserve mobilization unit called up from the East Province. The Easterners spoke with pronounced accents and were shorter than average, but they fought well. They rapidly occupied the west bank of the river and repelled a nighttime river crossing by Azanians in small boats. Artillery fire from both sides lit up the night like a thunderstorm and shook the ground like an earthquake. Suri had retired to a bunker after five minutes, having seen enough.

She had been pulled off the line upon the arrival of the combat troops from the 743rd. No comment had been made about her presence or her status as a *Bar Basiji*. The men of the relief force heard the story of the little ragtag band of engineers and security troops with incredulity. This was the 743rd's first taste of combat. Suri's band of muddy veterans accompanied her to the regimental HQ.

Suri had come out of the rain and the colonel in charge of the regiment had received her, listened to her report, nodded, and directed her to his command bunker. There she stayed, drinking tea and wishing for a clean uniform.

She was pondering the events of the last day when a soldier entered the bunker. He was carrying her briefcase.

"I was thinkin' this was you's, ma'am," he said.

Suri looked at the case with surprise, then guilt at having forgotten all about her charge.

"Thank you," she said and retrieved the case. She took the briefcase in her arms and returned to the colonel. She explained she was a courier and had a message to deliver to his superior, the military district commander. The colonel, probably not a little relieved to be rid of her, granted her a command car and a driver to take her there.

Suri said a hurried goodbye to her men, hoping she would see them again, alive.

Once she was away from the bunker, she told the driver, "You can come with me, but I'm driving."

After traveling through innumerable checkpoints and dodging through endless convoy traffic, Suri reached the town of 'Abad. The district HQ was housed in a commandeered council hall, having outgrown its peacetime location. Suri wiped her feet before entering but could not get all the mud off her boots.

She found the clean floors and strangely intact walls of the HQ bizarre. Men in clean uniforms with creases walked around with papers in their hands. Many stopped to stare at her. Her uniform was tattered and covered in mud and blood. She wondered if she even looked like a woman anymore.

She showed her security badge to a guard and was admitted to see the general. He was a middle-aged man, clearly a reservist, with a uniform that was too tight around his waist. He looked at her in surprise but didn't say anything about the condition of her uniform. He took the case from her hands.

"Thank you, Lieutenant," he said. "That will be all."

Suri saluted but did not leave. She was suddenly very curious about the contents of the case. What had been so important to bring her and Nasrin into the maelstrom of battle in the Karun Delta?

When she didn't depart, the general looked up at her, furrowing his brow. "Yes, Lieutenant?" he said.

"Sir," she said, trying to keep her voice from cracking with fatigue, "I would like to know what the message was. Was it important?"

The general raised his eyebrows. "That is a very irregular request," he said. "You are a courier, and you aren't supposed to ask what you are carrying."

"I know, sir," Suri said. "I'm sorry, sir."

"Quite," he said. He seemed to think over her request for a minute.

"Nevertheless," he said, "given your conduct over the last two days, perhaps…" he trailed off. He removed a key from his desk and unlocked the battered briefcase. Inside were reams of documents. Suri tried to keep her eyes away from the secrets inside.

The general took out the first few sheets and read them carefully. Suri waited motionlessly.

Finally, he spoke. "I'm afraid, Lieutenant, that these papers are the plans for an Azanian landing on the coast, as well as a parachute assault on the Delta Bridge."

Suri blinked twice and took in his words.

"You mean," she said, "I was too late?"

The general thought about it for a moment, and said, "No, Lieutenant Pahlavi, you were just in time. If the Azanians had seized the bridge, the defense of Persepolis would have been impossible. The enemy would have taken the city from the east. The message you carried may not have reached its destination in time, but you reached the bridge exactly when you were needed."

"So you know about what happened?" Suri said, surprised.

"Yes, of course," the general said. "Colonel Reynan of the Seven Hundred Forty-Third forwarded his report when he arrived."

"But Nasrin," Suri said. "She's dead."

"General Avesta's daughter?" the general said, "That is very unfortunate. He already lost his wife in the air raid. A double blow."

Suri blinked back tears. She was sad for Nasrin and hadn't thought of her father.

"I'm going to put you in for the Star Medal," the general said. "It's highly irregular, of course, you being a, well, a *Bar Basiji*."

Suri didn't know what to say, so she said, "Thank you, sir."

"Even the prince regent will hear of this," the general said. "You may have saved the empire from defeat."

Suri didn't believe him. All she'd done was to lead two dozen people to their deaths, including her best friend.

"In the meantime," the general continued, "you should get cleaned up. I'll make sure you are assigned a room in the officer's quarters. I'll report your arrival to your superiors."

"Thank you, sir," Suri said, feeling very tired.

"Dismissed," the general said.

This time, Suri saluted and turned on her heel to leave. She strode out into the office, where she waited for an orderly to supply her with new orders so she could stay at the officer's quarters in 'Abad.

When she arrived at her new room, Suri couldn't summon the strength to strip out of her uniform. Not wanting to dirty the linens of her bed, she collapsed on the floor with her boots on. Before she could fall asleep, she started to cry. Great, wracking sobs escaped her lips. She couldn't stop. Tears flowed out of her like a river.

"I'm sorry, Nasrin," she said. "I'm so sorry."

Forty-three

General Avesta looked at the map with satisfaction. The prince was with him in the war room under the Council of Ministers building. Both men had been pushed to the limits of their nerves by the events of the last day. First, the Delta Bridge had fallen to the enemy before any friendly unit could secure it. Azanian landing forces from the seacoast had raced to the bridge, and it seemed they must succeed in crossing it before they could be stopped.

Then, the Capital Corps, covered by the air corps, had successfully countered the Azanian force attacking from the west and cut it off from its supplies. The Azanians west of Persepolis were encircled. It was a great victory unless Persepolis fell to the attack from the sea.

Anxious hours passed until word came from a reconnaissance plane. The Delta bridge was destroyed! How? No one knew. Only when a friendly unit, the 743rd Motorized Infantry, arrived at the bridge was the incredible story told. A small group of stragglers had retaken the western span and blown it up! General Avesta made no show of it, but inside he knew he'd been preserved by luck or Fate. The bridge had been open, the Azanians poised to take Persepolis from the rear, and his own life and reputation ruined.

And now everywhere the Persians were triumphant. The western force was surrounded, and their breakout attempt had been stopped by the Primes and the Prince's Own Regiment. The eastern landing from the sea was contained behind the river, and more mobilization units were arriving. Soon there would be enough Persian regiments to push the Azanians back into the sea. In the air, the Persian Air Corps was sweeping the skies of enemy planes.

Avesta knew he'd accept the accolades flowing from the great victory. He was too human not to. But he also knew, deep down, the only person who really deserved the credit was whoever had blown the bridge. He would find out who they were and be generous in his thanks. To do anything else was to tempt Fate.

The Seed Storm was still coming, he reminded himself. No one would be able to fight during the storm. Who knew what would happen next?

Forty-four

Captain Aran watched the fragments of the Azanian Land Force pass his tanks on the road to Bandar. His tanks rolled north, the retreating men south.

Trucks full of raggedly dressed soldiers, many of them bandaged, rumbled past. Lines of men on foot lined both roadsides. There were only a few vehicles. Most of the tanks had burned the last of their fuel in the futile breakout attempts to the west. The Persians had counterattacked after each failed push, and the area held by the Land Force contracted to a pocket west of Persepolis.

Aran knew they were defeated. The only hope left was the sea. The fleet had evacuated some of the troops landed to the east of Persepolis and used them to take the port of Bandar. It had been a masterful operation, improvised under fire, but even a perfectly executed maneuver could do little but mitigate the horrible situation of the Azanian soldiers. It wasn't possible to hold back the approaching Persian tanks. Worse, the Seed Storm would arrive soon and annihilate anyone left in the open. To avoid capture and destruction, the land force would have to evacuate by sea.

Captain Aran's assignment was to lead the remnants of his company, a single platoon of *Mbwas*, and perform the role of the rearguard. He was to slow down the enemy for as long as possible to allow the maximum number of Azanian soldiers to escape.

He was exhausted and so were his men. They hadn't slept for days, and fatigue was causing a decline in performance. Aran had to kick his driver awake after every halt. Minds wandered and it was difficult to stay vigilant for danger.

The column of retreating soldiers seemed endless.

The sound of jet engines rose from the north. Men scattered in all directions and sought cover in irrigation ditches. Aran's column of tanks split with alternate tanks driving off the road to the left and right. None of the drivers paid much attention to what, or who, was in front of their tanks. Soldiers on foot had to get out of the way.

Aran pointed his roof-mounted machine gun at the sky in preparation for what was coming.

Two dark specks appeared and grew into a pair of Persian *Qahers*. Their wings were bare of bombs, but their noses sparked with cannon fire. The shells arrived before the sound of firing. Aran heard explosions behind him. He fired his machine gun without much hope of hitting the fast-moving planes. The roar of the jets passing low overhead overwhelmed him, and he ducked inside his tank.

When he emerged, the scene outside was chaos. Two of his tanks were burning, blasted open by 30mm shells. Wounded men cut down by shrapnel lay screaming in pain. Some were less lucky and did not move at all.

Aran's own tank was untouched. He'd been lucky this time.

He knew what he would have to do. He'd get out of his tank and do the best he could to help his fellow tankers. The wounded would be dressed and sent south. The tanks and men fit to fight would continue north.

As he gave orders and organized the remnant of his tank company, Aran heard artillery firing to the north. There would be no rest.

Forty-five

On a review stand in Capital Barracks, Suri Pahlavi stood at attention to receive the Star Medal from General Avesta. A band waited in the wings, and the field in front of her was filled with soldiers in formation. They came from many units. She saw the gray coats of the Capital Corps and the blue of the Prince's Own, as well as the humbler brown of the 743rd Motorized Infantry.

The general stood in front of her and waited for the medal citation to be read. His face was impassive.

The sergeant-major read, "For conspicuous gallantry and intrepidity above and beyond the call of duty. Lieutenant Pahlavi, *Bar Basiji*, took command of a leaderless unit and led them to retake the strategically vital Delta Bridge. After losing her commanding officer in an air attack, Lieutenant Pahlavi took command and assessed the situation. She recognized the enemy's objective as the Delta Bridge and immediately moved to foil them. By gathering stragglers from other units, she assembled a platoon-sized force and attacked the enemy positions around the bridge. By personally exposing herself repeatedly to enemy fire, Lieutenant Pahlavi successfully led her men to retake the western approaches to the bridge. Through improvising a vehicle-borne explosive, she successfully attacked the bridge span in order to arm explosive charges to destroy the bridge and deny its use to the enemy. Again under fire, she led her soldiers in a successful defense while the explosive charges were armed. After successfully preparing the bridge for destruction, Lieutenant Pahlavi was the last of her unit to step off the bridge to safety. She gave the order to destroy the bridge on her own initiative, and in so doing, prevented enemy forces from advancing on the capital city of New Persia."

Drums rolled, and General Avesta pinned the medal to her uniform blouse.

"Three cheers for Lieutenant Pahlavi!" bellowed the sergeant major.

The soldiers, as one voice, yelled, "HURRAH, HURRAH, HURRAH."

General Avesta shook Suri's hand. It took everything she had not to cry.

She saluted and executed a right face. She marched off the stage to the right and down the steps. The band began to play a march.

Suri found her spot in the line of medal recipients and fell in. She didn't know any of them, all men, but they all seemed nervous. She'd been the last to receive an award.

The music changed. The band switched to the royal march. The song was only played in the presence of the sovereign.

The prince regent, who had been standing in his place as colonel of the Prince's Own Regiment, took the stage.

He took off his hat.

"I am here to give the last award, as prince regent, as it is not a military award. The highest award for civilian valor is the Greatest Name medallion. Unfortunately, the award is posthumous," the prince said, his voice even.

"For conspicuous gallantry," he began, "when fighting to destroy the Delta Bridge—"

Suri couldn't stop the tears. They welled up unbidden from her deepest soul.

"...when faced with an enemy tank which threatened to kill her comrades and retake the bridge—"

Suri couldn't hear the words. She was struggling to suppress her sobs. She looked down the line at General Avesta. He stood ramrod-straight, his face impassive, but a single tear crawled down his cheek.

The prince read the rest of the citation. The drums rolled. He walked over to General Avesta and presented him with the boxed medallion.

At the end, the sergeant-major announced, "Hats off to Nasrin Avesta!"

The soldiers removed their covers as one. Total silence fell on the parade ground. Suri heard the flapping wings of a bird overhead. Time seemed to stop. The shadows of clouds passed over the field.

Don't let me blubber, God, Suri prayed. Embarrassed for making such a prayer, she thought, And Nasrin, if you're there, thank you. I miss you so much.

After one minute, the sergeant major called "Ready-two!" and the men replaced their hats on their heads.

The prince dismissed the colonels of the regiments, who dismissed their sergeant-majors, and on down the line. The formations of men atomized as the soldiers went their own ways, back to the barracks for most of them to prepare for the next round of the war.

Suri didn't leave. She was reluctant to go, but she knew she had one task to complete.

General Avesta came over to her. She saluted then wiped the tears from her face.

"You did well, Captain," Avesta said.

Suri blinked in surprise.

"You've been promoted," Avesta said. "It will be official tomorrow."

"Thank you, sir," Suri said.

"It's the least I can do," the general said. "I'd like to talk to you later about Nasrin."

"Yes, sir, of course," Suri said.

"Informally, I mean. I'd like to know more about her. We were not as close as I wish we were, in the end," he said.

Suri nodded.

"One more thing. I'd like to thank you," Avesta said, extending his hand.

Suri took it and asked, "For what?"

"For proving me right," Avesta said. "Without you, I would have lost the empire."

"Yes, sir. I don't quite understand," Suri said.

"It's quite all right," Avesta said, "I would be remiss if I didn't tell you."

He released her hand, and Suri saluted. Avesta returned the salute, and Suri strode away. Avesta watched her go, deep in thought.

She found her way to the motor pool outside her barracks. There, at her request, was a motorcycle. Where she had to go, she would go alone.

To the north, a cloud of dust and ash rose a kilometer into the sky. The storm was almost upon them.

Forty-six

Suri rode the motorcycle to the gates of airbase S-1 in the Sheban hills. The base buildings were heavily damaged from the fighting. The Azanians had bombed the base on the first day of the war, and both sides had fought over it when the Azanians took the airfield, and the Persians took it back.

Suri found Farad in the ready room, preparing a mission briefing. There were bullet holes in the walls. New maps hung over the remains of Azanian maps, which had been ripped down.

"Please, come in," Farad said. "There is no need for formalities."

"Yes," Suri said and came inside.

"It is a pleasure to see you," Farad said. "I was not expecting a visit."

"It is good to see you, too," Suri said.

"How is our friend Basir?" Farad asked. "I have not seen him since the war began."

"He is well, I hear," Suri said. "He's in the field, and I've only gotten letters and a telegram."

"I am glad to hear it," Farad said.

Suri could say nothing more. She struggled with emotion.

"If it is about Nasrin, I have been informed," Farad said. "I know she was with you when she…" he stopped. "When she passed."

"Yes," Suri choked out. "She was. She was very brave."

"I have heard the story," Farad said. "But I do not understand. How was it you two came to be together so far away from Persepolis? Why was Nasrin fighting the Azanians? I have many questions."

"I can answer them," Suri said, "but I have something I must give you."

"What?" Farad said.

"This," Suri said, and retrieved a small box from within her uniform blouse. "Nasrin would want you to have this."

Farad took the box. He opened it and saw what was inside.

"Is this?" he said, and tears formed in his eyes.

"It's her death ring, yes," Suri said.

Farad stood frozen, holding the box with the ring inside. The gold ring was inscribed with the Great Name and was to be placed with the body when it was buried.

Nasrin was buried beneath the rubble of the Delta Bridge, her body unreachable.

"Thank you," Farad said, "for bringing this to me." Then his legs gave way, and he knelt on the floor. Sobs overcame him.

Suri rushed over and put her arms around him. Her own tears came, and they cried together.

Forty-seven

Beneath the old archive building, a *Bar Basiji* brought a decoded message to Major Jahan. He rose to take it from her hand. He read it twice before sitting down. He wiped the sweat from his brow. The machine produced a lot of heat, and the air conditioning wasn't working again.

It was a short message, but he knew it was the most important message his code-breaking section had yet intercepted.

Sweat from his hands soaked through the paper where he held it. His mind raced as he tried to remember the proper procedure to disseminate a note like this.

His hand found the telephone.

"Operator. Yes, section six. Yes, get me the palace."

While he listened to the phone lines click in his ear as the switchboard operator connected him, he read it again.

It was intercepted from the Azanian weather reporting network. It wasn't a difficult code to crack, but it was read routinely because it improved the Persians' own weather forecasts.

PRIORITY ONE ALERT ALERT ALERT. SEED STORM SIGHTED NORTHERN WASTE. PROJECTED TRACK CENTRAL AZANIA. ARRIVAL WITHIN TWO WEEKS. ALERT ALERT ALERT. PRIORITY ONE.

Meet John L. Lynch

John L. Lynch is the author of New Persia and Endemic. He was a sailor in the US Navy and a soldier in the US Army National Guard. In the Navy, John was a CTR, a "Spook," and specialized in radio interception. He was stationed on Adak Island in the Aleutian chain and on Okinawa. After the military, John earned a BA in Political Science from Fort Lewis College.

Bringing his military experience to his writing is a natural fit for his books, which are about exceptional people in exceptional circumstances. Featuring soldiers in science fiction settings, John L. Lynch weaves together what is timeless about human nature with what is possible in the future.

Other Works From The Pen Of.
John L. Lynch

New Persia: Before the Storm - An impending war jeopardizes the lives of four friends living on a distant world.

Endemic - A mysterious disease draws a special operations team to the Congo, where they find something all their training and weaponry can't handle.

Letter to Our Readers

Enjoy this book?

You can make a difference

As an independent publisher, Wings ePress, Inc. does not have the financial clout of the large New York Publishers. We can't afford large magazine spreads or subway posters to tell people about our quality books.

But, we do have something much more effective and powerful than ads. We have a large base of loyal readers.

Honest Reviews help bring the attention of new readers to our books.

If you enjoyed this book, we would appreciate it if you would spend a few minutes posting a review on the site where you purchased this book or on the Wings ePress, Inc. webpages at: https://wingsepress. com/